The Book of Geezer

Also by John Teton

Appearing Live at The Final Test

Upsurge

ELEVATION: The Cave Logs of New Hale, Tibet

The Book of Geezer

John Teton

Scarlet Tanager
BOOKS
Oakland, California

Cover illustration copyright © 2020 by John Teton
Cover design by John Teton, Michael Ray Allison, Aidan Terry, Melanie Gendron, and Justin Mikkelsen
Typography and composition by Dickie Magidoff
Copyedited by Lisa K. Marietta

Scarlet Tanager Books
P.O. Box 20906
Oakland, CA 94620
www.scarlettanager.com

ISBN 978-1-7345313-0-5 (hardcover)
ISBN 978-1-7345313-1-2 (paperback)
ISBN 978-1-7345313-2-9 (e-book)
Library of Congress Control Number: 2020932017

The Book of Geezer is a work of fiction. Other than well-known real-life public figures, the names, characters, places, and incidents contained herein are the product of the author's imagination or are used fictitiously. In all other respects, any resemblance to actual persons living or dead or to business establishments is entirely coincidental.

Printed in the United States of America

First Edition

for
Jennifer

The Book of Geezer

Prologue

Scientific understanding, serenely enthroned as the pinnacle of Creation, gets put in its place pretty damn quick under a solar eclipse inching toward totality.

So thought the rangy, youngish black man hopping down from his dust-coated Jeep Gladiator on the side of one of Mexico's least-traveled coastal roads, squinting at the nearly eclipsed sun, its brilliance chiseled to a thin crescent by the silhouetted moon, and threatened further by clots of cloud floating its way.

A solitary researcher on a mission of discovery, he had numerous reasoning workbenches in his mind awaiting his attention, but with totality now just minutes away, pure enthrallment held sway. He marveled at how fortunate we Earthlings are to inhabit what might be the only planet among billions in this galaxy to have a moon positioned in a blessed sweet spot where its apparent diameter precisely matches that of the host sun, treating its planet's habitués every few years to such a breathtaking sight. He was obliged to suspend his allegiance to scientific rigor to ponder whether such rare symmetry might be a divine sign that a planet so situated has been singled out as a site for life to catapult from wriggling mindlessness to the greatest heights of intellectual prowess.

A flock of pelicans glided to a halt among the whitecaps a hundred yards out. Maybe the thinning of the crescent was getting too much even for them and they needed a little stillness to gather their wits.

With a little luck, this afternoon's eclipse might offer evidence of an even more extraordinary phenomenon that few to none of his billions of fellow humans had ever witnessed. No, more than a little—the odds against picking the one spot in an eight-thousand-mile-long moon shadow where the eclipse might trigger an extraordinarily rare terrain removal were astronomical. But, as he affixed a UV filter to his camera lens, he mused that fifteen years in aerospace R&D had taught him the rewards of patience, and if he had to gather data for decades to score the chance to witness an eclipse ground disappearance firsthand, gather he would.

With all that on his mind, he gave only a quick glance at the red-beaked Arctic terns perched on a narrow ledge halfway up a rocky promontory jutting into the Pacific, and they too were under the spell of the magic light. While the female fed some fish to their scruffy chick, her mate shivered at the strange sight above. Reminded by his offspring that breakfast wasn't over, he looked down to the ocean, cast in the sharp-shadowed, strangled amber light flickering on the whitecaps. Exchanging a look with his mate, he stretched and took off into a cruising float out over the water, surveying the ripples below for the faint, darting signature of fresh fish.

As the dark and silent juggernaut reached the threshold of totality, the photographer kept his trigger finger on the shutter button, sweeping the vista before him in search of the unknown something he'd come two thousand miles to discover.

A moment after the tern took his plunge, it came—a rippling, circular aurora growing in the near-dark sky overhead, followed by a deep, ripping rumble that shook the earth, tossing the photographer to the ground even as his camera motor whirred, snapping up a visual salad of off-balance pictures.

The shaken tern emerged from the turbulent waters, beheld the cliff, and cried out, dropping the family meal back into the sea. The chunk of land that had held his promontory, nest, and family had disappeared, leaving only exposed geological entrails in its wake. In the dim light of the late-afternoon starfield, foamy shock waves sloshed against the remainder of the sea wall, washing over its fresh crumbling rock and the adjoining beach and road.

The researcher jumped into his truck and maneuvered it toward the land's wound, training the truck's roof rack lights upon the site as the shrieking tern zoomed wildly back and forth past the torn cliff, lit solely by the truck's headlamps and the thin, blazing corona of the sun.

As the man got out to shoot more pictures for the remaining two minutes of totality, the tern mistook his curiosity for a sign that it was the human's power that had caused the catastrophe and flew to him with a panicky appeal to restore what he had destroyed.

Startled already by the disappearance of solid ground and cliff, and further weirded out by the bird hovering near his head, the researcher stood stunned for another minute as the blinding solar crescent emerged. When he recovered enough to reboard his vehicle, he was taken aback once more as the tern dove into the Jeep with him. Too intrigued to shoo the bird away, he shoved the Jeep into gear and drove off to the north.

Part One

The Calls of the Wild

1

Four living souls took note of an articulate bellow erupting from an American bullfrog in a long swamp lining the shore of the creek feeding into Merlo Lake in Northern California. A thousand feet overhead in the sunsetting sky, a cruising golden eagle altered its course, arcing down and west toward the swamp, which was coming alive with the chorus of the frog's fellow chanters, two thousand strong.

Relura Morell leapt off the porch of her parents' home and scrambled through the trunk of her car to find her Nikon. As she treaded into the swamp in search of her photographic prey, a great horned owl responded to her arrival with a ghostly call of *hooo . . . hoo-hoo-hoo . . . hoooo*. And sixty feet up in a nearby broadleaf maple, a northern mockingbird watched it all in uncharacteristic silence.

Another ten thousand feet up and forty miles east, Zeb Morell's eyes rejoiced at the sight of the tangerine and lime clouds layered above the western horizon as he guided his sailplane southwest to the landing strip at Santa Rosa.

I'll have Shangrilarian exult in a sky like this while flying over Zanzibar— hold on . . . eyes on this *sky, pal.*

What a blessing it was that Zeb's biggest problem was fending off such delectable images for Shangrilarian, his graphic novel hero, till he was back home on the ground. The hero of his new magnum opus kept imposing himself just beyond the windshield of Zeb's mind, undermining the discipline he had to apply to the task at hand, which was riding the fading Coast Range thermals onto an accurate glide path back to terra firma. But that was cool— part of his particular professional skill set was titrating just enough awakening of imagination to feed his writing session planned for later that night, but without letting it get the upper hand over his well-honed piloting mindset.

One could choke on a glut of blessings, which was how he regarded the hearty stream of images that flowed his way for review en route to publication in a ZM graphic novel. Yes, his sisters were sinking ever more impressive roots in their respective traditional fields (physics and biology), unintentionally casting shadows over his flights of fancy, but, for the time being, he was able to fend off the self-doubts such comparisons stirred up by remembering that he'd been able to pay for this glider outright with the royalties from his first graphic novel. Dammit, some people actually have made a living from art over the last few millennia, so why not him? Plus, he was filling in the gaps between royalties and hoped-for future publishing advances by occasionally taking on aspiring pilots as students. So, his blessings even included a real shot at prosperity, topped off with a view from the sky that would collapse anyone's attempt to take it in stride.

What the hell? There was a flying creature off his port wing, and he wasn't making this one up. It was a golden eagle, gliding parallel to him, scarcely six feet from his cockpit canopy . . . which was weird enough . . . but this one had turned her head and was staring straight at him, maintaining perfect, riveting eye contact, getting off on the stunning effect it was having on her human counterpart, sending chills through his innards.

Extraordinary weirdness was not new to Zeb. There was that singular night four years before when, at the age of seventeen, he and his twin sister, together with the intense former neighbor they called Geezer and an equally intense Arctic tern, had been swept into the sky over Antarctica, but he thought he had safely walled off that adventure in his mind. It was imperative to maintain a steady balance between reality and his fantastic imagination, where he mined the gems for his creative work. To succeed in both realms, he could not allow the wall between them to be sundered, and, so far, it had held. His artwork had grown, yielding abundant fantastical harvests within the safety of his imagination, most recently featuring a magnificent character he had named Shangrilarian, partly in honor of the single, extraordinary radiolarian he'd encountered on that mystifying night in his past. Meanwhile, Geezer, the unwilling pied piper whose trail they had followed to Antarctica, had met a different fate. Zeb and his sister had managed, through it all, to adjust admirably well to good old-fashioned Reality.

But now, an avian creature that was indisputably real seemed hell-bent on cracking open that wall. Birds do not stare at humans like that, even while perched, let alone in flight at forty-five knots. Zeb found himself jerking his head away, as one would try to put off a weirdo on the bus in Oakland, as if that would signify "Get lost" to an eagle who plainly had no intention of doing any such thing.

Please stop. I'd like to get home in one piece, physically and mentally.

Finally, the bird did split, but not before nodding at him, as if to tender him a supercilious salute, acknowledging to herself that she had delivered a message, as instructed.

I know why that bird bugged me so much. It reminded me of Shang, our abductor from four years ago. Well, calm down, pal. This was a perfectly normal flesh-blood-and-feathers bird, not some elegant monster in total control of our lives. So, it gave me a look and a momentary shiver—goody for Eagleface. Let's adapt that moment for a panel in Chapter 3 of the sequel, when Shangrilarian first flickers into existence during the coronation of the Zanzibarbarian queen. Let her get rattled instead of me. In my book, I'm God, remember? I can shuttle anything I want from the Real World into Shangrilarian's without fear of retribution or re-kidnapping. No worries—just enjoy your flight.

Zeb caught a few faint twilight glimmers of fireflies in a vineyard below. He estimated his altitude at five thousand feet. (He'd had to estimate since he'd covered the altimeter on his instrument panel a few months ago with a drawing of Shangrilarian. The compass too. He'd remove them if he got stuck in thick cloud cover, but otherwise he figured that doing without would sharpen his senses; most people these days were dulling them through device overuse.) Those lovely flying lanterns dancing among the grapes, so rare out West, couldn't compete in the Firefly Olympics with the champs his family saw in the Great Smokies during the road trip they took the summer after sophomore year, but the subtle little flares floating through the grapevines were yet another sprinkling of rewards for an early evening sky glide. Maybe he never would enjoy the granite stability of a career like the one Marlie was clearly headed for or the one Relura had already fashioned for herself, but as long as he could soar miles above the mountaintops in a marvelous engineless aircraft like his Schempp-Hirth Ventus-2a, he'd be just fine.

Probably best not to tell the girls about that bird. (I'm referring to Marlie and Relura, obviously—telling Alyssa is out of the question. It would be rather stupid to lob a bizarro grenade into a romance with a blissfully normal, superfine girlfriend.) The sisters (and I) are only four years into recovery. Give it another ten before indulging in such risky sharing. Marlie especially—blabbing to her about a bird phenomenon this unsettling just as she's trying to land a spot on a Hard Science League roster would be thoughtless. She's strong, but suppose I just let this one slide, eh? Now, let's focus on my approach. The runway's just six miles away.

At that very moment, Marlie Morell was enjoying her own sky view and wondering if Zeb was enjoying it too. *I hope Zeb's checking out the sight of Jupiter rising—wait—do I? I wouldn't want him to get distracted by memories of Geezer's last known obsession. Or imagine old Geezer flopping around out there as a space corpse.*

Hey, I'm driving here! I'm driving here! Geezer, get thee behind me!

Marlie wisely refocused her attention on the twisting dusk-dim road on Skyline Ridge in the hills west of Palo Alto. Her brother would appreciate the sight of the giant planet glimmering in the darkening eastern sky, but that sort of fare should be consumed only in small portions. At least that was true for her. Whatever the crazy hell had happened to them four years ago could remain manageable only as long as it was confined to quarters. With a degree in plasma science just months away and, even more important, a real shot at R&D financing for her (hopefully brilliant?) invention, she had to keep her nose as clean as a sterile operating room.

With the top down on her MG F (blueberry blue, in cherry condition despite the six-figure odometer reading) and the cool breeze off the bay enveloping her, she felt like she was skipping along wavetops toward a future brimming with possibilities. At times like this, which these days seemed to keep on coming, Marlie couldn't help seeing Nature's manifold displays of beauty as auguring success in her near future. Rather than having been bent out of shape by the exhilarating trauma of their very unplanned trip to space—*hush*—she'd gotten her act together. Not yet twenty-two, she was killing it—at Stanford, in her NASA Ames internship, and now as the leader of a bushy-tailed team of four smart pals she was about to dine with at the Chipmeister Brewery, all abuzz with the prospect of serious financing to build a prototype of her electromagnetic wave generator. (The recent addition to the team of a rakishly foxy electrical engineering grad student named Trey had nothing to do with her excitement about the project's potential. *Right?*)

Hustling impulses notwithstanding, Marlie was only too glad to spend a few extra miles to come up out of Portola Valley on the ridge road, where she could see the glittering colored lights streaming down the highway several miles below to the east. It was an automotive meditation—why choose the brain-frazzling, stomach-acid-churning, drunken-monkey chaos required to negotiate rush-hour traffic on US 101 when you could float above it in peace and quiet this sweet? She could hear a whinny from a quarter mile off or a hoot from a stirring owl no doubt monitoring her and other land-bound mammals crossing tonight's hunting field. This ride offered an infusion of pastoral mystery that complemented the animated wit-storm she'd be treating herself to at the restaurant.

She could hardly complain, able to hop within a single hour from research in one of the most sophisticated centers of astrophysics on the planet to a roadster sail through redwood forests, acre-wide vegetable gardens, and cattle pastures. This scene bore comparison to her parents' sweet spot in the placid countryside outside the greater Merlo Lake metro area (population 136), eighty-five miles north of San Francisco, where she'd grown up by a lake graced by eagles' nests, deer visitations, and the occasional coyote. Here, atop the Peninsula, she had access to all of that within sight of Ames, Stanford, and the throbbing heart of global high-tech.

Get a load of this hayfield on my left—that's got to be at least ten acres—and, oh, nice, a couple of quarter horses being led from their corral to the barn by two girls in their early teens—

Whaaaaat? An owl—Stop! Go away! You're creeping me out!

Normally, a great horned owl coasting along on the evening breeze by a road like this with dark coming on would have graced this happy hour with an auspicious mix of nature and magic, but there was nothing normal about this bird. It had deliberately cruised alongside Marlie at her eye level for ten full seconds, *staring right at her.* No, thank you—she'd exceeded her lifetime dose of weirdness on that night four years ago; she didn't need any more time in the Spookarama. But there it was—that owl's look could not be unseen. What was *that* about?

That owl reminded me of the one in Antarctica and . . . that other place.

Cut it out. Maybe I made it up. Some kind of lingering PTSD hallucination, an aftershock glitch.

Are you kidding? Evidence, girl: do not discount unexpected findings.

Do I tell Zeb, seeking comfort? Or keep my mouth shut, to avoid slipping into the Spookarama again? It's riding roughshod on my mellow either way.

Zeb had flashed on a concept for a great panel an hour after he landed the Ventus. Shape-shifting into its female aspect, Shangrilarian would sprout a couple of long pseudopodia, engulf the spaceship from Gargalon, and train all sixty of her eyes on the startled captain and crew on the bridge, staring fetchingly at them till they quaked.

Clearly, his imagination was repurposing the chills he'd gotten off the encounter with the googly eagle. And Shangrilarian was all the more seductive for positioning the rest of her marvelous, gigantic, unicellular form into the lovely, seductive pose being modeled for Zeb at that very moment by his muse and lover, Alyssa, in the wartime Craftsman house they were renting near downtown Oakland. As a dancer, Alyssa couldn't resist the temptation to add a Zeb Morell graphic novel to the collection of stages upon which one of her fine poses would appear in the year ahead.

The gravitational pull Zeb felt around Alyssa had so permeated his brain at that point, three months into their relationship, that it was affecting his imagination and, hence, his artwork. Nothing wrong with that—why not have a monster-creature superhero who exerted her dominance over the enemies of mankind with the power of her beauty? Shangrilarian's spellbinding powers could overwhelm evildoers on multiple sensory fronts. Behold how they're enveloped with breathtaking choral music emitted by vocal cord organelles lining her outer edges as they vibrate in the sun, mesmerizing all who beheld her sixteen-foot-tall stature! Then how about dazzling leaps to entirely different poses, followed by sinuous slides to others erotic or mysterious, all while emitting captivating tropical floral perfumes? The worst of the worst would fall helpless before such an onslaught of glory, rendered in painstaking detail by Zeb's ever-maturing draftsmanship, which could now give a crossbred offspring of artists like Ernst Haeckel and Roger Dean a run for their money.

Alyssa had multiple motives in modeling for the artiste. Deeming fifteen minutes plenty for this gig, she languorously slid into a sexy stretch she knew would disable any control Zeb's superego had over his id. Sure enough, within two seconds he flung his sketchpad to the side and dropped to the floor, draping himself around her.

"Are you trying to sabotage my career?"

"Poor Shangrilarian, powerless before an ordinary human female."

"Ordinary! Such obvious compliment fishing is beneath you, Alyssa. You've been extraordinary since you were a fetus." Lacking the confidence that his wit could top that line with something a bit more clever, he planted a kiss on her smiling mouth, and it was warmly received and reciprocated.

Twenty seconds of that was all that could be sustained by either party without a decision that would affect the course of the next few hours, so they separated enough to give their future-planning teams a chance to run out onto the court.

Catching his breath, Zeb asked, "Are we chucking the dinner-and-a-movie scenario?"

"I don't know. I'm so often mystified by the secrets lying beneath the shimmering surface of Zeb Morell."

Uh-oh. That reference to what Alyssa had dubbed The Secret signaled the need for more dodging ahead. She'd become suspicious when Zeb had come home blurting out something about his flight having been strange, before he realized that mentioning being stared down by an eagle could trigger questions about The Secret.

"Foxy Heart?"

Alyssa blatantly batted her eyes, which were just a few inches from Zeb's. "Yes?"

"I thought we were going to let that subject rest for a while."

"It has been a while. Three days, in fact."

He felt like saying, "Three years would be more like it," except with both of them only twenty-one years of age, envisioning their future together at least three years from then would be a recklessly bold move for him, and, he guessed, even for her. Instead, he got straight to the point.

"Alyssa, if I told you what happened to Marlie and me in our senior year, either you'd never take me seriously again or you'd skedaddle away."

"I won't judge you."

"It's not that we did anything wrong. I just wouldn't want you to be unsettled by it."

"Try me."

"Don't take it personally, Alyssa. It would be weird for anyone to hear."

Her eyes blazed. "Lay it on me or prepare to be goosed."

Zeb paused, pursed his lips for a moment, and looked away. "Okay, here it is, but don't tell anyone." After allowing for a dramatic pause to widen Alyssa's eyes, he whispered, "When we were seventeen, Marlie and I were taken by an alien to interplanetary space."

"Jerk!" she exclaimed and delivered on her threat. Zeb wrestled himself away from her, only to return with a more classical embrace.

"I love you, Alyssa."

"No stupid jokes. The least you could do is come up with something that's remotely possible. Did you think you saw Sasquatch in a forest? Or a UFO?"

"Let's move on, shall we?"

"It's hurtful that you don't trust me, Zeb. You think every human ear is a microphone attached to a recording device with a speaker-equipped playback system. I would never turn blabbermouth."

"I trust you as much as anyone." He was about to add "as long as we're together," but he caught himself in time. "But then you'd have to be burdened with a promise never to repeat it to anyone as long as you live."

"So? It will bring us closer together."

"But what's the rationale for telling?"

"What's the rationale for my loving you? What's the rationale for surveying the Hanakāpī'ai Falls from above?"

She scored points on that one. The very thought of their plan to go soaring in Hawaii in February was a romantic tour de force that could sweep up a lot of resistance, but there was one more legitimate reason for discretion.

"It's not just my secret, Alyssa. It's Marlie's too. She's very uptight about it, and I don't blame her. She has a lot on the line maintaining a rep for hardheaded science, and more to lose than I do if the secret gets out."

Zeb had to endure the disappointed look on Alyssa's exquisite face. He assuaged his guilt by telling himself that somewhere on the other side of the bay, Marlie was going about her business, secure in her brother's vow of loyal secrecy about the night in their teens that had shattered some assumptions about nature that they had shared with the rest of the human race.

Marlie, for the moment at least, was free of worry about The Secret. She'd even stuffed the chilling memory of being mad-dogged by an owl into a corner of her mind's back rooms. She was surfing some mighty exciting vibes with four of her smartest and most fun peers in the hubbub of a hot gourmet brewery in Palo Alto, just days before their big pitch meetings with three venture capital outfits on Sand Hill Road. Newcomer Trey added further whiz fizz to the high-end froth in which rapid-fire blue humor threaded through brainstorms of novel ways to stimulate gyroharmonic frequencies in the upper atmosphere.

She felt so lucky to have come up with an idea for building a more powerful aurora generator at a small fraction of the size and cost of the radio transmission systems employed by the navy. It could bust open the field of extraterrestrial aurora studies too, which might wend its way into a spaceflight run at Jupiter in the future. Getting this project off the ground could revolutionize plasma science and, by the way, get her set for life professionally and financially. And, hell, her exuberant teammates plowing through dishes of Kobe sliders and linguine Provençal were so entertaining to hang out with, she thought for a second that it almost didn't matter whether or not they succeeded. But just for a second. Success glimmered so close on the horizon she was positively giddy.

Marlie was gearing up to toss into the fray a fantasy about luring some Ames engineering specialists to their team as consultants when she felt her phone buzzing in the pocket of her jeans. Finding Relura incoming, she begged off the table chatter and turned to the side to take the call.

"Hey, girl—what's up? Egg production okay?"

Relura fielded her little sister's double entendre without comment. Marlie had been bugging her for news about a possible pregnancy, but Relura stuck with a literal interpretation referring to her hen management duties while house-sitting for the folks during their long weekend in New Orleans. "Except for broody Iridescence, they're all laying. We'll have surpluses for you and Zeb to take home from your visit this weekend."

"We're visiting this weekend?"

"I hope so. Hold on—I want to patch in Zeb."

Marlie glanced back at her crew while Relura three-wayed their brother into the conversation. When Trey caught her eye, she was tempted to postpone the conversation with her siblings, but she knew better. Something was up.

Zeb's cheerful voice came on the line. "Hey, Relura."

"What are you up to, Z?"

"Chillaxin' with Alyssa and Shangrilarian."

Marlie thought more than enough time had passed without her presence having been announced. "Relura informs me that we're staging a reunion tomorrow."

"Ah, both of you at once! A big deal must be afoot."

"Isn't it automatically a big deal whenever the three of us are together?"

Both twins recognized that as a classic deft Relura dodge, which confirmed their suspicions. Marlie feigned ignorance of its significance. "My, you must be getting lonesome up there without Sean."

"First of all, Sean is here. He's helping me cook." The twins heard the presentation of Relura's case interrupted by their brother-in-law whispering "Hey!" in the background in what the twins suspected was playful annoyance, a finding confirmed when Relura squealed "Yipe!" a moment later. Marlie figured Relura must have grabbed her husband's ass and suffered immediate retaliation. Either Relura thought her younger siblings wouldn't notice or she didn't care much if they did. How thinly the veneer of professional dignity lies on the surface of high-energy newlyweds. Marlie was delighted that the romance between her sister and her orthopedist hubby was flourishing with such élan, but she was tempted to suggest that they get a room.

"True, he is leaving tomorrow afternoon. The Niners are in town." Ah, yes—Sean had recently been added to the football squad's sports doc roster. "But I won't get lonesome here. I have two thousand frogs to keep me company."

No doubt. Relura was barely in her teens when the family had moved to the lake, and their proximity to the froggy metropolis in the swamp surrounding the feeding creek had catalyzed her fascination with the order Anura. No one was surprised when she headed to the pros as a herpetologist and was signed to a biomedical research team on the Peninsula.

"We haven't been together without the parents since summer," Relura continued.

"But the parents will be there, right? They're getting back from New Orleans tomorrow night."

"Not till after ten. If you two get here early enough we can have dinner together and, pardon the expression, hold a tribal council before I have to leave for the airport. I won't tell them you're there, and you can surprise them when they walk in."

Another attempt at artful dodging. Of course, Marlie couldn't pick up the folks in her tiny roadster on her way past the airport, but it was odd to have the twins arrive not all that long before Relura would have to make a four-hour airport run. Relura clearly wanted some alone-time with her sibs. The twins cooperated by not asking. Relura would get to the point in her own good time.

In the background, Marlie could hear Zeb laying out Relura's plan to Alyssa. He mentioned Relura's filial surprise motive, which didn't go very far explaining why Alyssa wasn't on the invitation list, despite Relura's having taken an immediate liking to her on the two occasions they'd met. Apparently, Zeb and Alyssa had plans to attend a dance concert Saturday night produced by Alyssa's favorite choreography comrade, so this wasn't the lightest of asks. Nonetheless, Alyssa accepted the inevitable with grace and charm.

Meanwhile, Trey had the rest of the dining team splitting up in laughter. Marlie felt torn when he looked at her. She really relished this dinner party, but there was no getting around the unusualness of Relura's move. The ease with which Zeb had scuttled part of his weekend with Alyssa meant that he had picked up on the same thing. Furthermore, it was unsettling that this was happening the same evening she'd been spooked by the owl. She was tempted to wonder if there might be some connection between the two, but let's not get too crazy here. It was true the three hadn't gotten together for a while, so, going with the certainty of the incoming tide, she told Relura, "I'm in," and signed off. She tried to refocus on her dining mates' dance of wit and guffaws even as internal questions about what else this weekend had in store gnawed away from below.

2

By the middle of the next afternoon, Marlie was feeling multiple high-tensile-strength wires competing to fix her attention on work, her social scene, and the prospect of a date request she felt coming over the horizon from Treyville, all of which yammered at her that this was an inappropriate time to take off for most of a weekend. Yet despite that—because of that tugging—she committed herself not only to the trip but to take Route 1 most of the way, forsaking the high speeds possible on US 101 for the lush forest, farmland, lagoon, bay, and ocean views of one of America's most scenic roads. She could take 101 for a speedier return on the way back the next day, but she wanted—needed—that time on the road to decompress.

Okay, it was more than decompression. Relura's call had rattled her a little on account of the sense that there was something offbeat—maybe weird—she *wanted* to discuss with them. The three of them had had a million lifetimes worth of weird four years ago, and it was so firm a policy to face that topic only rarely and gingerly, if at all, that *anything* weird had to be approached with caution to avoid reliving that night.

Aaaaand yet—part of her *wanted* to relive it. It was, in part, terrifying, but also thrilling. And somehow it seemed that she hadn't yet achieved the full equilibrium she'd need to go forward for the rest of her adult life if she didn't have a more solid foothold in the recollection of that night than she'd yet been able to achieve. She would not only immerse herself in the natural beauty of the non-hectic alternative route, she would open the gates of her consciousness to what had happened when she and Zeb were seventeen, and let come what may.

She tolerated the traffic plowing slowly through the heart of San Francisco and over the Golden Gate Bridge, salivating for the peace and quiet and luscious beauty of rural Northern California. As she turned off at Tam Valley Junction and headed across the coastal hills toward Muir Beach, what came was the evening of her first visit to Geezer Island, four years ago.

"I can see it all now—in the middle of the night, lightning flashes out of the eyes of the haunting Geezer, gliding along his castle roof, daring foolish would-be explorers to penetrate his defenses to discover what goes on within his dark castle." The high-school-senior edition of Zeb fished a pencil from his jacket pocket and began furiously sketching on the back of a yearbook photo flier he'd been handed at school in anticipation of graduation the following spring. "Imagine a sign like this shot from below with Geezer's actual house rising above it!"

In the roaring flare of this wild vision for the opening of a movie on the brink of production, the mundane trappings of the sauce and pasta shelves and the magazine rack in Batts's Country Store dimmed away from Zeb's vicinity. Marlie and two of their pals hovered over his shoulder as the hulking white-bearded ghost of black Geezer materialized behind the crenellations topping his tower.

"That'd make a dope poster, Z," nodded Zeb's fellow actor, J.D.

Nolan, the third actor in the troupe, looked askance. "A little too dope, if you ask me. It'll be pretty lame for us to make a big deal about spooky old Geezer when we can never get a shot of him."

"Don't be so sure," Zeb replied. "If we make a landing on the island and creep up to the haunted house, maybe Marlie can shoot him with her telephoto lens."

"If he doesn't take a shot at her first. A guy who's turned his place into a fortress must have paranoid rocks in his head."

"It's all right. I'm sure Marlie carries production insurance."

"No, I don't," interjected Marlie. "And we're not going to risk getting shot for trespassing either. We're going to get some exterior shots from the boat, hit the beach long enough for a shot of the fence, and fake the rest in our backyard." She poked her brother in the shoulder. "If we don't get back to the house soon, we're going to lose dusk light and the whole shoot. Get your markers."

The twins had no qualms about bossing each other around from time to time. Though born just eight minutes apart, other than their dark hair, fair skin, sharp intellects, and gymnastics-trained bodies—5'8" and 5'11", respectively—Marlie and Zeb didn't share many characteristics, but their bond to each other felt deep as the ocean and well able to withstand a little wolf-pup roughhousing.

Zeb's sketching zeal prevailed over her admonition, but she hardly noticed, as her attention was clutched by the new edition of *Astronomy* magazine, which she withdrew from the magazine rack. Between a small-type promise of an article on holography and the cover story headline "Darkness in the Antarctic Noon," a cartoon penguin peered through fancy mylar eclipse sunglasses.

Meanwhile, Nolan snapped up a sci-fi movie magazine heralding the imminent arrival of another Godzilla epic. "Hey, maybe we should put Godzilla in our video. The Indians who haven't been imprisoned in the mission eat some peyote and conjure up Godzilla to help them liberate the place."

J.D. grabbed the new issue of *Skater* magazine, his eye caught by a rhapsodic cover photo, shot from below, of a skateboarder inverted in the sky executing a kickflip above the sun, his arms outstretched. "What a stud!" he exclaimed.

Nolan peered over J.D.'s shoulder. "Who, the phony Photoshopper who faked that picture?"

"Photobullshit. This is Nick Rieger. I've seen him do stuff like this in videos."

Marlie rolled her eyes. "Oh, that's proof. Videos can't be faked." She brandished her magazine cover. "That skater's about as real as this penguin."

The dispute distracted Zeb from his artwork enough to notice Marlie's magazine. "Antarctica," he snarked. "What a waste of an eclipse. Why don't they do one here?"

Marlie pointed to the time on her phone. "Tick-tock, Zeb."

J.D. backed her up. "Let's go, man." Zeb sighed and headed to the shelf for school supplies.

Soon the group gathered near the cash register, Zeb now armed with a variety of sizes and colors of felt markers. On a nearby wall festooned with pictures of parties and family reunions, Zeb pointed to a black-and-white photo of a rural oxbow lake a few hundred yards across with homes scattered around its rim, captioned "Extending the Lake ('71)." "Have you guys seen this memento from Mr. Batts's trip down Memory Lane?"

J.D. and Nolan scrutinized the picture. A house hidden in the trees at the tip of the oxbow would soon be isolated by a dredger eating away at the spit of land connecting the house to a long driveway and the road lining Merlo Lake. A much younger Mr. Batts was among a crew of sweaty, shirtless men smoothing gravel near a Jeep Gladiator and a ship-shape Chevy Biscayne. "Hey, Mr. Batts," J.D. piped up. "Who'da thought you used to be so ripped?"

While checking out another customer's groceries, the now stocky Mr. Batts cast a glance at the photo and deadpanned, "What do you mean 'used to be'?"

Zeb carried on as docent. "Back in the day, Battsy must have been quite the laborer to make that crew. Those guys built Geezer's house and actually dug out a huge bunch of land between the house and the road so he could live on his own strange island. Geezer spent a gazillion dollars cutting himself off from the mainland so he wouldn't be interrupted from his schemes by solicitors and wayward travelers."

"How'd he make all that bank?" asked Nolan.

"Mr. Batts says he invented jets."

"Not quite, boys," Mr. Batts sighed. "Just some component of ramjet engines is all I heard. And all we did was put in the driveway and garage. He brought in a crew from Colorado to build the house, plus another crew from Kentucky to dig the basement. Coal mining outfit, we heard. It took them a full year and they were well-paid, but I suspect the tab was less than a gazillion."

"Whatever. Geezer spent plenty to create a moat around his evil castle. Now he's sighted about as often as Sasquatch."

Marlie saw Mr. Batts's twenty-year-old son Seth carrying boxes of groceries to the door. "Hey, Seth—you must have seen Geezer a bunch of times while you were dropping off his supplies, right? What's he like?"

"Sorry, Marlie. I just deliver the goods to the locker at his gate."

"Hey, I bet you're headed there right now with those boxes." Zeb glanced at Marlie with a conspiratorial eyebrow. "We could lie in wait for Geezer to make the pickup tonight."

"That could be midnight or 4 AM, who knows?"

"Yeah, but what a money shot."

Seth looked to his father, who intervened. "Kids, it might be best if you left the elderly gentleman alone."

"'Elderly gentleman'—come on, Mr. Batts, you must know his name, at least."

"Actually, no. He sends his lists to us under a business name."

"Which is?"

"Which doesn't fall in the category of your all's beeswax." Bidding his customer good-bye, he looked at Marlie, "Whatcha got, hon?" Marlie handed him the magazine. "You into penguins?"

"More like eclipses," said J.D.

"Wrong on both counts. I know about the eclipse. I'm getting this for the holography piece."

Zeb acted indignant. "You knew about a total eclipse coming? Why didn't you tell me? We coulda made plans to check it out."

"It's in Antarctica, Zeb."

"All the better."

Even Mr. Batts (not to mention everyone in Zeb's family) had learned to let Zeb's more outlandish remarks slide. He smiled at Marlie. "Holography, eh? I heard you were our local science fair champ with your lasers and such."

"Not just local, Mr. B," chimed in her proud twin. "National semifinalist."

"You've brought great honor upon Geyserville High."

"Hardly, Mr. B, but thanks."

Zeb wasn't done. "She cashed out with a cool two grand, all for a little homework on multiple varied-wavelength laser holography."

Marlie rolled her eyes while trying to stifle a smile. "That'll do, Zeb. Suppose we get our boat in the water before we lose the light."

Left unsaid but prominent in the twins' minds was *before the parents return and spot us landing on Geezer Island.* That wouldn't go so well. The objective was to get filmed o'ertopping the fortress walls surrounding Mission Santa Relura, their new appellation for Geezer Island. Come to think of it, it might be wise to get the shots they needed before the arrival of the mission's namesake: their older sister, who was also due at the house within the hour. Relura was sufficiently down with the twins to not get full-bore santa on them and stand in for the parents' rigor about the sanctity of neighbors' property rights. However, since she had accepted the commission from the higher-ups to chaperone the twins' stay at the house while they slipped off to Kauai for their twenty-eighth annual honeymoon, there'd be no point in pushing their luck.

So turned the wheels in Marlie's mind as she fiddled with the zoom lens in the shotgun seat as Zeb drove back along the county road from Batts's store toward home. However, on approach to the family manse with Zeb at the wheel of their mother's "Mom car," the despised mini-van, who should they find in the shadow of the setting sun pulled over in the driveway to Geezer's property but Seth. He was busy loading boxes of supplies into the

Castlekeeper's lockbox, a steel crate the size of a double-wide steamer trunk. Zeb pulled up, triggering a sigh in his sister as she summoned the patience for a further delay in the start of production. Zeb poked his face out the driver's window. "Saaaaay, there, Seth—how they hangin'?"

Transferring the third large box, Seth called out, "Not much different from the last time I saw you."

"I knew you were doing the drop. How would you feel about clueing us in as to what's in those boxes?"

"Not much different from the last time I saw you."

Nolan and J.D. ignored Zeb. They were too busy marveling at the decades-old carcass of the Chevy Biscayne, gone to its final rest buried under layers of crusty mold and decomposed leaves. Framed by the dramatic backdrop of Geezer's nine-foot-tall fence, which blocked the view of anything near ground level lying beyond, it was quite a set piece for an introduction to Geezer. Jungle-thick foliage bordering and overhanging the driveway all the way to the lake added a soupçon of natural decay to the whole.

"Mordor," Zeb declared.

J.D. mused, "Helluva life having to bushwhack your way through all that just to pick up your Raisin Bran."

"True that," Nolan responded. "But if he's doing it under cover of night, at least we know that, despite appearances to the contrary, Geezer lives!"

"Not necessarily," Zeb cautioned.

"Whaddya mean? Is he dead or is he still getting stuff from Batts's store?"

"Maybe both. All the more reason we should lie in wait to get him in the video."

"Right! We can make him out to be the mission's zombie head monk! The guy who enslaves the Indians and forces them to make history videos."

"Don't you kids have homework or something?" Seth suggested.

"Yes, sir, we do," Marlie interjected. "Glad you asked. Zeb, there's no time to spare. We aren't going to get every shot we need in one take. Would you kindly say good-bye?"

Before Zeb could summon a response, a bright-green Miata slid alongside them and paused. A window descended, revealing its twenty-five-year-old, auburn-haired driver glowing with health and grinning with glee. "Hi, boys and girl!"

"Relura!" hollered the twins.

Nolan informed J.D., "Zeb and Marlie's sister works with freaky frogs in a secret underground biotech lab down in San Francisco."

"Yeah?"

"South of the city, above ground, well-known, and anomalies rather than freaks, but otherwise yeah." Relura turned to check out the action at the delivery site. "Hey, Seth, are these youngsters making a nuisance of themselves?"

"Not too bad, as nuisances go. I was considerably worse at their age."

"Alas, me too, truth to tell." Turning back to the noisy van, she added, "I thought you were supposed to be shooting your video about now."

Marlie held up her camcorder. "Call is in three minutes."

"I'll let you get on with it, then. I'll help the folks pack. Bye!" And off she went, toward the modest house a couple hundred curving yards farther along the lakeshore.

Marlie said nothing as Zeb carried on bantering with Seth. She'd slipped into a marsh of complicated feelings about Geezer, a terrain she'd explored with her brother more than once. Their ghostly dark-skinned neighbor had been spotted no more than four or five times in the eight years the family had been living just down the lakeshore from him, and all of those times were late at night and all but two were from Zeb's window a good distance away. Geezer occupied a curious sector of their minds, a cerebral equivalent of the antigravity Mystery Spot promoted to tourists down near Santa Cruz.

Geezer catalyzed emotional concoctions of pity, admiration, and guilt that arose as much from the concept of Geezer as from the man himself. Pity because he was so old—from the wretched condition of his property, one had to assume he was too old to manage even the most minimal upkeep and too poor (or perhaps too hermetic) to hire anyone else to grant it a little cleanup every eon or two. Admiration because, despite his apparent infirmity and lack of support from any quarter, he did manage to stay alive on his own—and he did once have the smarts to earn that lucrative merit badge for technology back in the early days of jet R&D. And guilt because—well, face it. Here was this really elderly black man living all alone in a county with not all that many African Americans, yet, aside from a plate of cookies the twins' mother had once left on his locker with an invitation to brunch, the Morell family hadn't ever mustered much motivation or strategy to actively befriend their sorta next-door neighbor, or even to meet him, for that matter. Eight years on, they still didn't know his name. Back in the Appalachian holler where she'd spent her grade school years, the twins' mom, Jeanine, recalled that everybody knew who their neighbors were and, much of the time, what was going on with them as well.

And now Marlie and her brother were on the verge of doing something that felt a touch exploitative of him by deliberately encroaching—if only a few yards—onto his property when they knew damn well he'd be upset, maybe shaken up, if he knew about it. The least they could do was make it snappy. The guys in their Indian regalia will jump the fence and then Marlie will record them jumping back over. If the old man doesn't see them, what's the harm?

Well, she knew the harm. It lurked in the temptation to actually get Geezer on tape, which they just might succeed in doing if they kept watch late that night, when the old man was bound to crawl out of his house and then boat over to pick up the very boxes Seth was locking into the metal bin right now. Really, it was surprising he didn't demand smaller boxes from the Batts store. The guy could be pushing eighty or ninety—that was a guess, but he was obviously no spring rooster—so how could someone that beat up by time even lift the boxes out of the bin, much less get them down to the dock a couple hundred feet away? Maybe he used a combination of a wagon and a walker.

Never mind. There was nothing for it but to get the video footage needed for their U.S. History class term project as unobtrusively as possible. While composing her first shot with one hand, she used the other to poke Zeb in the shoulder. "It's dusk, buster. Let's get this show on the lake."

Zeb was absorbing the disappointment of watching Seth hoisting himself back into his truck cabin without having divulged a molecule of information, if he even had any to divulge. "Sorry, Zeb. Official Batts's Store Classified Info, y'know."

Zeb saluted Seth while firing up the mini-van. "Well, respect, dude. Customer loyalty is a two-way street, I get it. Peace, out."

On a narrow grassy beachhead farther down the lakeshore, pre-production buzz crackled in the evening air. As Marlie checked her camcorder, Zeb admired his new sign. Pretty slick, if he said so himself, especially for just twenty minutes' work in the garage—olde Spanish lettering "carved" into a background watercolored to look like rough-hewn oak.

The Mexican blanket his parents had picked up for him from a vendor hawking merchandise on an Acapulco beach wasn't quite Ohlone style, but it was the closest facsimile at hand. He swept it around his shoulders, summoning his proud inner brave en route to liberate his fellow Indians from the *misión*.

As upon the advent of D-Day, all logistics had been attended to and the expedition would be under way momentarily. Unlike D-Day, only four people had to be kept in the dark about the impending invasion: Geezer, Relura, and the twins' parents. However, Zeb wasn't sure just how much Relura already knew about their plan to use the family's fifteen-foot aluminum boat to traverse the two-hundred-yard expanse of lake to Geezer Island.

"Are you sure Relura believes we're going to stay in the boat over there?"

"I sure hope so," Marlie replied.

"How bad would it be if she knew the truth? She can keep a secret from the parents."

"Let's not put her on the spot. At twenty-five, she's susceptible to the parental-attitude virus."

"How do you know that?"

"I intuited it after she told me she'd heard Mom say, 'Those kids have no damn business hounding that man like a pack of paparazzi.' Her tone had a hint of suspicion."

"Fine. We keep the landing under wraps."

"I asked her to take over organizing dinner so the parents can pack. That way Mom won't be able to spy on us out the kitchen window."

"I'm sure her mind is already in Hawaii." A sound bet—Jeanine and Dan were bound to be effervescent over the prospect of hitting the Nā Pali coast on Kauai, the trailhead of which lay less than twenty-four hours in their future, following the flight they'd be taking out of San Francisco International after dinner.

Zeb sighed and turned his gaze to the island. Squatted in the lake, it made him think of an eternally sleeping dragon. "If only we could put this assignment off for eight months, when I'll have my glider pilot license. I could take you up in the sky for the first-ever high school video aerial shot of creepy Geezer Castle—that'd be the *bomb*. We might even discover what the hell the old man is up to in there."

"Save it for the sequel. We can't put this shoot off for eight seconds. Places, guys."

Marlie stepped into the rear of the craft, making room for Zeb, who gently placed his sign where it wouldn't be seen in the boat shots.

Zeb knew this video about liberating the Indians from Spain's California missions was more about liberating themselves from high school. It was obviously headed for Hokeyville, but so would be the videos by all the other senioritis victims jumping through one more hoop on course to graduation. At least theirs would have more color and snap than those of their classmates.

Even without an aerial view of the castle, Geezer Island had enough genuine spookiness to guarantee that.

J.D. scooted carefully around them, sporting a shaggy throw rug around his shoulders like an animal pelt, followed by Nolan attempting to keep his balance and as much nobility as he could muster with his face painted with football eye-black streaks. The players assumed their positions for Marlie's first shot, an upward angle on the Indians looking across the great lake toward their encounter with destiny. The gathering dusk amplified the gloom hanging heavily over the bit of Geezer's house not fully obscured by the ominous fence and the abundant overgrowth its owner had allowed to flourish for decades.

Marlie started filming with a hushed order. "Hurry up or we're gonna need night goggles for the camera." Out of habit, Zeb reached down to start the outboard motor. "Cut!" she declared in a hoarse whisper. "Good idea, Zeb—let's show the Ohlone braves operating an outboard."

"Oops." Zeb turned off the motor and readied himself to enter the frame, but his attempt to get in character was disrupted by a mockingbird's repetition of the motor sound from high in a eucalyptus tree at the lake's edge, causing the movie's cast to lose it in chuckles.

"You da man, Mock," Zeb called out. "We're buddies, Mock and me," he added, for the benefit of his friends.

"Bull," Nolan replied. "You're just a two-legged dog to that bird."

"Dead wrong, dude. He and I *talk* to each other. Get this." Zeb looked up to Mock in his treetop and projected a chirrupy *shave-and-a-haircut*. The boys allowed the bird a respectful moment of silence, only to hear the bird go off on a vocalizing spree of birdsongs accented with an occasional bark and squeak.

"Wow, you guys are tight," sniggered J.D.

Grousing, Zeb complained to Mock, "I feed you chocolate peanuts and this is the thanks I get?"

Nolan had barely chuckled, "Looks like Doctor Dolittle's gonna lose his license," when *two bits* echoed down from the treetop.

"Yes!" Zeb pumped his fist. "Gracias, pal!" Resuming his cool, he sneered at his friends. "Case closed."

"Will you people focus, *please*," Marlie fumed. "We don't have time to do this twice. Now let's see some nobility and courage that'll leap off the screen." The actors struck a pose that wasn't too embarrassing and took up paddling. "Now let's hear the song, nice and quiet-like."

Working their paddles, the boys reached into the lowest strata of their laryngeal ranges and came up with their newly minted cover of an old hymn:

Go down, Miwok
Way down in Mission Land
Tell old Padre
Let my people go

Marlie halted the recording and acknowledged that the performance wasn't half bad, but there wasn't much time for pride and joy. They rowed past a buoy floating in the water with a sign reading

PRIVATE PROPERTY BEYOND THIS LINE
NO TRESPASSING

Geezer's island loomed ever larger. Between slats in the fence walling off a dock at the edge of the island, they could glimpse Geezer's creaky boat, some twenty feet long with a bow pulpit, resting at a dock built on pillars rising from the lake. The rustling of leaves in the forest surrounding the old house lent a disquieting passacaglia to Mock's vocal play ringing hollow on the evening breeze.

J.D. wondered aloud, "I sure would like to know what goes on in that house."

"Same here," said Zeb. "Sometimes I've seen flashes coming from his roof."

"The place is probably crawling with rats," offered Nolan.

"Yeah, rats. Geezer's probably never taken out the garbage. He just keeps spreading it in layers on the floor, till now there's only an itty-bitty crawl space up near the ceiling. That's why he almost never comes out—it's too hard to get down."

Having secured her critical first shot, Marlie felt free to join the party. "I think he's got thousands of garlic bulbs hanging from the walls. Or totem poles made of squirrel heads. Real ones."

Zeb perked up. "Maybe we're underestimating the guy. The house is really a disguise for an underground playboy mansion, with a spa and movie theater and bowling alley and servants, and Geezer brings the babes in by secret underwater tunnel."

Their mirth evaporated as they reached the island. The Indians lifted their paddles into the boat, making as little sound as possible, and stepped ashore. Zeb wound the boat's rope around a tree and propped his mission sign on a vine crawling across the fence. Marlie lit a lantern and handed it to J.D. while scanning the fence up and down.

"I don't know, Zeb. I didn't realize how high this is."

"It don't bother me none. I'll go first. Nolan, gimme a leg up."

That was enough for him to reach the top of the fence, but the moment he did, a spark leapt at him from a wire at the top. He howled and tumbled to the ground.

"Holy crap!"

Marlie was horrified. "Are you okay?!"

"What happened?!"

"The damn thing shocked me! The old kook's got an electrocuting wire up there!"

J.D. whistled. "This guy's too much."

Nolan gave Marlie a look. "How 'bout we cut this shot and get the hell back in the boat?"

Rubbing his still-living head and body for reassurance, Zeb muttered, "How do we know he hasn't electrified the lake too?"

It had been all fun and games till it wasn't. Their faux spookiness having been shot through with the real thing, Marlie reached for levity, aiming the camcorder at her own face for a scarily well-hammed rendition of the final panicked, plaintive self-shot close-up of the camera girl from *The Blair Witch Project*. "I want our mom and J.D.'s mom and Nolan's mom to know I'm so, *so* sorry!" That said, she leapt into the boat and welcomed the sound of an eight-horsepower motor whisking them back to safe harbor at home.

Oookay, I think we've had about enough of that, thought Marlie, relieved to have returned her attention to the present, in which she was winding the convertible through apple orchards and vineyards not all that far from the lake. *Focus on the present. I don't want to greet my sibs weighted down by chilly memories. I shouldn't have gone down that path. Tonight is dedicated to fun!*

3

For Zeb, imagination-tripping could be as exciting—and as dangerous—as gunning his Kawasaki dual-sport motorcycle. Now that he'd biked two-thirds of the way to the folks' place, he'd decided to let himself have a run at the former.

Somewhere along a forlorn state highway crossing the Napa Valley, he was treating himself to a Fosters Freeze break, which brought with it the twin delights of a rest from the road and a chance to cut his imagination loose. Since that could be as harrowing as being passed by one eighteen-wheeler while he was passing another one, he snipped the wires restraining his creativity with due caution. Much of the time his fantasies were light fun, seeds to plant as verbal notes on his phone for later harvesting. But sometimes, traveling in Imaginationland, he'd find treacherous terrain under his wheels.

Evidently, he'd not shaken the spooking he'd gotten from that stalking eagle during his twilight glide the evening before. He'd often declared to his parents—and himself—that he granted top priority status to defensive driving while riding his bike, and accordingly he'd demonstrated rock-solid discipline prohibiting fantasizing on the road. During this trip up from Oakland he could feel his creative juices surging as he rode the bridge over the Carquinez Strait on one of the busiest superhighways in the West, so he made it his business to turn off onto a lightly traveled country road at the first opportunity. Now, at a comfortable remove from the teenagers hanging out at the far end of the parking lot, he took in the delights of a chocolate-vanilla swirl cone, set his eyes on the distant hills bounding the western edge of the valley, and let it rip.

Wow, he thought—brainstorming in the wake of last night's eagle stare-down didn't take long to deliver a shiver. He felt himself floating a few feet above Montparnasse sidewalk traffic in the heart of Paris. A hunched-over bag lady was sitting on a bench, of no interest to the glut of passing shoppers, beret-bearing students, and tourists trying to affect native cool. The sight of her nibbling bits of what looked like cracked corn she was plucking from a paper bag gripped him mid-float and he paused to investigate. The chatter and traffic sounds of the city dissolved to a white noise penetrated only by a nearly inaudible high-pitched squeal. He slowly approached her and bent over to see her face, which didn't move—except for her eyelids, which flickered open, fixed on him, and blinked a nictitating membrane. She had the eyes of a raptor—or else a raptor had the body of a bag lady.

Yeesh. Yeah, he could run with that image for a story about an invisible invasion of spying bird-people, *but let's move on, shall we? We'll just finish this here ice cream cone and get back up on the Kawasaki.* Hanging with the girls at the parents' would be a nice and easy respite from travels mental and physical. Maybe Relura's mystery is simply a scheme for a family vacation, like getting us all down to the Galápagos after all, seven years late being a whole lot better than never.

Actually, anything non-weird would suffice. For four years there'd been an unwritten rule about troubling the waters with harrowing memories. Relura had still not recovered from believing she'd led her siblings to their deaths after they'd been suddenly removed from her sight on a weekend jaunt. Knowing that they'd somehow survived and returned didn't quite settle her nerves or stomach. Among the three of them, references to that holiday on ice were rare and usually oblique. So not to worry—neither Relura nor Marlie would venture into weird waters, and neither would he. Maybe someday he'd confide about the eagle glare to a fellow pilot or some birdwatching freak to get a little perspective. As for Bagladybird, he should safely shove her toward the back door of his mind to make room for the sweet fall breezes of Napa Valley whooshing along his face as he continued his journey.

But keeping weirdness at bay turned out to be beyond his capabilities of the moment. That hypnotic eagle had blown the door to his memory vault, and the alluring glow from within beckoned and would brook no retreat. Instead of hopping back onto his bike, he succumbed to the sucking vortex and lay on his back. *A few minutes' reminiscence for now won't hurt. I mean, that night and the next morning—it was exciting, right? Just a taste, to get the lure out of my system. I can take it. Make a little withdrawal from the memory bank.*

*   *   *

Despite the passage of four years, Zeb remembered listening to the dinner table chatter from the kitchen island where he was making toasty-pies sandwiched in a metal bread holder over a gas range flame. It was necessary to monitor the ongoing family dinner conversation, lest it take a hazardous turn toward the aborted landing on the beach at Geezer Island scarcely an hour before.

"So, Relura, what does your research squadron hope to get out of this frog gland study?"

Dan Morell was trying to get a handle on what his older daughter's work involved. Marlie and her mother listened for Relura's answer over a scattering of Chinese food cartons on the dining room table.

"So far it's just basic research, but if we can isolate the glandular stimuli for new tissue growth in metamorphosing tadpoles, it might lead to a catalyst for nerve-lining repair in humans," Relura replied. "Maybe soup up people's memory function someday."

Her mother, Jeanine, smacked her lips after her final bite of Kung Pao tofu. "Well, get on with it, whatever-your-name-is."

The parents were in a good mood, as might be expected on the eve of an adventure that would take them far from the mainland grid deep into the exotic tropical wilderness of Kauai the very next day. Marlie was feeling pretty good too, since her video production crew had managed to squeeze a fairly spectacular gallon of lemonade out of a nearly fatal lemon. The shot of the toppling Indian recovering from a shocking security mechanism at La Misión de Santa Relura would add some colorful production value to their video— and they'd scored it without having to take Zeb to the emergency room or otherwise reveal their indulgence in the kind of trespassing misdemeanor they'd been admonished not to attempt.

"And what about that big video shoot of yours, Marlie?" asked her father.

"It was all just ducky, Dad. I'm certain we'll ace the project." Throughout most of the four seconds her response consumed, she did manage to avoid looking at her brother, whose ears had pricked at their father's inquiry, but at the last moment, she couldn't help exchanging a look with Zeb, and that was all it took.

Jeanine's head swiveled toward Zeb and caught him lobbing a look back to Marlie. "What?" she demanded.

"What what?"

"What happened with your video that we're not supposed to know about? Zeb?"

Zeb returned to the table bearing a plateful of apple-filled toasty-pies. "Words fail us."

"Words fail *you*," countered Marlie. "The shoot was a grand success. The class is gonna love it. Nobody else's video will have a scenic backdrop as cool as Geezer Island. We're going to say that the Indian collaborators in the mission put a hex on the wall."

"A hex?" Dan made no effort to disguise his doubts about the academic rigor of this assignment for what was supposed to be Advanced Placement U.S. History. "This is for history class at Hogwarts High?"

"Mrs. Holmes calls them twistory videos," Zeb explained. "We're supposed to put our own contemporary spin on what actually went down back in the day."

"That's encouraging. In ten years, there will be millions of video producers on unemployment."

"Hmmm—I'm afraid I detect creeping Geezeritis there, Pop."

"Sometimes old school is just plain old, Dad," added Marlie.

"Would you two stop referring to our neighbor as 'Geezer'? It's rude."

"Minor problem, Mom—no one knows his name!"

Zeb muttered, "Yet."

"I'd be a little more charitable if I were you, Zeb. Someday you're going to be an eccentric old man just like him."

Zeb emitted a gasp that was less than eighty percent jest. Dan would have piled on, but he was interrupted by sudden darkness and silence as the lights and stereo went out, only to return a moment later.

"It's the solar winds," offered Marlie.

"What exactly are the solar winds?" Jeanine inquired. Marlie noticed that her father was paying attention, glad that his wife had spared him having to ask.

"Streams of plasma; subatomic particles given off by the sun. It's what kicks up auroras in the atmosphere of some planets, including ours."

"Righto," said Relura. "We're going to get hammered by them this weekend. There could be blackouts."

Dan smiled at his wife. "Just think—by this time tomorrow, we'll be so far off the grid we wouldn't know if the whole world were freezing in the dark."

Jeanine arched an eyebrow for his benefit. "Grid or no grid, Dan, once we get in that tent, you and I are not going to be freezing."

The twins rolled their eyes in sync. "Excuse us," said Marlie, abruptly rising and picking up some empty plates. "Cleanup time."

"It's almost eight, Dan. Let's finish up packing. Relura, please get ready."

As Dan and Jeanine hustled upstairs, the twins in their wake, Zeb decided it was time for some truth-telling. "You know we love our sister, but I'm a little insulted that you think we need a babysitter. We're adults, Mom."

"You're high school students."

"For a few months."

Dan chimed in, "I should think you'd relish an opportunity for the three of you to be together on your own."

"This is all because of one off-the-books party Marlie and I threw, we know. That was a full year ago, parents! Now you don't trust us not to burn down the house."

"Of course we trust you not to burn down the house, Zeb, but with Marlie's science project and your flying lesson, it just makes sense to have Relura on hand to take care of the dog and the chickens."

"Yeah, right." Entering their bedroom, Jeanine and Dan set to shoving the final few items into their backpacks, eliciting from Zeb a change of subject. "I don't see why you can't take us on this vacation. What are we, dogdoo?"

"Guess what, Zeb: you are going to school this week, and your father and I are going to Hawaii."

"Hawaii's for tourists. Can't you think big? How about Antarctica? There's a solar eclipse about to go down in Antarctica."

"Why not the moon? We've never been there."

"I'm serious! You could take us all. Marlie and I still have our passports for the Galápagos trip."

"Which you canceled," Marlie added.

"I never promised we would visit Relura in the Galápagos. We only *considered* squandering a fortune on air travel, hotels, and a boat during an attack of financial insanity."

"You don't have to come," Zeb pointed out. "Relura can take us. And we wouldn't need old-fogy hotels. We can sleep on the planes."

Relura appeared in the doorway as her parents were testing the weight balance of their packs. "What's this about?"

"Get your jacket, Relura," Dan advised. "The twins want you to take them to Antarctica."

"Twins for sale," Jeanine threw in for good measure. "A dollar apiece or two for a nickel."

"Are you sure you want to go hiking? You and Dad could cancel Kauai and hang with us."

"And deprive you of quality time alone with your siblings? I don't think so."

Just for the hell of it, Marlie decided to shore up her brother's case. "Who could be a more perfect guide for a great trip to the Antarctic than ace naturalist and world traveler Relura Morell?!"

"Relura is a perfect guide and I would trust her to take you to the moon—"

"BING!"

"—if NASA would pay for it." Jeanine headed for the stairs, leading her husband by an affectionate hand.

Truth was, both twins were jealous of their parents getting to hike Kauai's spectacular coastal trail and camp beside a four-hundred-foot waterfall, but they were sufficiently well-mannered to tell their folks they loved them and wished them a great time. At the front door, car keys in hand, Relura told the twins, "I'll be back by eleven, thoroughly confident that the house will be intact and clean upon my return." A moment later, she and her parents were out the door and her siblings found themselves with a little "us time."

"And queen check," declared Marlie a few hours later, feigning self-confidence.

"And check check," responded Zeb with a swift move of said queen to a diagonal line of fire aimed at her king.

"I was afraid you'd see that," Marlie remarked, idly chewing another handful of popcorn. So she was behind; the game was still a satisfying way to pass the time indoors while a steady rain fell upon the neighborhood.

Crack-BOOM—the latest in a volley of thunderclaps in a series that had been unsettling them for the last half hour jolted Zeb out of his chair. "Whoops."

"Where are you going? This isn't over."

"Gotta check my window. I think I left it open when I filled Mock's dish."

Zeb bounded upstairs and discovered, indeed, a thin streak of rainwater lining the edge of his bed. In closing the door of that horseless barn, he noticed that, lo and behold, even in the depths of a fall storm, his one-customer diner on the garage roof outside his window was full. Mock was nibbling on a couple of chocolate peanuts and washing them down with sky-fresh water pooled in the cat food can under the Mock Diner sign Zeb had painted on a slab of walnut a few years ago.

This scene called for some observation, so Zeb flopped down on his bed. He heard Marlie call up the stairs, inquiring as to whether he'd be returning to the battlefield, and he called back, "I don't know." This chess game had gone on long enough, as it usually did when he played with Marlie; she could wait a couple of minutes.

He was still able to beat her about half the time, but he feared that the more time she spent sharpening her brain in science, the less frequent his victories would become. The first-place plaque awarded for her varied-wavelength holography research in the Northern California regional science fair competition vibrated in his mind as much as on her bedroom wall.

Yeah, he had a framed big-competition certificate of his own from last year's National Comics Contest Youth Division, but he doubted that would carry equal weight with the magisterial admissions committees at Berkeley and Stanford, where Marlie was a sure shoo-in. He sometimes wished his scholarly fires burned as brightly as those of his sister, but that was not going to happen. Between soaring and artistic visions, he was already Roman-riding two consuming passions displeased to be yoked together, and the specter of graduation just seven months away obliged him to juggle five courses at the same time. He understood the parents' pointed suggestion that he keep his GPA high enough to satisfy Berkeley, and he was sorta complying, but it was a struggle. A powerful magnet pulled at him all the time. Visions danced in his head to music too jazzed for sugarplums—like, for example, the one that just popped onto his inner screen: *a hummingbird the size of an aircraft carrier with headlights in its eye sockets and wings, and a hundred-foot beak that it pokes into the earth to suck up toxins to which it is immune, which it then carries to the edge of space, where it incinerates them with a blast of neutrino energy it absorbs photosynthetically from interstellar breezes of dark matter abounding throughout the galaxy—*

Ahem. Well, the point is that with an internal brook babbling such stories through his consciousness, beckoning him to bring them to life with pixel paint, it was no wonder that he so often wanted to explode the treadmill peddled by the parents-universidad-industrial complex. Hurl the pieces to the four winds; he preferred sailplane sorties off a tropical coast far from America while creating the Great American Graphic Novel.

Zeb's reverie of a revolution in personal policy was interrupted by the sound of Marlie ascending the stairs to her room. A young lady with limited patience for waiting around, Marlie wasn't going to sink roots into a dining room chair with no one else in the room.

Settling on her bed, Marlie switched on her bedside lamp and picked up her new magazine. Looking for the holography article, she cruised past the feature on the eclipse; sure, catching a glimpse of the sun's corona would be quite the kick for an astronomy buff, but she'd been only joking when she'd joined Zeb in ribbing their parents about Antarctica. Solar eclipses come along every year or two somewhere in the world easier to get to than Antarctica. She'd get her share in time.

There was another adventurous travel destination Marlie was dead serious about—space. Her brother's glider ambitions were fine for him, and she looked forward to checking out the NorCal terrain with him some day from a mile or two above, but she intended to reach altitudes measured hundreds or hundreds of thousands or even millions of miles above the surface of the Earth. She would shine as a mission scientist, courtesy of NASA or one of the private space-travel outfits in various stages of gestation. This dream required frequent refueling of confidence, given the fifteen-hundred-to-one odds against acceptance in the astronaut corps, but it would be a flight so magnificent as to justify the investment of more than a decade, even if it only lasted a few weeks.

Her need for understanding the physical principles of the universe was visceral, at one with the craving of her red blood cells for oxygen, but so far it had been confined to earthly quarters. In spaceflight—perhaps to another planet—she would be able to experience those principles in thrilling new dimensions. The brush of light across her helmeted face in the vacuum of space, the laws of motion, celestial mechanics—these axioms of nature on a cosmic scale demanded to be grasped. It's as if some conscious design process had selected these rules from among an infinite number of possibilities as worthy for the foundation of a universe. Who could emerge from a cave, having been whisked away by forces unseen, to a new country or a new world without thirsting to learn the lay of the new land and its various wonders and perils? What might the given physical parameters allow, and what would be beyond the pale of the possible?

Yet, incredibly, the vast majority of the species blessed with the capability to learn these secrets about our world and universe couldn't care less. The fire of Marlie's curiosity burned brightly as she bounded through the world surrounded by millions living out their lives in dim oblivion. *Life is so intensely rich in mysteries beckoning to be solved by the enterprise of physics.*

But there's no accounting for intellectual taste. Right across the hallway outside her room was someone with a pair of genomes nearly identical to hers but whose attitude toward physics was take it or leave it. Zeb had accumulated an impressive body of knowledge of zoology, which he was constantly putting to colorful use in his artwork, but for him the laws of physics were the way things had to be, and so be it. He appreciated that the world was constructed in such a way that he could fly miles into the sky without an engine, but the really juicy part of brain exploration was the freedom to imagine places, creatures, *and* rules of nature that needn't have a thing to do with old hamstringing reality.

At the moment, Zeb was training his imagination on his avian friend Mock. What goes on in Mock's mind on a night like this? And when Mock, that fine actor, impersonates characters, does he momentarily become them, whether human, dog, hammer, or boat motor?

Zeb was licking his chops to explore that terrain more extensively, when suddenly, from perhaps a hundred yards away, an odd sound broke into the trio being performed by wind, rain, and trees—an unfamiliar bird call, a few bright *kips* followed by a grating whirr. A moment later, when it sounded again, Mock spun around and took off into the air near his favorite perch, but this time he didn't settle there. Instead he entered into a curious aerial fandango with a strange bird, doubtless the source of the odd call.

Zeb yanked his binoculars from the hook near his desk and trained them on the scene, only to find something yet stranger coming through its lenses. Visible through the light rain, flashes appeared in a dome-like structure atop Geezer's roof. The dome was about twelve feet wide and five feet high, made of some transparent material fit into precisely curved struts. Zeb had seen that flashing display a couple of times in the last few years but always in the daytime, when it was harder to detect.

When the screw took another turn as the new bird flew over the dome, he stood up and barked in a hoarse voice, "Marlie—get the camera."

"I'm reading."

"Something fishy's going on at Geezer's."

Switching on the camera as she trudged into Zeb's room, Marlie followed Zeb's line of sight. Mock and the avian stranger were illuminated by the staccato flashes of light emanating from the dome atop Geezer Castle. She got the recording going in time to get a good look at them before the new bird suddenly seemed to fall, or dive, right into the dome and disappear.

The flickering lights went out at Geezer's, followed by a blinding flash everywhere.

*CrackCRACKA-**CRACK-BOOM!***

Holy shit—that was the loudest thunder the twins had ever heard in their lives. *Very* local. And now the power was out. For a moment Zeb wondered if the house might burn down after all.

"Whoa!"

"I've got this under control." Zeb heard Marlie stumble in the dark on her way back to her room. She messed around in a drawer for a second and then returned, waving a flashlight beam around the room. "Ah! And there was light!" she declared.

She expected a reply, but Zeb was silent, staring out his window. She joined him there as he picked up the binoculars again. Was it? Uh-oh . . . there was a fire all right—*on Geezer's roof.* Just a bit of orange flame flickering over there, but it was the real thing.

"A lightning fire . . . "

"The Geeze," said Zeb. "This could be real trouble."

"I'm calling 9–1–1." She plucked out her phone and tapped away at it, paused, and then dropped it on Zeb's desk. "No bars!"

"What could the fire department do anyway? Row a fire truck over there?"

"I wonder if Geezer even knows. He could be so decrepit he maybe couldn't even hear the lightning strike."

"There were those lights in the attic."

"That doesn't mean he was in there. He might not even be awake."

Zeb turned to his sister. "Don't you think we should do something to help an old man in trouble?"

Marlie was a little queasy about where this was heading, but she granted that it would be horrible if Geezer burned to death. "What are you getting at?"

"I think you know."

"What, now? In the dark?"

"No, tomorrow, when Geezer and the house and his little bird friend are soaked ashes."

The fire was diminishing and so was the rain. "I think the fire's on the way out, Zeb."

"We don't know what's going on inside. Maybe Geezer's bed caught fire. Or maybe he's unconscious from smoke inhalation."

Marlie mulled that over. "I guess we wouldn't have to worry about the fence with the power out."

"No fence problems—it looks ordained to me. We oughta go and drag him out of bed and tell him to grab his bird guest and get in our boat."

"If we barge in there, he might shoot us as intruders."

"Gunman Geezer? I shiver at the thought. All we have to do is call out who we are when we get there. If he doesn't want us coming in—and is conscious enough to let us know—we'll split."

Hmm. Marlie had to admit she'd love to see the inside of Geezer Castle. Sane or not, the old guy is an ex-inventor, kind of a kindred spirit. If he's grateful for their saving his life, maybe they could get him talking and find out how he passes his time. Does he regret fencing himself off from the whole world like that?

Buuuttt—the odds against that happening were a bit long. And pretending that invading his woodsy little fortress was purely a humanitarian move was a flimsy excuse for voyeurism. It would be a mite more honest to acknowledge that the temptations of the castle and potential revelations about the life of its keeper were so tasty that dipping their toes in any ethical or legal improprieties had to be forgivable.

No, switch off that rationalization bunk. This is serious! Either they're going to risk letting an old man go to his death and regret their cowardice the rest of their lives or they'd have to take action, moral ambiguities be damned. "All right," she announced. "Rescue patrol! Let's get a big screwdriver to jack open his front door."

They ran for their jackets and were headed out when Marlie pulled up short. "Of course, there's the Relura factor. She could be back any time."

"So? We'll put a note on the door. We might even get back before she does."

"Yeah. Maybe we'll have an interesting guest with us too."

Marlie scribbled a note on an empty grocery bag and grabbed some tape. In the candlelight Zeb read:

BACK IN A JIFF. STAY OUT OF TROUBLE.
LOVE, US

"Perfect. Let's do it."

Marlie taped the note to the front door while Zeb hustled down to the lakeside to untie their boat. A moment later they pushed off.

The light rain, the wind rolling through the trees, and the intermittent thunder rumbles masked the noise from the outboard. Marlie spoke close to Zeb's ear and kept her voice low. "This could be fun! It'll be quite the score if we find Geezer and convince him to come back to our place. We can make him a toasty-pie. That could be the highlight of his life if all he's been eating for twenty years is dog food. We could draw him out of his shell." Something told Zeb that was rather unlikely, but he kept his peace. "We could be heroes for saving his life!"

"You're assuming his life is still savable."

"Ew—what if the lightning did hit him and we find a burnt corpse?!"

They passed the buoy, pulled up where they had hitched the boat earlier in the day, and climbed out. Marlie took the lantern to the tree next to the fence and nodded to her brother. Zeb scaled nine feet up the trunk, clambered out on a branch, and poked through the ivy to touch the fence top. No shock. "We're goin' in."

Marlie handed Zeb the lantern, deftly finessed the tree, and joined him at the top. Together they dropped down onto the other side of the fence, scanned the terrain, and began making their way through the wooded darkness in the direction of the house of legend.

Traipsing slowly through the thickets and tangled tree roots, they were wondering how soon the house would emerge, when suddenly it appeared in front of them. The lantern illuminated little more than the front porch and a few rusty old appliances scattered around outside, but the flickering lightning provided glimpses of broad decay, peeling paint, and dark windows.

They stepped quietly up the steps and paused at the door.

"So, Zeb: we're doing this for Geezer's sake . . . right?"

"What do you mean?! If you were a hundred years old and all alone in a house on fire, wouldn't you appreciate some help?" Looking guilty nonetheless, Zeb tapped on the door, waited through a few beats of silence, then tapped again. Still nothing.

Marlie whispered, "I don't hear Geezer calling for help."

"Well," Zeb replied, "would you call for help if you were unconscious or paralyzed? We'd feel pretty stupid if we bailed and it turned out he'd been lying there in desperate condition a few feet from us." Absent a counter argument, Zeb jimmied the lock and gently pushed open the door.

A peal of laughter from the teenaged locals jolted Zeb back to the present. Ice cream joint. Reunion with the sisters. *Heck, what am I doing? Marlie might get to the house long before me and they'll both be pissed off. Pause the replay. I've got to fire up the bike.*

4

"To another triple conjunction!" declared Marlie, clinking long-neck beer bottles with her brother and sister in a toast to their reunion. She always felt good seeing those two faces, in this case by flickering home-campfire light on the patio of the parents' two-story house under a clear, starry sky. "Look—it's so clear you can see the Andromeda Galaxy."

Looking up in the direction she indicated, Zeb found the faint photon fuzz near Andromeda's knee. "You found that fast enough," he observed.

"It only takes a second or two if you know the trick. I trace it from Cassiopeia."

The Three all had significant others in their lives—indeed Relura counted her blessings every day for having found the man who was becoming the most important being in her life—but nothing could diminish the depth of the bond these siblings shared with each other. Now, over tamales Relura had scored from a nearby wayside tamale truck operation long adored by their family, they were wallowing in those comfortable spiritual waters out back of the family home. Crickets and frogs in the neighborhood had started up their random two-part choral improvisation. Low flames flickered up from a fire circle at their feet, a warming offset to the cool reflection of the crescent moon off the surface of the lake. The presence of the lake's dark island could stir unsettling memories of its rarely mentioned former resident, but present circumstances kept them at bay. Being together at home catalyzed a chemistry of fun and security and deep brain stimulation that radiated through the intersecting territories of their lives.

Marlie had arrived at dusk. She and Relura caught up on recent news, up to and including the club-dancing jaunt Marlie and a friend had taken at ten the night before. While the back-and-forth chatter was fun, it was a little odd to be back home when the place was parentless. The folks were flying back from New Orleans at an event the siblings' mother had planned for the hard-working staff of a posh Napa restaurant specializing in Cajun cuisine—an annual perk for which the owners whisked everyone off on an all-expenses-paid trip to the Crescent City for three days of deep gourmet diving. Jeanine had convinced Dan to take a little time away from Skywalker Sound, where he was responsible for adding rocket and weapon sounds to yet another sci-fi space opera, so that he could join in the festivities and add a helping hand with logistics. (More than once, their offspring had marveled in private that their father spent so many hours of his life engineering fake cinematic space epics, never dreaming that one vastly more fantastic had happened to two of his own children.) The parents' flight home was already in progress, and they were sure to arrive bushed late that evening but excited to find their entire brood with them at the house.

Relura and Marlie were always happy to spend time together and had a true bond as sisters. They always said that even if they had just met as strangers, they would have become fast friends through their ravenous hunger for unraveling the secrets of nature. That they were blessed with both genetic and intellectual sisterhood—and their colorful, handsome, devoted brother—was icing on the cake of life.

When Zeb puttered up the driveway on his bike, his sisters sauntered out to greet him. Together again, at last. Zeb assured them the ride up had transpired without mishap. He was queried about his flights of fancy and sailplanes for a few minutes, in which he informed them that he was steadily progressing up the ranks of sailplane aerobatics, having already logged four hundred hours and earned a gold badge en route to diamond, a rank he anticipated reaching in two or three years. Everyone understood that their adventure four years ago, for all its moments of quailing nerves and outright terror, had hooked him on flight as much as Marlie. He'd already begun sailplane training before "the incident," so, craving flight more than ever, it only made sense to build upon his flying start and become an ace pilot. Gliding a motorless aircraft using thermals, as birds have been doing for tens of millions of years, offered him an exciting way to feed his desire. Besides, it was the only option suitable to his temperament, which lacked the crazy level of academic discipline Marlie was exercising in the interest of her astronaut corps application that lay a few years in the future.

On to new business, declared Marlie's inner conversation monitor. She wasted no time launching an information-seeking missile at her beloved big sister.

"Okay, Relura, Zeb's here. Fess up—you have a cutesycake in the oven."

"Negative, Nosy. At least not yet, to my knowledge."

"But if you did, you'd tell me first, right?"

"She means *us*," Zeb corrected.

"Gee. I don't know. I might want to tell my husband first."

"Traitor. I've got big plans for that baby."

Zeb added, "I'll start him on flying lessons when he's in fourth grade."

"What if it's a girl?"

"All the better," Zeb replied. "Female pilots are inspiring."

"Damn right." Marlie knew her brother wholeheartedly supported her astronaut aspirations. She turned back to Relura. "No pressure, Relura. Niece or nephew, Aunt Marlie is all in."

"Nary a hint of pressure around here. When the parents left, Dad remarked, 'It's apple-picking season. What a perfect job for grandchildren!'"

"Subtle, Dad."

"Never mind that. Tell me something about your love life and what *you're* gestating."

"Those subjects could be connected over time, given that one of my tech crewmates is disconcertingly horny-making, but presently all's quiet on the love life front—but what I'm gestating scientifically could be as adventurous as any wild romance."

"The girl's a risk-taker."

"Oh, like you're not, flying around at ten thousand feet without a motor and banking your financial future on comics?"

"First of all—graphic novels, not comics, all right? And second, they're my financial present, not just the future. I've pulled in twenty-seven K already in royalties on Shangrilarian's debut, with more coming in, and the publisher has advanced me another ten on the sequel. But thanks for your confidence, Sis."

Marlie felt a twinge of guilt for having cast some leaden doubt on her brother's dreams. "Zeb, I'm sorry. You're a phenomenal talent. Chalk up my worries to ignorance about the graphic novel world. If anybody can make it there, you can. But talk about risky . . . " She paused a moment, weighing whether or not to refer to The Secret. "By the way, have any of your readers asked how you came by the name Shangrilarian?"

"A good many, in fact. I tell 'em it's a tribute to the alien that abducted my physicist sister Marlie Morell and me to outer space." For a moment Zeb took some satisfaction in Marlie's embarrassment at having asked such a neurotic question. "If you recall, Marlie, Shangrilarian emerged from an aerial sea that rests atop the highest peak in a Tibetan paradise. The humans who discovered him gave him that name as a tribute to the location, his visible skeleton as transparent as glass, his fluid movement, and his radially symmetrical icosahedral resting state." That answered her question but hadn't quite put her in her place for implying he was a risk freak. "Well, tell Relura about your risk-free endeavor."

Marlie appealed to their sister. "It's far from risk-free, I know that. Even if we get startup dough from the VCs with no debt, if I screw up, I may never get another shot."

"Pardon my ignorance, but 'VCs'?"

"Venture capitalists. I'm learning venture capitalese as a second language. Now phrases like term sheet, proof of concept, entrepreneur in residence, and uncapped financing roll off my tongue on Sand Hill Road."

"Better you than me," commented Zeb. "And to think it's all in the interest of burnishing your resume for a risk-free seat in a space capsule atop a five-million-pound rocket." He turned to Relura. "Of course, the Mars cruise is just a warm-up lap before voyaging to Jupiter."

"If I've proven myself on the Mars mission, I'll improve my chances of landing a place on the Jupiter team, which is obviously preferable since it has auroras."

"By the way," queried Zeb, "have any of your prospects asked how you came to be so interested in auroral phenomena?"

Marlie gave her brother a look of strained patience before turning to Relura. "So, how about your adventures in Frogland, Sis?"

"We'll get to that. What exactly are you pitching to your prospects, Marlie?"

The twins both noticed another Relura Deft Dodge and bookmarked that subject for later. Marlie accommodated her.

"It's a plasma density cloud inducer that could generate local auroras at a hundredth of the cost of systems currently used by the navy and others to do the same thing. By the way, mum's the word on this. Auroras have been found on our outer planets and even light years away in a different star system. The age of plasma science is still dawning, and this device could kick it up a full quantum leap."

Yet again, Zeb reflected on the obviousness of the connection between Marlie's fascination with auroras and the bizarre adventure that had befallen them when they were seventeen. Her embrace of the intellectual mores of acceptable science required serious compartmentalizing of that traumatic thrill. So, when she threw him an instinctive nervous glance, he nodded respectfully while keeping a poker face, which she saw right through. It was like having coffee with an ex-lover—the relationship might, over time, morph into a wonderful friendship as long as neither party ever referred to their former romance. Let her keep that adventure cordoned off at the back of her memory where no one would ever visit, save Marlie herself in the uncontrollable realm of her dreams.

Marlie wrenched the conversation's steering wheel in another direction. "So, Relura, your maybe-baby was not the reason you summoned us up here."

"No. But I do happen to have news from Frogland." The twins knew better than to ask if this were another dodge. Relura had a distinctive style of pacing herself in broaching ticklish subjects. "One of our projects involves investigating the effects of methane ebullition in wetlands on frog habitat, so I've been wanting to take a closer look around the swampy terrain surrounding our feeder creek."

"Ebullition?"

"That's when methane builds up in the soil until the pressure is so great it gets burped out. It's as if the marsh is breathing this stuff." She looked at Zeb. "Hey, there's an idea for one of your books, Z—make a character out of a swamp!"

"You're stalling. We know you've got something strange cooking. Let's get to the meat of it."

Relura nodded respectfully. "All right. I have an unusual animal incident to report." She was surprised to see that her siblings each sat up straighter in something like alarm, which intensified as each of the twins noticed the other doing likewise. "What?" Relura said, looking from one to the other.

"Nothing," said Marlie. "Go ahead."

"Yes, do. However, it just so happens that I've also got an unusual animal incident to report," said Zeb. Marlie's face then gave her away. "What, you too?" he pressed.

Marlie's discomfort in the presence of the scientifically weird was as predictable as the sunrise. Her ambivalence about the stalking owl forbade answering. "Please continue, Relura. You started this."

"I have to admit to some mixed feelings here. While you're the only people I could confide in about this without ringing a bunch of kooky bells, I'm still afraid of involving you in a pursuit of strange phenomena."

Zeb pronounced his diagnosis. "Relura's still suffering Post-Abduction Stress Disorder."

"Of course I am. Do you understand that my fate would have been worse than death if you had not reappeared after that disaster?"

"For God's sake, Relura, it's been four years and you're still freaking out?!"

"My point exactly. That was by far the worst day of my life. And your story about what had happened to you . . . "

"Our 'story'?" said Zeb. "I know you've harbored doubts all this time. You think most of what we told you was a shared hallucination."

Marlie rolled her eyes as Relura tried to suppress an embarrassed smile.

"Well, I do know you had a too-close encounter of the very scary kind, and that's bad enough."

"I'd like to know what you've told Sean," said Marlie.

"Almost nothing, though it feels dishonest, since we're going to spend the rest of our lives together. He does know something harrowing happened with you two on that trip."

"That's all right. I'm sure he'll survive without hearing the gory details." Marlie glanced at Zeb and got a funny vibe. "You haven't told Alyssa, have you?!" The only answer acceptable to Marlie would have been "Of course not!" and when Zeb didn't provide it, she exclaimed, "Are you trying to flush my career down the crapper?! The bank will surely forgive my $43,000 in student loans when they hear a blabbermouth has rendered my diploma as worthless as a used Kleenex."

"The ancients called the devil BeelZEBub for a reason."

"You wretch! How could you do that to me, Zeb?!"

"Calm down, and don't sweat the small stuff, or even the huge stuff if no one believes it. I made it sound like a joke, which is exactly how she took it."

"But she could have told a hundred people already!"

"No, she hasn't, because I asked her to tell no one."

"All the more reason she knows you're not kidding."

"*Au contraire*—she thinks that was part of the joke. Nobody on Earth knows but us, not even the parents."

"I had a close call with them last year. Mom found the metallic souvenir in my closet and showed it to Dad. They asked me about it."

"What did you say?"

"I told them I like putting interesting scrap from scientific gear to good use, like in my holography setup. A line like that and a cute wink might not be totally convincing, but often enough it can get me a change of subject."

"You think they're dumb enough to not know what you're doing?"

"Of course they knew—but they have to choose their battles. They proba-bly think I lifted it from the lab or dragged it out of a dumpster. They have no reason to connect it to Geezer, and they've stopped asking if we have any idea why he never returned."

For the first time that evening, they all looked across the dark lake at Geezer's island. After a moment's silence, Relura said, "Last year Mom checked with the county and found out the property taxes are still getting paid on Geezer's house. She told them she was interested in buying the property if it were to go to auction."

"You've got to be kidding!"

"I think she made that up as a cover for her curiosity. Turns out ol' Geezer was well prepared for the unexpected. He'd set up an account flush enough to provide for an automatic withdrawal of property taxes every year."

"You mean that place could just sit there turning into an overgrown Angkor Wat till somebody digs it up in a thousand years?"

Zeb recalled their speculations about Geezer's house during their first visit to the place, when they were shooting their high school history video. "Maybe by now it really *is* crawling with vermin."

Marlie had had enough about Geezer. "*Anyway*, Relura, it sounded like you were maybe kinda getting around to telling—"

"Listen!" interrupted Relura. "Did you hear that?"

"Hear what?"

"That odd frog call."

"I hear about a thousand frog sounds and, as far as I'm concerned, they're all odd."

"I've got something to show you." Relura stepped inside the porch door to retrieve her camera. "We've got to do this now because I have to leave for the airport soon." She took a deep breath. "Early yesterday evening I heard a loud, male bullfrog call just like that one thirty seconds ago, coming from the same direction. It was a really anomalous sound."

"Anomalous how?"

"The call starts with the good old-fashioned *jug-o-rum* theme, though a lot louder, but then he takes off on a more complex riff, articulated almost like human speech. As soon as I heard it, I grabbed my camera and tracked his sound about a hundred yards that way"—she nodded southwest—"and when I got there, here's what I found." She clicked her camera into playback mode and her four-inch LED screen lit up with a striking image of a large bullfrog staring right at the viewer.

"Wow," whispered Zeb. "That image is good enough for IMAX."

"Not quite, but for five thousand dollars I expect it to come close. Now, watch what he does here."

"How do you know he's a he?" asked Marlie.

"See his right tympanum? The tipoff is it's larger than his eye. There he's stock-still, staring at me—that isn't unusual. But be patient."

A moment later the frog hopped straight toward the camera, bugged his eyes, and released a long, guttural, syncopated belch. A barely visible flash of light appeared near his head.

Zeb arched an eyebrow. "A vulgar froggy mugger."

"And a musical one at that," Relura replied. "I've never heard a cadence like that from a bullfrog."

"And what was that little flash near his head?" asked Marlie.

"I assume that was a will-o'-the-wisp."

"A cold swamp flame?" suggested Marlie.

"Yeah, from oxidizing methane. Sightings aren't so common these days as wetlands get more depleted, but they're a little perk for those of us who hang around swamps. But focus on this." Suddenly the frog leapt six feet closer to the camera and repeated his vocalization. On the soundtrack, the twins could hear Relura muttering, "Hey!" as if she were afraid the frog was about to jump down her shirt. Her viewing audience was similarly taken aback.

"That was rude," commented Marlie.

"Rude or not, he seemed mighty damned determined about something. I intended to keep the camera on him for a while, but then I got distracted by *this*." The tinny camera speaker emitted a barely audible screech. On screen, the camera's point of view swung up to catch sight of an eagle swooping below the nearby treetops before taking off again. The recording came to a stop and Relura turned off the camera.

"Jesus!" exclaimed Zeb.

"What?" asked Relura. She was surprised not only at the intensity of Zeb's reaction but also by Marlie, whose wide eyes were darting between her siblings. Zeb appeared to be considering how to answer when all three of them heard that peculiar frog call, live, from down near the creek. "See? He's out there. We should go check him out. I've been studying frogs for seven years, and I've never encountered behavior or vocalizations like his." Marlie responded with an ambivalent shrug. "Come on, Marlie." Relura was familiar with her sister's discomfort with strange animal behavior, a lingering symptom of their traumatizing experience four years before. "We should get a look at this charmer before he disappears."

The three siblings trod quietly through the tall grass by the red glow of Relura's field light, listening carefully to the massive amphibious Anura choir that performed every night at that time of year, waiting for the next eruption of Relura's burping orator. The farther they got from the house, the darker it got, and the more outstanding became the stellar panorama above.

When they got within forty yards of the frog concert, the musicians stilled. Relura halted their drive forward so as to encourage her siren caller to come forth. When he obliged, he inundated their aural environment with a *jug-o-rum* so close and loud that Marlie squeaked. The creature appeared five paces in front of them, his huge eyes reflecting back the red glow of Relura's light. After a moment's recovery, Marlie hastened to assure her siblings that she was fine with the frog showing up; she'd just been a little startled.

Zeb and Relura would like to have reassured her that there was nothing to be embarrassed about, but they were bound up in the frog's spell. They were awaiting his next move, which turned out to be an impressive leap straight toward the twins. Marlie wanted to hang tough, but she couldn't stop herself from stepping back a few inches. The frog was now just six feet away. Zeb thought he was behaving like a suspect found by detectives who knows he's been caught but is not going to fess up. For his part, the frog glared at the twins as if they were the suspects instead of him.

A passing fly buzzed his last as the frog's long, slimy weapon shot out of his mouth to snare a snack. As he swallowed it, the humans saw his eyes retract a bit toward the interior of his skull.

Zeb whispered, "Was that eye thing really necessary?"

"It helps him swallow," replied Relura. "He's multipurposing his eyeballs."

Marlie spotted an opportunity to redeem herself from her display of squeamishness. "Cut him a little slack, Zeb. I'll bet you'd retract your balls for a moment if it would aid your digestion." But she wasn't really taking this encounter in stride. The frog continued to maintain eye contact with her and Zeb, sliding his glare back and forth between the two of them. Nothing was easing her digestion; her stomach was in knots.

"I'm tempted to take him," Relura offered.

"Don't!" replied Marlie, a little more urgently than she intended.

"A brain scan could prove revelatory."

"I thought it was time for you to go to the airport."

"Perhaps you can let the frog go this time, Lura," advised Zeb.

Suddenly they heard Marlie's voice exclaim, "You wretch!" from behind them and yet somehow higher up, even though she was standing right next to them as still and silent as a dolmen. All three of them felt a shot of gooseflesh.

"It's Mock!" exclaimed Zeb. He and his sisters took a moment to catch their breath. Then he called up in the direction from which the sound had come, "Hey, Mock—how ya doin'?"

Zeb's old childhood avian pal responded in Relura's voice. "It feels dishonest."

That was unsettling. The twins became further unsettled when the bull-frog leapt right between the twins. "That'll do for now," said Marlie.

"Aren't you curious to see where he's headed?" asked Zeb, even though he knew how his twin would respond to an invitation to experience more animal weirdness: the same as if she'd been offered a paregoric cocktail.

"The party's over."

"Fine," said Relura, charitably. "At least you got to see my guy. I'm tempted to look for him again after I get back from the airport."

As she led the way back to the house, she put an arm around Zeb's shoulders. "Say, little brother, I could have sworn you reacted to the end of my video with something like alarm. Care to explain?"

After a moment's hesitation, Zeb laid out the facts of his golden eagle shared-flight encounter from the evening before. "The bird got up in my grill and stared at me for what must have been ten seconds." His sisters refrained from mentioning the obvious, leaving it to Zeb to train a spotlight on it. "The eagle on your video headed off to the east, which was right where I was flying just after sunset. It's hard to avoid the conclusion that it was the same bird."

"Oh, it's just an ordinary eagle-and-frog spy team," observed Marlie with a nervous chuckle. "Who knows what hell there'll be to pay if animals start monitoring us the way Relura studies frogs in her lab? What's next? Crickets? Bacteria? I'd hate to have ninety trillion spies in my intestines." About her own encounter with the owl, she said nothing.

Knowing her sister well, Relura knew there was something else going on. She recalled that Marlie had also shown some alarm at the eagle video, but she didn't press the matter. Zeb wasn't quite so lenient. "What is it with you, Marles? You're wired tighter than a violin's E string."

"It's nothing," stated Marlie, thus revealing that "it" was indeed something. Relura decided to let her be. Perhaps later that night she could get her sister to unwind a bit. For now, she stated her intention to research the records for any reports of similar behavior among frogs, adding, "I don't know what to say about your avian co-pilot, Zeb. I'm sure it wasn't the first time a sailplane pilot has encountered a bird close by."

"It wasn't my first time either. It was just the first time I'd been mad-dogged by one."

The three continued their walk back to the house quietly, until the silence was broken by the grating sound of Zeb's voice filtered through the vocal cords of a mockingbird overhead. "Vulgar froggy mugger!" Marlie forced an audible chuckle out of herself in a vain attempt to cover her fear that, after four long years of relative calm, something creepy was gaining on her again, slowly but surely accelerating by the minute.

An hour after Relura's departure for the airport, Zeb was idly sketching a new landscape for Shangrilarian's next adventure. He'd chatted with Marlie for a while but he could tell that the moment to chew over this odd business with the frog and the eagle—and whatever else seemed to be troubling Marlie—had not yet arrived. There'd be time for that. Relura had called to say that the parents' plane was delayed; they wouldn't be home till at least half past ten.

The pleasure Zeb had taken earlier in the evening in being back with his sisters was now alloyed with some nameless background anxiety. He'd barely begun to process his chilling encounter in the sky with the eagle when the matter had become compounded with not only Relura's frog confrontation but the apparent connection between the two.

After poking around in his imagination for a new trick for Shangrilarian involving specialized brains lining its pseudopodia, Zeb found he couldn't keep his mind on his work. He felt compelled to figure out why, when the conversation had turned to the incident with Geezer, it had ruffled his feathers so much. He turned off his light and stared out the window at Geezer Island. Part of him regarded the memory of Geezer with affection. True, the old coot had seemed to pose a mortal threat when they first encountered him that fateful night, but in the end, hadn't he revealed a good side?

Ah—of course—I know why that eagle got under my skin. Her stare reminded me of our first sight of Shang. It still makes my skin prickle to recall that ice-cold shock. And yet sometimes I can't resist sinking into that memory hole.

Meanwhile, his twin sister's thoughts were close by. That had often been the case, even when they were physically far apart, and now Marlie was just a few yards away on her bed across the hall. She'd gone to her room a half hour before to steady herself for another chapter in the story that had begun with the great horned owl's nerve-rattling fly-by. Like her brother, she'd soon made the connection between being stared at by a large bird and the throat-tightening memory of having been ripped away from everything she'd known at the age of seventeen. That was hard to avoid when she'd opened her closet to hang up her jacket and seen the metal souvenir from that event stuck in the corner. It always set up a fight between her memory of that fantastical event and the powerful grip of accepted physics. The intellectual struggle could get so exhausting, she'd set up humorless sentinels on the parapets of her intellect to guard against intrusions by that bizarre one-night journey from her past. By comparison, that adventure made Dorothy Gale's fictional tornado-driven saga seem about as extraordinary as a butter dish.

Zeb's awfully quiet over there. I'll bet he's giving in to the Memory Stalker . . . as I'm about to do, against my will. Sometimes I have to, as an exercise in mental health preservation. It's as if I must recall what happened that night in detail to assure myself that it was not a psychotic episode, which would be much worse. Every once in a while, to assure myself I'm not insane, I must revisit the event that only seemed *insane.*

I literally shivered when we opened that creaky door.

Part Two

A Night in the Sun

5

With the innocent audacity of age seventeen, Marlie stopped Zeb with a hand on his shoulder and called out, "Mr. Neighbor? Don't be afraid; it's us, the twins from across the lake."

No response. Louder: "We saw a fire on your roof and . . . and thought we should come over to help." In the ensuing silence, Marlie tried once more. "Mister?"

"If he were conscious, we'd know it by now."

They stepped softly into a narrow foyer with rooms off to the left and right. They looked left, peering into the lantern's advancing glow, and turned the corner. The room was very narrow and long, extending all along the north side of the house. The wooden floor was bare except for an old throw rug. In one corner stood an empty card table and a chair. A spartan, neatly made single bed hugged the adjoining wall. The place looked little used, somewhat dusty and yellowed around the edges.

"The motel that time forgot," said Marlie.

"Maybe it's a guest room."

"Right—for the guests who overparty at Geezer's all-night bashes."

At the far end of the room, they turned and found a bathroom. Marlie's flashlight came to a sharp halt when its beam fell on the floor of the shower stall, where a couple of dirty boot prints were on display on a wet floor. "Uh. Oh."

"Well, he ain't unconscious, unless he's walking in his sleep."

"So, where the hell is he?"

"I believe our work is done, Zeb. Let's split."

They exited the bathroom and continued clockwise around the house, passing through a narrow kitchen before returning to the foyer, where, instead of heading for the door, they stopped, their faces puzzled in the flickering lightning. "This place seemed a heck of a lot larger from outside," said Zeb. "There's some square footage missing. And how about the whole second floor, maybe a third? But there's no stairway."

Marlie didn't reply. She was looking toward the back of the house. "Those wet boot prints in the shower stall? How often do you wear boots in the shower?"

Swallowing, she headed back to the bathroom, her brother in tow. She swept the shower stall with the flashlight beam, past an empty built-in metal soap dish and grip bar, then jerked the beam back to the corner. The two walls didn't quite abut—-there was a tiny slit between them. Wide-eyed, Zeb put his hand on the grip bar and gave it a sideways tug. The whole wall moved a few inches to the side, revealing a dark space of unknowable dimensions.

Marlie drew a deep breath. "Oh, boy. This dude may be decrepit, but he's a decrepit creepster. It's time to reconsider." But Zeb hadn't taken his hand from the grip, and Marlie hadn't budged. Zeb slid the wall three feet to the side and they were staring into the maw of a dark stairwell bounded on one side by a structure of large crisscrossing wooden beams extending into the darkness in all directions. A curving stairway leading downward penetrated the darkness. "Holy shit, Zeb. All signs point to getting the hell out of this house."

"So, Geezer was trudging around his house wearing boots. But we know he's not conscious now. He's probably overcome by smoke in his basement. Didn't we come all this way to save him?"

Marlie's eyes strained at her brother's reasoning—scratch that, his rationalization—but she didn't protest. And when Zeb began descending the stairway, she followed right behind. "Mister?"

As they reached the bottom of the stairway, a piercing, scratchy, demonic shriek echoed off the invisible walls. Her scalp prickling, Marlie aimed her light toward the source of the sound and discovered, to her relief, a thoroughly non-demonic gray-and-white, red-beaked bird, perched on what appeared to be the balustrade of a mezzanine circling the room above them. A quick sweep of their surroundings ensured that, apart from the bird that Zeb took to be some kind of tern, they were alone.

"Whew!" exclaimed Zeb in an instinctive hush. "That bird is the one we saw entering the house from the top."

Their light beams toured their surroundings. The "room" was the inside of a wide chamber stretching up three stories above ground and surrounded by a wood and metal grid similar to an electrical power transmission tower. The grid walls were slanted slightly inward toward the ceiling, more conical than cylindrical. The walls slanted outward to the floor, or possibly even beyond the floor, down to a lower basement.

"Yikes!"

"Looks like we've stepped into a cage. A mighty big cage."

Against the far wall was a cot and a rumpled blanket. The walls were covered with annotated charts, diagrams, and photographs. Scientific equipment and machining tools abounded.

Zeb's beam lit upon an ancient set of free weights and a treadmill. "Relics from his youth. Kinda sad." He pulled out his phone and took a few pictures of their skin-prickling surroundings, including one of the tern that seemed to be staring straight at him.

"Let's keep it down, shall we? I don't know where Geezer is, but right now he'd have every right to shoot us as intruders."

"Yeah . . . but . . . do you want to leave?"

Marlie's non-answer was her answer. Her flashlight beam had reached a wall covered with charts, graphs, writing, and photos of the sun—sunspots, solar prominences, eclipses, and the solar surface—all of it arranged in a timeline that stretched high up along the wall. "Apparently the old boy used to be fixated on the sun. Eclipses in particular, it looks like. And there's a whole bunch of stuff arranged in a timeline. It's like a lab log." She noticed several hand-sized grip bars protruding an inch out of the wall. "Seems like he was once a rock climber." She hoisted herself up, studying the handwriting inscribed by each document.

Meanwhile, Zeb was inspecting an array of scientific equipment set within the central column of the grid. One was labeled "Emerson spectrohelio-graph." Other gauges and meters were labeled with indecipherable abbreviations. On a workbench stood a three-foot-tall contraption built like the chamber's infrastructure, except that the miniature bore a top shaped like a mushroom cap. Engraved on the side was *Wardenclyffe 3*. "This thing's named 'Wardenclyffe,'" he said out loud.

Examining the timeline, Marlie murmured, "Maybe Cliff was Geezer's warden in a nuthouse somewhere."

"Nope," said Zeb. He spelled it out for her. "It's engraved on a weird machine shaped like a cross between a narrow cone and a gun. It kinda looks like this cage we're in."

"Ah—Wardenclyffe! That was the name of a fantastic electrical transmission tower designed by Nikola Tesla."

"What, in some comic book?"

"No, it was the real deal, or was supposed to be, like a hundred-plus years ago. Tesla was a world-class inventor, a mortal rival of Edison. Just the kind of brilliant nutcase who would spark the imagination of an inventor, which Geezer was, supposedly. But if you think that's strange, you should see what he's tacked up here."

"What?"

"There are a lot of photos, some originals, others from books and magazines, in a section he's labeled 'Suspected Eclipse Ground Disappearances.'"

"Oooookay. From when?"

"Fairly recent, a lot of them, if 'recent' means the last forty or fifty years, but some go way back. Like, centuries."

"From where?"

"Everywhere. This first one is out of *National Geographic*. It's a rock painting on a canyon wall over a river bed. The label says 'Fitzroy R., Western Australia, site of tenth century TSE.'"

"TSE?"

"Total Solar Eclipse—that's the abbreviation used in the article I just read about Antarctica. Here it's written by a picture of a primitive drawing of a large bird with giant eyes next to the sun's corona. Listen to what he's inscribed on some of these. 'South coast, New Guinea, April 1926—Local legend of cocoa trees stolen by aurora god.' 'China '25—Iron miner reports "eye" aurora near eclipse, barn owl grove gone.' 'June '37, Chiskeel, Labrador—Two fishing boats lost.' 'Shekina Island, Sea of Japan, December '48—Falconer loses bird and quarter acre. Beach reduced suddenly one hundred yards.' 'August '59—Kenyan cattle herder claimed flamingo pond suddenly deepened three meters after dry thunder during eclipse.'"

While Marlie droned on, slowly scaling the wall, Zeb was silent, but not for lack of interest in his sister's report. He was absorbed in other findings. Shelved above the workbench were samples of rock and soil labeled *Chiskeel, Fitzroy River, Papua, Kenya, Kahoolawe, Shekina I.*, and *Puerto Ángel*.

"Listen to this," Marlie continued. "Here he's got a set of three pictures featuring his bird pal, that tern. The first one's captioned 'Puerto Ángel, Mexico, '70' and it shows the tern flying near a cliff in dim light, and he's outlined part of the cliff and labeled it 'ground disappearance area.' Above that is a pencil sketch that looks like a circular aurora. Next to that, there's another picture showing the tern in a tree at the edge of a truck stop and another where he's perched on a Jeep, captioned 'Oregon, Feb. '79: Tern followed me all the way home.' In those last two the bird's looking straight at the camera."

"What makes you think those are all the same bird?"

"Ol' Geeze went to considerable lengths to establish that. He's got a blow-up of the bird's head from the Mexico picture, with a circle drawn around an odd white feather sticking out above the bird's left eye, and here's another, sharper enlargement of the bird in the Oregon shot with an arrow pointing to the same feather. And he's scrawled above them 'SAME TERN— associates me w/ the event?'"

"What the hell was this guy up to? Wait, here's a ladder." Zeb began climbing up a ladder next to the slanted wall leading up to the mezzanine from which the tern watched him. "I like this bird, but he's staring at me a little too intensely."

"I doubt you need to fear that little feather ball."

"I'm not afraid he'll attack. He just looks like he's gauging me."

"Hey, here are some Hubble pictures of auroras. Not just on Earth, either—Jupiter, Saturn, Neptune. And he's written underneath them: 'What's the EGD–aurora connection?' Then get this: 'Jan. '87, Finland—missed by 102 mi. What's behind the aurora?' What does he mean 'missed'?"

"Quiet—did you hear a crackly hissing sound?"

Marlie stopped reading and listened. "I'm . . . not sure. Where'd it come from?"

"Up near the tern, maybe." They held still, listening, but the odd sound had abated. Zeb refocused on the wall near the ladder. "Hold on—here's your guy Tesla." Craning his neck, Zeb read more scribbling beneath two black-and-white photos cut from an old magazine, one of which showed a man electrified, with long sparks streaming from his hands. "Tesla's got lightning coming out of himself in a lab, and Geezer's written 'HOW MUCH DID TESLA KNOW?' And there's another picture of an electric power tower, like twenty stories high, that looks like that model on the workbench, and he's labeled it 'Wardenclyffe, 1903.' Must be what you were talking about."

"I'm not done with this timeline. Here he's got 'July '91, hillside Kahoolawe, Hawaii. Hummingbird haven, possible EGD, missed by 32 miles.' 'Missed' again. And WHOA! Here's one dated *today*, and under that he's written 'Tern reappears 10:38 PM, TSE minus 62 hrs.'"

"That's less than an hour ago!"

"Uhhhh . . . yeah."

Zeb thought back for a moment. "But he's obviously not around now. He must have taken off somewhere right before we came out to the lake."

"I didn't hear his boat."

By now, the twins' paths up the wall had almost merged. Zeb took a deep breath when he noticed a map between them near the top of the ladder. It showed Antarctica, the Southern Ocean, and the tip of South America, with an eclipse path marked and one area circled and inscribed with a note that read: "Ideal target: small island w/ seabirds on eclipse path = 2000–10000 times greater chance of a hit! COMB THIS SPOT FOR NEAREST ISLAND 62º S, 58º W."

"He's talking about the eclipse two days from now."

Zeb was audibly short of breath. "Got a pen?" Marlie checked her pockets. "Never mind, I won't forget this: sixty-two degrees south, fifty-eight west."

His head had now reached the mezzanine floor, from which a lever jutted out. The tern was a couple of feet away, its gaze now fixed on the ceiling. Marlie was staring at the ladder.

"What?" he asked when he noticed her intense gaze.

She shook her head. "Just . . . wondering . . . We're already at the mezzanine, so why does the ladder extend up to the ceiling?"

"Maybe it has to do with this thing," Zeb replied as he reached to pull the lever.

"Zeb, don't!" she cried, but it was too late. The lever triggered a hydraulic release that opened a trap door in the dome, which let in a gust of cold, damp wind, the sound of electrical static . . . and the blood-curdling sight of the powerful frame of Geezer turning around to discover the cause of the interruption as his blazing acetylene welding torch illuminated the dome above him and lit up the raindrops like cascading balls of lightning.

Whipping off his welding helmet, Geezer shouted in a voice of storm-whipped gravel, *"WHAT THE HELL?!"*

The twins froze in terror at the lightning-lit fury of Black Zeus. Geezer slammed down a switch, ceasing the sparks, and stuck his arm through the trap door, attempting to seize Zeb. Marlie screamed and Zeb sprang to life, sliding down the ladder. "Slide, Marlie! Down!"

She didn't need to be told. She grabbed the stair's handrail and firepoled down twenty feet, landing on the chamber floor one second before Zeb's leap from the fourth stair. Hearing Geezer jump through the trap door, Marlie called out, "We're sorry, mister! We only came to save you from the fire!"

The twins tore back across the floor and up the stairs to the hidden door, glancing back terrified at the sight of the old man tearing down the ladder with the agility of a Green Beret. Marlie's voice quavered, "He's going to kill us!"

"Go, go!"

They raced out of the bathroom, through the house, out the front door, down the stairs, and into the woods, trying not to slip in the mud, all with Geezer, growling in fury, pounding four seconds behind them.

"Ohmigod . . . what if he shoots us?!"

"Shoot a couple of kids? He'd have to be crazy."

"Well?"

At the island's edge, the twins climbed over the fence and leapt into the boat. Zeb hit the outboard and they began to pull away, just as Geezer appeared at the water's edge and hurled himself into the lake. The twins' hearts reached their throats as they beheld the titan swimming toward them with amazing strength, actually gaining on them until the outboard punched up to a fifteen-knot kick, opening up a widening lead over their thrashing pursuer. Their strain of relief was soon sickened by fear, however, as they saw Geezer halt and then heard his booming voice over the wind and the motor as he shouted, "SAY NOTHING!"

They were startled again, now by the sound of a car horn honking from their side of the lake. Relura was turning into their driveway. She jumped out of her car and ran to the beach, calling to her siblings, whose pallor shimmered in the moonlight.

Relura watched them cut the engine and paddle the boat to the lake's edge while the distant swimmer returned to the island in smooth strokes. "What in the name of *God* are you doing?! Can't you be left alone without doing something insane?!" Wet from the rain, and still catching their breath, the twins tied up the boat. For a moment the only sounds were the pounding of their hearts and Geezer's final strokes as he climbed onto his island. "And is that who I think it is, trying to drown himself?"

"That thing isn't gonna drown," said Marlie as they watched him climb out of the water and over the fence with the ease of a cougar. "It's SuperGeezer."

6

Their faces glowing with the reflected light from their laptop LCDs, Marlie and Zeb scarcely noticed Relura entering the room bearing steaming mugs. Marlie sat at Zeb's desk, huddled in a blanket, her hair still wet from the rain, and dug deep into web research on Tesla and terns. Zeb's portfolio was transportation logistics to and in the Antarctic. "*Oh*, yeah," he grinned, nodding his head at his screen. "We're going, all right." When a marshmallow bobbing on hot cocoa intruded on his visual field, he looked up at Relura. "Thanks, Sis. We're heading south tomorrow. *Way* south."

"Piece o' cake, Zeb. We'll pluck fifteen grand off the money tree in the backyard and head out for a fun-filled weekend in Antarctica."

"Aaanh!" Zeb had hit his vocal basketball court buzzer. "Fourteen hundred apiece is more like it, round trip. We throw in a little more for the puddle jumper and a bribe for the fisherman and we're in."

"A bribe for the fisherman?"

"To get to the path of totality. There are millions of fishermen sitting around during the off-season you can hire to give you a lift. Patagonian toothfish hunters."

"Neither the parents nor I are springing for Patagonian toothfish hunters, intercontinental jets, hotels, or anything else connected to such a nutty escapade."

"Marlie and I each can afford fourteen benjamins, thanks to our prize money, with room to spare."

"'Nikola Tesla, 1856–1943. Inventor of radio devices, X-ray technology, alternating current,'" read Marlie off her screen, assuming that Zeb would be interested, but not caring much one way or the other. "Blah, blah . . . 'Tesla's *Wardenclyffe* transmission tower on Long Island was designed to pump the Earth's natural charge by running a low-frequency current in a free charge plasma to generate a current powerful enough to allow virtually no-cost wireless communications, broadcasting, and unlimited electrical power worldwide. The respected inventor's credibility suffered when he claimed that radio signals he intercepted from outer space originated from alien civilizations.'"

That historical tidbit failed to distract Relura from the argument at hand. "Zeb, the idea of your bopping down to the South Pole when you've never even been out of the country is a delirious figment of your imagination."

"You've been out of the country plenty and you'll be with us all the way, watching over us just as the good parents intended," he countered.

"'I could feel the pulse of the globe,' wrote Tesla," Marlie continued. "'I had observed something possibly of incalculable consequences to mankind.'"

Vaguely annoyed that Marlie wasn't doing her part to bring Relura around, Zeb continued pressing his case. He turned his laptop to Relura's sightline. "And look at this." He'd placed two pictures side by side. "This is the bird hanging out with Geezer right now." He held his cell phone photo next to the video clip of an identical bird resting on a snowy pine snag. "This is *Sterna paradisaea*, an Arctic tern, the planet's greatest migrator. This little wonder can fly up to sixty thousand miles in a single year, from Arctic to Antarctic and back."

"Well, goody for Arc. What's that got to do with your sallying off to Antarctica?"

"Well, 'Arc' appears to be an eclipse nut like Geezer and seems to have scheduled a migratory visit to Geezer's cuckoo crib right now. I've got to wonder if the bird is planning to hitch a ride with Geezer all the way to Antarctica. You must be curious how that's going to go down, Zoology Girl! This trip would be a great career move for you!"

That earned a fond half-smile from Relura, who was delighted by Zeb's love of animals, even if their wondrous natural states were constantly being transmuted by his artistic hands into fantasy creatures. The poster on his wall of Ernst Haeckel's fabulous nineteenth-century drawings of protozoa was surrounded by hand-drawn chimerical concoctions from Zeb's imagination, which knew no bounds. But she recognized a blatant ploy when she saw one.

"Don't try to spin me, Zeb." She watched as Zeb bounded to his closet, dumped the contents of his school backpack on the floor, and began stuffing it with clothes, his binoculars, and his travel toothbrush.

"I'm not spinning—"

"You are spinning out of control. Your destination should be the Land of Nod. Down that cocoa. It's a calming alternative to a straitjacket."

"Straitjacket?! I'm the sane one here!"

"You think it's sane to go boating in a lightning storm in the middle of the night?"

"We were trying to save the life of a decrepit old man!"

That got Marlie's attention. "Ha. I wish I were that decrepit. Geezer was coming at us like a great white shark. The only lives that needed saving were ours. If he'd gotten to us, he might have strangled us both at the same time, one hand per neck. Who knows what he'd do if he found us hounding him in Antarctica?"

"Kindly don't join your brother's Nutcase Brigade, Marlie. All that's happened is that you trespassed on the private property of an elderly gentleman—"

"—an elderly Aquaman—"

"—an old man who happens to be in better shape than you expected, and he got upset with you. Quite understandably, I might add."

Zeb became flushed with frustration. "And who happens to be the key to what could be the greatest event of our lives!"

"Of our lives? Really? Solar eclipses happen every year or two."

"Not here, they don't." He handed Relura a list of future eclipses from Marlie's magazine. "Check it out. Besides, this one's in Antarctica! It's gorgeous down there, all those brilliant icebergs."

"You'd have to get to the moons of Saturn to see anything that amazing," chimed in Marlie, "and that would take thirty years and forty billion dollars."

"Thank you, Marlie." Zeb absorbed the pleasant surprise of a little support from his former wombmate. "We can get this done with what's in our savings and be back in three or four days! And even Saturn wouldn't reveal what Geezer's onto with the EGDs."

Relura was unmoved. "Ah, yes, this is the mission to solve the eclipse ground disappearance mystery. Look, it's time for one of you to write a note of apology to Geezer. We can drop it off at his locker box in the morning."

Zeb looked out the window for a second and said, "Okay." From the mess on his desk he dug out a textbook with a title page featuring the image made famous by Flammarion of a man poking his head through the firmament toward mysteries beyond the stars. He ripped it out and started writing on it.

"Hey! The school's going to make you pay for that." Her brother scribbled on the drawing, ignoring her.

"Geezer's an explorer of historic proportions, like Magellan, Shackleton, and especially this guy." He thrust his apology note at Relura. "Here's Geezer in a past life."

Above Flammarion's cosmic wonderer, Zeb had drawn an eclipsed sun among the stars, written *SuperGeezer* on the man's cloak, and scrawled above the textbook title:

> *We're sorry, Mr. Neighbor, but we hope you'll take us*
> *with you to Antarctica. Our sister's the old fogy—*
> YOU'RE OUR HERO!
> *Marlie & Zeb Morell, The Twins Who Meant Well*

"How amusing," Relura intoned, giving Zeb a fake-deadly glare, his ideal reward. She tossed the note on the floor. Zeb picked it up and stuffed it and the eclipse article into his pack.

"Fine. I'll give it to Geezer in Antarctica."

Marlie had gone back to studying her screen. She read, "'The disturbances I had observed might be due to an intelligent control, perhaps the greeting of one planet to another . . . . What a tremendous stir this would make in the world!' Maybe Tesla was gifted with visionary superpower. No moss grew on that dude's brain."

Noticing Zeb's dissatisfaction with Marlie's return to the sidelines, Relura saw an opportunity. "Marlie doesn't seem to share your zeal for this caper. I guess you're pretty much on your own."

"Are you kidding? Marlie's all in," he declared, unable to conceal his shred of doubt.

Relura invited Marlie to chime in. "Wellllll, Geezer's references to odd auroras are certainly intriguing, as is the bit about ground disappearances . . ." Zeb tensed up waiting for the imminent "but." "But on the other hand, we're running against some unfriendly odds due to the possibilities of clouds, Geezer's disinclination to share knowledge with others, and the chance of his murdering us, so I've gotta say, I'm a little uncertain about blowing the biggest windfall of my life on a bet that we're going to draw three aces."

"Toldja, Zeb." Words no guy enjoys hearing from his big sister.

"Think about it, Zeb," said Marlie. "What if we die of shame over our stupidity for blowing our life savings chasing some weirdo who might never even leave his house?"

"What if, what if! At least we'll be alive! What if we stay home and die from the agony of thinking what we're missing? You are such a *traitor*!" Zeb couldn't control himself, even though—in fact, especially because—he suspected that Marlie wanted to go as much as he did. "Back at Geezer's you were as excited as I was."

Marlie thought that any case to be made could wait till morning. "Maybe this whole eclipse ground disappearance 'mystery' is just part of a creepy old man's fantasy life. And yours."

"Bullshit. Do the right thing, Marlie."

Marlie closed her computer and got up to head to her bedroom, escorted by Relura, who commented, "Thank God at least one of you is level-headed."

"Perfect, level-headed Marlie," Zeb snarled from across the hall, "who breaks into an old man's house in the middle of the night, climbs his walls, and scares him berserk."

This was too delicious for Marlie to ignore. "I was led astray, but in the warmth of my big sister's arms I've become level-headed and perfect again."

"*Aaanh!*" Zeb buzzed, louder than ever. "Barfmaking, Marlie—two shots."

As Marlie climbed into bed, she smiled at her sister. "I love getting Zeb, but I gotta admit Geezer's scene was pretty incredible."

"Sleep it off, hon."

Zeb's silence from across the hall told the tale: he'd taken a hit. Agreement between his sisters usually conjured a fortress that was unbreachable by his volleys of conscience or common sense. But his ears perked up when he heard Marlie quietly tell Relura, "I mean—a total eclipse in Antarctica? That would be sweet."

"Daylight is a great antidote for delirium, Marlie." Relura kissed her sister good-night and returned to Zeb's room.

"I'm really disappointed, Relura. You—a scientist!—passing up the chance to get in on an astonishing phenomenon of nature."

"Nothing phenomenal has happened, Zeb. We're back to reality now. This is all in your imagination, which *is* phenomenal and will inspire a lot of people some day."

"Not if it gets snuffed by 'reality'—but it won't because I won't let it. Reality's stranger than you think, woman."

"That may be, but come daylight, you'll find it's not as strange as *you* think. Get some sleep and tomorrow we can have an adventure closer to home than Antarctica, maybe hike up to the top of Mount Tam."

Relura gave him a hug and exited to the hallway, where she paused to regard the dark island through Zeb's window. Turning, she noticed Marlie doing likewise. Was there a dim light emanating from a window in Geezer's house? Did it matter? If not, why was it hard to turn away?

*   *   *

Marlie floated up in a world of black, white, and sepia, rising alongside a cage of some kind—no, it was Wardenclyffe Tower on Long Island at the turn of the last century. An antiquarian automobile sputtered and horse carriages clopped on the ground below. As she neared the top, a giant came into view, gripping the tower like King Kong on the Empire State Building, but this was Geezer, who turned toward her, grabbing her shoulder as electrical charges flowed along his skin and he hissed, "Sis!"

Marlie shivered and opened her eyes to find her brother prodding her awake in the dim pre-dawn light of a passenger jet. Through her sleepy skein of confusion, she heard him yammering about arriving somewhere soon. It felt like a replay—hadn't Zeb already done this to her moments ago? No, that was hours ago, a whole day, they'd been home, yes, he'd roused her from sleep very early yesterday, the morning after their chilling escape from their furious neighbor.

Fragments of the last twenty-four hours began to reassemble themselves in her memory. She recalled Zeb's eyes wild in the darkness when he'd said, "Marlie, get up, *now*! Geezer's getting away! Pack your stuff—we've got to follow him." He'd handed her his binoculars and gone down the hall to awaken Relura, who gamely padded to Zeb's room and witnessed Geezer boating across the lake with two valises and what looked like a trombone case. Arc was flying lazy circles overhead, following Geezer like an aerial golden retriever.

On their front porch with their packs, they'd urged their weary sister to hurry to her car. In the distance a garage door opened—had to be that structure near Geezer's gate by the road. Relura offered to indulge them a few minutes' drive to track Geezer, out of curiosity. They entered the road after he left his property in an old-model Jeep. They were positive that Geezer was off to Antarctica. They implored Relura to take them there that very day.

She'd agreed only to follow Geezer for a while. She entered the freeway behind him, tracking him as he weaved from lane to lane, stretching beyond the speed limit, Zeb eyeing him all the while with his binoculars. Geezer exited the freeway and Relura maneuvered her car in pursuit, keeping a careful distance from the Jeep. Geezer unwittingly led them along a back road to the Sonoma County Airport. They'd hidden behind an office building on-site and seen Geezer drive into one of the hangars.

The sound of high-powered jet engines sheared the sunrise as a sleek private jet poked its nose out of the hangar. They begged Relura again, insisting that they had the coordinates of Geezer's destination, which were perfect for viewing the coming eclipse. Spying Arc flying free inside the aircraft, they changed tack—forget Geezer, they told her, think whales and penguins. The sun hadn't set for a month down there, and then all of a sudden there'd be darkness, starlight, and a ring of white fire over an Antarctic iceberg. That alone would make it all worthwhile. They'd be her slaves for life if only she'd stop by her place in the city, grab an overnight bag and her passport, and head on to SFO. She wouldn't have to do a thing other than be the responsible adult.

Relura reached the nearby intersection with a sign that read

San Francisco	**60 >**
< Geyserville	**17**

and turned right. She smiled. It would be an early graduation present. Her siblings' goosefleshed cheers filled the car until they were drowned out by the roar of the jet's engines ripping through the morning as Geezer lifted off the runway and into the sky.

Within six hours they were lunching on an Aero Argentinas jumbo jet seven miles above the Panama Canal. They'd fidgeted and tried to watch a movie but fallen asleep until Zeb had woken Marlie to alert her that they would soon be landing in Buenos Aires, where they would get another flight to Ushuaia, at the tail end of South America, where they would then get a boat that would take them to the Antarctic path of a total solar eclipse. Was this smart? Or might they be careening toward death at the hands of a crazy man or perhaps the flukes of an angry whale in a mood to capsize them into the Southern Ocean?

The spray off the swells of the Southern Ocean wet Zeb's face in the open cockpit of his glider as he skimmed the sea top like a shearwater beneath towering thunderheads. A small jet pulled up alongside him, matching his much slower speed, its pilot—wearing welder's goggles atop his dark face—taunting him with a menacing grin. A living Arctic tern sat as a steely figurehead anchored to the plane's nose cone and eyed him while the jet's engines blasted the screams of hundreds of seabirds. It was Geezer, all right, taunting him, gunning his engines and zooming ahead, churning up a wake that swallowed the glider, tugging it down to the ocean's depths, where a raspy voice called out "Señorita!"

Zeb awoke to the leftover smells of decades of toothfish hauls and the sight of a fisherman rousing his older sister from sleep. Disoriented, he struggled to fit this new puzzle piece into the still-fuzzy array of his last twelve hours—or was it eighteen? Who knows, with little to no nighttime? But yes, there was the change to a prop plane in Buenos Aires and the haggling to charter an off-season fishing boat in Tierra del Fuego, after the near-certain spotting of Geezer's aircraft at the Ushuaia airport. Right—they'd interrupted the pilothouse paint job being conducted by the grizzled owner of the equally grizzled forty-five-foot steel-hulled trawler *Eva de la Plata*, equipped with wader boots, fishing tackle, nets, ice tanks, and a fiberglass dinghy. By flashing a copious bundle of pesos, they'd persuaded him to take their gringo party of three out on the open sea, where the constant engine drone had lulled Zeb to sleep on a narrow foam-covered bench below deck.

There had been an earlier interruption to his slumber, that one courtesy of Relura, who'd jostled Marlie and him awake to enjoy a nature-lover's bonus for this *très cher* jaunt, a chance to commune with a pair of sperm whales arcing slowly above the water's surface within forty yards of the boat. That was something they'd have bloody well missed if they'd spent the weekend in a boring house in a landlocked chunk of Sonoma County, CA! What a beauty! They'd struggled to keep their cocoa from spilling out of their mugs while staring in silent awe at their cetacean fellow travelers. But the sun looked fickle and—*urp*—those long waves were greening the gills of his sisters, and even his glider time hadn't completely immunized him from this upside-downside of sea travel.

A tinny tango issued from the pilothouse radio and then slowly descended into white noise, a plaintive soundtrack to their recognition that, rare and thrilling wildlife notwithstanding, they were gazing into a void of gray sea and sky. They'd sat on the engine housing, huddling in their jackets against the damp chill with prayerful glances as a gathering mist delivered its soft threat. *No, not rain, no!* Geezer yes or Geezer no, they had to at least see the sun's corona for their money. The weather just had to clear up by the time they got to the big ol' iceberg at 62° S, 58° W.

Queasy on the long waves and aching for a break in the clouds, Zeb glanced at his dry-mouthed sisters and they exchanged glum looks before retreating to their beds. To distract himself from his guilt and nausea, he tried to extract some English meaning from a flier about the *Eva de la Plata*, boasting of its owner's successes in getting sport fishermen to their happy fishing grounds. The flier contained information about how to reach Señor Cebolla on his boat via satellite. That was interesting, wasn't it? Please? *Almost heaved there. You've never gotten airsick in all that glider time. Hold it together!*

Their captain—what was he saying to Relura?

"*¿Señorita? ¿Así es como querías el sol, no?*"

Not many vocabulary fragments remained from his Spanish classes, but it was clear that the guy was waking them to see the show with the front-row-ticket prices. Or was it to *hear* something? His ears were flooded with a cacophony of bird calls, the likes of which he'd never heard, not even in his mp3 album of nature sounds.

In dimmed daylight, the fisherman waved around Zeb's map with the coordinates marked on it.

"*Señorita, hemos llegado a la locación que querías.*"

"*Sí . . . sí. Muchas gracias,*" she'd answered. "*Ya vamos.*"

As the boatman went back to his business, Zeb stuffed the flier in his jacket pocket and joined his sisters in bolting to the smudged window, where, in quick squints, he discovered a clear sky—*thank God!*—highlighted by a crescent sun. "The sun's being gobbled up!"

They rushed out on deck, Marlie bearing her camera and some mylar she'd picked up at the Buenos Aires airport gift shop. Zeb whipped his binocs out of their case. The chorus of birds singing in chaotic disharmony grew deafening, and then *another* three-inch-headline event seized their attention: they were approaching a giant iceberg—a stunning arabesque of ice less than two hundred yards off, a frozen, abstract-expressionist cathedral stretching five stories into the near-violet sky, its soaring white buttresses tinged with yellow shadows under the struggling sun.

And there was more: "*¡No estamos solos, amigos. Miren allá!*"

They were not alone. The iceberg was playing host to a riotous flock of avians they could see—and, they suspected, one human they couldn't. Sure enough, another fishing boat was anchored nearby and, lying on the icy "beach" a couple of feet above the water was, oddly enough, a rubber Zodiac skiff. Odder yet, there was a motley flock of birds flying around the iceberg, most of whom were settling on what must have been a plateau near the top, obscured by a surrounding rim of ice.

Exactly who had landed that skiff on the iceberg? Relura got straight to the point with their pilot. "*¿Señor, llama al otro barco por radio, y preguntales porque estar aquí?*"

"*Sí, señorita.*"

The skipper put the engine on idle within a couple hundred feet of the iceberg and radioed the other boat. Shags, petrels, gulls, pelicans, and albatrosses continued to approach the iceberg in formations—and there was an Arctic tern, and the twins were pretty damn sure they knew which Arctic tern it was. Then a rolling visual shock wave erupted as Relura shouted, "God! There's an *owl* in there! And *what?!*"

Zeb trained his binoculars on the birds hovering and then alighting on the hidden plateau. Six of them—a barn owl, a flamingo, a toucan, a falcon, a swallow, and a hummingbird—joined the Arctic tern in flying spirals up a hundred feet toward the sun before swooping back down to the plateau.

"*El otro pescador dice que el a cargado a un viejo y unos quantos pajaros,*" reported the fisherman.

Marlie cried, "Relura, what's he saying?!"

Relura replied, "Geezer must be up there . . . "

"*Los pájaros vuelaron ase al iceberg, y el viejo fue com los pájaros para estar con ellos.*"

"The pilot of the other boat says that an old man followed the birds up onto the iceberg."

Then it was the fisherman's turn to exclaim in surprise, "*¿Que pasa?*"

Three albatrosses were approaching the iceberg, one of which bore a crouching flamingo on its back. Three sibling jaws dropped as the arriving birds landed behind the arching wall of ice near the top of the iceberg. The flamingo joined the others in the aerial spiral dance.

The fisherman pointed to his dinghy. "*¿Quiere el barco chico?*"

Relura reminded her wide-eyed twins that they could see the eclipse from the boat.

"So freaking what, Relura—we can't see Geezer from here!"

Zeb and Relura looked to Marlie. Swallowing her apprehensions, she mustered restrained bravado and announced, "This is our stop. We gotta get off."

Reluctantly, Relura untied the dinghy from the boat railing and told the fisherman, "*Señor Albrezo, solamente vamos a tardar unos minutos.*"

"*Claro, esta bien.*"

The fisherman helped them lower the dinghy over the side and, bidding them caution, held the rope while they descended the ladder.

The three siblings moved across the short stretch of sea in the sharp-shadowed light toward the immense ice castle looming ever larger over them, their speed the net of driving curiosity braked by growing apprehension about unknowable risks.

A tiny peep from the upper branches of Marlie's mind inquired if it were too late to turn back now. *No harder than returning to the top of a cliff halfway through a hundred-foot dive. We're seeing this one through.* Zeb felt his hair standing on end. That unnatural assembly of birds made it crystal clear that something extremely eerie was going down. He leapt from the dinghy to the narrow ice beach and helped his sisters drag the dinghy out of the water, keeping an eye on the avian dance visible over the plateau walls and under the slimming crescent sun.

The varying arcs flown by the flamingo, swallow, falcon, toucan, hummingbird, and owl decreased in height till they fluttered down to rest out of sight on the hidden plateau. Arc, indefatigable, continued his flying frenzy as intermittent sparks shot up alongside him from the plateau.

"Our man's up there, Zeb."

"Let's do it."

"Do what?" Relura demanded to know in a shaky voice as she secured the dinghy to a block of ice at the shore.

"Worry not, Sis," called Zeb, worrying her plenty as he began to scale the fifty-foot-high ice cliff. Marlie followed close behind, fighting off dizziness from the deafening bird sounds swelling and eddying around them.

More high-powered sparks shot upward in the darkening sky from the plateau, leading Zeb to speed up his climb on the craggy ice. Growing fearful for his safety, Marlie hurried to catch up to him in case he should suddenly need a helping hand.

Near the top of the wall, Zeb's right foot slipped for a moment. Relura shouted, "Come back, you two!" loud enough to be heard up above. Seconds later the haunting apparition of Geezer appeared above them, clad in an old Air Force parka and holding Wardenclyffe 3 on his shoulder like a rocket launcher spitting lightning bolts toward the sun. His welder's goggles hid his eyes but not his scorching fury.

"IDIOTS!"

Zeb began slipping again, yelling this time in what appeared to be the beginning of a final plunge. His sisters called out in horror, but Geezer, still holding his heavy contraption in one arm, dropped to one knee, seized the boy's reaching arm, and with the aplomb of an orchestra conductor lifting his baton, swung Zeb onto the plateau, pale and breathless.

Relura moved laterally to a spot under Zeb and called up to Geezer, "Thank you, sir, so much!"

"Shut up, lady!" he roared with the guttural blast of an angry demigod. "Get these brats outta here or you're going to regret bringing them here as long as you live!" He then refocused his attention on the Wardenclyffe, adding, "But that may be just a matter of seconds."

Having scaled the cliff to join her brother and Geezer atop the plateau, Marlie froze in terror, too spellbound to pay much heed to the hundreds of birds gawking at them.

Totality hit, freeing the distant stars and the corona of our closest one to shine in the darkness. Geezer stepped back to the center of the plateau with the Wardenclyffe on one shoulder and Arc perched on the other. "Stay back," he growled. "This charge could kill you, and if it does, it's your own damn fault." He aimed the Wardenclyffe right at the eclipsed sun and shot crackling lightning bolts at his target. The din and the birds' shrieks drowned out Relura's cries to *Come back down now, carefully!*

A rippling, iris-like aurora unrolled from the zenith, filling the darkness beyond the sun's corona and enshrouding them with a filmy column of swirling plasma. The twins looked in speechless alarm at Relura down below them on the ice. With a deafening sound of sucked sea and the breaking of an ice mountain, Relura seemed to fall below them, farther and faster by the second, along with the iceberg, the boats, and the sea, all plummeting into invisibility far beneath the piece of ice holding Geezer, the twins, and Arc. The entire moonshadow-striped Earth filled their view, falling in space, until they found themselves slowing and swaying over the surface of the moon.

7

The shock of apparently imminent death stopped Marlie's tears and breath in place. Zeb tried to focus on extracting a thrilling revelation from the event, as a bulwark against his fears and his fraught conscience, which was overwhelmed with guilt for having pushed Marlie to join him on this surely fatal caper. For a moment he couldn't even look at her, but when he did, he saw her following Geezer's and Arc's eyes straight up. Doing likewise, he beheld the starlight of outer space shining through a faint blue-tinged rim of atmospheric haze atop a transparent swirl stretching upward two hundred feet. Geezer threw his goggles off and his hands up and roared in ecstasy, "EUREKA!"

Marlie gasped. Overhead a glowing narrow triangular plank appeared from on high and began lowering to their level, revealing an immense eye, a thousand feet across, positioning itself to regard them through the faint electromagnetic membrane containing them. A bird-like creature that must have been two miles high, made of opalescent yellow and green auroral light, was perched on the moon, where it had placed the mysterious container in which it had captured the Earthlings, along with a good-sized chunk of Antarctic air and ice.

The creature fluttered back to stretch its wings and then lowered its head again for a more protracted examination. The plank Marlie had seen was its lower beak, easily two thousand feet long, now pointing sideways so its owner could inspect them with its left eye, whose pupil alone was the size of her parents' property back home.

Marlie had told herself countless times that she'd give anything to experience space travel, but she hadn't meant to include her life among the necessary sacrifices. And yet it looked like that's precisely the trade-off she'd unwittingly made by stalking a crazy codger more than halfway down the world. It was a dolorous surprise served on an unimaginably glorious platter —the blinding solar sphere in infinite skyless blackness, the Earth seen from the viewing platform of the moon in its resplendent entirety for the first time in more than half a century, and for the first time ever by a woman—and *this thing*, whatever it was.

Swept in battling winds of awe, disbelief, and profound regret, Zeb pushed himself to look at Marlie, but he found in her no reproach. They were in this together, and whatever had happened, it wasn't fatal. At least not yet.

Elated, Geezer paid them no heed. Arc, maintaining sharp eye contact with their kidnapper, emitted a scratchy demand in Ternese. The three humans saw that it was Arc that the aurorabird was paying attention to, not them. Fascinated, the creature's granular iris performed kaleidoscopic pattern shifts. It lifted its head, opened its beak, and trumpeted a sound like a million-bird choral arpeggio muffled by storm winds but powerful enough to send rough temblors through the Earthlings' patch of ice. Colored translucent light in the aurorabird's body rippled for miles on each side. Glowing diaphanous streaks rose and fell in waves along its surface, through which sun, stars, and Earth shone on.

Marlie was the first to get her voice back. "Mister . . . would you *kindly* enlighten us as to what the freaking hell is going on?"

"In particular, sir," Zeb asked, "what is that *creature*?!"

"And in even more particular, if it's not too much to ask, have you any idea how, or if, we will ever return to Earth?"

A grin creased Geezer's rough face. He didn't take his eyes off the aurorabird. "You twerps nearly destroyed my life's work," he muttered, breathing the sigh of a hugely satisfied soul. "But not quite," he added before going silent again.

Thanks for the help, G, thought Zeb.

"That's it?" asked Marlie. More silence. "Nothing?"

That thought train was derailed as the creature's call erupted again, knocking its captives off balance. It reached down, secured its treasure by slipping its lower beak through a hole near the top of its plasmic container, and lifted off, flying them away from Earth and moon both, like a pelican gliding on solar wind. It folded its wings back along its body in a long dive in the direction of the brilliant sun. Behind them, the bright moon diminished to the size of the stripe-shadowed Earth underneath it. Soon it was nothing but a bright spot suspended over Earth's southern hemisphere, then a dot near a glowing blue disk, while ahead the sun grew ever larger.

Geezer wedged Wardenclyffe 3 into a fissure on the iceberg floor at the base of an ice hillock about five feet high. He stepped up to the forward edge of the ice hill and folded his arms over his chest like a schooner captain pleased with the craftsmanship of the shipbuilders who'd spent years constructing a vessel that could sail so strong and true.

Zeb saw an opportunity in this shift in Geezer's mood. He stepped around him and up a few inches on the ice to match Geezer's eye level. "Mister, my name is Zeb Morell." Marlie nodded her approval to carry on. "My sister is Marlie." Geezer deigned to cast a quick glance his way, but Zeb understood the gesture derived more from a need to monitor the situation than any sign of respect. "And you are?"

Geezer rolled his eyes above his firm, wide nose, muttered a curse under his breath, and returned to regarding the underside of the creature's head above them. Apparently, he regarded as ludicrous the premise that Zeb and his sister were entitled to know his name.

Zeb thought to himself that maybe, come to think of it, the imperious nutcase didn't have a name. *Maybe his kingly hauteur had been so apparent even at birth—he must have had a birth, come on—that even as a newborn he'd emanated a powerful vibe that he was already too cool for school and didn't need no stinkin' name tags, and had thus intimidated his parents (or designers?) into refraining from assigning him any.*

But, no, let's not get too crazy. Dad once pointed out that the old man must have registered a property title with the county, one he'd apparently purchased after cashing in a bundle of chips on at least one big payday. Plus, he must have licensed that airplane. He has to have had a name somewhere along the line. Dammit, he does have one even as he stands here right in front of us, fixated on the vast face of the aurorabird he'd hunted down over thirty-odd years. But, alas, that's irrelevant, since we obviously don't merit a perfunctory "Next question," much less being granted the knighthood entitling us to learn His Royal Name. (Note to self: Let's not complain about this to Marlie. She's got enough to be bummed about. She's a rock, but Geezer's a stone-cold rock grinder. Approach with caution.)

"Mister—as Marlie said, we'd really appreciate knowing what's going on here." Geezer took a deep breath and stared ahead. Maybe he was hoping the kid would give up and shut up. "All right, could you tell us your name, at least? We haven't had anything to call you but Geeze—"

"Mr. G," Marlie interjected.

"Yeah, 'Mr. G.' How's that?"

"Suit yourself," the old man responded.

Let's see, thought Marlie. *There was "Say nothing!," "Idiots!," and that comment about our nearly ruining his life's work, so "Suit yourself" constituted a fifteen percent increase in the total number of words spoken to us in our whole lives by the man in whose wake we've been swept up into deep space. We're making progress! I'll give it another go.*

"Mr. G, please share with us what you know about this creature—"

"Aurora birdealis," suggested Zeb.

"—this aurorabird, such as what it is *doing* with us . . . or . . . whether we're going to . . . "

"—live, say, another five minutes—"

"Yes, will we survive? That hits the old nail on the head. Any chance, literally, on Earth?"

Geezer replied, "I've got a mind to push you both right through this gauzy wall."

There's a friendly traveling companion, thought Marlie, but since his remark seemed more a muse than a threat, she kept her focus on assessing their situation. For one thing, whatever this jar was made of had maintained the conditions of atmosphere, temperature, and even gravity that had surrounded them on the Antarctic iceberg, even though they'd gotten near enough to the sun that it now appeared twice its usual size and yet no more painful to glance at than normal. Nonetheless, the question of survival presented itself to her and Zeb at least, if not to Geezer, who was squinting at the sun in evident satisfaction.

Zeb decided to combat the silence by changing the subject. "Our kidnapper looks like a pouchless pelican." No comment. "Say, Marlie, I doubt it's escaped your notice that this aurorabird must be moving about a million miles every time it flaps its wings."

"Accelerating too."

"Maybe we're going to bust the so-called speed limit of light. I always suspected that was mad scientist bullshit."

Marlie was put off by Zeb's attitude toward her hero, Einstein, although she had to admit she'd harbored her own doubts about the constitutionality of that law. *But let's get to the point.* "Mr. G, are we going to the sun?" she asked, even though it did seem like a dumb question at this point, as the sun was now eight times larger than it normally appeared.

To her surprise, Geezer, no doubt noting the ashen look on her face, acknowledged her existence. "Sure looks that way."

"Well, sir, since you've studied situations like this, does our future hold a chance in hell, or incineration in hell?"

Geezer recommended his practice of silence. Marlie had to swallow Geezer's complete lack of interest in conversing or returning to Earth. To right her inner gyroscope and to show Zeb that she was not crumbling in fear, she looked his way and pointed far to the left at a bright disk the size of the moon on a normal night back home. "Check out Venus."

Zeb had noted their neighboring planet already, but what under normal circumstances would have been unforgettable to see had been shunted from his attention by the sight and fate that lay straight ahead. He pondered how they might flip the attitude of the fried piper who'd led them (well, to be fair, not intentionally) on this magnificent life-threatening jaunt. They were going to need all the help they could get. "Y'see, Mr. G, we're really sorry about invading your house. We saw the fire and figured you might have been injured or suffering smoke inhalation. We thought that maybe we could save your life."

"We were going to make you a toasty-pie," added Marlie, under no illusions that that line was a slam-dunk icebreaker. She thought she'd detected a fleeting flicker of sympathy in Geezer's stifled smirk, but that glimmer of hope was soon snuffed out by the spectacle of the great gossamer beast hurtling them ever closer to the sun. "We admit it—we blew it. And we hope that you will at least forgive us enough to tell us what this auroral monster that seized us *is*."

Arc squawked by Geezer's ear. Perhaps that led Geezer to soften a little at the trace of panic in Marlie's voice. "You think I'm hiding classified information? I can only guess, same as you."

"And your guess is . . . ?"

"Maybe it's some kind of gaseous or plasmic life form, composed of loosely bound atoms and molecules that expand in high solar winds, exciting auroras in its body and rendering it visible."

"And what's this weird carrying case it's got us trapped in?"

"Could be the bird can mold plasma. Make itself a handy trapping net."

"So, we're specimens in a see-through monster's firefly jar," Zeb concluded.

"More like a beaker constructed as the eye of a protective plasma cyclone that maintains the conditions of our original environment. It polarizes the sunlight so we're not blinded. Atmosphere, magnetic field, even temperature. Otherwise we'd have already roasted like an ovenful of floating Christmas geese."

Christmas? Geezer? That association struck Marlie as about as likely as a polar bear casually dropping a reference to limbo dancing. Not exactly a Geezerish thing. But who knows? The old boy had to know about Christmas. Maybe he'd wished somebody a merry one in a previous life, perhaps in a spontaneous moment at an aircraft factory holiday fete. The thought of Geezer partying in a social setting was a little unsettling—but so was the sight of Venus and Mercury slipping behind the sun as she and her companions were led ever closer to a ten-million-degree hot star.

She chided herself to stay on point; there was no telling when he might clam up again. Why waste an opportunity to bone up on an aspect of physics they hadn't covered in her AP course at Geyserville High?

"Thank you, Mr. G. Care to tell us a little about all that research into electromagnetism you've been conducting, and the famous Wardenclyffe 3 you were firing at the sky? That'd be a big help too."

Geezer looked at Marlie for a few seconds, which constituted an all-time record, and actually answered her again. "Decades ago, I chanced upon a geological disturbance during a total solar eclipse in Mexico. Looking into the historical record, I discovered common elements in accounts of similar events during other eclipses. They were rare, but they all shared indications of aurora-like anomalies, and I grew determined to figure out what was behind them."

Dang, Marlie, thought Zeb, *this is right up your alley, or a nearby alley anyway. You and Geeze have got a thing going. He's a chatterbox now.*

"Nikola Tesla had planned to use his wireless power-generation tower in New York to send electromagnetic charges across interplanetary space to communicate with alien species. I realized Tesla might have been onto something that could be relevant to these eclipse ground disappearances if there were some intentional design behind them. But even if not, I could run some experiments on the phenomenon and try to invent a device to generate aurora triggers that I could use during total eclipses. I drew on Tesla's work generating high-voltage, high-frequency charges using coils, plasma lamps, and air-core transformers to build my own portable miniature Wardenclyffe.

"Meanwhile, I looked for patterns and came up with calculations to estimate the precise locations where eclipse ground disappearances were most likely to occur. This one in Antarctica looked like my best bet ever. I'd have a hundred and forty-seven seconds of totality to try it out. Then you punks showed up."

Arc took off from Geezer's shoulder and launched into a narrow spiral up the plasma jar. That burned a question mark into Zeb's mind. "We said we're sorry, Mr. G," he said. "And I'm glad we actually didn't destroy your experiment. So how about telling us what your tern has to do with all of this?"

Geezer glanced up at Arc with a crooked smile. "That bird is older'n me in tern years, but he's got of a helluva will to live, and I think I know why. He's been part of this story ever since Mexico. He lost his nest, and his family with it, during the ground break in that eclipse. I saw it happen. And for some reason he associated me with the event and got it into his noggin that I was going to chase these things the way he tracks his migration routes with the magnetite in his brain."

"Magnetite?"

Zeb never minded a chance to enlighten his brilliant sister, and a conversation that veered into zoology sometimes gave him such an opportunity. "Magnetite's an iron ore mineral in the brains of migrating birds, Marles. It helps them navigate."

"Some say it can pick up on solar-wind variations," Geezer added.

"Ah," Marlie nodded, beginning to connect the dots.

"The tern has been able to sense when TSEs are imminent and has shown up at my place more than twenty times since then to accompany me to various eclipse sites, and we've gotten closer to the ground disappearances every time. I guess he's been thinking I might somehow help him recapture what he lost that day." Geezer frowned, as if he were embarrassed for having been pushed to expose so many of his private thoughts. "That better satisfy you," he declared. "I'm done talking."

That makes sense, Marlie thought, *since we're probably done living.* They were so close to the sun it was filling nearly half their view. Numerous sunspots of various sizes dotted its surface like black lakes in a prairie of fire. One of them lay straight ahead.

"We're being shanghaied to a sunspot," she observed in the dry tone of a lab technician.

"Maybe our shanghaier's going to return us to the iceberg after borrowing us for an hour."

Marlie tilted her head up toward that of their kidnapper and called out, "Glad to oblige, Shang!"

"Good name for the beast, Sis. That's a step toward controlling him."

"Naming ain't taming," she replied as she sat down on a chunk of ice, becoming increasingly morose. "I was being ironic. I don't mind being borrowed for an hour of tourism, but I'd prefer not to sizzle and evaporate as a result."

Zeb noticed that Geezer had returned to stoic mode with Arc perched on his shoulder. Seeing no prospects for engaging him any further, Zeb joined Marlie on the ice bench. With her eyes fixed on the sunspot, she muttered to Zeb, "Relura's in Antarctica, probably calling in the Argentina Coast Guard, thinking we've drowned or God knows what. She's going to feel bad enough to die of guilt. And Mom and Dad . . . "

"Hey, lay off, Sis. We're not dead yet. Giving up is a bad move."

"That's rich—of course! Let's ask Shang to reconsider his plans." She glanced behind her at the bluish star-like object she assumed had to be Earth. Meanwhile, straight ahead one sunspot dominated the view, a vast black hole framed by fires of the sun.

Her orientation to the sunspot suddenly became hard to sustain, however, because the aurorabird had begun swinging them in great arcs. At one point the sun was entirely on their right, at another on their left.

Fighting off dizziness, Marlie asked, "*Now* what?"

"Looks like it's looking over its shoulder. Hard to imagine what a creature like that could be afraid of."

"I think its whole trip is sneaky. Kinda how it acted on the moon, like it was hiding while peeking at the Earth."

"Maybe that's why it hits Earth during eclipses—so it can case the joint in daylight and then make its move while its targets are dazzled by the sun's corona."

At last they penetrated the photosphere, surrounded by immense dynamic sheets of white flame, while the sunspot grew closer and closer. As they approached the level of the solar surface, brilliant, arcing yellow-orange fires of the sun lined the distant horizon all the way around them, like a forest fire seen from the middle of a great dark lake. They heard a muffled roar and soft, syncopated explosions far away. With one more sweep of its wings, the aurorabird soared straight into the "spot."

Zeb lunged toward the front of the jar. "Hey! This is no spot—it's a tunnel!"

Behind them the tunnel opening receded into the distance, visible as a circle of fire narrowing around a view of a few stars, including one blue "star" that was probably Earth. Adjusting to the darkness, they made out subtle colors pumping and gushing around vertical stripes in the tunnel walls, which changed gradually from red-orange and orange to yellow and yellow-green. Behind them Zeb noticed a faint moving aurora following them but keeping its distance. "Look, I think there's another one of these things following us!" Marlie gave him a heavy-lidded look: *That can't be good.* Zeb stared at the tunnel walls sweeping past them. "It's like descending into the Grand Canyon, all these levels. Mr. G—what do you think this flowing stuff is?"

"Solar fuel's my guess."

Eventually, the aurorabird slowed. Its great head turned to survey the vertical stripes. It fixed on a yellow-green one to its left, made a hard turn, and headed in that direction, taking them into a canyon of vague dimensions filled with yellow-green fog.

Their flight then came to a halt. The aurorabird swept aside a curtain of light with its wings and placed its avian and human passengers and their little chunk of Antarctica in a foggy space illuminated only by a dim glow of indeterminate origin. A representation of a total solar eclipse appeared, dangling overhead like a charming bauble hung over a crib by an adoring new parent.

The three humans and their avian companion shared a stunned silence. Geezer looked up and down the high chamber wall, his faced creased with a wide smile. Arc performed an aerial survey of the wall as if seeking a way out. A bit of the fog outside the plasma jar was pushed aside as if wisped by a breeze, but it revealed only darkness, and that only for a moment before the fog reinstated itself all around.

Zeb felt like he needed split vision as he kept a curious eye on Geezer and a wary one on his sister, who broke the silence with a slow, understated assessment of their situation.

"Hoe-lee shit."

Geezer nodded with evident delight. "Not too shabby, friends."

Zeb tried to brighten his sister's mood, knowing he'd need her to keep her wits about her, no matter what was about to happen. "Pretty trippy, doncha think?!"

Marlie shared neither Geezer's state of beatitude nor Zeb's feigned cheer at being incarcerated with a crazy stranger looking at the least predictable future in human history. When her brother confronted her, face to face, and said, "Marlie? Anybody home?" she had nothing to give but somber silence, even when Zeb added, "Please grunt if alive."

Switching strategy, Zeb turned to Geezer, hoping a dash of concern over Marlie's funk might have softened him. "So, Mr. G, think you've scored enough info to check that Eclipse Ground Disappearances box yet?" Geezer's glance in his direction made Zeb hope he might be making headway. "I sure hope so, since this project consumed your whole life!"

Geezer chewed the inside of his cheek a moment. "It's cost me some."

Opportunity! "Why'd you turn yourself into such a secretive hermit? An interesting dude like you could have been a town hero."

"What a sad loss," Geezer commented, letting the sarcasm acid seep in. "I wasn't going to let a pack of media wolves and scientific poseurs get their grimy paws on me or let anybody think of me as a nut job."

"Hey, that worked," Marlie grumbled too far under her breath for Geezer to hear, maybe. Didn't matter much.

"My objective was to learn what was seizing Earth specimens during eclipses."

"A discovery to die for," Marlie chimed in.

Zeb regarded his sister's downer as an obstacle to his extraction of information from Geezer, but Geezer wasn't troubled by it. "The only leverage Death had on me was the threat of busting my mission. He lost that battle but good. I'm mostly rip-snorting fine, but I'd have been happy as an elk in clover if I were here alone." *Ouch.* "Not knowing what was going on with these eclipses was intolerable."

"Well, Cap'n," said Zeb, trying to keep things light, "you sure caught the culprit's attention with your ray gun."

"That's not a gun, dummy. I wasn't out to kill anything."

"I know. You were trying to draw the grabber's attention with your Tesla rays."

"Which it wasn't interested in, turns out."

"It's interested in us."

"Don't flatter yourself." Geezer nodded toward Arc, who was hopping around and wing-flapping. "It's interested in him. We're just a few incidental insects taking up space in a birder's prized aviary."

On cue, the aurorabird's doting eye reappeared at their level near the bottom of the aviary, tracking Arc's flight and ignoring the non-winged Earthlings. When Arc settled on the ice behind the hillock, blocked from the humans' view, the aurorabird brought one of its wingtips to the aviary wall near its new pet and tapped on it a few times, poking a hole in the jar wall. Some white fog seeped in before the aurorabird could smooth it over.

Having completed his experiment, the aurorabird turned away and glided back out to the tunnel from which they'd come. Geezer promptly scampered over the ice hill to observe the location of the hole up close. Sensing Geezer's interest in hiding what he was up to, Zeb sneaked a look at him. *Seems like he's sussing out the fog. Apparently, it's breathable.*

Geezer turned his head and caught Zeb observing him. Too late to duck, Zeb said, "Whatcha up to there, Mr. G?"

Geezer's glare was crystal clear: Minding my own business. Zeb swallowed and backed off. Draining energy and bravado, he stole a look at Marlie out of the corner of his eye. Sitting on an ice chunk near the opposite wall, she hadn't seen the look Geezer had flung at her brother, but she knew it wasn't good. "None of our business?"

"To put it mildly."

Zeb ambled over to her. It was time to take stock. They sat together quietly in their first moment of stillness since they had awakened on the fishing boat very far away.

"Well. Interesting place to die, doncha think?"

"Marlie, would you stop with the 'die' business? Don't be so damn negative."

"For God's sake, Zeb, wake up. We're in for it. I'm hungry, and the nearest food is ninety-three million miles away."

"For all you know, this aurora thingy just likes to borrow birds for a few minutes before returning them."

"Oh, yeah—I remember that from a National Geographic special on Thingies of the Sun."

"Ha-ha." Zeb wasn't up for joining his sister in a jest fest. She'd just rejected his affectionate attempt to shore up her spirits, plus he had something else on his mind. He knew Geezer was trying to conceal what he was up to, and Zeb aimed to find out what it was. But since he'd just been caught spying, he'd need to let a little more time go by for Geezer to let down his guard.

In the meantime, he sat with Marlie, back to back on the other side of the ice hill, both with their eyes closed, neither wanting to acknowledge to the other the chilling new fears mushrooming out of the ones they'd arrived with. He tried to direct his thoughts toward the pure interestingness of their captor. He wanted to crawl right inside that creature's two-hundred-foot-diameter pupil and scrounge around back there to see what made him tick. Was there an optic nerve the size of a jungle liana bristling with electromagnetic fevers, or maybe a field of brain lobes with deep fissures that could entrap him forever?

But before long, his thoughts migrated back to the iceberg in the Southern Sea, where their older sister at that very moment must be beyond panic-stricken, terrified at what the future held for her and their parents, assisting the two fishermen and their dinghies and dragnets, combing the iceberg and surrounding water, struggling to get mayday calls to the Argentine Naval Prefecture. His zealous campaign to spend his fortune flying to Antarctica didn't seem so smart anymore.

"I'm . . . really sorry about this, Marlie. I should never have pushed for chasing Geezer."

"I was in with it," she replied. "His crazy research lab got to me too." That kindness conferred, the curtain came down on her ability to converse. Ashen-faced and short of breath, she pictured their parents tanned and ebullient coming off the trail in Hawaii a few days hence, returning to civilization and cell tower range, and picking up a frighteningly somber voice mail from Relura. And the call that would follow, and their father trying to find out what horror was streaming through the half-inch speaker on his wife's phone, and the ensuing arrhythmias that would threaten their hearts and lives. Swallowing hard, Marlie scooted around and put her head on her brother's shoulder. She opened her eyes for a reality check, and the reality she saw made her close them just as fast.

Geezer knew little and cared less about the kids' problems. The hole the aurorabird had dug in the wall of the plasmic aviary had set off klaxon alerts that were inaudible to everyone else but deafening to Geezer's curiosity. *No, punk, he had not yet scored enough info about eclipse ground disappearances.* There was something behind that wall crying out to be seen and *he would see it.*

Geezer pushed his right hand against the plasmic wall but found it sturdily resistant to pressure. Problem-solving—he couldn't be sure what the properties of this plasmic membrane might be, but there was a chance it might be susceptible to some kind of impact from the Tesla charges produced by his Wardenclyffe. Maybe he could use that to sensitize or prime a section of the wall with an ultra-low-powered charge. He couldn't help but remember the concern J. Robert Oppenheimer had had pre-Trinity about the possibility of Earth's atmosphere being ignited by the first atomic bomb test. Of course, there was no reason to fear a firestorm resulting from an experiment with a low-watt Wardenclyffe charge, but what if the charge were to jangle delicate current flows enough to make the entire chamber dissolve? That'd turn out to be one helluva caper capper.

But what did he have to lose? It had to be tried. He rose to glimpse the twins and, noticing that they were resting with their eyes closed, he crept over to the crevice where he'd stowed the Wardenclyffe, retrieved it, brushed the snow off its surface, and brought it back to the test site. Setting its power level to minimum, he aimed it at the spot in the chamber wall where the aurorabird had dug. He applied a one-second charge over an area several inches in diameter. He pressed his hand against the charge-treated spot and, sure enough, there was some give. It felt like sticking his hand into a cool, tingling, swift current of wind that felt sandy even though it was transparent to the white fog that clung to the outer aviary wall.

He retracted his hand in a scooping motion, creating a whooshing sound and leaving a hand-sized hole a half foot deep in the wall. Arc hopped onto his shoulder, every bit as intense in focus as his human partner. Geezer considered his options. He cast a glance over his shoulder to make sure he wasn't being observed by the neighbors who'd followed him here like face flies.

He needn't have worried about that. The twins were sinking ever deeper into their own concerns—namely survival, finding a ride home, and what might happen if they couldn't. Marlie's stomach clenched, imagining the memorial service their parents would have to hold for them, with Relura looking like she was contemplating guilt-wracked suicide standing alongside their parents staring at two flickering candles.

That was a cheery Christmas-morn image compared to the nightmare haunting Zeb, in which Marlie and he were splayed out on the icy aviary floor, dirty and emaciated, eating their boots, while Geezer gnawed on raw tern meat, eyeing the twins and contemplating his next course.

Meanwhile, the real Mr. G was proceeding with the business at hand. He knelt down and dug a wider hole in the aviary wall, deeper and deeper, till, at about a foot and a half, he broke through to the exterior, and white fog began seeping into the aviary. Arc took one look at that passageway, darted into it, and disappeared.

Geezer began furiously widening the opening till it was big enough for his head. He could see Arc fluttering on the other side, awaiting him. After checking once more to ensure that the twins were preoccupied, he pushed his head through the hole in the swirling plasma wall.

8

Geezer's shoulders were stuck in the plasma jar's wall, but he'd poked his head through to the other side (inadvertently mimicking Flammarion's famous cosmic discoverer) and now beheld in amazement a dark body of water some forty feet beneath him. It was perhaps twenty miles across and was cloaked in night-like darkness illuminated only by some dim light sources, which he couldn't yet see. Over time, that oversized pelican must have put together for itself an entire inland sea! His heart ratcheted up; he was not about to waste precious seconds charging the jar wall and digging a wider hole. He pulled back to get better purchase on the ice with his feet and then shoved himself with full force through the wall and climbed out onto a narrow cliff that extended around the sea in both directions.

For the first time, he could see from the outside the plasmic jar in which he'd been captured. It towered above him, and there were half a dozen more such gigantic beakers of varying sizes set like lighthouses on the curving cliff bordering the sea, each with an artificial total solar eclipse suspended above it.

The whole sea and the high shore around it were encased by some kind of protective dome. No surprise there, given that he and Arc both still existed as flesh-and-blood creatures rather than twenty-million-degree organic vapor. Since the now-absent aurorabird had been fooling around in there, the dome had to be at least ten miles high, maybe more. It was designed with a sprinkling of a few thousand stars that were obviously fake but apparently good enough in the aurorabird's judgment to add a nice decorative touch to his not-so-little play area. Geezer had to admire the industriousness of his kidnapper; it must have taken quite a few trips to the Earth depot to build this place, but then the same dedication to task could be admired in the slow, tiny Earthlings who had established the pyramids, Rome, the scientific method, and aviation.

Geezer's lifelong dream of discovering the secret behind the eclipse ground disappearances was coming true beyond his wildest imaginings, a thrill like Galileo's first sighting of the rings of Saturn, multiplied a thousandfold. The hell with the small-brained fools who would have laughed at him had he been foolish enough to share what he was searching for during those long, lonely decades—this mind-boggling revelation justified every last hour of it.

With those other beakers beckoning, there was no time to waste. He had to get cracking and investigate them. But what if the brats discovered he was missing and tried to follow him through the hole? That wouldn't do. He looked back. The aviary's wall hole seemed to be repairing itself, which, come to think of it, was a little unsettling. That might present problems when he wanted to return.

But what "when"? Where was it written he had to return anywhere? There was plenty more to explore right here, some of which might be quite a bit preferable to being cooped up with a couple of nosy teenagers on a block of ice. Not terribly nice, granted, to abandon the cubs that way, but they'd brought it on themselves by stalking him for thousands of miles. He could go back to check on them after a while, but why should he? He'd toiled for this as long as the Israelites had slogged through the desert sands in search of their promised land, so having reached his, he wasn't about to squander his opportunities playing nanny. He had met his destiny.

Arc fluttered about patiently as Geezer took time for a deep breath to mull over his very careful next steps. The cliff was as narrow as a window ledge and of uncertain stability. He could test it gingerly and try to make his way down the catwalk to the next beaker a couple hundred yards away. Several times larger than the one they'd arrived in, it had something moving inside it that demanded inspection. Employing delicate footwork along the ledge, Geezer would mosey on down the shore to check it out, counting on trusty Sancho Arcpanza to follow along.

In the cage Zeb had dubbed "the Antarctijar," the twins were ever deeper inside their nightmares, still unaware that they were now alone in a birdless aviary. Compared with what they were enduring in their imaginations, dealing with a dangerous old crank would have been a welcome relief from the grotesque internal sequelae they were suffering from in the current phase of their colorful destruction disorder.

Zeb, for example, had moved on down the narrative line from Geezer relishing finger-lickin' tern meat. Now, the crazed, hollow-eyed abomination aimed the Wardenclyffe right at him—*Zap!*—and flash-fried him to meat with burnt hair slipping off the bone. Poor Marlie beat on Geezer with her bony hands until he zapped her too while slurping a wee bit of juice out of what remained of Zeb's left trapezius. The vibe alone from his overdeveloped imagination heated Marlie's mental temperature another twenty degrees.

But now she awoke. Relief!—if awakening from one nightmare to another counts. She'd heard a silent internal buzzer go off, alerting her that something new and discordant had appeared in the real world. Her eyes snapped open to absorb iceberg, aviary, still alive, what? *Ack!* A huge eye staring at them. "Zeb—it's back!"

Zeb came to, shook off the ugly specter tormenting him, and saw what Marlie was pointing to. It was an aurorabird eye, but not the same as before. It was smaller, almost by half. As the creature pulled its head back to regard them with both eyes, he could see that its body was smaller in proportion to its head. Indeed, the whole creature was smaller than before, and its auroral glow was milder, a speckled tan with simpler, random surface patterning.

"Oh, it's not the same one," said Marlie. "I'll bet it's the one that followed us down the tunnel."

"I haven't studied aurorabird ethology, but this smacks of sneaky interference on the part of a little brother."

"What counts as younger around here? A couple of years?"

"Could be a couple of hours or a couple of millennia, for all we know."

Little Brother's expression changed, looking to Marlie for all the world like cunning. "This dude is creeping me out. I'd rather dance with the guy that brung us."

It was all-hands-on-deck time. "Hey, Mr. G!" called Zeb, but Mr. G didn't respond. Zeb jumped up and leapt to the top of the ice hill. Geezer was nowhere to be seen, nor was Arc, but he shouted "Mr. G?!" again anyway.

Marlie got up to see for herself and thus missed Little Brother's standing up, lowering his head, grabbing the aviary in his beak, and shaking it, throwing her and Zeb off balance.

Outside, the jar shaking had thrown Geezer off balance too, and he was now hanging from the cliff by his fingertips. Maybe this body of water was a pond to the aurorabird, but in Earthling terms it was a treacherous sea with waves that would tax an English Channel swimmer. When a second yank lifted the aviary off its moorings, Geezer was knocked down deep into the tossing waters below. Before he even hit the water, back first, Geezer saw the aviary carried out of the dome by the aurorabird—or *some* aurorabird. The one that had just fled with the coop didn't quite look like the one that had led them to this corner; maybe it was another one altogether. Either way, it was a good thing Geezer hadn't banked on returning to Earth, because the only option for a ride home now vanished as his body splashed into the inner sea. As for those kids headed for God knows what, well, *c'est la vie* in the sun.

Oh, there'd be some kerfluffle back in California when the children's sister had to report to her parents and the police what had happened in Antarctica, and that wasn't pleasant, nor was it comfortable to contemplate what new fate was bedeviling those kids, but time was a-wasting out here in the dark sea. It was time to put those concerns aside in a small, leak-proof compartment and focus on the task at hand—namely, swimming on down to the big beaker and attempting to scale the cliff beneath it to see just what was what.

Geezer didn't mind a little exercise after being cooped up in a plasma cage for hours. He hadn't thought about the water temperature, seeing as how he hadn't contemplated going for a swim, but now that a dive had been foisted upon him, he was relieved to find the water more than tolerable. Salty, too. The goofy aurorabird must have imported many a shipment of sea water and shorelines from Earth's tropical zones.

Not only was Geezer unfazed by his fall into the sea, he found it exhilarating, and touching too, since Arc had plunged underwater with him and was following him back up to the surface. The bird's concern reminded him that they had a job to do. Here's hoping the kids enjoyed the next stops on their tour; he and Arc were plenty pleased with theirs. The dimly lit plasma jar closest to them, looming over the sea not far away, would soon receive visitors.

9

With the pilfered Antarctijar containing Zeb and Marlie hanging from its beak, Little Brother flew back through the secret yellow-green striped passage connecting the cave to the main tunnel. Each of the twins was tempted to say something along the lines of *What the hell now?!* but there was no point. Each knew the other was enduring the same mixed malady of excitement, depression, and fear. They had little to say to each other, till Zeb broke the silence with an observation that brought no comfort.

"I saw Geezer trying to dig a hole in the jar wall. He must have escaped through it."

"Escaped to what? More fun in the sun? He's probably dead by now, or deathbound, and Arc too."

Zeb's optimism had finally drained out. He had nothing. It wasn't like they'd been handed an options menu. Back when he was only a few months into sailplane flight instruction, emergency response sequences had been drilled into him. He'd been indoctrinated with the mindset that there must always be options, things you could do to avoid or at least minimize disaster, but that belief had just crumbled. His sister's life and his own were utterly at the mercy of a being that made the Loch Ness monster look no stranger than a cocker spaniel.

Zeb's uncharacteristic gloom only deepened Marlie's. She forced herself to focus on where they were headed next. When their new captor reached the main tunnel, he emerged and turned left, the same direction they'd traveled in before. Over the next ten minutes, the sunfire-rimmed stovepipe view of space through the tunnel entrance back at the sun's surface grew vanishingly small.

As Little Brother flew them toward a soft blue-violet light, Marlie thought she heard Zeb ask her something, but her systemic response to this cascade of craziness was to cocoon herself in silence. *He probably said something vaguely amusing or some groundless pep-talky Zebism. Goody. Go ahead, God, Aurorabird, whoever, whatever. Bring it. At this point, you think I care?*

Zeb had said something, but it was addressed to the creature from whose beak they were suspended: "Oh, driver, you need to turn around; our house is in the opposite direction. And please first stop by your brother's place and pick up our friends." But since his real target was as unresponsive as the pretend one, he abruptly canceled his open-mike act and joined Marlie in quiet, uneasy contemplation of the great unknown ahead.

It wouldn't be unknown for long. That blue-violet light was getting larger, and there was movement within it. In less than a minute they slowed and coasted into a place so strange that both twins' jaws dropped at once.

A vast, spherical hollow bathed in blue-violet light opened up before them, populated by aurorabirds of various sizes and hues as far as the eye could see. This place had to be hundreds of miles in diameter, judging from their perspective view of the creatures farthest away. Some of the aurorabirds were suspended in exotic yoga-like poses, languidly floating in space, while others communed in small groups or gravitated toward a great, shimmering, transparent globe at the hollow's center. The twins were going to get a better look at that soon, for their new captor was taking a short cut toward another sector of this spacy cave that would bring them close by.

Okay, thought Marlie, actually smiling, *that fits. The sun has a nucleus with a lake the size of a small county inside it attracting stoned-looking aurorabirds alighting on its slow-rolling waves and bobbing like glowing sea lions.* She could hear them emitting soft, rhythmic hums tracing melodic lines around the reverberating echoes of what she guessed was the thrumming of the sun's power plant. What better nucleus for an immense spa of magical indolence than a globular spiritual lake?

Zeb was smiling too, watching the streams of aurorabirds entering and leaving the cave through tunnels dotting its surface in many directions. Upon arrival, most of them collapsed briefly into blobs like beached jellyfish before re-energizing themselves and wandering about or navigating their way down to the lake globe. Maybe he was getting as stoned as the bobbing aurorabirds, because this latest twist in the saga taking them ever farther from the lives they'd known for the entirety of their seventeen years struck him as so ridiculously strange it set him giggling.

Little Brother wasn't giggling. He was on a mission that took him and his stolen treasure toward a cluster of aurorabirds about his size hanging out on the outskirts of the hollow. He seemed to be making a concerted effort to avoid the larger ones. When he reached the group, he halted and held up his jar for their inspection and hushed squeaks.

Now surrounded by six more gigantic eyes, Marlie finally spoke up. "I always wanted to be an object of fascination to the cool kids' clique."

"Hang in there, babe. This isn't necessarily a bad thing," said Zeb, and for the first time in two days Marlie laughed. Zeb was a little abashed but stuck by his guns. "All I'm saying is, let's see where this is going. Maybe there will be some angle we can work here." Rushing to his own defense in advance of further ridicule, he added, "Either way, as a scientist you've got to admit this is an interesting development."

"It does beat the pants off AP physics lab."

The young aurorabird gang was mighty animated over the tiny human creatures their pal had shown up with—excited enough, unfortunately for them, to have drawn the attention of a few much larger aurorabirds who had glided by while show-and-tell was in full swing. Little Brother caught on and tried to quiet his buddies, but it was too late. The twins saw one of the giants coming straight at them, causing Little Brother to jerk his prized jar backward in a vain attempt to hide it behind his back. Zeb figured that quailing body language must be universal, because Little Brother shrank like a molested sea anemone. Between that and the way his buddies had skedaddled, somebody was in trouble.

A moment later, the prisoners were brought back around to the front, and what they saw made them swallow in awe. The new arrival towering over Little Brother was three times his size and the most flagrantly vivid aurorabird they'd yet seen, with purple and gold light streaming across its skin and dynamic fractal patterning, especially in its eyes. It lowered its head for a good look at the captured humans. Its face swelled with indignant anger at Little Brother, who swallowed hard while seeming to plead his case.

"Looks like Big Mammy's not pleased," Marlie observed.

"Mammy? I was thinking Big Pappy."

"Care to try and determine its sex?"

"I'll pass, thanks."

"Fine. Let's call it MammyPappy."

"Deal."

That frothy exchange did little to quell the immanent question of whether the coming change in their fortunes would be for good or ill, but there wasn't much time to speculate. MammyPappy snatched Little Brother in its huge beak, toppling the twins onto the snow. It steered toward the sunspot tunnel they'd arrived from and then, with a powerful sweep of its wings, flew into it with the delinquent and his booty in tow, one dangling thing in the mouth of another.

10

The novelty of this latest twist in their adventure did little to distract Marlie from the sense that they were zooming through a rainbow tunnel of death, but at least this return trip offered the possibility that they might be reunited with the two terrestrial companions with whom they'd spent their rest stop. Geezer was an unreliable—probably dangerous—character, but she couldn't help feeling a little attached to him. On balance, they might be better off with him than without.

That speculative reverie was interrupted when MammyPappy let loose with a deafening honk and accelerated through the tunnel so fast the stripes in the tunnel wall blended into a polychromatic blur. They whipped by the yellow-green region, dashing any hope of gathering reinforcements at Shang's den.

The creature slowed as it approached the end of the tunnel where the sunspot opened to space. The distant forest of fire rimming the sunspot at the solar surface surrounded them. Both twins had assumed they were en route to some other destination in the solar system, but when MammyPappy turned toward the flames, Marlie lost it. "No!" she screamed, "it's going to vaporize us! Stop, you freaking idiot! Take us home!"

"Chill out, Marlie," Zeb implored her. Panic was not on the list of advised steps in the face of flight emergencies. "We haven't roasted so far," he added, but Marlie had already begun to quiet down, recognizing the futility of yelling at an ionized electromagnetic archaeopteryx thousands of times her size.

MammyPappy slowed as she-he approached the roaring, orange-white conflagration. The twins saw arcing, skyscraper-sized flames growing to the height of mountains, lightstreams of such blinding intensity that even with the protection of the plasmic jar wall, the twins had to squint.

MammyPappy set their jar down on the sunspot's rim—a soft landing on a beach of fire. The closest flares were too vast for their form to be discerned, but the twins stared in wonder as, in the distance, untold thousands of immense flares performed spectacular acrobatic leaps into space like highly trained dancers committed in blazing body and soul to the orgiastic worship of Terpsichore.

"Looks like a freaking rave out here," said Zeb. Marlie nodded; words were out of stock amidst her internal churning of apprehension and awe.

With Little Brother glumly hunched alongside the human captives, MammyPappy scanned the crowd. Other aurorabirds arrived, stretched out, and allowed their bodies to glow like hot coals. A few on the outskirts remained stationary in meditative poses, but the auroral skins of those closer to the fray ignited in fire, and those propelled themselves into the thicket of dancing flames.

When MammyPappy's own skin reached the glowing-coal stage, she-he set forth into the crowd, dragging the captives along, flying low enough to surveil the heads of the smaller dancers. All around Zeb and Marlie, inflamed ravers formed elegant patterns with each other mid-leap, momentarily losing their individuality in brilliant kaleidoscopic shock waves before gently floating back down to regain their original forms. One blazing ballerina soared up a hundred miles and executed an octuple back flip on the way down, changing tints along its edges all the while.

Most of the creatures were too frenzied to pay heed to MammyPappy or its odd cargo, but a few who caught on came in for a close gawk. One of them got one good look at MammyPappy and its cargo and fled in the opposite direction.

"Zeb! That's our hijacker from Antarctica!"

"Shang!"

MammyPappy bellowed a great avian choral honk into the surrounding thunderous bonfire and took off after the scamp, quickly zooming ahead of him and cutting off his escape. MammyPappy then stopped and suspended the twins' Antarctic cage in front of its offspring's huge face and erupted with a thunderous demand for an explanation of the apparent contraband. The kid kidnapper cowered and peeped a few meek honks before halting and moving in for a closer inspection, looking puzzled.

"I think our pal just realized that he's in danger of a royal auroral ass-whipping for messing with us tide pool organisms."

"And that his prize bird is missing," Zeb speculated.

"Maybe he'll be forced to take us back where he got us!"

Shang's eyes slid over to Little Brother with a sibling-shrinking glare. MammyPappy shoved the specimen jar in the older brother's beak, swung a wing toward the sunspot, and barked a command. Shang then found himself grabbed by his auroral scruff and lifted away by MammyPappy, leaving Little Brother behind. Zeb noted the resignation in Shang's body language and thought he could feature it in a cool panel in a future graphic novel. But then he recalled that getting back to his drawing desk would require getting back to Earth first, the odds against which were literally astronomical.

When Zeb was thirteen, a well-connected friend of his mother had scored a ride for him in the Goodyear Blimp, which kept a *pied à terre* in Oakland. The glory of gliding over the Bay Area from within the panoramic windows in the underbelly of the aircraft ignited the spark that later led to his taking up sailplane flight three years later.

That early inspiration came back to him now as he and his sister were transported in a compartment beneath their monstrous living carrier, surveying the landscape of thousands of solar-flare ravers in their multimillion-degree club. Half of him wanted to exult in the marriage of his lust for the fantastic and the adventure he was living moment by heart-throbbing moment; but the other half glanced at his sister, who, as usual, was grounded in a classical science outlook that didn't brook fantasy when reality was pounding on the door, especially when reality was fantastical enough. The look on her face stung Zeb with a reminder that this whole Auroralark Ascending romance they were living held little hope for their lives lasting more than a few hours, if that. Therein lay a downer of unspeakable dimensions.

Such was the nature of his temperament as MammyPappy & Son reached their home sunspot and banked a turn back down the tunnel. Once again, both captors and captives were enveloped in near darkness illuminated only by the dim glow of rainbow stripes blurring by on all sides. When they finally slowed in the yellow-green region, his mind was too much of a jumble to cast odds one way or the other as to whether things were about to get better or worse.

11

The grim solemnity with which Marlie faced the return to Shang's den was leavened with anticipation of relief. In her psych elective, they'd learned about a consciousness determinant a Harvard psychologist had called the Uncertainty Principle, which made the unpredictability of subatomic particle momentum and position look as logical as Swiss watchworks. According to the theory, people often find the grating pressure of extensive uncertainty so unsettling they will deliberately tip their fate toward an available unhappy resolution rather than endure a further prolonged battle to effect a happier one. Thus, she found consolation in the imminence of the end to their ordeal, a fate-sealing slam of all doors to the future that she and her brother might have enjoyed if only they'd had the good sense to stay in their parents' comfy nest when Geezer set forth on his pre-dawn lake-crossing a couple of century-days before.

Thus enervated, she looked at Zeb, sighed, and mused, "I'm guessing MammyPappy's ordered its kid to go to his room."

"Maybe we'll have a reunion with Geeze and Arc after all."

"Goody."

"Hey, you didn't really want to leave them in some unknown solar hellhole, did you?"

"Fine—bring on a reunion. Then what?"

She got her answer soon enough, as the four travelers decelerated on approach to the aurorabird's secret passage. When they reached the foggy cave, their bow wave blew a break in the fog and revealed the incredible domed land and seascape that Shang had built with half a dozen enormous jars like the one in which they'd been housed. "Jesus! Look at this thing! A whole collection of plasmic jars, and an ocean to boot. You think those other jars are discards? Or does he keep other victims in there?!"

"You mean dead ones?"

"Who knows? Dead or alive—either way our kidnapper is even more bizarre than I thought."

"Welcome to Shang's Seaside Zoo."

Throughout this exchange the fog began to thin out, as if driven away by winds off the dark ocean. Zeb kept his eyes peeled for any further clues he might mine as to what was going on outside their jar and what might have happened to their missing travel companions. Marlie was tracking the creatures' movements far overhead when Zeb seized her arm.

"Marlie—look! In the sea! It's Geezer! And Arc!"

Marlie followed Zeb's pointing finger to the sea below the gigantic plasmic jar nearest their own. Geezer was pulling hard swim strokes in their direction, with Arc flying around just above his head. The old man appeared undaunted by the waves—hardly a surprise after his formidable performance giving chase to them in their boat on the lake back home, but Zeb was impressed nonetheless. "Still the gold medalist."

"For now, but if they're not rescued from the ocean, they're doomed to die! We've got to figure out a way to get them back in here."

Meanwhile, overhead, MammyPappy's kaleidoscopic eyes looked ready to pop out of its kinetic head. She-he thrust a wingtip toward the nearby jar and honk-growled a demand at its offspring. Apparently, Shang's collecting habit was a serious no-no.

"They don't seem to even notice Geezer and Arc."

Zeb caught Shang casting a furtive glance over his shoulder down in the ocean. "No, Shang knows they're down there but doesn't want MammyPappy to catch on."

"Well, bullshit! He's not getting away with that!" Marlie leapt to the top of the ice hill, waved her arms, and pointed down to the sea, screaming, "Save our friends, you solar freaks! They're drowning down there!" That last exaggeration of passion didn't matter much, given the creatures' ignorance of English, but the truth was things weren't looking too good for the human at sea with his pet bird.

Zeb joined Marlie in raising a ruckus, and Shang caught on quickly, but instead of making any move to help, he tried to hide the twins from his parent. "That bastard," exclaimed Marlie. "He doesn't want to save them!"

"I'm not so sure about that. Maybe he just doesn't want MammyPappy to know about the extra contraband so he can preserve them."

"Or maybe just Arc, at least, no matter what happens to us."

Zeb looked down at Geezer and hollered, "Mr. G!"

"He can't hear you, Zeb. We can't even hear those waves in here."

"No, but he can see us, and so does Arc."

No sooner had Zeb spoken than Arc flew right up to their eye level, flapping his wings in a frenzy. "I think they want back in here, Marles."

"I thought Geezer couldn't stand us."

"Maybe being lost in a solar sea has changed his mind."

By then Arc had caught MammyPappy's eye, which lowered into view looking so huge that, by comparison, the flapping bird could be a solitary dust mote floating in front of an IMAX screen. Arc tried to draw the monster's attention to Geezer splashing his way toward the Antarctic jar.

Shang and the four Earthlings felt the reverberations of a MammyPappy anger storm. She-he picked up Shang by the tail feathers and whipped him back and forth over the sea four times before setting the harried creature back down in front of his jar collection. With a guilty twitch, Shang set about the task he'd been ordered to execute.

The twins suspected it had to do with plucking Geezer and Arc out of the sea, but they couldn't figure out how the gigantic creature was going to pull it off. Expecting a creature with a couple of ten-thousand-foot-long wings to pick up a six-foot, three-inch human—let alone a one-foot, two-inch bird—out of an ocean was a lot to ask. It would be like using a pair of salad tongs to remove two specific germs from a swimming pool.

Shang was too clever to be vexed by a little problem like that. For one thing, he was able to improve visibility all around by using his huge wings to sweep most of the nearby fog out to sea. Then all he had to do was dig a hole in the jar wall and scoop up a bunch of sea water where the specimens were, and *voilà*. The only problem was that hole-poking and sea-scooping were precise operations, not exactly fit for Shang's wingtips. His first clumsy attempt plunged the jar into the sea and nearly drowned the twins with a mini-tsunami that failed to include the target bird (and human). The wave tossed the twins in different directions, but at least the immediate fear of each sibling for the other's welfare was quickly assuaged as most of the water spilled back out of the hole.

As they recovered their wits, they noticed Shang casting a sheepish glance at MammyPappy, whose temper was not improving. Neither was the twins' state of nerves. The water itself wasn't very cold, but in contact with the iceberg floor it got really cold really soon. Thoroughly drenched, they scampered for higher ground to get their legs out of the chilly spillage so they could figure out what to do next.

As they brainstormed, Arc flew into the jar through the hole, momentarily brightening the twins' hopes before they realized that the bird's return didn't mark much progress toward the goal. There was a much larger flightless organism down in the sea who would have a tougher time getting through that hole. The tern fluttered around as if assessing the situation himself and then, as easily as he had entered, he flew back out down to sea level to be with his partner.

MammyPappy and the twins were now on the same page, determined to get the remaining Earthling back in the jar. In the wake of Shang's botched rescue attempt, Marlie's face lit up in sync with her brother's. "We can help these giants."

"And I know how," said Zeb. "We'll make a chain!"

"Are you sure we can lift the Geeze in here? He must weigh two hundred."

"Hey, what was all our time in the gym for if not for this?"

"How prescient of the parents."

"Brace yourself against the ice by the hole and spot me as I lean out. I'll reach down and, if Shang's got any brains, he'll lower us close enough so I can grab Geezer. Once we've leveraged my center of gravity back over the edge, the two of us can lift Geezer to where he can get his hands up to the ledge. From there he can do the rest himself."

They scrambled into position at the portal, where Marlie wrapped one arm tightly around a solid ice peak protruding from the floor of the iceberg. Zeb gripped her by the wrist, scooted to the edge, and waved to the immense creature overhead, convincing himself that the aurorabird winked in response.

When the aurorabird lurched the jar, readying it for its second grand swipe over the sea, Zeb felt the thrill of flight he'd gotten addicted to in sailplanes. He was swept above the sea in an arc stretching swiftly toward Geezer from a hundred yards away. Zeb could tell Marlie's hold on the ice had slipped a little before she repositioned herself for an even tighter hold, but neither one commented on that glitch because the contact with Geezer was only seconds away.

Treading water, Geezer was plenty clear as to what they were aiming to do, and he was cooperating all the way. He kept his eye on the moving jar and Zeb's outreached hand as they flew overhead, but Shang hadn't lowered the jar close enough for contact. Having overshot the mark, the creature stopped and tried wiggling into a more precise position to match Zeb's and Geezer's outstretched arms, but what he thought to be a little wiggle was an earthquake to the twins. "I'm losing my grip!" yelled Marlie.

"Brace yourself against the portal edge!" shouted Zeb, and the moment she did, he let go and fell into the sea.

"Zeb!" screamed Marlie into the dark sea where her brother had disappeared.

Geezer did a surface dive and a moment later reemerged, holding Zeb by the arm much as he'd done in Antarctica. As the two looked at each other for an instant, Zeb heard Marlie call from the jar portal overhead, "Why did you let go?!"

"Had to!" he shouted. "You'd never have gotten back to a secure position and we'd both have fallen in!" He looked back at Geezer just long enough to ascertain that the old man was still intent on cooperating with them. He turned to Marlie. "Shang will do it again. This time, reach for me, and once I'm up there, I'll grab Geez—Mr. G!"

Zeb heard Marlie holler back her agreement as he turned to Geezer, who was treading water alongside him. "Thanks, Mr. G."

Geezer demanded to know where they'd gone, and Zeb started to explain. "Another auroracreature—"

"A small one—I saw it."

"That one took us toward the center of the sun. That giant found us there and took us to the sun's surface—" Zeb took a deep breath. "It's too much to explain now. We're trying to get you back in the aurorabird's mason jar. You can't swim forever, Mr. G." Zeb heard Marlie cry out and looked up to see her hanging halfway out of the jar as Shang lifted it up a hundred feet to be ready for another swipe over the sea.

As the jar came swooping down toward them with Marlie reaching out as far as she dared, Zeb suddenly felt himself being grabbed by the hips and tossed up several feet in the air; he'd just become a ball passed by an ace water polo center. He admired Geezer's timing, because he reached his upward peak at the precise moment Marlie passed overhead and, with her old uneven-bars skills kicking in, she and Zeb finessed a mutual forearm grasp. As Zeb swung out over the waves, Marlie tugged him up high enough to reach the ice wall at the edge of the portal, and in three more seconds he'd hefted himself back inside.

Marlie smiled when he said "Thanks," but what meant the most to her was the evidence on his face of his pride in having a strong, can-do sister. It was partly that pride that made him glow, true, but there was more. "I saw bioluminescence underwater, Marles."

That caught her up short. Marlie hadn't thought about life inhabiting Shang's inner sea, but with Shang still fixed on completing the present game plan, there was no time for debriefing. "Tell me later, Zeb. We've barely got seconds before our next shot at saving Geezer."

Marlie pinioned herself into position around the ice blocks by the portal's edge as Zeb placed himself at the opening. He flashed on the World War II British paratroopers looking down on Italy from gliders in the moment before jumping. While maintaining a tight grip on his sister's forearm, Zeb prepared for Shang's swift sweep just over the water. Geezer already had his right arm raised, and a second later Zeb had him dangling over the water with Arc swirling around him, evidently cheering him on. But Shang, being a novice at this sort of thing, apparently thought he could help secure his catch by yanking the jar upward. Instead, that knocked a block of ice onto Marlie's head, nearly unmooring her enough to dump all three of them into the sea. Geezer, understanding the risk to his saviors, let go of Zeb from fifty feet over the water and executed a perfect back flip dive with vertical entry.

"Crap!"

"Not to worry, Marles, we've got this. Shang's gotta be smart enough not to try that jerking thing again." Marlie nodded, and the two of them got into position for the next swing, which was already beginning.

Drenched by the cold waves sloshing around their legs, the twins anchored themselves, looking down upon Arc and the spot where Geezer had disappeared. By the time he emerged, Shang already had them swinging out over the sea, headed toward Geezer, who waited like a slugger poised for the next pitch. When Zeb's hand was one half second away, he lurched up from the sea surface and—*thwap*—landed a solid grip on the kid's forearm. This time Shang slowed to a standstill while, slowly and carefully, Zeb pulled Geezer up to the portal edge. With adroit flexion of his arms, torso, and leg muscles, Geezer climbed into the jar, followed by Arc, and stood up.

"Glad you decided to rejoin us, Mr. G," said Zeb with a smile.

Geezer understood that Zeb's declarative remark was probably also a question as to *why* he'd rejoined them, but grateful as he was for their help, he wasn't about to answer that, much less grovel in gratitude. He did manage to mutter "Good work," after which he crossed over to the wall facing the rest of the jars, where the remaining fog was still clinging to much of the plasmic tower. Arc settled on his shoulder with an intense expression worthy of a dog catching the scent of a nearby bear.

The twins took a much-deserved deep breath and wondered aloud how much time they had to strategize before events overtook them yet again.

Their answer came quickly: none. The Antarctic jar was suddenly lifted up again, and its passengers could see Shang gulping, glancing ruefully at MammyPappy for a moment before moving their jar laterally along the cliff.

The entire jar began to tilt over. A sideways palm tree punched a hole near the floor of the iceberg, breaking up the side of the jar. Marlie cried, "Look out!" as they were thrust nearly upside down into another space they couldn't make out because of the ice, snow, cold sea water, and each other's bodies falling all around them. They slid down the side of the jar toward the hole, with broken ice and snow burying them in whiteness.

They landed with another splash, this time in surf a couple feet deep that was as warm as the water they were already drenched with was cold. Marlie heard Zeb curse and call out to her, but she couldn't answer immediately. She was pulling hard in an attempt to get her left leg out from under a packed snow boulder that was now covered by the palm branches of a coconut tree. She couldn't see because her face was covered with snow. A moment later a large, rough hand swept the snow off her face and she looked up into Geezer's grizzled face. Zeb appeared alongside him and the two of them lifted the branches and heavy ice off her leg. Once liberated, she joined them standing in knee-deep water and surveying their new environs.

They were in a plasma jar, all right, but it wasn't the same one they'd been trapped in before. The top of the Antarctijar was poking through into the new one until Shang withdrew it, under the disapproving eye of Mammy-Pappy. In evident embarrassment, with the busted, wilting Antarctijar hanging listlessly from his wingtip, Shang dropped it into the sea.

The new jar was much larger than the other; Zeb estimated it was some two hundred feet across. A wide smile appeared on Geezer's face as he stepped onto a tropical shore, pulling off his jacket and opening his shirt against the humid heat.

"Where are we?" asked Marlie.

"Mexico, you might say," Geezer answered.

"*Hunh?!*"

"I get it, Zeb. This must be one of those land grabs Shang made before he took us."

"Long before, children," said Geezer. "Long before."

As the twins removed their soaking parkas and rucksacks, Geezer cheered, "Goddam, yes!" as he watched two adult female Arctic terns wheel down from the top of the Mexican cliff toward Arc, who was flapping snow out of his wings while fluttering to regain his bearings in the air. When one of the females called out, Arc swiveled in mid-air and locked eyes with her. They began flying around each other in an aerial joy dance, eventually retreating to a home on the cliff wall. Arc met his daughter, and the warmth between them charged the tropical air.

"A family reunion, it looks like," observed Zeb.

"I could use one of those," replied Marlie.

Geezer warned them to brace themselves as he pointed to Shang bringing his wingtip down to the jar containing them. This time, instead of lifting and tossing them about, the creature brought another jar in their direction and plunged it through their wall, and in another moment a chunk of new landscape slid into view alongside the Mexican cliff. It was a small platter of savannah, complete with a little waterhole in which a toppled, shocked flamingo was flailing about. The three terns sailed down to greet it.

"What a peculiar beauty," murmured Marlie, relishing the first post-Pangea get-together of Africa, Mexico, and Antarctica. It didn't last long, though. After tilting the savannah enough to leave the flamingo behind, Shang slipped the foreign landscape out of the jar, leaving the population of the Mexican plasmic jar increased by one.

Then the humans on the beach were rocked again as a thicket of bamboo and banana trees entwined in vine appeared in their little sky, pointing down to their heads, an upside-down swatch of rain forest with rain falling upward. An agitated toucan flapped its wings and flew down to join its fellow birds as the patch of rain forest was pulled away.

Regarding the motley coterie of birds, Zeb thought how odd it must be for these species who likely had never seen the likes of each other on Earth to be thrust together in these most extraordinary circumstances.

Not done yet, Shang slipped the rain forest away and charged on, astonishing the human and growing avian population of the Mexican plasma jar with a bewildering succession of biome plates penetrating its walls just long enough to liberate the bedazzled newcomers—a hummingbird surprised while extracting nectar from pampas wildflowers, a barn owl swooping down from the eaves of a prairie farm stable, a swallow halting its darting dance over an evergreen forest creek to join her distant cousins on and above the beach, and a falcon mid-hover over a tilted conical volcanic hill, flying into a new sky as its original one slipped away.

Slack-jawed, Geezer and the twins beheld this cavalcade of stars stolen from Earth. Marlie suspected that even hardened, jaded Geezer had goose-flesh like her brother and herself. The perverse thought flashed through her mind that even if they did die that day, it would have been worth it to have witnessed such an extraordinary solution to a great mystery that had been lurking in far corners of the Earth for centuries.

Zeb's asking her "You okay?" brought her around. "I think we may be go for launch, Sis."

She looked up at the two auroracreatures towering above them. Mammy-Pappy removed the total solar eclipse bauble at the top of their jar and tossed it into the mini-ocean. The giant creature swept its wings back in a universal gesture that crossed boundaries of species to command "Let's go!" Obediently, Shang took a forlorn look at the site of his former collection of aviaries, seized the looped top of the Mexican jar in his beak, and took off. Gliding like an osprey, with MammyPappy close behind keeping a sharp eye on him, Shang left his domed niche and flew through his secret passage and up the main tunnel leading out of the sun.

12

Two auroracreatures, nine birds, and three humans zoomed back up the sunspot tunnel toward the rim of orange-white fire at its end. Geezer trained his eyes on the widening circle of space straight ahead. The twins had dropped out of his consciousness once again.

Countless, largely disconnected thoughts tried to jam their way into Zeb's mind like rush-hour passengers on a Tokyo subway. No single one struck him as adequate to share with his sister at a time of such frightening and exhilarating tension, but the one that won out was this:

"Marlie—these birds—you've noticed they're the same species we saw on the Antarctic iceberg, right?" She nodded. "I can't help but wonder if the birds holding that flying séance knew or suspected that their departed were still alive somewhere."

Again, she replied with only a nod. Her approach to wrestling with the Great Hulking Uncertainty differed from her brother's. Among the myriad questions swirling in her mental cyclone was whether their next stop was a permanent one in the fiery dance hall theatrics of the solar-surface ravers.

Evidently not. Their captor shot out of the sunspot entry like an auroral bat out of hell, MammyPappy on his rippling tailfeathers, sparing the twins little time to behold the ravers' blazing ecstatic acrobatics etching graceful prominences into the blackness of space on all sides.

Leaving the sun behind, Marlie felt liberated. For all its color and drama, the sun had become a claustrophobia-inducing cloak around her spirit. Now, she was living her dream of interplanetary space travel, and for the second time, no less. Yet it was hardly the untrammeled joy she'd anticipated since first lapping up the images of new astronaut recruits in *Astronomy* magazine at the age of ten. With mounting odds of imminent death, she and her brother were far from ripe enough to share Geezer's end-of-life fulfillment bliss. Making it into space was transcendent; not so, dying out there before graduating from high school.

Bugged by morbid musings, Marlie hungered for more of a distraction than the chattering birds and the sight of sharp Mercury and opalescent Venus far off on opposite sides of their trajectory. She hoped her loquacious brother would provide one for her, but as he too seemed engrossed in thought, a conversation starter popped out of her own mouth.

"Zeb, what was that about seeing lights underwater when you fell into the sea?"

Zeb perked up. His own ambivalence about their very-near-future fate welcomed the relief. "Oh, yeah—I saw a bunch of bioluminescent zooplankton. Arc dove down with me and gobbled up some of it."

"Ah, that makes sense. Shang would hardly have filtered his pilfered sea water."

"I imagine he lavished as much love and care on his hobby as any basement-train-set freak, and now it's come to an end."

"Poor thing. Cue the violins."

They were far enough from the sun to see the entire disk framed by its corona, its brilliant dominance beginning to yield to darker space lit by millions of far more distant stars. Shang dutifully maintained a straight course toward blue Earth gleaming straight ahead.

"Dare we hope?" asked Marlie.

"Yeah, we dare! Shang knows better than to mess with MammyPappy." Zeb did his best to imitate MammyPappy's honk voice, articulating, "Take those things back where you got them!" He noticed a small, telltale sign of relaxation in his sister's brow. "Never thought I'd be more desperate to see Antarctica than I was two days ago."

"Hey, maybe it won't return us to Relura. What'll we do then?"

"No point in kidnapped beggars being choosy. Anywhere on Earth will be just fine. We can take it from there."

Throughout this exchange, Geezer had kept his gaze fixed on Earth. The sun had diminished to a quarter of the sky behind them and was getting smaller by the moment. Time to look ahead, thought Zeb. Once they'd gotten back home (should they be so fortunate), maybe Geezer would be a mite more open to friendship with him and Marlie. True, the guy was an inveterate hermit, but after all, they'd been through so much together. Zeb was sure there'd be a lot to learn from such a creative mind. Marlie ought to appreciate that as much as he would. He piped up, "We're sure glad we got you back out of that faraway ocean, Mr. G."

No acknowledgment. Zeb figured Geezer was wrestling with the question of how to deal with the two young problems he'd briefly divested himself of. Marlie welcomed the possibility of a change of pace and decided to help out. "Zeb told me about the bioluminescence in Shang's sea, Mr. G. You must have seen that while we were gone, hunh?"

Geezer snapped his head in her direction. "Where did that pipsqueak aurorabird take you? And how did that big dog come into the picture?" His expression had zero percent smile content, as might be expected from someone who wanted the facts, ma'am, now.

"Saaay," smiled Zeb, with impolitic bravado. "Now we're the ones with some secret knowledge. Let's work a little trade here, whaddya say, Mr. G? Maybe you could help our friendship along by telling us your name."

Marlie rolled her eyes at her brother in unspoken rebuke. "That's not necessary, Mr. G, much as we would like to get to know you."

Zeb didn't want to be obnoxious. He simply believed that a modest needling at someone's quirks could sometimes prompt an improvement in their behavior. It worked that way between himself and Marlie every little once in a while. "How about your phone number, Mr. G? That way, if we all make it back, we can let you know when we're coming over to your house to play."

"My brother means nothing of the sort, Mr. G. We will never come over to your island again without permission. He just wants to know a little more about you. I do too. I'm kind of a budding inventor myself, and the chance to learn more about how a successful one thinks and accomplishes things— why, that'd be wonderful."

Geezer remained mum, focused on the bright blue planet straight ahead. Mercury shone brightly too—that was a landmark which, under other circumstances, would have prompted a cheerful tourist's comment from Marlie, but she was concerned that she'd ventured too far into Geezer's business. Maybe Geezer was wondering how the hell she knew that he'd invented anything. Maybe he thought she'd rummaged through his things (which she had, but only through notes about eclipse ground disappearances). "You know, word gets around," she added airily. "Mr. Batts told us you were an all-star in post-war aeronautical engineering."

Still no dice. Zeb took the hint and changed tack. "I was kidding, Mr. G. Of course we're not going to badger you about your name or your past or anything else. And, to answer your questions, the little one took us to a spacy blue spa where a whole gaggle of aurorabirds came to chill. I think he was showing us off to his chums till his MammyPappy chanced upon him and dragged us up to the surface of the sun to find Shang. It was wild up there. A million auroracreatures getting their raving freak on in cosmic fire dances. Once MammyPappy found Shang, it wasn't long before we were back at his hideout."

"Not all of the firebirds were rave freaks, Zeb. A few looked like they were meditating—remember, with their heads fixed and their eyes wide open, like the ones we saw in the center of the spa?"

"She has a point, but you get the picture. So now it's your turn, hopefully. We'd really like to know what else you saw under the dome during your long swim."

The twins noted a quick movement of Geezer's eyes, which made them suspect that he had seen something of interest, but whether that were true or merely the product of their ongoing gnawing curiosity about everything Geezer was not about to be revealed.

The flow of their conversation, such as it was, was interrupted by a loud blare from MammyPappy, which startled the birds as much as the humans. Shang swung his head around to see his parent with what the twins suspected was an effort to convey submissive disappointment. Shang got one more blast of noise in the face for his trouble, after which MammyPappy began a wide turn back to the sun.

"Was that MammyPappese for 'Put those things back where you got 'em and git your ass back home!'?"

"Looked like."

Off to the right, gibbous Venus shone far more brightly than ever seen from Earth. Zeb's underlying fear of somehow meeting his maker on this trip came to the fore, tempered by the reassuring sight of Earth up ahead, now perceivable to the naked eye as a bright disk. "We're almost home, thank God."

"Yes, if by 'almost' you mean less than twenty-six million miles to go."

"Jeez—I just realized, if frisky Shang here isn't really careful, our landing could hurt Relura. Or worse."

"That assumes she hasn't already killed herself in guilt and grief."

"Uh-uh—keep it positive."

"And that our driver won't total this jar. How do we know his skills are any better than a sixteen-year-old on crystal?"

"Marlie, kindly get a grip!" Her reply: an uneasy sigh. Zeb decided to have another go at Geezer. "Mr. G, got any idea what you'll do, now that you've solved the great mystery of—"

"Zeb!"

Zeb had interrupted himself before Marlie's alarm. Shang had swung them around again to look behind him. That was unexpected. Was Shang checking to see if MammyPappy had returned to tail him?

Shang steered them again, reversing the turn too far to have Earth at twelve o'clock. He had another bright point of light in his sights and now began to accelerate straight toward it.

"What's this creature up to?" asked Marlie with a squeak in her voice, showing some agitation that the birds seemed to share, hopping around the jar.

"That's not Mars, is it?"

"Mars is on the other side of the sun."

Zeb thought of asking Geezer where they were headed, but he noticed a grin sprouting on the old man's face and thought better of it. Instead, he picked up his rucksack, yanked the zipper open, and grabbed his binoculars, spilling a compass, a folded paper, and an old Snickers bar onto the beach. Rejoining Marlie, he trained the binocs on their new destination and breathed "Whoa!" For the first time, Arc alighted on Zeb's shoulder, with a wary glance at Geezer.

"What?!" demanded Marlie. Zeb handed her the binoculars. Even from several million miles farther away than she'd ever observed it before, there was no mistaking the yellowish planet with four moons easily discernable with eight-power magnification. "Jupiter! What the hell?!"

"I . . . hate to say it, but maybe Shang wants to hide us again, somewhere MammyPappy won't suspect."

Marlie wheeled around to see the Earth slipping behind them. Arc lifted off from Zeb's shoulder and joined the other birds, who were becoming agitated.

"The hits just keep on coming," Geezer muttered to himself in a tone the twins recognized as glee filtered through the now-familiar Geezer emotional compression circuitry.

"What are you talking about?" Marlie challenged Geezer. "Don't you see what this idiot is doing? He's taking us to Jupiter!"

"Exactly," nodded Geezer with enraging satisfaction.

She shouted upward, toward the huge lower side of Shang's beak, "You freak! Take us back to Earth!" Shang was not overcome with pity. He sped up. She shouted at Geezer, "What is it with you?! Don't you care about staying alive?"

"Ain't nobody ever been as alive as I am right now," he replied. "Setting aside how I feel about being yoked to you yokels, you've got turkey wattles for brains if you don't appreciate what we're on the verge of discovering."

Zeb shared his sister's antipathy for death from youthful starvation, but Geezer's last comment had caught his attention. "What do you mean?"

Geezer had returned to his default silence, his eyes set on Jupiter, apparently wishing the twins were anywhere else in the solar system. Zeb noticed that Arc's palship with Geezer had plummeted into the deep freeze. The tern could readily perceive the pleasure his old ally was taking in this turn of events. Arc hadn't spent a lifetime pining for a reunion with his family so they could die together in a gauzy canister in the vast darkness of space. Indeed, all of the birds were unsettled. Surely they all recalled the traumatic moment when they had first found themselves in space being dragged far from Earth, and they didn't relish a reprise.

Marlie slumped against the slab of cliff adjoining the mashed-up Mexican beach, watching Zeb pace up and down. "Geezer's a big help. We're finished."

"Now, hold on, Marlie." Zeb sidled up to her and lowered his voice to a whisper. "No giving up. We can think outside the Mexijar, right?"

Her eyes narrowed as she looked around in silence. Zeb could almost hear her mental engine revving into higher gear. "Right you are," she whispered.

"Okay," he replied, lowering his voice as well. "I'm waiting. What's your angle?"

"My angle is to get MammyPappy back on the case for a little auroral ass-kicking."

"That fool left a jillion miles back."

"I realize that, but maybe she-he-it will respond to a blast from the Wardenclyffe. That worked on Shang when Geezer fired it on the iceberg."

Geezer's eyes slid to the side. Nothing like someone whispering near you to perk up your hearing. Something suspicious was afoot with his stalkers. He wasn't about to get jumpy around them, though. What trouble could the punks make? Let 'em try.

Marlie hissed, "Let's grab that thing and call 'the big dog' before it's too late."

"I like the way you think, but Geezer did say 'that thing' could kill us. It'd be a shame to kill ourselves trying to save ourselves."

"It didn't kill him. I saw how he operated it in Antarctica. He pulled that lever on the underside like a trigger."

Zeb followed her surreptitious examination of the Wardenclyffe, which had survived the tumble into the Mexijar by landing in soft sand. Noting Geezer's suspicion, he looked away, pretending to be interested in the cacophonous jitters of the nine birds, a tableau that would have fascinated him had he not been wrestling with how to deal with his sister's imminent desperation play. An attempt at stealing the Wardenclyffe from right under its inventor might not end well, and a panicky firing of it by total novices would only heighten the risk-benefit ratio. He felt obliged to advise Marlie that this move could be a potentially fatal gut-shocker.

She weighed the choices in a two-hand balance scale. "Possible gut-shocker versus definite death in outer space, Mom and Dad getting a couple of empty coffins for their anniversary, and Relura's life train-wrecked." Zeb had no comeback. "There's no time to waste, Zeb. Are you in?"

Zeb took a deep breath. "With Geezer ten yards away, we'll be lucky to get off one shot. The sun's only half the apparent size we're used to, and for MammyPappy to catch on, our aim has to be perfect. I'll hold the back end and you level the barrel."

"Three . . . two . . . .one."

They rose and walked quietly toward the Wardenclyffe. While Marlie blocked Geezer's line of sight, Zeb lifted the peculiar machine, shook off the sand, and walked it a few yards farther toward the far wall of the Mexijar.

That was all it took to draw Geezer's attention. "HEY!" he bellowed as he leapt toward them.

Together they raised the device, with Marlie holding the barrel over her shoulder and aiming it at the sun. With Geezer one stride away at high velocity, Zeb yanked the firing lever, but Geezer's flying tackle was already in progress. All three of them landed in the surf, scattering water and sand onto their faces and the nearby birds as an electromagnetic blast spurted out of the barrel.

"Marles! Are you okay?" Zeb called instinctively, but he could see that she was fine, wiping the spray from her eyes.

"Dolts!" bellowed Geezer. "Sticking your noses where they don't belong—"

Geezer cut himself off when he noticed the twins looking over his shoulder with their jaws hanging open. Marlie breathed, "Ohmigod!"

He turned and beheld a dazzling auroral tapestry of intricately designed complex geometric patterns filling half their view of space, whorls and crystals of soft colored light knit together, slowly floating outside the jar. As the figures gently receded, the twins, and even Geezer and the birds, were spellbound. Then their outlines became visible and Zeb cried out, "Radiolaria!"

Dozens of microorganisms of the sea, but writ huge on the canvas of interplanetary space, wheeled slowly outside the Mexijar, a bouquet of kaleidoscopic blossoms drifting apart in a slow-motion solar breeze. Similar to the creatures on the Haeckel poster in Zeb's room but as large as tall office buildings, they transfixed the birds as much as the humans, who stared in awe as they got to their feet.

"How strange . . . millions of miles from the nearest sea."

"Not quite," said Zeb, slapping a foot into the surf. "Our fall splashed some sea water right into the Wardenclyffe's blast."

Geezer mumbled to himself, "The charge galvanized the organisms' subatomic structure!"

Shang glanced behind himself, perhaps mildly puzzled, but not enough to slow his advance to the outer solar system. The receding radiolaria floated apart from each other.

On any other night, Marlie's intellect would have been ablaze with desire to unravel the mystery of the physical phenomenon she'd just witnessed, but the departure of the giant radiolaria permitted the threat to their lives to immediately fall back into place with a deadening thud. Zeb's protective optimism had better traction on his spirits, but only barely. He struggled to come up with something that would keep their thoughts above water, his early pilot training kicking in with a reminder that depression depresses problem-solving.

"And I thought I'd seen it all."

"I honestly can't tell if that remark was serious, ironic, or a desperate attempt at good cheer."

He sighed, "All three."

Geezer sensed the darkening of the local emotional weather. Disinclined to have his mind-buzzing groove rained on, he stepped away from his companions. Near Zeb's rucksack, his eyes fell upon the surf-drenched paper stuck under the candy bar. Curious, he picked it up.

It was Zeb's apology note, concocted under duress by Relura's command, way back in Earth's Northern California, with the cosmic discoverer's Super-Geezer cloak under the eclipsed sun and "YOU'RE OUR HERO!" scrawled above it. Against his will he was thrown for a loop. He set to mulling as the twins' accommodation to reality seeped into his consciousness.

"No MammyPappy in sight, Z."

"Ain't no sunshine and she's gone."

"We're on the losing side of an endgame we know nothing about."

"I admit, insisting we chase Geezer to the end of the Earth was a little hotheaded."

The nine birds seemed dispirited, whether from the twins' sinking spirits or their own instinctive recognition of the peril they were facing. They fluttered around on the sand near the twins. Arc looked askance at Geezer, who paid him no heed.

"You didn't force me, Zeb. I was as hot to trot as you were."

Geezer looked to the twins as Marlie said, "If by some miracle we make it back home, I will never underestimate the value of a single hour of life. But given our present odds, maybe we should start thinking about how we're going to handle our lives ending out here."

Geezer's antennae picked up that conversation while his eyes moved from the distant radiolaria to the Wardenclyffe on the beach. He was struck with an idea that inflamed him with a silent epiphany. "Not so fast, pests," he blurted. The agile codger picked up the Wardenclyffe and stomped around to confront the twins, wiping the sand off the machine and making adjustments on it. The twins were shaken awake from their deep immersion in melancholy.

"Now listen up. That stumblebum act of yours might have saved your lives. It showed what this instrument can do to living organisms in an environment of intense solar winds if there's no ten-mile blanket of atmosphere in the way. All it needed was a massive wireless transmission system to interact with." He jerked a thumb over his shoulder toward the sun. "And back there we've got the biggest one within four light years.

"The charge reaching us from the sun must be a hundred billion times more powerful than the charge from this device, but the device was a hundred billion times closer to the plankton—"

"—so, we had an apparent size equivalency like the sun and the moon in an eclipse," Marlie interrupted. Geezer paused an instant as it dawned on him that the kid was a smart cookie, which pleased Zeb and her both and gave her time to add, "and since we were aiming the Wardenclyffe at the sun, the organic molecules were optimally positioned to be affected by the charge."

"You've got it, princess. That zap must have galvanized the subatomic particles in the solar wind, turning them into lit fuses that set off a chain reaction that overcame the strong intra-atomic force holding protons and neutrons together in every atom in the cell. In the vacuum of space, every atom expanded . . . must have been at least a hundred thousand times!"

Geezer thrust the Wardenclyffe into Zeb's arms. "What's up, Mr. G?"

"What's up is your one and only prayer at getting home, so you can spy on your parents instead of me. That'll make us all happy. Step back to the far side of this cage and aim this thing like you did before. Both of you." He put his hands on their backs to nudge them where he wanted them. "We're gonna align you, me, and the sun."

"What?!" demanded the twins in unison.

"You're gonna pull that ignition lever and light me up like those radiolaria so I can get this behemoth's attention."

"Now I *know* you're crazy, Geeze."

"*Geeze?!*"

Zeb picked up Marlie's thread. "With all due respect, sir, that really is quite insane. We're not going to—"

"Don't give me any shit! You've already screwed me over once, stalking me to Antarctica."

"You warned us that a blast from that thing could be fatal."

"If it were mishandled. But with your great skill and finesse you just aurorized a bunch of radiolaria. I'm willing to bet you can do the same to me, and once I'm out there I might be able to coerce this plasmic behemoth into returning us to Earth."

"We're not into manslaughter. Sorry."

Geezer paused two seconds, long enough to come up with another tack. "All right, after I kick this creature's ass back toward Earth, maybe you can reconstitute me. Get to where I'm lined up with the sun on the outside of this can, reverse the polarity on the Wardenclyffe, and pull the trigger. If the strong intra-atomic force takes hold again, I might pop in here without a scratch. Next thing you know, maybe I'll be back in business at home, making sure you two never find me again."

"*Maybe?!*" exclaimed Marlie.

"Or maybe not?!" added Zeb.

"Do as you're told." He spat on the sand for emphasis.

"That was crude," Marlie commented.

"Alternatively, I could blast you two to oblivion so I don't have to think about you anymore."

"Oh," said Zeb, "so you want to be rid of us so bad you'll give up your life."

"This transformation could be the crowning achievement of my life, which has been going on a piece longer than yours. I've got my own reasons for doing this."

"Like what?" Marlie inquired.

"Stop your yapping and get this done." Geezer unzipped his left boot, pulled a thin wrapped sheaf of hundred-dollar bills from the lining, peeled off a bunch, and stuffed them in Zeb's rucksack. "This is in case you get back to the right planet and find yourselves a long way from home."

"So that business about you being 'reconstituted' was b.s.?"

"Who knows? What if I don't make it back, but you do, and Sparky here doesn't put you back where he found us?" The twins stole a look at each other and Geezer saw an opening. "That bright little spot at two o'clock is an asteroid. Every second we're getting closer to Jupiter. I'm offering you your one and only chance at ever seeing your sister and parents again, so stop being fools.

"Now focus: You're going to have to blast me at high power and pray I survive long enough to get the jump on this plasmic thief. I've got more than thirty trillion cells for you to hit, so you've got to keep your aim sharp and plug away till I'm completely out of here. I don't fancy sacrificing a free ride to the outer solar system in vain, so you damn well better not blow it!"

Zeb took a deep breath and looked at his sister. "How's your stomach?"

"Its knots have knots."

"But can you do this? Because he might be right."

She closed her eyes a moment. "I'm not up for handling a life-or-death decision."

"*Not* handling this one is a decision. Between Geezer and our family, there are six lives at stake; fifteen if you count the birds. And the time for decision could be gone in a minute."

Offering Marlie no quarter to dither, Geezer pointed to the ignition lever. "This spring-lock tab is the safety. When we're lined up, pull that first, then the lever, and let it rip." He left them and crossed the beach to gauge the spot on the far side of the Mexijar most likely to line up with the sun. Planting his feet, he pressed his back against the jar wall and commanded, "Zap me!"

Marlie turned pale at the sight of Geezer's head-shaped annular eclipse of the sun. Zeb snapped, "Marlie!" The gravity in Mr. Optimist's tone of voice brought her around. She placed herself in front of Zeb and grasped the near end of the Wardenclyffe's barrel.

"Fire!" bellowed Geezer.

She took a deep breath, steadied the barrel toward the sun, and grimaced. "Do it."

Zeb gulped and pulled the ignition lever on the Wardenclyffe. With a roar like a jet engine punctuated by staccato drum beats, a lightning-like blaze shot out of the barrel and hit Geezer full in the face. An auroral glow emanated from his hair, eyebrows, and eyelashes, soon becoming too bright for the twins to make out details. Arc and his eight fellow birds hovered nearby in fixed position like stars in a living constellation. The longest twenty seconds of the twins' lives had begun, each second a capacious cavern overflowing with second thoughts demanding full hearings.

Zeb was vaguely aware that Shang was flying past another asteroid, but at the moment he couldn't care less. Concern about their whereabouts was subsumed in his realization that, even though Marlie rarely subordinated her better judgment to his, in this instance she had relied and acted upon his insistence that doing as Geezer had commanded was the right and necessary thing to do, so whatever calamity was about to ensue would be on him.

The fertility of Zeb's imagination worked against him. What if Geezer turned into a chimera with a giant eyeball embedded in his scalp, glaring at him in condemnation for having been so stupid as to follow Geezer's order, even though it had been delivered as a threat? Or a liver bouillabaisse with floating molars, alveoli, kneecap chips, and toe tips? Worse, Zeb knew Marlie's similar fears were peppered with a loss of trust in his judgment that would likely last till their dying moments—which, come to think of it, might not be very far off, and yet the idea of that being her final thought still hurt like a sting from a rat-sized wasp.

As the fifth second crossed to the sixth, a new impulse jumped into Zeb's view. Maybe it wasn't too late to stop and prevent the worst. They shouldn't succumb to the weakness that had trapped countless souls since time immemorial—doubling down on terrible mistakes they'd begun as if that would somehow snuff out gnawing doubts despite their inner recognition that they were making a very bad thing all the worse. Such mental spasms were perversions *in extremis* of that Uncertainty Principle Marlie had yammered about from time to time. Part of him determined to never again judge those people so harshly, but another part responded that committing to an act of evil with greater intensity only intensified the cowardice, stupidity, and inherent cruelty in the act. It would be far better to stop immediately and attempt to salvage what might be salvaged. But it was too late. He had committed like a base runner stealing second and, having committed, had dragged his trusting sister along behind.

As the seconds crept on and more and more of Geezer's body became invisible in the brilliant glow emanating from his interior, Zeb's guilt was compounded by an irrepressible jolt of pleasure. *Yes, pleasure, or an even more perverse visceral thrill that's demolished any sense of morality clamoring for respect from a tiny vestigial nook in my soul. Like an insane, all-powerful mythical deity, I'm in the thrall of the magnitude and gravity of the wild physical phenomenon we've set in motion. And Marlie must be torn by the same ambivalence. I polluted her soul along with my own, inflicting damage not only on our former neighbor but on the person I love above all others.*

By the twelfth second, Marlie knew Zeb was beating himself up over this. *However, you can't share nine months in the womb plus seventeen years in the air world with someone without knowing what they're feeling, so guilt notwithstanding, I know I'm not alone in reveling in this outrageous thrill. Geezer's head and neck have disappeared, or somehow melded with the vibrating auroral mass filling our view. The blinding glow emanating from his remaining skin pores is opening to us, and us alone, a vast new territory for science, merging biology and physics. So maybe I'm bad for loving this, but I must pay attention because I can learn something incredibly interesting here, and learning is always a good thing—and especially learning something nobody else knows, a genuine discovery. So, Zeb, keep firing until the deed is done.*

When Geezer finally vanished altogether, Zeb ended the Wardenclyffe blast. The birds fell out of position onto the shoreline in a daze, as depleted as Marlie and her brother. Time remained dilated, allowing her to wonder what lay ahead in the next tumultuous minute of their lives, which were relentlessly approaching yet another corner.

It was silent now, but for Arc's pecking at the sandy spot and jar wall where Geezer had last stood. Marlie knew if she simply turned her head, she would see Jupiter brighter than ever before, possibly even as a brilliant little disk rather than just a point of light. That was a lure, but she hesitated, knowing that turning would lead to locking eyes with someone she loved and with whom she had just conspired in shameful manslaughter.

And what of their victim? Could he possibly have survived in some form? Had they doomed him to existence in some terrible freakish state worse than death? Might his attack on Shang destroy them all? Or might he take vengeance on them, whom he had railed against as brats, punks, and pests, and do them in first? Or might he just shine it on and head to Jupiter? That was all he wanted anyway.

"Marlie?"

She looked over at Zeb with a tight, synthetic smile.

"You all right?"

That merited raucous laughter the way a spark would ignite kindling, but current circumstances permitted her only tremulous questions. "Where— where did he go? Did we kill him?"

With no clue to fashion into an intelligent response, Zeb shrugged nervously, disappointed in himself for disappointing her. Had it not been for those magnificent radiolaria and the hours of incredible adventure that had preceded them, he would never have agreed to blast Geezer. Perhaps the damned obsession with the fantastical that had propelled his forays into illustrated storytelling had pushed him over the brink into a cataclysmic failure of judgment. Yes, Geezer had threatened them, but Zeb had wanted to do it. He'd goaded himself into buying Geezer's suggestion that his transmogrification might be reversed, but that just provided him cover for satisfying his curiosity's rapacious lust. He had let himself be played, and Marlie knew it as well as he.

Suddenly his self-censure collapsed in yet another wave of astonishment so thrilling his tear ducts stung. A great forest of dark-brown spires and towers tinted with green and hints of orange was rising slowly in their awed view of space outside the jar. Zeb flashed on a vast Bryce Canyon amphitheater that had somehow become aurorized and shot through with intense colors. He heard the tone of Marlie's dismay, though not her words, for it was dawning on him just what they were beholding. "That's the top of one of Geezer's irises!"

The full eye, the height of a Douglas fir, appeared before them. Like a retreating octopus, Geezer swept himself backward so they could see what they had wrought.

"Geezer!" Marlie exclaimed.

Zeb replied in a hush, *"AuroraGeezer."*

Now thousands of feet tall, larger than any human figure in the history of the world by many orders of magnitude, Geezer granted his former traveling companions a genuine half-grin and flew away, employing the body mechanics of swimming on the solar wind. He sneaked up on Shang, who was merrily focused on Jupiter. When Geezer suddenly shot out in front of him, Shang dropped his jaw in shock, causing the Mexijar to slip to the end of his beak. Shang caught himself in time, jerking his beak upward and darting to the side to get a handle on what was going on. Before he had a chance to reason it out, his harasser sped toward him with the frenzied fury of a gang of crows chasing a nest-threatening hawk.

Inside the jar, the twins lost their balance and fell onto the beach, soaked with a mix of warm sea water and cold melt from the iceberg fragments that Shang had spilled into the Mexijar. Arc and his fellow agitated birds fluttered down onto cliff ledges and the beach in a vain quest for stability. Looking up from their odd, very low angle, the twins could see dark crimson threading into Shang's colors as his defenses were aroused.

The appearance of their enormous ally injected the twins with a rush of hope. Seeing Shang dumbfounded by the sight of the gigantic auroral human made the joy jolt all the more delicious. But the shakeup they'd had to endure as a result of Shang's first dodge made them uneasy too. This battle was far from over. Geezer had retreated, cutting a swath through the solar waves to put some distance between himself and his target in order to give himself a long flying charge in his next assault. The comfort of the Mexijar's eleven remaining passengers was of no concern to Geezer, for their lives were at stake.

Looking up, the twins and the birds saw Geezer coming straight at Shang at triple the speed of his previous drive. Shang dove beneath Geezer with the agility of a swift, shaking the Mexican beach with the equivalent of an 8.5 temblor. Zeb saw birds crashing into each other and a boulder knocked loose from the cliff rolling straight toward his sister. He leapt to his feet to drag her out of the path of danger, but she beat him to her own rescue by executing a back flip over the half-ton ball of limestone, leaving them both grateful for all seven years of their gymnastics training.

The birds weren't so lucky. Arc seated himself on Zeb's shoulder, apparently unhurt, but they'd witnessed a collision between the toucan, the swallow, and the flamingo that left the first two limping and the flamingo with difficulty straightening its neck. "If this goes on much longer, I don't know how they're going to survive," Zeb said, watching Geezer retreat again. "A thirty-pound rock or ice ball can do a lot of damage to a bird."

"We've got to prevent them from crashing into each other." Marlie paused, then stared at the jar wall for a moment. "I have an idea how to do that. It may be super dumb, but we can't be picky."

Zeb's opinion was that Marlie hadn't had a super-dumb idea since they were six, when, fancying herself Wonder Woman, she'd jumped off the garage roof into a snow drift and broken her arm on the lawn mower buried underneath it. Whatever it might be, her scheme merited a serious hearing. "What is it?"

"Remember how we heard Geezer using the Wardenclyffe when he was hiding behind the ice hill before he cut out of the Antarctic jar?"

"Yeah, after he told me to get lost."

"The machine was really quiet. He must have set it on ultra-low power and used it to manipulate the wall itself to carve out his escape hatch."

"Okay . . ."

"Well, if a tiny dose of 'clyffe blasting makes this wall substance malleable, maybe we could use it to shape individual pods that would keep the birds from crashing into each other or getting battered by falling stones."

"Hunh—they'd have their own transparent plasma-shielded theater boxes for the show."

"Look out!" Marlie cried as Geezer suddenly appeared behind Zeb, coming back at Shang in a ferocious horizontal dive. Zeb didn't waste precious fractions of a second turning to observe the threat for himself. He bounded toward Marlie, away from the cliff wall, and braced for trouble.

Shang was ready for Geezer's attack and held his position just long enough to fool his tormentor with a last-second feint followed by a dodge in the opposite direction. More toppling, splashing, and sandstorming ensued, leaving both the birds and their would-be protectors gasping.

Zeb and Marlie needed no further discussion. Zeb pulled the Wardenclyffe out from the sand in which it was half buried and brushed it off while hauling it over to the jar wall. Marlie held out her arm for Arc, who landed on it as if they'd known each other for years. When she hustled to Zeb's side, needing full use of her arms to help aim the 'clyffe, Arc hopped onto her shoulder.

Zeb set the dial to "Min" while Marlie held the barrel of the device a few inches from a spot on the jar wall. Zeb pulled the trigger for half a second, and a gush of what looked like high-frequency heat waves exited the barrel. The spot on the wall sagged slightly, and Marlie reached in for a gentle pull. The plasma submitted itself to her will and came away sticking to her hand like translucent whipped egg whites, leaving a cozy dent in the wall.

When Zeb offered Arc his hand, Arc ignored him and flew up to the cliff where his mate and grown chick were watching. With a gentle peck, he nudged his offspring from her roost and guided her down to the twins' new plasmic bird safety pod, and she obligingly hopped into it. As Zeb pulled the plasma around her, he exchanged a startled look with his sister. "Man, these terns are smart," he observed as they moved on to dig out another pod.

"All these birds had better be smart," said Marlie, "because even if we tuck away another one every fifteen seconds, we're gonna be lucky to get them all in."

In fact, all the birds had caught on. The way they hovered around Arc and the twins made it clear that they grasped the dimensions of the crisis and the solution at hand. There was no time to waste with seven more birds in need of similar protection before Geezer caused another jarquake.

Zeb delivered another low-power current to the jar wall. As Marlie sculpted another petite plasma nook and ushered the hummingbird into it, he said, "If we're running out of time, we can let the falcon fare for herself for one more dive. She's tough and agile enough to handle it."

Keeping an eye on Geezer gaining altitude and arcing around to face them, Marlie had another worrisome thought. "If Shang figures out that Geezer is doing this for our benefit, he might threaten to dump or crush us."

"No way," replied Zeb. "Shang won't risk hurting the birds. He wants them for keeps."

By the time Arc, his mate, the flamingo, the swallow, the owl, and the toucan were safely ensconced in their safety pods, Geezer had begun his next attack and there was no way the falcon could be protected in time. Somehow, she sensed both her peril and the most logical means at hand to face it: hovering high above the jar floor. Geezer pulled his arms down in a powerful breast stroke, and gliding his lower body around as he approached Shang, he leaned into a flying karate kick near Shang's head. Shang saw the blow coming and yanked his trajectory sixty degrees away to escape Geezer, drenching the twins with Mexican beach surf. Shang shot far clear of Geezer and reset his trajectory toward Jupiter, leaving Geezer behind.

Zeb exhaled, surveying the scene for new damage. Marlie was in good shape, as was the falcon. "Shang knows what's up. He must rue the day he snapped up an Earth bird sample contaminated by humans." He joined Marlie on the other side of the jar to complete construction on their avian housing development. As they finished and looked for Geezer to get ready for the next jousting, they noticed that Shang was sweeping into a wide turn, keeping it going till he was facing the opposite direction—redirecting his flight path straight toward Earth.

Marlie exclaimed, "Holy cow—did Geezer just win this war for us?"

"Apparently MammyPappy proposes but Geezer disposes."

A smile stole over Zeb's face. Adventure, shmadventure—he had no desire to die at seventeen languishing in outer space. He high-fived his sister, who let out a *Whoop!* of relief.

Shang glanced briefly behind him, hoping against hope that the truant officer might have changed his mind, but no such luck. Geezer was following behind, close enough for the twins to see his expression of bemused satisfaction.

Marlie thought that Shang might actually be tiring. Having seen Shang and his pals dancing at the solar rave, she wouldn't have thought that possible, but if it were true, it would be all the better for their next task. "All right, Zeb, let's get ready to bring our fighter pilot home. We should wave Geezer around to the other side to place him between us and the sun. Then we'll put the 'clyffe current into reverse."

Zeb trotted over to retrieve the Wardenclyffe while Marlie faced Geezer and started waving her arms like a ramp guide at SFO directing a 747 to its parking place at the gate. Geezer wasn't paying her any heed. He was concentrating on keeping Shang in line. "What the hell? Can't he see what I'm doing?!"

Zeb was about to reply when their lives took another abrupt turn. Shang had spun around and shot up high above Geezer, plunging the twins back into the sea and bouncing all the birds around inside their pods. Zeb wiped the salty water out of his eyes and located his sister behind him, climbing back toward shore. "Hell—Shang faked us out, the creep!"

Looking back at Geezer, they could see his embarrassed rage at having been played by an adolescent solar creature. They could imagine his growl as he built up speed to get back in Shang's face. Were his and his sister's lives not on the line, Zeb would have loved to admire the killer ballet moves being executed by Geezer's powerful three-dimensional swimming and Shang's grand wing sweeps. Good stuff to incorporate into a graphic novel on another day, but of more immediate concern was whether they would live to *see* another day. His binoculars lay crushed under an ice boulder that, come to think of it, must have hit him on the head on the way down, given the painful lump he could feel forming on the vertex of his skull.

Meanwhile, Shang's newfound power was sweeping them up and away from Earth so fast that Marlie noted slight changes in the positions of nearby stars. They had to be going pretty damned fast for that to be perceivable. It brought back to her—and not for the first time since they'd left Antarctica—the dubious nature of Einstein's claim that the speed of light could never be exceeded, but that thought too had to be set aside in the exigencies of the moment.

She looked at Zeb to inquire *What now?!* but he was spellbound by the emerging scenery, the splendor of which had escaped her notice. Shang had led them on a climb so high above the plane of the solar system—must have been two million miles already—that looking down afforded a view of the asteroid belt. The asteroids were much farther apart from each other than the conventional depictions in movies and illustrations, but there were enough of them glittering in the sunlight to look like a curved path of glowing pebbles.

Fine, a jar with a view, thought Marlie, *but there's a major emergency here.* Shang was flying ever faster toward Jupiter, stretching out the gap between them and Geezer. Marlie was getting short of breath. "We've got to do something, Zeb. We know Geezer can subject Shang to some fierce hounding once he's in range, but he's falling behind."

"The Wardenclyffe . . . "

"What about it?"

"There's got to be some way we can use it to slow Shang down or give him some second thoughts about ditching Earth and Geezer. Maybe we could fire it in the direction he's traveling, like a reverse-thrust braking maneuver with a jet engine."

"That ain't gonna happen, Z, much as I appreciate your effort to emulate the Geeze's engine-design proficiency. That thing's not a jet engine—it emits only electromagnetic charges—*but* it still might do us some good. If we aim the Wardenclyffe straight up at the top of the jar, we can blast Shang right in the head."

"The underside of his beak, maybe, but why? It probably won't hurt him."

"I know, but it might distract him or tickle him or annoy him or just plain get in his auroral grill so much he can't concentrate on evading Geezer. Anything that could induce him to bail on his whole project."

"Geezer's closing the gap," Zeb noticed. Shang noticed too and tried to lurch into a higher gear, but it didn't help much. "Maybe he is getting tuckered out."

When Geezer got too close for comfort, Shang tried dodging left and right like a running back trying to shake off a frenzied safety. The twins were getting knocked about again, but desperation prevented them from succumbing to helplessness. Zeb grabbed the Wardenclyffe, twisted the output dial to "Max," lifted it toward the top of the jar, and fired.

The artificial lightning unnerved Shang. When he angled his head to the side in an effort to see why he was getting struck, the twins could see his eyes widened in shock. He seemed to lose balance, allowing Geezer to assail him mercilessly. Though getting knocked off his own feet repeatedly, Zeb kept getting up and firing at the hole at the top of the Mexijar, and Geezer kept driving at Shang with harrowing kicks until, finally, exhausted by the ordeal, Shang stopped moving. Geezer and the twins followed suit. With one last resigned look at Jupiter, Shang heaved a sigh, swooped his great wings into a broad turn, and sailed Earthward.

The birds and twins were stunned, still far too aware of Shang's capacity for deception to believe they might make it all the way back to their home planet without yet another dreadful surprise, but Shang kept on going toward the blue-and-white half-Earth and its crescent satellite shining up ahead. All the while Geezer stayed on Shang's tail like a cattle dog expertly needling a headstrong dogie.

Once inside Mars's orbit, Marlie began to breathe a bit more easily, allowing her thoughts to return to rescuing their rescuer. "I think Shang is going all the way this time, and Geezer must realize it too. Let's prep our deaurorization plan."

"Okay. I'll set up the 'clyffe while you signal Geeze to get into position between us and the sun. At this speed, it won't be easy to maintain that alignment in flight, but Geezer's become an ace fighter pilot."

"It should become easier as Shang decelerates." Marlie made a quick internal calculation at the speed they must be traveling and her stomach sank. "I mean, he's got to slow down, doesn't he?"

Her question wasn't rhetorical, but Zeb had nothing on hand with which to reassure her, so he stuck to business. "Get Geezer's attention. He's on the wrong side of the jar."

Marlie hustled back into space-traffic-controller mode, catching Geezer's eye and making broad, sharply defined gestures that would have been crystal clear to a border collie. Oddly, Geezer slowed his swimming strokes enough to slip behind Shang and out of Marlie's range.

"What the hell is Geezer doing?!" Marlie cried.

"He could be wiped out."

"I get that, but why doesn't he get over to the other side so we can restore him before it's too late?! He's not even trying!"

Zeb felt a chill and leapt into signaling action himself, waving his arms around in Geezer's direction, trying haplessly to get his attention. "Come on, G-Man, don't waste time!"

They reached the orbit of the moon, off to the left, flying so fast that its phase changed from a thin crescent to a quarter moon in less than ten seconds. Geezer maintained his position just behind Shang, even though Shang seemed to be slowing down. "Maybe he's waiting till the last moment."

"This *is* the last moment! He's copping out!"

"He's freaking insane."

Deceleration notwithstanding, they were still hurtling toward Earth at great speed. Both twins jumped back into signaling action at the back of the Mexijar, waving wildly to Geezer in a last, desperate effort to let them restore him to his original form. Geezer did sidle up alongside them, but his only response was a shooing gesture fit for an annoying mutt begging for a chunk of the steak his neighbor was enjoying on his front porch.

"Geezer never intended to let us get him back!" Zeb exclaimed. "That bit about reversing the charge on the Wardenclyffe was a pure sucker play."

Wilted in defeat, the twins faced forward again and were greeted with their first good view of Earth since their abduction. A flow of relief trickled into their bloodstreams as they caught sight of Antarctica. They looked at each other, and the thought that they might be back in Relura's arms within minutes lit their faces with smiles—but they were faint smiles, dimmed by fear for their own lives, as well as those of Geezer and their avian companions. Their misery over having ended the human life of the mysterious neighbor they'd met on good old *terra firma* was twisted by resentment of his having abandoned them. They were overwhelmed by growing terror for their immediate future—a mélange of nightmares of incineration, crushing g-forces, possibly drowning by being reinserted into Earth deep into the Pacific Ocean. Overlapping panoplies of stark images rode roughshod over Zeb's and Marlie's minds, cataracts of grief and horror too fast, internally loud, and breathtaking to permit sharing. They shuddered at the possibilities of re-entry—lung squashing, skull stretching, iceberg crashing, ocean submerging, and waves washing over a litter of bird and human fragments. Deep sorrow emerged for the loss of their lives by means no one would ever be able to imagine, much less learn. It would leave behind an inexplicable tragedy for their parents to try to survive, compounded by the helplessness of their suddenly-only child Relura, wracked by guilt forever.

Marlie heard Zeb mutter something about what an f-ing stupid fool he'd been to drag them to the end of the world. There was no time left for smart-ass cleverness. "Zeb," said Marlie with wet eyes, "please know that I was all in for this trip and that I love you."

Zeb looked at her in frightened gratitude as they continued to slow. "The feeling's mutual, Marlie. You know it."

Shang glanced momentarily back at Geezer, who was still tailing him, and then angled into a slight turn. That smacked the twins as another surprise, and, except for the last one, Shang's surprises had never been good. He was steering them away from the South Pole, headed north. Night shadow was creeping away from the Americas. Whenever Shang made the slightest change in angle, deceleration forces pinned them against different parts of the jar wall, where they hung like riders on a Gravitron.

"Where do you think we'll hit?" asked Marlie between clenched teeth.

"Thousands of miles from Relura is all I know. If we survive this descent and aren't dumped in the ocean, I really don't give a damn. Here comes the atmosphere!"

They hit the atmosphere near an ocean coast, and Zeb discovered that Shang didn't know much about executing a smooth landing approach in Earth's gravity field. The twins fell into the surf of the jar, only to then feel the entire jar itself tilt sideways so that its seabed stood vertically over its cliff fragment, which had become the new ground, and covered them with sea water. The twins slid down the seabed wall, past sea stars and falling, gasping fish. When they reached the bottom, the cliff was again upended and the entire mass of sea water fell onto them like a thin fifty-foot tidal wave.

The twins hollered to each other over the fierce noise of wind rushing outside the decelerating jar. As they reached the familiar passenger jet altitude of seven miles, they could just make out an ocean coast on the planet's surface through the blender chaos of waves and sand sloshing all around them, but the view was too obscured to identify just where they were. When their vessel slowed to a halt with a great splash and grinding of rock against rock, a loose boulder toppled a palm tree that crashed down onto the Wardenclyffe, smashing it to pieces. The plasma of the birds' safety pods and the walls of the jar evanesced, freeing Arc, his family, and all the other birds to flap their wings, delirious with their newfound freedom in the long-craved airy space of Earth.

As Zeb cleared the water from his eyes, his first thought was to find Marlie, but his first sight was of a full, clear blue sky, which lasted less than a second before he was washed over by a fresh wave as tall as he. Glad to find he could move his arms and legs, he spun around to find Marlie getting her bearings and rubbing future bruises.

"Marlie!" shouted Zeb. "You okay?"

"I think so. You?"

He nodded and rose to behold the cliff that they'd traveled alongside since Shang had dumped them out of the Antarctic jar in his solar den. It now fit sloppily into a space that seemed custom-carved for it in a continental wall adorned above by palm trees with fronds swaying lazily in a balmy breeze.

Marlie plucked from the water a piece of Geezer's machine with the *Wardenclyffe 3* engraving still intact and then joined Zeb in a drenched toddle to dry land. When they reached it, they exchanged a high five that slid to an exhausted hug en route to an Earth-embracing flop upon the beach. When Marlie cried, "Thank God!" Zeb could barely hear her through the din of the calling pelicans and gulls swirling around the prodigal terns and their exotic avian comrades.

Wondering why Zeb hadn't responded in kind, Marlie noticed that he was staring over her shoulder. She turned and realized he had been fixated on the cliff, where the three terns were settling on a small shelf about thirty feet up. "Look familiar?" he asked.

Her eyes widened. "Dang—it's that place in the picture on Geezer's wall back home, where he first saw Arc!"

"Welcome to Mexico, Sister." They stood up and Zeb swung an arm in the opposite direction, toward a cluster of random boxy buildings about a mile up the coast. "Downtown's thataway."

"Civilization means a shot at cell service!"

"Relura might be glad to hear from us." Zeb pulled the waterproofing baggie from his jacket pocket and yanked out his phone and some well-preserved pieces of paper.

"I didn't notice a cell tower on that iceberg."

"Neither did I, but I did notice that our fisherman's flier mentioned a co-op phone number with a satellite radio hookup." He triumphantly waved before her the flier he'd picked up on the *Eva de la Plata*.

"Good call," said Marlie, "and an even better one to follow." She looked around at the exotic surroundings. "I guess hefty roaming charges will apply, though."

"Who cares? We're rich, remember?" Zeb waved the wad of Geezer dough at her and handed her his phone. "Here—your Spanish is better than mine."

"That doesn't mean much, but fine, read off the number."

He did so and awaited the results, observing Arc and his family heading out on a breakfast flight a hundred yards offshore. Soon he heard Marlie prattling on in fractured Spanglish trying to convey to the receptionist at the fishermen's co-op in Ushuaia how important it was to reach the *Eva de la Plata*. When she was put on hold, he noticed how nervously she was stirring the sand with her foot, reflecting the anxiety they both felt about Relura having suffered hellaciously every single minute since they were abducted. Deciding to help by offering her a distraction, he mused, "I almost wish you'd blown me up with Geezer. I could have been in on Operation Rescue Marlie and sailed on out to Jupiter."

Marlie checked her phone to make sure her call hadn't been dropped. "Nice idea—but what if Geezer's gizmo had run out of gas halfway through your transformation? You'd look pretty cute with an aurorized head the size of a sequoia atop your normal body, but it might prove hard to get a prom date." Slightly indignant that that image hadn't generated at least a chuckle from Zeb, she added, "Anyway, you can be proud, big guy. When it all came down to choosing between a quickie zoom in space dogging a crazy coot or decades more life on Earth, you stepped up and made the tough call."

"I'm all that, Sis, but I'll still miss the old guy. AuroraGeezer was a larger-than-life hero, like a Michael Jordan who could jump into interplanetary space." He stopped talking for a moment to give Marlie's Spanglish a shot at impressing someone else at the Ushuaia fishermen's co-op with the urgency of contacting the *Eva de la Plata*.

When she was put back on hold, he commented, "I bet Geezer's house will really feel haunted now that he's gone. So gone."

"Gone to a better place, as far as he's concerned. However many days or hours he's got left will be an orgy of discovery."

"That's our boy."

"Hush!" Marlie shouted at him, covering her other ear to shut out the sound of the ocean waves accompanying the crazy chorus of bird calls. *"Sí, señor, muchas gracias, quiero hablar con Relura Morell—la mujer Americana—* Hello? Hello?! Are you there? *¿Me puedes escuchar?"* She looked at Zeb in agony. "I think it's our fisherdude, but he keeps cutting out! Hello? *¿Relura Morell, ella existe? ¡Relura Morell, por favor!"* Zeb leapt over to Marlie's side and planted his ear next to Marlie's phone. "Ohmigod—I think she's there! He's calling her over!"

The twins' eyes widened as their ears teased out of the tinny phone speaker the voice of the sister they feared they'd never hear again. "Hello?! . . . RELURA! IT'S ME!"

Zeb poked his face closer to the phone's microphone. "AND ME! WE'RE ALIVE!"

They heard Relura's screaming cry of blended relief, joy, and dismay. *"Oh, thank God, thank God! WHERE ARE YOU?!"*

"DON'T CRY, RELURA—WE'RE OKAY!"

Whatever Relura said next was fragmented beyond recognition by cut-outs, except for *"Where . . . scared . . . can you hear . . ."* Marlie shifted into slow-shout gear as she started trotting toward the village, nodding to Zeb to join her. "RELURA, YOU'RE CUTTING OUT." Marlie turned to Zeb exclaiming, "This is so frustrating! Reception here sucks. It's got to be better up in town. Let's go!" Zeb didn't reply, but she scarcely noticed as she rushed to shout back into the phone, "RELURA, WE'LL CALL YOU BACK IN TEN MINUTES."

Only then did she realize that Zeb's head had been tilted up to the sky with his mouth hanging open. When he whispered her name, she looked up and understood. Two vast auroral figures—the heads of Shang and Geezer himself—dim but clearly visible even in the bright-blue morning-lit sky, looked down upon them as if the twins were the most mesmerizing spectacle in existence, instead of themselves. But they differed sharply—Shang's face steamed with anger at his opponent for having forced him to abandon his treasured birds, who just now had joined the twins in sighting their former captor and fled to all points on the compass. Geezer's glowing face radiated satisfaction of cosmic intensity. He nodded gallantly to his opposite number, who appeared to honk in displeasure before flying off east, toward the morning sun.

"Geezer!" Zeb called in irrational awe, knowing his hero couldn't hear him. But apparently Geezer could see enough to get the point. He graced them with one of his rare half-grins and launched his great transparent being into flight in the opposite direction, to the planet with scores of moons and a red storm four times the size of the Earth, three hundred million miles away, leaving in his wake an evanescing comet tail.

Marlie stood thunderstruck and speechless until finally the circumstances of the moment put her back in gear. "We've got to go, Z. Every additional second we make Relura wait is an unnecessary injury. We can talk about this some other time."

Marlie picked up the fragment of Wardenclyffe 3 that had fallen on the beach, while Zeb kept his eyes on the sky where Geezer had greeted them seconds before. He felt like saluting Geezer but instead restrained his ardor and called out, "Au revoir, AuroraMan!" and joined Marlie in jogging north to Puerto Ángel.

Part Three

The Fall of the House of Geezer

13

The intense finale of Marlie's recollection of their crisis four years in the past began to dissolve to her dreamy present. As she lay on her bed without opening her eyes, current reality seeped quietly under the door of her consciousness. It was a few hours past the dinner with Relura, there'd been a swamp hike, Relura left, Zeb was across the hall. Perhaps he, too, had gotten sucked into the past. It wouldn't be surprising given the disrupting influence of the weird animal sightings and the rare talk about their long-gone neighbor and his dark island house. It's not all that hard to trigger memories of terrifying splendor in someone whose life has been hijacked by a creature as fascinating as Shang or introduced to electromagnetic properties hitherto not even guessed at in centuries of physics work by extremely smart people. Sometimes the image of Shang's huge eyes looming over her could make her head shiver—yeah, like that slight shaking she just felt under her head. Except that was more like a plopping on her pillow, which didn't fit with her dream, so she opened her eyes and *SCREAMED*, for two very real mini-monster eyes were inches from her own, boring holes of fear into her mind.

It was Relura's frog, squatting almost on her face, greeting her with his phlegmy, ominous rumble.

Marlie bolted off her bed and out of her room, colliding with her brother headed the opposite way to see what the hell had happened. Zeb thought she'd discovered a guy in her room with a severed head or a raised cleaver.

Marlie pointed to her visitor. "That freaking frog freak!" she shrieked. "He jumped onto my pillow!"

Without getting obnoxious about it, Zeb's constitution did have minimum standards of machismo, which forbade revealing that he was startled. Gathering himself together, he said, "Well, have a taste of serendipity, wontcha?"

"Would you kindly get him out of my room, and house, and county?"

Both of them expected Zeb to come up with a pithy answer as to what needed to come next, but the frog beat him to the punch. In four quick hops, he exited the bedroom, leaping right between his hosts and out into the hallway, where he halted, turned around, stared at them, and emitted a speech-like croak that tied up both twins' tongues for several seconds.

When the frog repeated this behavior, advancing toward the front hallway, and again treated them to a demanding froggy bark, it was time to acknowledge the obvious. "It is hard to avoid the conclusion that he wants us to follow him," Zeb observed.

"Yeah? Well, I'm not getting a nice Lassie vibe off that slime ball. I'm going for the broom."

"Now, hold on jest a goldarn minute there, Marlie. The frog isn't hurting us, and I can't imagine how he could, given that our combined mass is at least a hundred times his. You've gotta admit this is a very curious development. What do we have to lose by going along with him for a little bit? I think Relura would disown us if we abrogated our investigatory responsibilities here."

The frog hopped another few yards down the hall toward the front door and hurled another insistent *jug-o-rum* their way.

"Get your jacket and flashlight, Marlie. You know you want to."

Zeb's pep talk had the desired effect, and a minute later the twins were following their wide-mouthed leader down to the lake's edge. He led them to their aluminum boat and, with one more flourish, he hopped into the craft and unleashed his most demanding croak yet.

"You've got to be kidding," Marlie muttered.

"He's angling for a field trip. I wonder where to."

As if he were answering a direct question, the frog pointed his nose straight at Geezer Island, croaked again, and then looked back at the twins.

Somehow the frog's gesture struck them both as so obvious they had to laugh. A nervous laugh, to be sure, but a laugh nonetheless, for there was no "Why us?" about it. If anybody on Earth were going to get sucked into a return to Geezer's abandoned house, it would be they.

Zeb addressed his sister with a smile. "Well?"

"You've got to be kidding!" came a reply in Marlie's voice and with the same intonation as her reaction to the news that their mother had inquired about buying Geezer's island. This time, however, it issued from the mouth of Mock, who fluttered down to the lakeside party and perched on the boat's stern.

Zeb greeted the new arrival with delight. "Say, if it ain't me old pal Mock! I heard you up in the trees a while ago."

Zeb's avian buddy from his teenaged years at home was not in the mood for lying back with a cold one and chatting about old times. He addressed Zeb in Zeb's voice: "Are you dumb enough to not know what he's doing?"

That tasered the twins' sensibilities. They recalled that Zeb had said something like that to Marlie about their parents over tamales earlier that evening, but this was no mindless echo. The bird had altered Zeb's original line in a way that was jarringly well adapted to the present situation. It was a double wallop, a sharp warning in a manner conveying intelligence way too acute for a bird-brain. Even more disquieting, the frog responded by hopping up to Mock and blasting a loud croaking retort at his face. The frog seemed to have understood what Mock had said and was not amused.

Uh-oh. Given their history, Zeb had reason to be leery about the possibility of being on the verge of an earthquaking discovery. Against the advice of his well-grounded intellect, he took a chance and asked Mock to explain why the frog wanted them to cross the lake to the island.

"Don't!" Mock replied, in Marlie's voice. Immediately the frog launched into a tirade directed at Mock, to which Mock responded in a mix of the frog's voice and his own natural sounds. The similarity between the cadence and tonalities of both animals and human conversation shattered every belief the twins—like everyone else—had held about the limitations of animal communication. The twins had heard many a frog before, and Zeb had practically adopted Mock as a pet in the past, but there'd never been even a hint of communication on such a sophisticated level. If these animals had intended to keep that ability under wraps, their cover was now blown.

After a few more heated exchanges with the frog, Mock turned to the twins with what looked for all the world like embarrassment and deep regret. Articulating his speech in his default mockingbird voice, he sighed, looked the twins in the eyes, and said, "Now you know."

Marlie glanced at her brother in shared dismay. Then she swallowed hard, tossed her tightly coiled resistance overboard, and exclaimed, "No, we do not, Mock!" The frog gave Mock a hard look. "I hope you and this frog are not able to understand what we're saying, or what any human says, but if you are . . . how long has this been going on?" Marlie swallowed again. "And how many other animals are capable of it? And what have you and the frog been arguing about? Why is he trying to get us to the old man's island? And what are you warning us about?!"

Zeb smiled. His full awareness of the absurdity of what was transpiring couldn't tarnish his pleasure in seeing that his sister had freed herself from the talons of standard-issue science, for the moment at least. The apparent evidence that a bird could understand them sent chills coursing up and down their backs.

It was weird seeing a bird roll his eyes, but there's no getting around that that's just what Mock did. He cleared his throat, muttered something he immediately stifled, and then blurted in non-dulcet tones, "All right, screw it. Yeah, I understand you—everything you say. And I've been able to the whole time you've lived here. The same goes for my big-mouthed associate here."

The twins were stupefied. It wasn't because of the bird's use of human language—they'd heard Mock and a few parrots perform verbal stunts with the tonalities of his avian voice box many a time. What stunned them was that the bird's vocabulary, sentence structure, and attitude seemed on a par with those of a human being. They wondered if they were the first people to witness this phenomenon.

Mock seemed very uncomfortable about having hit them with this revelation and went silent, but Marlie was too rattled to let it slide. "Well, Mock. If you don't mind, how many other—"

"I heard your questions, lady. Forgive my clamming up on you. I was just a little pissed off at the Croaky Kid for violating the cardinal rule: intelligent animals must keep quiet around two-leggers. He knows damn well we're not supposed to let on that we're watching you. *I* follow the rule. My Arctic mate, who joined you in Antarctica, *he* followed the rule. *Everydamnbody* I've ever known has followed the rule, but this frog had to go and blow it." He jerked the muscles on one side of his face enough to fling a sneer in the frog's direction. "You dope!"

The twins had become short of breath, but they stopped breathing altogether when they witnessed the frog sneer right back at Mock while releasing a slow burp.

Mock hopped closer to Zeb. "Look, bud, I liked you when you were a kid, the chocolate peanuts, the whole bit, and I still do. You were a good chum. But I had to mislead you. We've got rules, for everybody's good."

"'Everybody'?!" stammered Marlie. "Who's everybody? Are you telling us that every rooster and raccoon walking around here is as smart as we are?"

"Hayell no, woman. Creatures with our brand of brainpower make up an itty-bitty fraction of one percent of all animals. Those of us with smarts and mission-critical jobs are precious few and scattered around the world."

Jobs? What in blazes did the bird mean by that? Dumbstruck, Zeb imagined high-intelligence humming in a pigeon on the rooftop overlooking a riot, a mouse in a cathedral, a fly in a club, an ant trolling a wall overlooking a clandestine encounter in the woods, a bear in a circus overhearing members of the audience, a dolphin watching gill netters, a microbe in an examining room, a cat in a dowager villain's lap.

Eventually Mock took pity and deigned to elaborate without further prompting. "Look, we're reporters, all right? Those of us with high-powered brains have reporting instincts bound into our DNA, alongside the same animal instincts you have. We watch you." He turned to Marlie. "You too. Every chippie and Charlie we observe, including the rest of your family, and everybody who lives or visits here. I've got reporters all over this territory who send me the news. Then it's my job to edit it together so those of the froggy persuasion can send it on to the big shots."

"*What* 'reporters'?" cried Marlie. "And *what* 'big shots'? And sent *how*?"

"Our reporters are the animals and insects who are just as clever as you guys. They learn whatever lingos you are using and pick up on your chatter. They check out what's going on all around the planet—your conversations, your broadcast goodies, what's up with nature, and send it all to editors like me. Been doing it for ages—since your lot was a passel of cave people, anyway."

The frog deliberately rolled onto his back and released a guttural garble, apparently making some kind of statement of disgust at Mock's blabberfest. "Don't give me any crap, Croaky." Mock was good and indignant now. "You started this by treating these kids like they were your little dogies to get on down to this lake. You think they wouldn't notice something fishy about that?"

After a moment's silence was broken by a snort from the frog, Zeb confronted his old friend, affecting a pose that he was taking it all in stride. "Fine. You're in the news media, Mock. So how about answering my sister's questions? How does the frog 'transmit' these news bulletins?"

"It's the magic of electromagnetism, kid. Croaky goes to work every night while hanging out with a horde of ordinary frogs who haven't the slightest idea what he's really up to, even though his signals become visible every now and then in the presence of methane."

Zeb's eyebrows jumped. "Ah—Marlie, like that little flash on Relura's video, remember?" She nodded.

"I heard your big sister shrug that off as a swamp gas effect," said Mock. "Few humans even notice that much. We can always count on you to have rationalizers on board to hide from uncomfortable truths. We especially appreciate the ones parading as experts with labs, webcams, and trap cameras. Even if you did catch Croaky in the act of transmission, you wouldn't suspect what he's really up to."

Marlie felt a touch of nausea for asking a serious question of a bird, but she could no longer stop herself. "What *is* he really up to? Who's receiving these transmissions?!" she demanded.

The frog replied with a loud garble. The twins looked to Mock for a translation. "He said, 'Good question!' We'd like to learn as much ourselves. All we know is that each transmitter targets a whale somewhere at sea, but what the whales do with the info is a mystery. It's been bugging Froggy his whole life, same as the rest of us."

"Well, what's the prevailing theory? You must have made guesses."

"Nah—not me. This has been going on so long, most of us don't jabber about it, except for the occasional waterhole joke. But Croaky Boy, he's obsessed." The frog lifted his chin in pride. "He believes that the whales relay the records to historians beneath the sea floor who store them in methane archives. He fancies them as protectors, like the monks during your so-called Dark Ages, keeping records safe for some future civilization."

"The sea floor?" Zeb looked to Marlie. "There's methane down there?"

"Methane's all over the place, Z," said Marlie. "Natural gas deposits, the Arctic, outer space and distant planets, *and* the ocean floor." She looked straight at the frog. "Well, what's the evidence for this sea-bottom-historians scenario?"

"Absolutely none," Mock replied. "That's just a bloated figment of the frog's imagination. For all we know, the ones who put this whole system in motion up and left eons ago. Maybe we're mindlessly doing all this reporting for nothing—y'know, like the deluded Japanese soldiers who hid in the jungles of Guam and Mindanao for decades after World War II, certain that the war was still raging.

"But Froggy, his confidence is unshakable. He's never let it rest, so when he received a mysterious message this week, he flipped out."

"What mysterious message? And what's it got to do with pushing us to invade the old man's island?"

Mock exchanged a look with the frog, who *jug-o-rummed* insistently for a few seconds, trying Mock's patience. "Señor Frog is under the impression that one of the great Recipients of his transmissions promised to reveal all to him if he could get you two into your old neighbor's house, where a secret clue is stored in the basement. It's made him all the crazier because"—another vulgar-sounding croak in the face from the frog interrupted his flow— "because he's afraid someone else might get to the secret first."

Marlie frowned. "So why doesn't he just go over there and leave us out of it? He can swim."

"He claims the Recipients won't deliver the prize, whatever that is, unless he can get the two of you into the house with him." The frog interjected a croak of emphatic confirmation, which Mock ignored. "That's why he cooked up the scheme of spooking you to attention with your owl and the eagle that hounded your brother in his sailplane."

Zeb looked at Marlie. "What owl?"

Marlie looked abashed. "I was going to tell you. A great horned owl followed me along Skyline Ridge last night, eyeballing me just like your eagle flying partner."

"Jesus. I had a feeling you were hiding something when Relura was here. Why didn't you tell us then?"

"I was trying to toe the line on the crazy for a while."

Mock continued. "You've got to watch Mr. Slimy. He's been known to make stuff up in the past." The frog bristled at this and leapt at Mock, who flew over his head and landed on the other side of the boat. "He once peddled a story to an albatross that the Recipients had sent him a secret message promising the bird a promotion if she'd fly him to a humpbacked whale he'd been transmitting to near Maui. He later admitted he'd made up the whole thing as part of a scheme to investigate the sea-bottom archives." He paused long enough to let the frog finish blaring an extended angry burp. "He's the Croaky Boy Who Cried Hidden Historian."

Hesitantly, Marlie stepped into the boat, sat down on the aft bench, and lowered her head. The frog offered her a welcoming croak. Zeb looked at her in dismay.

"What, are you up for going to Geezer's now?!"

"I . . . no. I'm just feeling a little faint. I'll be all right in a moment."

Mock was taken aback by Zeb's interest. "I warn you, Zeb, you have no idea what kind of stunt Croaky Boy's capable of." The frog unleashed a caustic croak. "But now he says the wise course is to stay here and forget his earlier demand." The frog bounced up within an inch of Mock and unleashed what was apparently a stream of invective. Marlie demanded to know what the frog had really said. "Okay, I lied. Froggy wants you to believe that by joining him on this expedition, you'll share in the joy of discovering the truth about the Recipients."

The frog burped in Mock's face. "That was uncalled for," growled Mock, much annoyed by what he and the twins perceived as a satisfied grin on the frog's spotted face.

The recollection of another local denizen becoming obsessed with a mysterious phenomenon several years ago flickered across Zeb's consciousness. He tried to put that thought out of his mind. Taking a deep breath, he arched an eyebrow at his sister, a neon sign of his interest in taking up Froggy on his suggestion.

"Zeb, how can you be seduced by a creepy frog and ignore the advice of your longtime bird buddy?"

"Mock's being ultra-careful, just like Mom and Dad—but how could we live with ourselves if we turn down this opportunity?"

"When have I heard that line before?"

"It was true four years ago, too. If we hadn't gone to Antarctica, we'd have lost all respect for ourselves." Marlie looked away, avoiding Zeb, Mock, the frog, and Geezer Island. But for Zeb, the opportunity to discover an electromagnetic historical archive run by animals with human-scale intelligence could not be ignored. He had to get Marlie on board.

Then inspiration struck. "Who knows what we might find in Geezer's den? Maybe we can turn up the schematics for Wardenclyffe 3!"

Zeb knew he'd connected with the fat part of the bat when he saw Marlie's eyes widen. There was no getting around Geezer's having invented an extraordinary device for controlled electromagnetic radiation, the design of which might possess incalculable value for the magnum opus Marlie was trying to get off the ground.

Marlie blinked. "You're really ready to go over there again, after all that happened last time?"

"I'm not proposing a trip to town, much less a trip to Antarctica. All that happened last time was we got chased out of the house by the owner. That's not likely to happen this time. Let's just go and check it out." Zeb turned to his bird friend. "Mock, you could come with us and keep an eye on the frog and translate in case he speaks up again."

Marlie took a deep breath. When she suggested they leave a note for Relura, Zeb knew he was home free. "Why bother? Relura probably won't be back for at least half an hour. We can be in and out easy by then."

Marlie scooted over to the next bench to make room for Zeb, who stepped into the boat with a big smile. "We're doing the right thing, Marles. Who knows what secrets of the universe we might unlock?"

"Stop selling," she said, reaching for the throttle on the outboard. "In the words of another starry-eyed fool, you had me at 'schematics.'"

"Oh, boy," sighed Mock as he fluttered up into the air while the frog emitted another satisfied double *jug-o-rum.*

Marlie moved the boat away from the shore toward the dark island in the middle of the lake, but at a fearfully slow pace. Zeb knew she was treading through a jungle of apprehension about what lay ahead. Even in the moonlight, he could see her gulp.

Meanwhile his imagination's night shift hummed along at its usual feverish pitch. Glancing at the frog out of the corner of his eye, he wondered what fantasies were jacking up the creature's little brain. It was obvious he was het up about this expedition. Perhaps he imagined himself invited to join an elite brotherhood of superfrogs whom he could assist in an evolutionary leap over humans to surpass us in thought and planetary control, just as they already outmatched us in jumping ability. Such a delusion could only be expected among intelligent members of a species that had suffered so much decline in population and habitat due to the outrages perpetrated by humans upon their fragile environment. Maybe the frog was convinced that such an anointment was just what lay in store for him at Geezer's, with all the certainty of a girl convinced that the fancy dinner her beau was taking her to would be the setting for his popping the question. Perhaps the Recipients—whoever they were—would whisk him away that very night in a protective bubble straight to the bottom of the Pacific Ocean, where he would be introduced to the true king of the world as the hot rookie prince they'd been scouting for years.

The boat's bumping against the island shore jolted Zeb back to reality. Their return to Geezer's house was now less than two minutes off.

The frog leapt out of the boat instantly and hopped in stages to the top of the fence, beneath a tree branch where Mock had just settled. Marlie followed, much more slowly. *Steady as she goes, even if she's nervous and scared,* Zeb was thinking when she turned to him and said, "My skin is crawling."

"Anything that makes life zing is good, the way I see it," Zeb replied, neglecting to mention that his skin was prickling too. Determined not to let Marlie register his doubts, he tromped over to the fence and pointed at the two animals sitting at the top. "No frog fry happening here. The Geeze's electrocution system must be kaput." He hoisted himself up the nearby tree with a sturdy limb hanging out over the fence and jumped down on the other side. "C'mon, Sis."

14

Marlie kept quiet as she followed her brother over the fence into Geezerland with her heart quickening. The frog hopped along right in front of them, as if to balance the competing needs to get inside the house as fast as possible while monitoring his human catch for signs of wavering will.

As a professional fantasist, Zeb adored the sight of the looming house when it first appeared through a break in the trees. It was nearly buried in a tangle of tree branches, vines, moss, and the nests of birds and squirrels. He made mental notes of numerous details for future use in his work, like the mournful look that lush clumps of moss resembling drooping eyebrows gave the two main windows, where specks of reflected moonlight transformed the glass into the eyes of a cat much larger than an elephant. Part of him wanted the house to rise up off the ground in angered alarm at their intrusion upon the sacred privacy of whatever dark ritual meditation it was carrying on within.

Marlie's concerns left little room for such entertainment. It occurred to her that a very real earthbound danger could be awaiting them in that house. Suppose some violent, armed vagrant was squatting in there? *What? No one's moved Geezer's boat in four years, and no bad guy would want to hassle with going back and forth across the lake. Let's be reasonable.* Or perhaps they'd disturb squatters of the rabid rodent variety. Maybe Geezer himself has been lying in wait for them for years, seeking revenge for their having invaded his scientific sanctum four years ago and threatened his expedition to the Antarctic eclipse.

I said reasonable.

Perhaps he'd somehow regenerated himself as a normal human and had returned home and died, leaving a dusty corpse for their viewing pleasure.

Enough! Keep that train of thought to yourself. Better yet, drop it. It's not helpful.

They reached the front, where Mock awaited them on the railing. For the second time in her life, Marlie wondered if she were on the verge of committing criminal trespassing. *But why mention it? Zeb will pooh-pooh it, just as he did before. Suck it up, girl.* "We're going in," she announced, beating her brother to the punch.

The front door was unbolted and it opened readily. Geezer must have figured that anyone sufficiently motivated and capable of getting past his perimeter fence wasn't going to be deterred by a deadbolt, especially when there were unbarred windows a few feet away.

The twins smelled musty dust but nothing nasty like dead rodents (or humans). Training their flashlights around the dark environs of the main floor, they found the same barren appearance that met them on their first visit—a few items of little-used furniture, now overlain with a skein of cobwebs. Mock explained that, while the frog had never been inside the house, he'd known for years about the secret chamber in the center of the house and was croaking a demand to be led to it. The twins stepped carefully toward the bathroom at the back of the house, with Mock fluttering around them, punctuating the silence with intermittent nervous chirps.

"There's a lotta schmutz making this door stick in its groove," observed Zeb as he tried to slide the shower stall entrance to the inside of the chamber, but with some extra force he shoved it aside and braced himself for the return to Geezer's true former home. The frog's next demanding *jug-o-rum* needed no translation—he wanted his human partners to shine some light on the stairway, which Marlie provided. Mock flew ahead, ever watchful for the safety of his friends.

They descended past the shadowy wooden spar structure into the bottom of the laboratory. The circular chamber wall festooned with photos, diagrams, and the elaborate timeline of eclipse ground disappearances that had consumed most of Geezer's adult life were exactly as they'd been discovered during the twins' first time there. And why not? The old man had been in the house only one night since the twins had shown up all those years ago.

Marlie tracked her flashlight beam across the timeline to its climax predicting the site of the Antarctic EGD and got some gooseflesh on her scalp. Mock, perched on the mezzanine rail, spoke first. "Get in and get out, always a good policy."

The twins were too captivated by what they were seeing for polite conversation. Every picture and chart felt luminous in significance now that they knew where it all had led once they'd reached the top of the iceberg in the Southern Sea.

The frog hopped about between the two moving flashlight beams, undoubtedly wishing he weren't beholden to the humans for his source of light. He was behind Marlie when Zeb's light reached the section with pictures of Nikola Tesla, but then he shot across the chamber onto the worktable to stare at those photos, croaking a brief monologue. Marlie looked to Mock for help. "The frog knows all about Tesla," explained Mock. "He was enraptured with the wild Tesla-style electrical discharges that appeared from time to time in the dome at the top."

"Maybe the frog is Tesla, reborn," commented Zeb. "He seems nutty enough."

By then, absent any grand epiphanies, Marlie's enthusiasm for this adventure was beginning to wane. "I'm not seeing any gold doubloons or diamond-crowned Recipients offering enlightenment. I'm thinking we should face it that Nikola the Second suckered us just like he did that albatross. It's time to go home. This place is creeping me out."

The frog hurled a loud protest burp. "Don't pay her any heed, Nik," said Zeb. "She isn't going to want to leave here without those Wardenclyffe schematics."

"Oh, right." Marlie was embarrassed to see how her discomfort had almost sabotaged the mission. "I'll be right down. Those lower shelves next to the cot look promising."

While Marlie combed through the documents she found on the shelves, Zeb picked up a magnifying glass and examined some of the drawings of the earlier eclipse events, especially those where witnesses had sketched what they could see of Shang. He thought how perplexed the artists must have been. Too bad for them that they hadn't had Geezer's money, engineering skills, and decades of free time to pursue the matter.

"Oh, baby!" Marlie was lifting a sheaf of blueprints from the shelves she'd been rummaging through. "We're eating tonight!"

"What?!"

"Schematics! Blueprints! Techno details galore!" she sang as she brought the documents over to the worktable. Zeb trained his flashlight beam on them as she pored over them.

"Toldja," said Zeb, relieved that he wasn't going to catch any grief from Marlie for having pushed this venture across the lake.

"Here's a blueprint for Tesla's original Wardenclyffe and another for a smaller tower labeled Wardenclyffe 2, maybe an early draft that Tesla never built. And *here* are the plans for Geezer's machine, Wardenclyffe 3 itself!"

"Goooooooooaal!"

"God, I want to take this home, but it does feel like burglary."

"Old Geeze ain't equipped to come back for this, Marles, nor is it likely to interest him at this point, if he even exists. Either this document rots to dust or stays in your hands, where it can do some good."

"Look at this thing—the original tower on Long Island had pipes and catacombs and tunnels and wires extending hundreds of feet into the ground. The hidden underground part of this contraption was even bigger than the tower itself, which was almost twenty stories high! It was all part of his plan to make an antenna powerful enough to transmit electricity across the world and communicate with other planets."

"Gotta love the guy's ambition. He and Geezer were two peas from the same odd pod."

Throughout this discovery, Nikola the Frog had remained fixated on the photo of his namesake, but now he turned back to continue his tour of the premises. Marlie suspected that he was getting antsy for the advent of the Recipients to unveil their identity and the great opportunity they had in mind for him.

"It's all rubbish, if you ask me," commented Mock from his perch on the mezzanine.

"That's harsh, Mock. Marlie loves this stuff. It's right up her alley."

Nikola was scouring the lab floor looking for clues and started a little croakfest. Zeb asked Mock what he was saying. "He says he's found a trap door in the floor and wants you to open it. But I suggest not." Switching to Marlie's voice, he added, "This place is creeping me out."

"Yeah, our work is done here, Zeb," said Marlie nervously, in spite of herself.

Nik mustered an angry croak, along the lines of "*Your* work, maybe. We've got an appointment coming up here."

Zeb didn't respond. He was staring at the ceiling that served as the floor of the dome. "Ah, the famous dome," observed Marlie. "Hard to forget Geezer up there with his Thor helmet, glowering at us."

"This is the perfect opportunity to give that dome a look-see," said Zeb. He climbed the ladder to the mezzanine and the lever he'd pulled four years ago that had revealed Geezer.

Marlie tried her voice in Mockish impersonation and imitated the bird for a change. "I suggest not."

"Just a second, Sis." Zeb wrenched open the iris that revealed the twelve-feet-diameter dome and beheld the moon and stars shining through it. "This whole dome is laced with little wires, and there's a sliding panel like an observatory's window." He opened up the panel to the atmosphere and the cool evening breeze.

An unexpected sound reached them. There was a vehicle in the distance, which was uncommon at that time of the evening in that rural part of the county. Zeb climbed up and stuck his head out the dome window for a look. "Hey—car coming. Less than a mile off."

"That settles it, Zeb. If that's Relura and the parents and we're not home, it'll wreck the surprise. Plus, they'll notice the boat missing and then they'll spot it over here on the island and we'll have a shitstorm on our hands. Let's opt out, on the double."

"I don't want to leave just because there's a random car out on the road," protested Zeb. Nikola bellowed his agreement.

Mock's peacemaking instincts rose to the fore. "I'll check it out. Back in no time," he declared and flew out the window in the direction of the road.

Nikola recommenced his search of the premises in a panic that the twins—the supposedly vital secret catalyst that would bring about his reward from the Recipients—might be on the verge of leaving. Marlie noted his behavior and called up to her brother, "I don't think Nikola was kidding about having received a secret message. He's plenty agitated."

A strange vacuum-like rush of wind arose above them. Zeb looked around trying to make sense of the increasing noise and glimmering light swirls in the sky. "What's that?!" Marlie hollered as she climbed the ladder to join Zeb in the dome.

"Zeb! Marlie!" shouted Mock flying their way. "GET OUT OF THERE!" but his warning was too late, for an immense force shook the house like a powerful earthquake and began to rip and slice through it, causing wood and metal and concrete to shatter and the entire contents of the lab to be shaken about. The twins' stomachs leapt into their throats as they found themselves rising into the sky.

"NOOOOO!" screamed Marlie, "NOT AGAIN!" They were enveloped in a too-familiar gauzy transparent bubble suspended a hundred feet above ground and were held there just long enough to see the bottomless hole that had been ripped out of the center of Geezer's house, Relura's car screeching to a halt in their driveway across the lake, and Relura and their parents stumbling out of her car in horror and dismay. Directly above the twins loomed a figure of shimmering auroral light akin to what they'd first witnessed above the Antarctic iceberg, but this time peering down at them was the immense, crazed, craggy face of AuroraGeezer, examining the core of his former home and his kidnapped passengers in menacing glee before lurching them into the night sky.

15

"Oh, shit—Houston, we have a problem," said Zeb, attempting to radiate aviator right stuff as Geezer swept them first out over the ocean and then, scarcely ten seconds later, beyond the moon into deep space away from the sun. "And this time, Geezer's not riding to the rescue."

Marlie remained silent. The appeal of interplanetary travel to the aspiring astronaut had its limits when their lives were on the line. Zeb feared—again—that his sister might be trapped in a funk bus with Catatonia on the manifest.

Even if he could prevent that, they were already trapped for real in a plasma jar about the size of Geezer's gigantic thumb. The old man had apparently tapped into the power to craft such an instrument by virtue of his having become an auroral creature like their former captor, Shang. The jar wasn't much taller than Geezer's house, but since the twins were still up in the dome, they were high enough to see out into space even after Geezer stuffed the lower two-thirds of the jar into the upper pocket of his aurorized parka.

The twins had gotten free of Shang during their prior abduction, but that was with Geezer's help, which was not on offer at present. Recognizing the gravity of the situation, Zeb's crisis-management mindset kicked in as surely as that of a test pilot's. In a jam, Zeb knew to adhere to the emergency plan, which begins with swift evaluation of what's going wrong with the aircraft—except first he made sure his fellow passenger was okay. "Marles?"

Any response she might have come up with was derailed by the third passenger on board, whom she'd briefly forgotten about. Nikola had jumped in between their heads to get a better view out of the dome and unleashed a celebratory croak. "Oh, for God's sake!" muttered Marlie. The puny beast was messing with her state of shock.

"Our stowaway," remarked Zeb. He sighed, gave up for the moment on conversing with Marlie, and cut to the chase. He shoved Nik out of the way, earning a frog belch near his ear in return. Placing his face at the top of the dome, Zeb hollered, "MISTER G! WHAT GIVES?!"

Geezer glanced down, but it wasn't clear whether he could hear what Zeb had said. Whatever the case, he was not in a mood to chat. The expression on his huge face, looming more than a thousand feet above them, may have suggested—at best—patience. Geezer lifted his gaze toward his direction of travel, leaving the passengers with an unobstructed view of his nostrils, but not much else.

"Not a good sign, Zeb." Marlie could see Zeb's inner search for an encouraging comeback and his disappointment at coming up empty-handed. "I'll bet he's heading to Jupiter, right where he was gung-ho to take us last time." She pointed at a reddish object far to the left. "That's Mars—this express ain't stopping there." She knew that her brother's flight-loving side had to be stirred up, but she could see it was tempered by her fear and some of his own. She changed the subject. "The green goblin seems plenty pleased. He must be convinced that Geezer is one of the Recipients."

"Who cares? I just want to know what Geezer is up to. He must have wanted us pretty bad if he ripped up his house to get us."

"Looks like he wanted his house too."

"At least his lab."

Zeb joined Marlie sitting on the sill of the domed window capping their tower-like cage. Marlie shook her head in self-recrimination. "We aurorized him four years ago and now he has total power over our lives. We did this to ourselves."

"So? We'd never have made it back to Earth otherwise, and our lives would have ended as disappeared, dead high school students. Let's focus on the problem at hand, shall we? Somewhere there's got to be a solution." Zeb banged on the dome with his open palm. "Hey, Mr. G!"

"You mean 'Hey, Mr. Schmuck,'" Marlie grumbled.

"DON'T BE RUDE, CHILDREN." A sonic shock wave nearly knocked the twins off the sill down to the chamber floor below. It was Geezer's raspy voice all right, but raked by static and rumbling vibrations like those recorded during northern lights displays on Earth, amplified to deafening volume. "You'll catch more attention from a flying man with honey than with vinegar," he continued. Marlie recoiled from the double punch of embarrassment, having been heard insulting Geezer and subjected to his supercilious jest reminding her of how utterly powerless they were before him. From his position, Geezer could afford to be generous. "Not to worry, little ones. Sure, you're startled, but you're in for a *tremendous* reward, a lick of just the kind of cream you curious cats love."

The reverberation from Geezer's emphatic "tremendous" struck the twins like a thunderclap that knocked the wind out of them. Catching her breath, Marlie said, "I hope he doesn't have much to say besides, 'I'm taking you home now.'"

Zeb shouted upward again. "That's mighty kind of you, Mr. G, and thanks a bundle for the joy ride, but the one reward we'd really cherish right about now is to be escorted back to Earth."

"Safely, while you're at it!" shouted Marlie. "And preferably home, though Mexico will do." She frowned and turned to her brother. "Say—how do you suppose Geezer heard me call him a schmuck? You could barely hear me."

Zeb's eyes slid over to Nik, whose unmistakable smirk left Marlie in open-mouthed dismay at the frog's perfidy. "If Geezer can receive Nik's transmissions from millions of miles away, it can't be too hard when the frog's right in his pocket."

"Note to self: There's a rat in our cell." Nik shot Marlie a wide-mouthed grimace.

Geezer clucked his tongue. "You're going to appreciate that frog, girlie. If it weren't for him, you'd have missed out on one of the greatest revelations in the solar system. He's hooked into a wireless field-news reporting system covering stories from all around the world. Thanks to him, we've got a shot at discovering who's receiving them."

Zeb noticed Nik's head jerking back as he released a staccato series of displeased croaks, which Geezer noticed. "Don't bust a cranial artery, Froggy. I never said I was one of the Recipients. What I told you in our brief chat was that your doing a little favor for a former neighbor would lead to your *discovering* the Recipients, and that's what we're about to do, at long last."

"Oh!" exclaimed Zeb. "Nik has been thinking that *you're* one of the Recipients."

"Who's Nik?"

"We named the frog after Nikola Tesla."

"Ha!" boomed Geezer. Nik was taken aback, as if unsure how to take that. When Geezer followed up with a wink, a thumbs-up, and a bellow of "What good taste!" Nik puffed out his vocal sac. "Though I doubt the original would appreciate the comparison."

Marlie cut into Geezer's guttural chuckle. "As we were *saying*, your kind offer of revelation notwithstanding, we would prefer that you return us to the planet from which you hijacked us."

"Believe me, I'd prefer to do this run solo, without the nuisance of complaints from the hired help—"

"Hired, my ass. We didn't sign up for this, and we wouldn't have 'hired on' even for all the money in the world."

"—but I need four normal hands to pull it off, and presently I have none. As for your compensation, no shower of money could measure up to the rich rewards of secret knowledge you're about to reap."

Marlie gave Zeb a look, bugged that he had stopped contributing to her campaign for repatriation. "Look, Marles—we know this guy. He was bullheaded even before we aurorized him. He's not about to turn back right when he thinks victory is within his grasp. Maybe it makes more sense to go with the flow. He did get us back home last time. In the meantime, maybe we can get something out of this excursion other than a terrifying tease." Marlie bore this speech with a look of betrayal.

"You'll get plenty more than a tease, popcorns," bellowed Geezer. "Listen up. I've got a story with a helluva punchline for you."

"As you wish," said Zeb. At the moment, there was no choice but to settle in for another ride on the solar wind. Grateful that Geezer's plasma jar was as comfortably protective as Shang's had been, Zeb took off his jacket, stuffed it behind his head for a pillow, lay back, and looked at his sister. "Marles?"

Marlie heaved a sigh of resignation and called up to the grizzled specter hurtling them through space. "Go ahead, big guy—hit us with your best shot."

As she settled in with her feet pointing toward Zeb's, both of them had to swat away unsettling thoughts about the state of things back home—panic, without doubt, pure and anything but simple. What the hell had happened on Geezer Island? The noise of the house being torn asunder must have been heard by a couple hundred people, even in that rural part of the county. That would have been plenty disturbing for Relura, even without seeing the core of the house rising into the night sky, her recurring nightmare of the last four years suddenly made all too real, this time in the presence of their parents. Had Relura seen her siblings' faces in the dome looking down on her from a hundred feet above? Or, if not, had she seen their empty boat across the lake and scrambled to get another boat to reach the island and search for bodies in the wake of a bizarre boomless explosion?

Then other images flowed into the twins' minds through the cracks in their consciousness. What of the rest of their present lives—Zeb's girlfriend and his book, Marlie's school and startup crew and their brink-of-break-through visions, and countless more reverberating mini-losses foaming in the overwhelming swell of fate that was just beginning.

Marlie looked out the dome and noted Geezer's World War II–era wrist-watch still strapped to his wrist, now aurorized and enlarged to the size of a skating rink. It had a lunar subdial showing the phase of the moon—as quaintly irrelevant as the time of day for someone who had not set foot on Earth for years. But time meant plenty to Marlie in terms of survival in the woeful trap where she and Zeb found themselves now. There was nothing for it at the moment but to let Geezer lay out some historical tidbits from his last four years and whatever he'd choose to reveal of his present scheme. Neither reason nor strategy had a place at the table now; everything had succumbed to a surreal miasma.

These musings were interrupted by a rolling sensation as the starscape above them appeared to rotate. It reminded Marlie of a planetarium show she'd once seen, in which the audience had the sense of being on a celestial carousel as the scenery revolved all around. She and Zeb realized that Geezer had decided to turn onto his back. As AuroraGeezer, he wasn't tied to the physics regulating swimmers and sailors or even birds on Earth. He could assume whatever position or movement struck his fancy and still fly very fast indeed. As this new movement revealed another hemisphere of stars, Geezer placed his hands behind his head for a moment before he accelerated to an even greater speed, by sweeping his arms in an upward-facing breast stroke. Marlie sensed that he was edging ever closer to the speed of light, and half expected to see twirling cosmic cop lights coming up behind them.

That image scattered abruptly as Geezer began his tale. "That house of mine you broke into four Earth years ago was no ordinary pad," Geezer began. Zeb was determined to ignore the annoying static corrupting the old man's baritone. He had long been able to train the focus of his brain's reticular formation on a good story when one came along, and Geezer's tale promised to be a doozy.

"It was my laboratory for the principal research project of my life for over forty years," he began. Geezer explained how, as a young retiree with an affinity for mechanics (aeronautical by profession, celestial by agnostic spirituality), he'd journeyed to a remote spot on the coast of Mexico to witness a total eclipse of the sun and chanced upon what he came to call an "eclipse ground disappearance," taking place in aurora-imbued darkness. He acknowledged that his present prisoners—whom he referred to as "passengers," as if they'd signed up for a Princess Cruise to Jupiter—were well aware of the eclipse locale, since it was the very place their aurorabird captor had deposited them after their merry jaunt to the sun. Zeb vividly recalled the panicky moment he had searched for Marlie in the surf when he emerged from the ocean just off the beach in Mexico.

The ancient astronaut's rime rumbled on. The rupture of the Mexican beach and cliff, stalked by the tern who had lost his family to an unseen kidnapper, disturbed his sleep for weeks. At the dawn of what should have been the luxurious bliss of early retirement, Geezer was bedeviled by a natural phenomenon that had blasted apart the pillars upon which his understanding of the natural world had been constructed.

The agitation would continue until he could devise a plan that would resolve two contradictory objectives. That the bizarre ground disappearances were associated with an auroral event was beyond question. He would need to build a laboratory large enough to carry on research leading to the development of predictive, recording, measurement, and analytical tools to study a rare artifact of solar wind both on-site and in distant locations. At the same time, despite its capacious size, this laboratory would have to be inconspicuous to avoid arousing the suspicion or curiosity of others who might live nearby.

"How'd that work out?" asked Marlie, not quite loud enough to derail Geezer's recital. He carried on, pointing out the obvious: that he was a recluse by nature and the last thing he needed was having to explain what he'd witnessed in Mexico to a passel of looky-loos and media hounds who would slap him with a reputation as a crackpot.

Meshing these conflicting objectives was made all the more complicated by his decision to design the lab with a large, extraordinary structure that, absent a clever disguise, would draw attention to itself from anyone who came within a mile of it. But he thought it through and came up with the perfect solution—building the lab in its full dimensions within the disguise of a normal residential house. Obviously, he told them, the house could not be sited in a noisy, light-polluted, densely populated place like the Oakland of his childhood.

"You mean you were a kid once?" interrupted Marlie, only half jesting, which was enough to amuse Nik, who croak-chuckled his approval.

"Briefly. Don't hold it against me."

Siting the house in an industrial colony like El Segundo, south of Los Angeles, where he'd honed his inventing skills, wouldn't be much better, nor would it fare well in a suburb surrounded by nosy picket-fencers. Yet it also couldn't be plunked in the middle of a vast open space like a desert or farmland, where it would stand out too much. No, Geezer's dream house called for the appearance of a modestly isolated, commonplace middle-class home. The solution that would govern the rest of his Earthly existence finally crystallized on a forested island he created from a spit of land sticking into a lake in the lightly inhabited outskirts of Sonoma, California.

The specs for his facility called for a subterranean section dug deep into the earth. He could employ locals for some of the work, like lake-dredging, trucking, and siding, but to avoid local gossip that the digging and tunneling could invite, he brought in laborers from mining communities in Colorado and Kentucky.

The ease with which he could afford such extravagance, let alone the sophisticated materials and instrumentation in the lab itself, made him thankful all over again for his earlier meteoric success as an inventor and for the protections of the U.S. Patent Office. He possessed the freedom, motive, and means to delve into the historical record and the science underlying the phenomenon he'd witnessed in Mexico, with a view toward developing a portable artificial solar wind generator that might be capable of catalyzing similar incidents. Safety measures would be necessary to minimize the risk to lab, home, and life, and if they failed, those were the breaks. Hiding eternally under a comforter would not suit someone for whom earthshaking discovery was the principal reason for living.

He committed to facing down a knotty scientific problem. Clearly, auroras and solar winds were involved, plus there were birds and solar eclipses, but perhaps one or more of these factors were unrelated to the ground disappearances. To get a handle on it all, he would have to find a way to catalyze or attract the kind of aurora that had ripped substantial chunks of Earth into the sky. He figured his best shot at getting at the solar wind piece of the puzzle was to build a high-voltage transmitter powered by a private, off-the-grid underground generator.

Ah, thought Marlie, *so that was the origin of the aurora bug I was to catch decades later. Geezer was Patient Zero—well, he'd caught it from Tesla, but he'd caught it good, and my parents had gone and built their house practically next door, exposing me to an admittedly fascinating contagion.*

She visualized the scheme Geezer described, topping the lab with a dome that could function as a projection lens. Ultimately, he aimed to create a miniaturized version of the entire system that he could transport to eclipses along with gear capable of recording the event and measuring its electromagnetic characteristics. He regarded eclipses taking place during solar wind storms as especially desirable conditions for testing his apparatus.

Occasional visits from the tern whom the twins had later named Arc added enchanting grace notes of mystery to the research. Geezer soon recognized that the bird was coming when total solar eclipses were imminent somewhere on the planet. Further, once Geezer had a crude prototype of his device and began traveling to TSE sites, the bird insisted on staying by his side, so he began transporting him along with his instrumentation. Why not? Anything he could do to replicate the conditions of the incident in Mexico might be to the good. The bird could feed himself readily enough when they were at or near the sea.

As he looked out at a couple of distant twinkling asteroids coming into view, Zeb thought about the many instances he'd come across of birds possessing a lot more intelligence than they've been given credit for. *Making a derogatory epithet out of "bird-brain" is more ignorant than any bird. Crows, finches, magpies, and vultures use tools. How many dogs or horses can claim that? And some Chinese fishermen have employed birds who could count to at least seven. A lot of birds are more tuned in to the environment than humans. How many of us can navigate across the world without maps like Arc and his kin? A lot of birds can outpace us in predicting weather, even earthquakes. But solar eclipses? Arc was in a league of his own on that one.*

Geezer's still explaining himself. Pay attention.

"Once I put together the prototype for my portable solar wind charger—"

"—which you christened Wardenclyffe 3," Zeb offered. Geezer hesitated a moment before acknowledging that fact. "Which you did because . . . "

"I suggest you two listen up and cut the interrogation." Marlie's annoyance at this dismissal was doubled by Nik giving her a haughty look and a gratuitous *harrumph*. Recognizing the pointlessness of pressing her demand to someone who had complete control of their destiny, she settled back in aggrieved silence.

Though he was a touch too weird to serve as a mentor, Geezer did inspire some respect in Marlie, as he recounted the arduous R&D that went into his high-tech concoctions. The determination he demonstrated in dragging his gear and a wild bird to TSE sites all over the world for decades on end made many scientific luminaries look like pallid slackers by comparison. His confidence in his ultimate success was built on air. Many years and eclipses passed without his witnessing or generating a single ground disappearance event, but along the way he learned of several such events that had occurred elsewhere. Those were in the eclipse paths at various distances from the sites he'd selected, and it appeared his site predictions were getting closer and closer each time.

Then, finally, Antarctica.

Geezer's staticky, gravelly baritone was becoming steadily more animated. "By the time I got to that iceberg, I had the perfect setup. Even with the convocation of birds, I had everything under control, until you two showed up." Marlie thought it was a bit petty of Geezer to be holding a grudge against them after all this time, during which he'd gotten to promenade around the solar system thanks to their assistance with the Wardenclyffe, but never mind. "Suddenly I was caught in a kiddie rescue op on the ice and ended up having to fire the device with one hand. I realized that posed a risk to you too, but I wasn't going to miss the chance of a lifetime on your account. If you got snatched with me, too bad for you."

"No reason to get crazy saving kids' lives."

Geezer didn't comment on Marlie's sardonic remark, but she could swear she saw him grin. Nik delivered a satisfied, croakish equivalent of "Damn right." Zeb's expression suggested that she should let Geezer get on with the story.

"Well, you two think you know the next chapter in this saga, but you missed its climax."

"The climax was our getting delivered alive back to Earth," Marlie reminded him.

"For *you*. The climax I'm talking about got the greatest discovery in the history of science rolling, one that's rolling still and picking up speed by the minute."

Not knowing what Geezer was talking about, Marlie couldn't assess that outlandish claim, but it did occur to her that Geezer himself was picking up speed, because the outer planets seemed to be getting larger and brighter fast enough to hint that they might be closing in on the speed of light. She would have pressed him on that matter but for the intoxicating revelations unspooling from his recitation.

It turned out that during the time Zeb and Marlie had spent at the mercy of Shang's presumed younger sibling, Geezer and Arc weren't just frolicking in the imported sea. They'd approached the plasma jar Shang had stationed along the cliff adjacent to the Antarctic jar, the one they would soon find out Shang had plucked from Mexico many years before. During a brief break in the fog, they'd witnessed Arc's mate at the edge of the jar facing down toward the sea in an intense, eyes-open meditative pose. Arc had flown up to the jar and, like someone peering into an illuminated house at night, he was able to see his wife before she saw him. Once he squawked in excitement, she recognized his call, despite the passage of decades. However, the couple's joy was frustrated, for there was no way for either of them to penetrate the plasma wall separating them. Nor could Geezer help, since he was stuck down in the sea, below a forty-foot-high vertical cliff.

Geezer was pleased for his companion's partial good fortune, but his focus was on several beams of light that became visible in little gusts of methane floating in and above the surface of the sea. The thinner beams emanated from all the jars arrayed along the cliff, including the one with which Arc had become so taken. The beams converged on one target—a blue whale who held its great head above the water to receive the signals for a long time, facing away from the jars, with its eyes wide open as if fixed on something far away. In a wafting cloud of methane, Geezer and Arc saw one more beam, a thicker, rapidly fluctuating stream of light, extending from the whale's head up from the sea in the opposite direction.

The whale-head mystery begged for some unraveling, but there was no time for that. Arc knew something was up and he flew into the beam in the methane cloud. He faced it and his lower beak *dropped*—Geezer had never seen that before. He swam over as fast as he could and arrived in time to see a remnant of the beam for about seven seconds before the whale lowered its head into the water.

The image stream consisted of a rapid-fire series of scenes, like a desultory movie montage. Since the thinner beams from the array of plasma jars had been aimed at the whale, Geezer figured that the scenes might have originated as projections from Arc's mate and perhaps other captive birds in Shang's collection. Among the scenes were visual recordings of Shang's arrival with the Antarctic jar, Arc's first foray outside the jar, and Geezer's plunge into the sea.

The twins knew what these beams signified. Mock had laid it all out for them. Apparently, the birds in Shang's keeping were among the elite intelligent animals capable of and responsible for making sure the news stayed on, even in a realm where the provinciality of "24/7" had no meaning whatsoever. The signals the birds and their whale partner were transmitting evidently included not just the captives' news reports but also their internal visualizations. Shang must have been fully aware of this news-gathering enterprise, for he'd taken the trouble to import, all the way from Earth, a whale and enough water to provide it a marine home in the center of the solar system.

Zeb could feel gooseflesh rising on his scalp. "I *knew* you'd seen something weird down in Shang's sea that you weren't telling us, Mr. G. And it explains a lot!"

"I'll say," Marlie replied, "like what kind of birds Shang was capturing."

"And what those meditating aurorabirds in the blue spa at the center of the sun were up to."

"And the ones at the edge of the rave on the solar surface."

"What it doesn't explain is what the whale was doing with those signals. He sure wasn't carrying them down to the bottom of the ocean around Hawaii."

A smile swept over Geezer's craggy face. "I've got a theory about that, youngsters."

Zeb noticed Nik becoming increasingly flummoxed. If his whole construct of sea-bottom historians was colorful garbage, who and where were the Recipients?

Geezer barreled on. With an emotional brew of equal parts fascination and dread, the twins realized they'd better let him make his case, and the sooner the better. "You recall what followed—your return to the aurorabird's domain under the auspices of its overlord, our acrobatic reunion over Shang's inner sea, the merging of microworlds in Shang's Mexico jar, the retreat from the sun under pressure from the beast you called 'MammyPappy,' and your incomprehensible disinterest in becoming two of the first three people in the history of the human race to visit Jupiter—"

"I'm interested now!" Marlie interjected. "I just prefer to do it with astronauts equipped with state-of-the-art engineering versus a manic hermit and an aurorabird the size of Mount Everest."

"My, aren't you the peachy princess of professionalism!" Geezer saluted her in auroral insincerity. "It's that kind of narrow-mindedness that made me realize it was in my best interest to get rid of you and your brother. Hence the speed with which I facilitated getting your sorry asses dropped off back on Earth.

"Now I reckon that my good deed might have led you to think I was Mr. Sweetie Nice Guy—"

"I wouldn't go that far, but please continue."

"It might help if we stopped interrupting him," Zeb admonished her. She grudgingly agreed.

"As it happened, while sacrificing my familiar mortal coil to harass Mr. Shang for your benefit, I had an ulterior motive. Becoming aurorized like those radiolaria you accidentally zapped would enable me to explore the solar system without a couple of nuisances mucking things up, at least until I could find out who was receiving these report signals."

Unable to resist a little interrupting himself, Zeb exclaimed, "So that's why you were so fired up about having snared a spot on what you thought was Shang's Jupiter Express! You figured you'd find the Recipients there!"

"Bingo, boyo. I'd offer you a sunflower seed that's been buried in the depths of my parka pocket all this time, but it's bigger than you are now and would spoil your appetite. But you're right—my plan was to find the whale's transmission again and track it all the way to its destination."

"Ah-ha!" Marlie lit up. "And you took us out over the ocean near Hawaii before zooming us into space. You were picking up a whale's signal beam as a guidance system, and you're riding it like a carrier wave right now!"

"And by 'destination' you mean Recipient Central!"

"I'd never have recruited you if you weren't such a clever pair of whippersnappers."

Marlie replied rhetorically, "You're referring to what you've done to us as recruitment?"

Geezer didn't respond. He was distracted by Nik's hoppin' and croakin' dance, the froggy equivalent of a catcher whose pitcher had just completed a no-hitter to win the pennant. The giddy frog was acting as if Geezer's hand was on the verge of pulling aside the curtain of mystery hiding the Recipients. He capped off his celebration by snapping into his mouth a fly that must have joined them when the dome window was open for Mock's departure back on Earth. Nik smacked his wide lips in deep satisfaction.

The twins did not share Nik's elation. Geezer's reference to appetite had brought to their minds the issue of survival and the great unknown of how long they were going to be cooped up in this crazy wizard's pocket. Some high-moxie initiative would be in order eventually, but for the moment, the best move was no move—keep quiet and let the guy get to the point or, as he had put it, the punchline.

"I had my work cut out for me, but I had all the time in the world to do it. Shang's pet whale had transmitted an ultra-long-range signal that I would ride all the way to the promised land. The only problem was how to find it in interplanetary space."

That would be a problem, all right. Returning to Shang's hidey-hole to find his pet whale could be a risky business. He'd have to find the right sun-spot entry and hope that Shang hadn't relocated his terrarium, with its inland sea, to evade MammyPappy's scrutiny. Geezer decided to take his chances and head straight on to Jupiter, with its copious supply of methane that could render the signals visible.

Along the way, it occurred to Geezer that, as a newly minted aurora-creature, he might have acquired Shang's turf-snatching superpower. He decided to take a crack at it on Jupiter's giant moon, Ganymede. He found that a rapid motion of his hands stirring the solar winds was all it took to create a plasma swirl that he could employ as a grabbing tool on the satellite's surface. His first swipe attempt netted him a motley mix of rock, ice, water vapor, and some thin atmosphere in a portable plasmic package—no eclipse necessary. The experiment confirmed Zeb's suspicion that Shang conducted his land grabs during eclipses as a matter of choice. Eclipses offered him a way to snatch his victims while they were bedazzled by the sun's corona.

Geezer's success brought him little satisfaction. He was desperate to find the intangible signal that he'd seen just once, almost five hundred million miles away. He released his handcrafted jar into its future as a tiny, odd addition to the Jupiter system and then returned to his main mission.

"As I wandered in space over the following few Earth weeks, I began to see how all the various puzzle pieces fit together. What I'd seen in the methane mist radiating from Shang's birds and their whale compadre was no accident, nor was it an isolated incident. As we left the sun back then, you'd described some similar behavior among the flaming auroracreatures you saw on the solar surface." Zeb nodded to Marlie, acknowledging Geezer's point.

"And that wasn't all. That whale-bird broadcasting team shook something loose from my memory bank. I knew I'd seen something like that before, and recently, in a different context. Then it hit me: back on Earth in the Southern Ocean, not far from the iceberg where we'd gotten plucked away, in the dimming light of the partial eclipse I'd seen a sperm whale behave in the same hypnotic posture as Shang's whale pet. And in both cases the whales were near a gaggle of unusually intelligent birds. Looked to me like some kind of reporting network involving birds and whales was going on on both the Earth and the sun."

"*Crrroooaaakoribbit!*"

Geezer rushed on, ignoring Nik's escalating fever. "I recalled what you of the twerp squad had said shortly after Shang took us away from the sun, about aurorabirds meditating in their so-called spa and on the sun's surface. I figured they could have been in on the reporting operation too."

"An operation reporting to whom, exactly?" Marlie prodded.

"Patience, colleagues." Marlie couldn't keep herself from scoffing at that appellation. Geezer looked faintly annoyed that she was trying to stuff his long-planned story into a box of her preferred dimensions. "I soared the solar winds throughout the solar system for the next three years—Earth years—looking for that signal and the mysterious Recipients it was intended for. It was a long and lonely quest, but in the end my persistence paid off."

"You found the Recipients?!" exclaimed Zeb and Marlie in unison, as Nik recommended jumping around the dome sill.

"I found the beam I'd been hankering for ever since I was bobbing in the aurorabird's hidden sea."

"Where?!" asked Zeb, noting that their last question had still not been answered.

"And it turned out the beam was even better than I'd expected." Ignored again. Can't be surprised—if the crochety crank was difficult to deal with in flesh-and-blood form, there was no reason to assume he'd become cream-puff sweet when he was four years older and four thousand feet taller. "It was a composite, merging the signals from all the long-distance transmitters from both Earth and the sun.

"That was an arresting discovery, but it stripped away only one of the Recipients' seven veils. From that point on, I studied the beam for months on end in a fruitless search for clues to the final answer, getting nowhere—until just recently, when a path to that promised land opened up." Geezer looked down at his Earthling captives and added, "I have you, my trusty frog, to thank for that." At this acknowledgment, Nik's vocal sac engorged near to bursting before he let loose with a deafening croak of pride and anticipation.

Geezer described how a serendipitous appearance of his old house in one of the frog's transmissions helped him formulate a plot to tear away those last six veils. Seeing Relura tiptoeing through Frog City in the foreground set in motion what he modestly considered a brilliant scheme to get his auroral hands on something he could use to great effect—the core of his old house.

"Grand idea!" said Marlie. "If you wanted your wacky, creaky house so much, why didn't you just grab it and leave us out of it?"

"Good question, young woman!"

"I see I've been promoted from 'girlie.'"

"You promoted yourself. I've seen signs of the project you're working on with your college pals. We're kindred research spirits, you and I. When I needed a couple of old-fashioned humans to pull this off, you and your brother, for two different reasons, were the perfect candidates."

Marlie was annoyed at herself for feeling a glow of pride. *Get a grip. You're being whipped about by a reflex developed from years of craving and relishing praise from professors, mentors, and venture capitalists, but consider the source, for God's sake: an aurorized ruffian inventor-kidnapper with sixteen-foot-long eyelashes.*

Marlie grabbed her consciousness back to focus on Geezer. He was recounting how he had recognized Relura immediately, even though he'd only seen her once, on the iceberg, and that got him thinking about the twins. "Despite your egregious interference in my affairs four years ago, it was clear you weren't dumb and you possessed healthy curiosity instincts."

The twins sniffed Geezer's effort to ingratiate himself, but it worked in spite of their suspicions. He lauded the progress they were making in their careers—a budding research scientist investigating plasma science (no big surprise there) and a skilled pilot and artist cashing in on images he'd confected courtesy of the auroracreatures they'd stumbled upon years before. For the human helpers he'd need to carry out his new mission, the best bets were the ones who had accompanied him on his earlier one.

"Of course, getting you on board wouldn't be easy. I couldn't exactly send you an embossed calligraphic invitation or a neatly drafted memorandum. Plus, you'd proven less than enthusiastic about this kind of travel last time around. But I had someone I was pretty sure would help me out: the creature you've christened Nikola." Nik belched another fiercely proud croak. "Yes, indeed—without that frog, you, my human friends, wouldn't be here."

Marlie turned to the frog and remarked dryly, "Thanks, Nik." She stared for a moment trying to figure out why the frog wasn't responding, only to be treated to the sight of Nik's skin splitting down the middle of his back and belly, allowing him to extricate his arms and legs. He concluded his ritual by pushing the discarded skin up to his mouth and gobbling it up. "Ew! You are *weird*, dude!"

"Mmm-mmm—finger-lickin' good, Marlie!" said Zeb cheerfully. "Don't knock Nik's cuisine till you've tried it. Besides, in a few days he'll do it again, and by then you might be hungry enough to ask him to share it with you." That got her burning, so he added, "It's not my preferred snack, but I like watching him do it. It's a circle-of-life kinda thing."

"Oh my God." Marlie felt like shedding her own skin, now that Zeb was getting under it again with gross animal facts meant to put her off balance. *Okay, life science has its superfine processes and the ongoing mysteries of evolution, but it's so messy—viruses, corpses, mucus, poop, battles to the death. If the guy likes learning about science so much, why couldn't he have chosen pure, clean physics?*

Geezer wrenched the conversation back where he wanted it. "Knowing you youngsters would be apprehensive about signing on to this project, I needed to coax you into making yourselves available without too much information, and 'Nikola' was the perfect foil.

"I knew of his zeal for unmasking the Recipients, so one recent night when your family was away, I lowered my face into the sky above your local swamp. That packed a wallop the local amphibious population wasn't used to. Imagine a couple thousand frogs going totally silent in one instant and then breaking out in a screaming, croaking hysteria the next. But not Nikola—he was spellbound. He knew I was talking to him. It was easy to make visions of meeting sugarplum Recipients dance in his head. All that could be his if only he would get the twins who live nearby into my island house, when all would be revealed.

"Then I vanished. I knew he'd assume I was one of the Recipients, but a little deception in his own best interests was essential to motivate him. I knew he'd appreciate the big payoff for joining forces with me once we made it across the goal line, and so will you!"

"What do you mean, join forces with you?" Marlie protested. "What do you want us to *do*?!"

"Hush, puppy—all will become clear in time. We've got a way to go before this flight lands. I suggest you just lie back and rest up for a revelation."

Zeb hadn't said anything for a few minutes because his attention was split between Geezer's disconcerting story and a bright spot of light he'd been keeping an eye on. Actually, it was a cluster of several spots of light, a number of small faint ones hovering near a much larger one that was a good fifth of the size of the moon from Earth. He looked at Marlie while nodding in that direction. "Jupiter, right?"

True enough, the giant planet hung off in space, still very far away but large enough that they could make out its multicolored atmospheric bands. "You can even see its auroras."

Marlie did feel a reflexive thrill at the sight of the red, green, and purple auroras at Jupiter's poles, but her expression soon shifted to puzzled alarm, for Jupiter was at eleven o'clock, not their heading. "Geezer, where are you taking us?!"

Geezer looked down in disapproval at the impudent face at the top of his pocketed plasma jar. "'Geezer'? You might want to rethink the wisdom of addressing me disrespectfully, missy."

Zeb interjected, "We'd be pleased to use your real name, sir, if you'd divulge it. And let us know where you're taking us while you're at it."

"Zeb! The binocs!"

That doesn't sound good. Marlie's alarm even brought Geezer up short. Zeb handed Marlie the binoculars sitting on Geezer's shelf. Within a moment of training them on another bright object far ahead and to the right, she exclaimed, "That's Saturn—we're not headed there either! This maniac must be taking us to Uranus—the *outer* outer solar system!"

"Oh, *now* we're up Shit Creek! At Saturn we'd be a hop, skip, and a jump from home."

"Real funny, Z. Uranus happens to be farther from Saturn than Saturn is from Earth." Marlie retrained the binoculars on Saturn for a glimpse of its polar auroras, but she was too agitated to enjoy it for more than a second. She jerked her head back toward Geezer. "Hey, Mr. G! How about a damned itinerary for tonight's kidnapping?!"

"Calm down," rumbled Geezer. That marked the second time this evening she'd been so instructed, and she was tiring of it quickly. "I have too much respect for you to drag you on a mission that didn't have a fat payoff you'll relish the rest of your life." She was sufficiently shaky that the mere reference to the possibility of a rest-of-her-life offered a modicum of reassurance. "You're correct—this express doesn't stop at Jupiter. I was wrong about the target of the whales' transmissions.

"But all good things in time, children. Your best bet at present is to lie back and get some rest. You're going to need it." With that, the old man had the audacity to shove the plasma jar containing his old home laboratory deeper into his pocket.

It was pretty dark down there. Flicking on his flashlight enabled Zeb to illuminate the lab but not their captor's intentions. The old buzzard had them right where he wanted them, and there was nothing they could do about it.

Marlie resisted the impulse to remind Zeb that Mock had warned them against falling under the frog's sway. The best play would be to hang with her brother in a friendly, peaceable mode conducive to creative problem-solving. She joined him in stretching out on the curved dome sill, where they retained at least a little view of the stars through the dome. It was a gorgeous visual balm for their present and coming distress.

"Don't get too cozy over there, Z. We've got to huddle up and figure a way out of this fix."

"Old Geeze has got us by the gizzards, all right. I've not had much training in the art of escaping aurorized jacket pockets in interplanetary space."

"We escaped once."

"With some space-age technology and the aid of someone eager to be aurorized himself."

Marlie was hoping to see her brother's eyes narrow in brainstorm mode, but instead he was focusing on Nik, who was taking small hops up the dome's latticework toward its apex, stopping a couple of times to look over his shoulder at them. "Let's not ignore the possibility that a frog can be a mole, Sis."

Abashed at her carelessness in having broached the subject of upsetting Geezer's plans with his staunch ally nearby, she careened into strategizing a counterespionage maneuver.

"Oh, Nikola . . ." she called in a soft, musical tone. "Come here, baby frog." Nik froze, allowing only his eyes to move, sliding toward the femme fatale a few feet below him. She reached up ever so gently and stroked his slimy sloping expanse of chin. "I am so sorry for having given you a hard time. I'm sure you've had more than your share of those, all those herons, snakes, and nasty cats. They look down on you because you're small, but with the lightning-like adeptness of your tongue, your leaps many times your height, and the bewitching beauty of your great big eyes, you eclipse them all." Nik radiated suspicion laid low by a hungry ego. "I don't need you to turn into a prince—in a way, you already are a prince. You can handle yourself no matter what this crazy auroraman throws at you. But I—I'm in need of your princely wisdom and secrecy to save my life."

Unable to help himself, Nik emitted a little throat-clearing sound and motioned his head toward Zeb, a clear case of "Him too?"

"Of course. But he's just my brother, *mon cher.*"

The frog recoiled, his eyes bugging out as he hugged his hind legs.

"Big whoops, Marlie," chuckled Zeb. "Cardinal rule: Don't speak French to an intelligent frog."

Damn, girl, Marlie chided herself, tempted to think she'd actually been getting somewhere coaxing Nik into her corner for the match of wits she'd fantasized coming with Geezer. "How clumsy of me, Nikky. What I meant was, 'My dear, we must bring Zeb back too, else my family will blame me for negligence resulting in the death of their only son and brother. You can understand that."

Nik understood, all right, and hopped defiantly up to her face to deliver a croak reeking of frog-skin breath.

"You think you're smarter than me because you go to Stanford!" Zeb kindly translated on Nik's behalf. "I could eat a smarty-pants like you for lunch with a side of my discarded skin!" On cue, Nik flicked his obscenely long tongue at Marlie's nose and hopped back up to the dome apex to raise a loud, croaking alarm. Zeb was amused in spite of—well, because of—himself as he watched his sister swipe her nose with her jacket sleeve. "I admit I'm no virtuoso negotiator with venture capitalists, Sis, but I advise you to skip that blatant cooing tactic in your next pitch meeting."

"At least I tried," Marlie muttered, attempting to quell her embarrassment until she heard Geezer's guttural growl from above.

"I've got some advice for you, too, missy: Recognize that you're in it up to your nostrils. A little patience and trust will do you wonders."

Once she was sure Geezer wasn't looking her way, Marlie stared at the handful of stars they could still make out, sighed, and fought off a little stinging of the eyes. She took up the binoculars again and scanned the outer solar system for Saturn and Uranus, hoping to assuage her anxiety by noting the pattern of auroras at their poles. Dim and distant as they were, the auroras shone in the clarity of space like feather-soft jewels, but the relief they afforded her pain was short-lived. She had a boatload of dreams and some very dear souls she wanted to hang with back home, and the ever-diminishing odds of having any opportunity to do so in the future were getting her very down indeed. *But there's no crying in spaceflight; think positively. Come to think about it, thank goodness Zeb and I went through that wild ordeal four years ago. It taught us that there could always be a way out if we keep our wits about us.*

Yeah? How do we get around that the family back home has to be near drowning in crisis floodwaters? Not so easy to gloss over that. What in God's name had Relura thought when she saw that old house ripped apart from across the lake, the boat tied up at the island, and no siblings around? Did she see Zeb and me in the dome, wide-eyed in shared shock? If not, she'd want to get to the island ASAP, but how, with no boat? By waking some neighbors or the volunteer fire department with an emergency call about an auroracreature or some such creature having devoured a house with her siblings in it and fled into space? How much had the parents seen? How much had Relura been obliged to blow their minds about the Antarctic expedition?

Marlie clamped her eyelids down, determined to stanch her frenzying thought flow. She focused on her breathing, which, miraculously, lulled her into sleepy drifting, so even though her brow was furrowed, she was en route to unconsciousness. She hoped that her brother, for his sake, would do likewise, but when she opened her eyes to check on him, she saw him leaving her side to descend to the lab proper to fetch a pencil and paper. Moments later he was back on the mezzanine exercising his go-to anxiety deflection mechanism: reveling in his imagination as he drew on the back of an invoice he'd found from Ramcartt Electrofuel Technologies of Alberta, Canada.

Marlie envied Zeb's capacity for escape to worlds of his own imagining. How marvelous it would be to have such mastery of drawn lines! The guy could draw a perfect circle three feet in diameter freehand on a whiteboard. He could capture the essential appearance and personality of anyone they knew in a four-minute sketch. At parties, people could call out names for him to caricature and he would respond with a drawn rendition as entertaining as any standard from the American songbook demanded of a first-class dance band. Lucky boy.

Zeb was excited by early minings of ideas for his Shangrilarian sequel. One chapter would place his hero in an aerial dogfight with a pilot of the enemy air force. Sixteen feet tall and with the power of supersonic flight, he would have no difficulty ascending to the airman's cockpit canopy at forty thousand feet altitude and freaking him out with dazzling pseudopodia poses, disabling the enemy without firing a shot.

Ah, well. Their fraught circumstances prohibited Zeb from delving deeply into the intricacies of scene staging. Better, he decided, to indulge his love of creature elegance and simply commit to paper a series of drawings of his hero in glorious poses, equal parts martial arts, modern dance, and invertebrate dervish whirls. That afforded him a good twenty minutes of enchanting cerebral stimulation. But eventually anxiety burbling beneath the surface sapped that glory of its fun and lured him toward sleep. Marlie had the right idea. A sweet escape from reality beckoned.

16

The twins awoke at the eruption of a croak. Nikola was attempting to stand on his hind legs, hoping in vain for a better view of their destination than could be achieved from the plasma jar's position deep in Geezer's pocket. Certain that his mentor would heed his appeals, Nikola went off on a full-throated *jug-o-rum* jag. Surely the Recipients of the countless transmissions he'd relayed over the course of his life must be near, perhaps even awaiting his arrival as an ambassador from the kingdom of Earth's animal reporters and then—*and then*—they would welcome him into their ranks, grateful for his dedicated service to the cause!

At any rate, that's how Zeb interpreted Nik's agitated dance moves and vocal licks. But Zeb had other things on his mind, and he could see that his sister did as well—such as what in blazes Geezer was about to do to them as they approached a gigantic world with half a dozen faint rings, a plethora of moons, and a blue so uniform as to make Earth look like a spherical rioting rainbow.

Marlie's first word in two hours was "Neptune!" spoken with the weight of the planet looming high overhead. "We're ten times farther than we ever were with Shang. And—shoulda known—so much methane that its blue can be seen from Earth with binoculars." Zeb nodded while staring in wonder at the circle of azure rapidly filling their view. Marlie stood and shouted upward, "Say, Mr. G! What's happening?"

"Patience, Ms. Morell. In a matter of minutes, almost all will be revealed."

Zeb knew Marlie wasn't going to let that rest. "What do you mean 'almost'?" she called. But she received no reply, and her face sank in recognition that Geezer had a perfect hand and they were cardless.

Geezer decelerated as they entered Neptune's atmosphere and were swallowed up in an azure storm of blustering winds. Geezer lifted the plasma specimen jar higher in his pocket, affording his passengers a broader view of their surroundings.

"Look!" Zeb pointed down to a thin ray of light beneath them, a luminescent beam filled with sparkling particles racing forward. "Mr. G—you've found your magic beam?"

"I found it before we left good old Earth, friends. I've been able to follow it all along because I can feel it, even when I can't see it. You need methane for it to become visible, and we've just entered an ocean of that. The show's about to begin. Hang on."

Marlie's stomach swooped up toward her throat in sync with Geezer's sudden maneuver tilting down toward the beam. She could see that it wasn't so thin after all, with its true width becoming more apparent the closer they got to it.

As a pilot, Zeb had developed a keen eye for estimating altitudes, and hence the heights of very large features, like mountains. As Geezer began flying them alongside the beam, still decelerating, Zeb pegged its diameter to be at least a mile wide. From the side, the pulses of light tearing through the light tube were indecipherable, but the twins were pretty sure that was about to change. Their captain gradually turned into the beam, penetrating it to its center, and then slowly brought them around to a halt, facing head-on as astonishing a sight any they'd ever seen—and they'd seen Shang's inner sea and aurorabirds raving on the sun's surface and mellowing in its indigo center.

It was like standing in the blast of a mile-wide firehose in which the substance of the torrent was imagery instead of water. More than imagery, there were sounds and smells and tactile sensations, all coming at the hearing-smelling-feeling viewers in a ceaseless flash flood, flowing toward and past them in dozens of small-diameter circular channels packed within the larger circular beam like glass fibers bundled together in a fiber-optic cable.

Once inside the beam, the stormy Neptunian winds faded into the distance. Now the twins' minds were buffeted by the fierce speed of the scene flow, making it impossible to make sense of what they were seeing. Zeb noticed that even the phlegmatic frog appeared contorted in a mental mix of excitement and dismay. But MC Geezer knew how to dial it up. Telling the audience, "Your moment's coming, kids," he moved his hands into position directly in front of them, at first obscuring their view and then gradually spreading his hands apart like a widening viewfinder, just enough to create a space in which each sub-stream could be clearly seen and felt, one at a time. Thus isolated, the sensations associated with each scene—each *report*—were lifted above the white noise, stretched out in time, and slowed enough to be experienced much as the original reporters and editors had initially prepared them.

It was an awesome onslaught: summaries and snapshots of romances and wars, urban and termite hill construction sites, crimes and sporting events, milk cows and sunning lizards, political shenanigans and children's games, ladybugs and apex predators, gatherings in boardrooms, stadiums, and dim alleys, surgeries and surgeonfish, clear-cutting and sewing circles, scientific experiments and religious services, on and on. The twins smelled gardenias, dank beaches, and barbecue smoke and felt the feather-light brush of spiders' webs, the vibrations of jack-hammers, the humidity of tropical jungles, and the dawn-cool surface of moonlit lapis lazuli glimmering in the walls of the Taj Mahal. They heard country, Afrobeat, heavy metal, K-pop, string quartets, calypso, acid jazz, samba, and the sinuous melodies of Hindi ballads; and the roars of tigers and rioters, the crashing of waves and cars, freight train horns and burbling brooks; and the voices of birds and animals and even insects, all of it overlaying the scenes like context provided by commentators, which they may well have been. The whales apparently responsible for these very transmissions were seen from above as observed by avian reporters.

And it was not Earth alone featured in this show. Geezer's frame revealed exotic animated tableaux of solar dancers, including a Busby Berkeleyesque slowly spinning circle of interlocked aurorabirds in the sun's photosphere arrayed like the spokes of a great wheel at a ship's helm.

After letting his dumbstruck passengers marinate in wonder for a while, Geezer re-entered their consciousness with his gravelly basso profundo voice-over, schooling them in physics so far beyond "classical" as to make Marlie's elite seminars at Stanford look like monastic alchemy apprenticeships in the Middle Ages. Having read into the history of science on her own (and incidentally having lived through a honking paradigm-busting adventure in her teens), Marlie was less smug than many in her discipline about the durability of presently treasured tenets of physics. She was a soft target for Geezer's salvos aimed at the giants of the past, as well as the millions who'd been spoon-fed in school on their various dictates. "Don't be too surprised by violations of the supposed laws of physics you've witnessed so far," Geezer advised them. "There are more to come."

Marlie asked what that last remark was supposed to mean, but Geezer did not elaborate. "Isaac Newton was as ignorant as an oyster about X-rays," he pointed out. "It's of no concern to electromagnetic radiation that the man on the street is as oblivious to it as the Neanderthal before him. The cylinder puncturing Flatland doesn't care if some lowlife perceives it as a circular line.

"The understanding humans have of natural phenomena is limited by your stage of evolution. You two happen to be the first lucky ducks to have won a free chartered cruise to a world with a magnetic field that juices up the transmissions of intelligent animal reporters—signals that include electromagnetic stimuli not just for your vision but for all your senses!

"I know you're shaken as your old-hat science atavisms are quaking, kids. Your little bodies are surely churning up doubts and stomach acid. But in the face of startling new facts, you'd best let go of the tattered old myths your teachers taught you in school. Otherwise you're like bunnies convinced of a meadow's stillness, unaware that it's spinning at nearly a thousand miles an hour around the planet's axis and revolving sixty times faster around the sun."

Both Zeb and Marlie did feel their inner bunnies reeling, but Zeb, for the time being, kinda enjoyed it. What a trip! He wasn't used to real life presenting him with an adventure as wild as any he imagined as an artist. For Marlie, however, even as a veteran of intrasolar travel, this jolt was already the latest in a series of a-bit-too-muchness, and Geezer wasn't letting up.

Nor was Nikola. The big-screen extravaganza washing over them was a delightful example of the kind of work he'd been participating in for years as part of Earth's transmission network. But he hadn't forgotten why he'd been lured into this journey, and he erupted with a few hearty croaks to give Geezer a piece of his mind, which Zeb believed he himself understood.

"Mr. G, I grant this is humdinger entertainment," Zeb remarked. "Great score! But your accomplice here is raising a good point. This is hardly the punchline you were promising. Where is this grand show's target audience?"

"Hold on, young man—permit me to show you something."

As if we had a choice, Marlie commented to herself. Geezer swept them out of the beam and flew alongside it at a distance for a minute till it hit a broad crystalline surface angled at about forty-five degrees, from which it shot upward. They followed the beam to the top of the planet's atmosphere, at which point it appeared to vanish in the darkness of space, where methane molecules were few and far between.

Atop the Neptunian atmosphere, Geezer removed the plasma jar from his pocket and held it in front of him. Thankfully, he held it at arm's length, a quarter mile from his auroral face, permitting his captives to see his entire head, rather than treating them to an extreme close-up view of his gnarly nose. His three passengers readied themselves. *Here it comes—the reveal.*

"I searched all over Jupiter for almost two years without finding that whale's signal. I continued the quest on Saturn, and that failed too. Uranus was next, and again, zip. Even here on Neptune it took months of exploring before I finally came upon that beam—but as you can see, though it's a most colorful clue, it ain't the treasure. This doesn't tell us a thing about the Recipients because Neptune is only a booster that refracts the beam and relays the action somewhere else. So, I re-latched myself onto the beam and followed it out toward the Kuiper belt."

"Where Pluto hangs out?" Zeb asked Marlie.

"Pluto and thousands of other mini-planets, with plenty of methane."

"The Kuiper belt is immense. Taking some risks that I might lose track of it, I kept following that beam for a long time before I had to retreat because, even though the signal kept accelerating faster than ever, the journey dragged on endlessly. I'd spent all that time on the trail of these news junkies only to come up with another boatload of nothing. It seems like they really don't want the ants in the anthill to have any idea they're being watched. That must be why they set up the elaborate secret spy system with smart reporters and transmitters like Nikola and your mockingbird buddy." The frog jutted out his throat sac and his pancake chin with the pride of an aide-de-camp being praised by a dictator before a full military assembly.

"Well, I don't give up easy. The Recipients' determination to stay hidden only made me all the more determined to find them. To beat them at their game, I realized I'd have to change mine, so I returned here to Neptune to study the signal beam for clues.

"By then, nearly four Earth years had gone by since I'd persuaded our aurorabird to put you kids back where you belonged. For a couple of months, I scrutinized countless telecasts from those whales and their aurorabird counterparts without catching a break. The thought of giving up began to infect my mind, when suddenly the solution hit me in the eyes—an image appeared of your sister traipsing through the swamp with my old house in the background. The sight of that house sparked a real epiphany. I realized I'd built the answer to my problem into my lab long ago during the R&D for my portable artificial solar wind generator."

"Your what?"

"The device I brought to Antarctica. I had created a solar wind wave in an attempt to trigger whatever was responsible for the TSE ground grabs, but it turned out to have a very handy ancillary use out near the asteroids."

"You mean Wardenclyffe 3."

"Exactly."

"And why did you give it that name?" asked Marlie. Zeb knew that Marlie, to steady herself in the intensifying swells of uncertainty about what Geezer had up his gauzy sleeve, had grabbed onto the prospect of learning something about physics and the thinking of an Inventors Hall of Fame–class mind. Meanwhile, Zeb handled his own re-centering by surveying the constellations, which had been hidden from view when they were beneath the clouds. The three-billion-mile difference in vantage point as compared to what could be seen from Earth didn't seem to affect their appearance to Zeb. The closest star in Canis Major was still eighteen thousand times farther away from Earth than Neptune. For his part, Nik maintained his squatting stare at his revered leader.

"Wardenclyffe was the name Nikola Tesla gave to his fantastically ambitious creation on Long Island."

"His transmission tower, I know." Marlie didn't want Geezer thinking she was some illiterate science duffer.

"Wireless transmission of messages and images was the selling point he presented to investors and the press, but he had bigger plans for it. *Far* bigger. He was convinced he could grip an inherent electrical power of the planet itself that could be channeled into an energy source and a worldwide communications system that could be expanded to establish contact with civilizations on other planets."

The twins had known that, but they weren't about to interrupt Geezer again. Where was he going with this? Geezer was really getting fired up now, perhaps to amp up their enthusiasm for what lay ahead. He'd moved on to Tesla's work on non-dispersive charged-particle-beam projection and his scheme to accelerate tungsten particles to tremendous speeds with high-voltage electrostatic repulsion.

"Marlie, didn't you once say you thought Geezer had used tungsten in Wardenclyffe 3?"

"I suspected as much. It's a very special metal. It's got the highest melting point of all elements and a higher density than lead, on a par with gold and uranium, and yet it's still ductile."

"An A for the day, young lady," boomed Geezer. "You were holding an intricate bundle of the stuff when you zapped me in the asteroid belt."

"Not to be too blunt about it, Mr. G," nudged Zeb, "but Wardenclyffe 3 was smashed to smithereens on the Mexican coast years ago. So, what does any of this have to do with your grand epiphany seeing your house in one of Nik's reports, or your even grander scheme to unmask the Recipients?"

"Everything, my boy—because the only thing I could use to ride that signal beam all the way to the finish line is a similar device vastly more powerful than the one I brought to that iceberg, and now we've got it."

"Really? And what and where might that be?"

"It's called Wardenclyffe 2, friends, and you're standing in it!"

"Jesus!" hollered Marlie, bounding down the ladder. "I knew there was something familiar about this place!" Zeb felt the hairs on his neck rise. He watched his sister scurry around the lab, knowing she was looking for the old photo of Tesla's Wardenclyffe Tower in New York. While he awaited Marlie's return, he surveyed the metal wires laced through the tower's mushroom-cap dome. He craned his neck to look through the dome and down the sides of the tower below, appreciating for the first time the unusual shape of the structure—unusual, but not original, because, as Marlie's photo confirmed when she clambered up to his side, the lab that Geezer had built was a smaller but precise replica of Tesla's tower that had been demolished a century ago.

"You've been traveling in a 23.5 percent scale reproduction of Wardenclyffe Tower. Back in California, where it was camouflaged as a house, I even replicated Tesla's tunnel system."

"Tunnels?!"

"By 1904, Tesla had a shaft twelve stories deep dug into the earth on Long Island, from which a set of tunnels hundreds of feet long radiated out in every direction, all so he could field wires that he believed would grip the Earth's natural electric resonance, to serve as the tower's power source. I did likewise, with tunnels for my tungsten oxide cables extending beneath the lake in four directions, including one that went right under the spot where your parents built their house. When I plucked out the tower with you in it, the wires from the tunnels remained attached at the bottom of the tower. They're still connected to the caging laced into the tower walls and the rim of the metal oxide-treated conductive polycarbonate dome."

"Wires?" was the only question of the many tumbling around in Marlie's brain that found escape via her mouth.

"You may see them before long." That was the latest in a string of inscrutable pearls Geezer had been casting that called out for explanations, but Marlie abandoned herself to the information flow that Geezer alone controlled. "I needed to amplify plasmas in deep space, and Wardenclyffe 3 had proven it could do that when you zapped the radiolarian and then me. I'd had to sacrifice much of the capacity of the tower in miniaturizing the technology for the portable unit, but in that revelation here on Neptune, I realized that the tower's full power was there for the taking, back home."

"The tower's full power?" cried Marlie. "What are you talking about?!"

"I'm referring, children, to the nuclear reactor you'll find neatly tucked into the laboratory basement beneath you." Zeb and Marlie glanced down at the bottom of the lab and, without a word, hastened down the ladder from the mezzanine. The curious frog hopped along at their heels, as Geezer called after them, "And you, my dear colleagues, are going to operate it!"

As both Zeb and Marlie were reeling from the phrase *nuclear reactor*, Geezer carried on. "The micro-reactor of my own design is a central component of my invention, the NSAG—a Nuclear Simulated Aurora Generator. It's the heart of the system with which I created auroral charges during research and development of Wardenclyffe 3. The NSAG mimics solar winds with highly collimated femtosecond-scale megavolt pulses.

"We're at T-minus four minutes. If you'd be so kind, please take a Phillips screwdriver and the magnifying glass from the workbench and lift the circular steel plate on the lab floor between the workstation and the bed. That's the reactor chamber door."

"What, this manhole cover?"

"Lift it up by the handle in the center and climb down the ladder. Both of you."

Marlie looked to Zeb, wondering if he wanted to follow that order. He shrugged, "Might as well see what he wants us to do." He lifted the disk and slid it to the side. A metal ladder of the type that ascended to the top of the water tower outside of town (way back home) plunged into the technological abyss below. Zeb led the way down the ladder, followed by Marlie. Nik remained at the top, watching their every move.

"Pilot Man, find the junction box on the side of the NSAG near the ladder, about five feet up from the basement floor, and unscrew the moisture-proofing cover over the sliders that control the NSAG's polarity and charge level. You've got to set the charge level to fifteen percent above Minimum. That ought to do the trick."

"Just what trick might that be? Wardenclyffe 2 is a hundred times larger than Wardenclyffe 3."

"With electrons exiting through a hole in the drift tube plate, I'm expecting it will cause the tower to function like a vertical guided missile, adhering to the report signal-beam path like a maglev vactrain sliding through its tube." Zeb noted that Geezer had not commented on the size differential between the two models, nor was he leaving time for Zeb to pursue the point. "Inventor Lady, position yourself on the opposite side of the reactor, where you'll find the pulse duration control. Set that at five femtoseconds as soon as the polarity switch is moved all the way to the left. That setting must be changed within two seconds after the polarity is reversed. Immediately after that your brother can pull the power lever—that's the wide black acrylic handle next to the junction box."

"Exactly five femtoseconds? I can barely see that tiny gauge. Z, hand me the magnifying glass, willya?" Finding what she was after, she pocketed the glass and called up to Geezer. "These two sets of controls are only four feet apart. Couldn't one person do both?"

"I don't want to give a raw beginner too much to do. We can't afford any screwups here. Even if I dragged another couple of eager beavers out here from Earth, there's no replacing that laboratory."

Charmer, thought Marlie as she muttered, "W.T.F.?" Zeb permitted himself a half-grin at their situation's absurdity, which was growing exponentially.

"The moment that power switch is pulled, you've got to haul ass up the ladder and stand against the walls. A wide circle will open in the chamber floor, and the NSAG will take care of the rest." After a moment's silence, Geezer added, "I'd do it all myself but for my current lack of normal-sized meat hands. All we're after here is a few intelligent operations requiring fingers a tiny fraction of the size of mine."

"I see," Marlie called out, looking up through the manhole opening and dome to the top half of AuroraGeezer's gossamer face staring down at them. "It's for these few seconds of risky business that you dragged us three billion miles from home. Zeb and I are some ultimately replaceable flunkies in your ongoing R&D operation."

"Don't be foolish, little woman! Why would I subject my able assistants to a high risk of loss? I may need you for other tasks later as we up our game." At five-foot-eight, Marlie wasn't used to being called little, but the pointlessness of any objection now was only too clear. Geezer continued, "You should be thanking me. I selected you from a field of billions of human beings, and not just because I knew you could execute these maneuvers. I knew you would exult in our imminent triumphant victory!"

Really? I'm afraid that any exulting I do will be quickly punctured by another of your grand surprises.

"Now, there are a couple of things to keep in mind when we pull the trigger. There will be lightning-like electrical arcs shooting up toward the dome. They should be harmless for a short time, as long as you avoid direct contact with them."

"But of course. And the other?"

"I must admit that our positive experience with Wardenclyffe 3 is not a guarantee of just how this larger instrument will perform in our present circumstances, so it may be wise to expect the unexpected. But rest assured that I've got your back in case there are side effects that need attending to. Now, while I align your jar with the sun, kindly get cracking! That plasma jar you're in won't last forever."

Neither twin budged. "The nervous bunnies again! Shape up! We're on the verge of converting that laboratory tower into a guidance-system-equipped engine that can solve our entire trans-Neptunian transport problem. All you have to do is—"

"Look, Mr. Geezer," Zeb interrupted, "I've managed scores of aircraft landings in difficult conditions that no nervous bunny could handle, and I—"

"That's why I knew you were the man for the job." Zeb's silence over the following second gave Geezer leave to forge ahead, with evident pride in his brilliant NSAG lab repurposing scheme. "Along with you, Ms. Morell, being the woman for the job."

Marlie found this pandering totally transparent but was certain that Geezer knew as much and didn't care. She wanted badly to rip him for playing so cavalierly with their lives, but she knew that, after all the trouble he'd gone to to get this far, he was in no mood to change his mind. She asked Zeb, "What if we refuse?" but Geezer, operating with either super-hearing or telepathy, was on to her.

"Our interests are perfectly aligned, missy. You help me get to the end of this treasure hunt, share in the rewards of historic discovery, and then I'll do my best to help you get home."

Marlie took one more swing at getting Zeb to come up with an escape. "That plasma jar won't last forever?" she hissed. "What's *that* supposed to mean?! Is this jar just going to expire and leave us fast-frozen and blown around in Neptune's hurricanes?! Notice how Geezer words things: He's *expecting* the NSAG will cause the tower to function like a guided missile. *He'll do his best* to help us get home. Setting the charge at the level he's guessing at *ought* to do the trick. And, by the way, *what trick*? The electrical arcs *should* be harmless. There *might be side effects* that will need attending to. *Expect the unexpected. There are no guarantees.* If we get fried, *there's no replacing the laboratory.* And what's he got in mind for *later as we up our game?*"

"Good questions, Marles."

"We could be in the auroral hands of a crazed killer."

"Geezer's too smart and devoted an explorer to think so destructively."

"Are you kidding? Tesla dreamed up superweapons. So did Leonardo da Vinci. What about all the physics heroes at Los Alamos? Who knows what Geezer might want to entertain himself with out in deep space all by his lonesome for years on end? And maybe he has no idea that he's either crazy or a killer or both."

For Zeb, the intellectual thrill ride of this adventure and the firm grip of realism mitigated the desperation taking hold of Marlie. He put his hands on her shoulders. "Do we really have a choice here, Sis? We're billions of miles from anything and everything but this."

"Chop, chop!" Geezer bellowed from above. Marlie could feel the final sand grains falling through the hourglass before they would fulfill the destiny Geezer had forced on them. She saw (as did Zeb, more than he would let on) the whole trip to the sun when they were seventeen in a disturbing new light. What had seemed for four years as a nearly cataclysmic life event against which all future dramatic events would unavoidably be measured was now no more than a blipping precursor to whatever this would turn out to be. Zeb glanced her way before unscrewing the cover to the polarity and charge sliders. Marlie felt the jar move. Looking out through the dome, she saw that Geezer was lining up the jar with the sun. She was about to ask him why when Geezer's staticky vocal rumbles vibrated her body again as he barked, "Let's hit it!" She yielded to Fate gripping her hand and placing it on the pulse duration control. A moment before she turned it, she heard one last announcement from on high.

"Oh—that punchline? Coming right up!"

17

A nerve-jangling rumble emanated from beneath their feet. Vibrations shaking the floor and their bones made them splay themselves against the chamber walls (*the Gravitron again!*), which were vibrating too. A spark arced up from the hole in the floor toward the dome, followed by another and then a steady stream.

Oh, Tesla would have doffed his cap at this, thought Marlie, *but no amazement is worth dying for.* The wire-lacing in the dome was glowing—perhaps she could get a better glimpse of the effect of all this voltage up there if she edged a little closer to the stream while peering upward. She inched closer . . .

"Marlie!"

Zeb felt the upratcheting power of the vibrations and the disturbing proximity of his sister to the supercharged cool fire, and when he saw her stumble at the next temblor, he shot across the floor and managed to pull her back, only to fall partly into the brilliant geyser himself.

"Zeb!"

"Uh-oh!" he uttered as he felt a great chill radiate through his body. "Get back!" he roared, "It's . . . SHOCKING!"

Marlie froze in horror as she watched her brother tremble and glow, becoming larger by the second, towering over her at a height of ten feet, turning diaphanous as his head reached the ceiling, his entire body enlarging exponentially far beyond the boundaries of the lab, the plasma jar, and out into space, his sneakered feet now three stories high and growing. Her brother, whom she'd been almost as close to in the twenty-one years since her birth as during the nine months before it, was *becoming aurorized.*

"Holy God!" Zeb hollered, now nearly the four-thousand-foot height of Geezer, who looked on, impressed, at the shining jar he was still holding at arm's length. After casting an angry glance at Geezer, Zeb leaned over to look into the jar, now so small compared to himself that he could place it in his own jacket pocket if he so chose. "Marlie!"

Inside the jar, Marlie scrambled up the ladder to the dome, breathless, wide-eyed, and wary of the spark stream shooting up nearby. She was hoping for a wider view of her brother and the ancient specter she saw as their tormentor. "Zeb! Zeb!" she cried. *"What the hell?!"*

His voice came through the dome, tense and loving. "I've got this, Marles!" She saw him rise up and grab Geezer's left forearm and reach for the plasma jar, only to be blocked by Geezer's right. Zeb, still gymnastics-agile, darted under Geezer's arm, shot his hand to the jar, and stole it. He moved away from Geezer and slowly reached his fingertips to the plasma boundary. Necessity having mothered an instantaneous adjustment to his new incarnation, he reached ever so carefully inside the open dome window and took hold of Marlie's tiny hand with his gigantic fingertips. It reminded him of having once rescued a mosquito hawk by taking hold of the tip of one of its legs. "This was for the best, Marlie," he called down to her in his staticky voice. "I'll deal with Geezer, and you will get home!"

"Not alone, I won't!" she shouted back as she jumped into the spark stream, immediately taking on the brilliant spark-fueled glow all over her body, then expanding and swiftly outgrowing the lab and the jar, rising in space as an aurorized young woman, still and forever her twin brother's teammate.

As Geezer looked on, Zeb handed him the unpeopled but still glowing plasma jar and embraced his sister. Her eyes shone with the first aurorized tears in the history of the solar system.

Zeb pulled back enough to look at Marlie and plastered an ambivalent grin on his face. "Your first spacewalk!"

Another Zeb stab at humor in the face of real trouble, a familiar gesture from the persona she had nicknamed Wittydumdum when they were in junior high. She shook her head in silent appreciation till their moment was interrupted by the bellowing alert from Geezer as he held the plasma jar out in front of him once more. "She's gonna blow!"

The plasma jar filled with phosphorescent silver light and caused the tower within to expand far beyond the jar, swallowing Geezer's hand and arm and all three of its original human passengers. The entire core of Geezer's old island house rebirthed itself as an aurorized tower with Marlie, Geezer, and Zeb now enveloped within it, afloat just beneath the dome and slowly, out of habit, settling down to the floor, where Geezer dropped the now humanless little jar.

Zeb was pleased to see Marlie chuckling to herself. Between the spectacle of the largest dwelling in human history (ten miles in height, Zeb estimated), the possibility that they were now inhabiting what Geezer had described as an electromagnetic guided missile, and the total craziness of their situation, Marlie's central nervous system had hit a mandatory laugh switch. Zeb's spirits elevated with Marlie's, despite it all.

"Hey, check out that spark stream on the dome, Marlie. It's got the tungsten veins up there glowing like the radial canals in the exumbrella of a jellyfish. And get a load of what's hanging out of the bottom of this thing!" Since the floor, like the tower's walls, was also now auroral, they could see long tendrils extending beneath the tower. "Those must be the tungsten oxide cables Geezer told us he'd laid into his tunnels under the island and lake back home."

"BING!" Geezer had apparently decided that Zeb's smarts deserved a quiz-show reward chime. Marlie was irritated by the sound, and irritated at herself for being gratified by it.

"They look like jellyfish tentacles." Zeb looked to Geezer. "Gotta admit—nice design, bro!"

"I can't say I envisioned the place looking quite this impressive when I built it, but thank you. Now if you'll excuse me, an NSAG adjustment must be made."

As Geezer descended to the NSAG chamber, Zeb joined Marlie in taking in the view, which became easier to behold once Geezer halted the upward charge from the reactor. The transparent auroral lab walls permitted a stirring view of the vistas of Neptune, the solar system, and the stars, while thin luminescent currents laced around them like nerve charges extending all the way from the tungsten "tentacles" beneath the lab floor up through the walls to the dome.

Then the whole place began to rise upward like a rocket at liftoff. Geezer returned to the lab and nodded appreciatively at his surroundings and the mile-and-a-half-diameter dome overhead. "Home sweet home!" he exclaimed.

The new reality was still sinking into Marlie's consciousness. Her auroral being looked at Geezer for the first time in stunned dismay. "You knew this was going to happen all along!"

Taking in the somber expression on her transmogrified face, Geezer paused his meditation on his wondrous success, composed himself, and graciously managed an acknowledgment of the crisis into which he'd thrust his young companions. "It occurred to me it was possible. I understand if you're a bit rattled, but my money says you'll thank me later." Seemingly on cue—whether in confirmation or mockery—the whole tower, an obelisk of auroral light, began to slip upward ever more swiftly away from both Neptune and the sun, toward the still more distant stars. "Settle in for the ride, kids. You done good and deserve the payoff coming your way."

18

The sight of the starfield sliding downward in opposition to the tower's upward trajectory had made Geezer forget all about his one-time ally. He looked down at the floor, scanning the corners of his auroral lab. "Say, what happened to our friend Nikola? I'd have thought he'd have joined the party by now."

Marlie wasn't moved to join the search, but Zeb glanced at the floor under the table and found it frogless. "I guess he croaked."

Marlie rolled her eyes. A kind chuckle was out of the question. *It's way too soon for jokes about death, Wittydumdum, even a good one, which that wasn't. The croaker we have to worry about is the grim one with a scythe. Don't you smell him?*

Geezer shook his head in pity. "Poor little buffo. He deserved a crack at this after all he'd done for us."

As the tower's pace accelerated upward, Marlie turned her attention back to Geezer. "Precisely what's the 'this' Nik's missing a crack at, if I may ask?"

"An interstellar journey culminating in discovery of the Recipients, little lady."

Marlie's eyes narrowed. "What do you mean 'interstellar'? The nearest star is more than *four years away at the speed of light!*" As Geezer considered his reply, Marlie noticed her brother's consternation. He was aware of the basic facts, but she decided to underscore them for him. "If you reduce our entire solar system to the size of a baseball field, the nearest star is ten miles away." She was ambivalent about hitting him with that downer analogy but felt justified by a growing urge to rope Zeb into coming up with a potent countermeasure, pronto.

Geezer's counter-countermeasure instincts were in full swing. "You can't assume anything about how far away the Recipients reside," he remarked. "For all you know, we'll come upon them in the next five minutes."

Zeb swallowed, signaling his agreement with Marlie's assessment of the gravity of their situation. She called his attention to the constellations overhead in their direction of travel. "Check out the Doppler effect on the starlight."

Light coming from Scorpio, Sagittarius, Capricorn, and other nearby constellations that Zeb knew as well as he knew the features of their backyard looked slightly repositioned and a bit bluish. Behind them, Gemini, the twins' stellar mascot, appeared to be contracting and somewhat reddened. No funnies from Zeb about that: their velocity had increased and was still increasing.

Geezer roamed around his former home and took a deep breath of satisfaction. "Yep, the last time the three of us were together inside this laboratory, you were scattering like cockroaches. Now you stand on the brink of cosmic discovery."

Marlie was not in the mood to partake of Geezer's chatter. Under her breath she suggested to Zeb that they take advantage of their newfound powers. Asking him to follow her, she floated up past the lab's mezzanine to the dome. Zeb tagged along, unable to suppress his delight at the easiest flight of his life. Ensconced in a spot beyond Geezer's hearing range, Marlie scanned down her gigantic diaphanous body and murmured, "I've got to admit that being light enough to fly feels great, but I have no intention of thanking His Craziness, because the odds of our getting home safely have just plummeted from point oh one to point *oh shit!*"

"I don't think we should discount the possibility that His Craziness might yet help us. Last time he seemed to think deaurorization was possible. He wanted us to use Wardenclyffe 3 on him to pull it off."

"Unless that was a load of b.s. he was feeding us to get us to do what he wanted."

"Maybe, but don't forget that last time he did save us from a permanent fate as Shang's prisoners. And if there were anything to his deaurorizing theory, this honking SuperWardenclyffe might somehow be put to good use. Assuming we make it back to Earth, of course."

Far behind the tower's transparent walls, stars slid slowly downward, passing from view vertically at the casual pace of farmhouses sliding past your window during a ride through the countryside. Marlie felt the blood in her face drain in the same direction, toward her solar plexus. "There are so many stars directly underneath us, I'm having trouble visually tethering us to the sun."

"It would be unwise to get lost."

"Very. We must at least commit this arrangement of stars to memory. The sun is located in a part of the Milky Way called the Orion Arm, and if this flying crib keeps on keeping on, we may need that image as a landmark to find our way home."

"Yes, my friends," began Geezer, adopting the regal demeanor of a famous professor, accustomed to decades of adulation, leading a nature seminar on board an alumni cruise motoring up the Amazon. "Our familiar constellations—Cassiopeia, Pegasus, Andromeda—they're all dissipating. But those are just doodles perceived by the local yokels of Earth. One achieves a new perspective on things out here." He pointed grandly to a tuft of fuzzy starlight high up behind them. "Except, naturally, the Andromeda Galaxy. That belle hasn't budged."

"Of course not," snapped Marlie. "It's a hundred thousand times farther away. If that's your idea of cheerful news, kindly keep it to yourself." She noticed in Zeb's expression a conflicting mix of bemusement and serious concern. She lowered her voice. "Finding the sun, and therefore Earth, again is going to be a bitch. Dead reckoning where X marks the spot will be as worthless as Hansel and Gretl's bread crumbs. That doesn't seem to be a problem for Geezer, though. What evidence is there he ever intended to help us get back this time?"

"Hard to believe he'd want to be cooped up with us in this thing for the rest of his life. He's got something in mind. Otherwise he'd have devised a way to dump us and keep his towermobile to himself."

"Wow, that's reassuring. You're convinced Geezer's not envisioning our future as frozen corpses wafting through the Kuiper belt. But consider: being conscripted as his Igor and Igorella to do flunky chores for him for the next nine years might not be any better."

"Yes, sir, and mademoiselle," Geezer piped up from below. "You and I stand atop the mountain separating the Valleys of Ignorance and Revelations. We're on the verge of becoming the first formerly Earthly souls to learn the identity of the Recipients and their reason for collecting all the information the animals of our former habitat have labored so long and hard to provide them."

"Frankly, my dear, I don't give a damn," replied Marlie at a volume barely loud enough for Geezer to hear. He looked up at her and shook his head in sorrowful pity before turning back to enjoy the magnificent illusion of the stars slow-falling around them.

"You don't?" asked Zeb, surprised. "I mean, you give at least a little bitty damn, right? I do."

"I might, if I thought about it, but at the moment I'm a little preoccupied with the scenery. We're moving at unnerving velocity and still accelerating. Is this thing going to exceed the speed of light?"

Marlie had ceased whispering and thus enabled Geezer to hear her. From his position down on the lab floor, roaming around to catch the view of different parts of the starfield, he called up, "Who knows, children? We're proving that the possibilities for interstellar travel are limitless."

Well aware of how Geezer's comments would roil his sister, Zeb watched the scrum of emotions playing on her face and tried to figure out how to respond. Marlie wasn't used to being treated like a naïve ninny, much less a child, when it came to things astronomical, or otherwise. Yet he knew that Geezer's trashing of Einsteinian orthodoxy about the impossibility of anything exceeding the speed of light had some traction in her thinking. She'd expounded on the subject just a few weeks ago, while sipping espresso with him and Alyssa at a North Beach café. "I love Einstein, but that absolutist papal bull about the impossibility of anything exceeding the speed of light smacks of epic, blinders-on presumptuousness," she'd declared. "It's like a revered baboon elder telling the other baboons that nothing in the universe can exceed the speed of a cheetah. You'd think Einstein would have learned from Copernicus and Newton that the truth of a scientist's discoveries might be contextual."

"Maybe you were right about the need to edit the cosmic speed limit out of the rule book Marles. And why not?" Zeb asked. "Scientific revolutions, paradigm shifts—they're part of the game, right?"

"Word!" declaimed Geezer from below, apparently confident that his young listeners would understand that he was mocking a linguistic fad they might fancy while simultaneously applauding the wisdom of Zeb's observation.

"Wow," exclaimed Zeb. "I'd never have guessed that the hermit keeper of Geezer Castle knew any voguey pop culture claptrap."

Geezer hopped up to the dome and alighted so close to the twins that his intense eyes burrowed into theirs. "For months I've been certain that aurorization would intensify not just matter but also forces, like the thrust from the

NSAG. In this frictionless environment, we should be able to keep on accelerating well past the speed of light, and when that happens—"

A shock wave smacked into the tower, knocking all three of them together and off the dome sill into floating chaos. In a few seconds they recombobulated themselves and discovered that the starfield below the tower had disappeared. The stars ahead of them were turning bluer and flooding past in a cataract so torrential that individual points of light could no longer be discerned any more than individual water droplets in the middle of Class VI rapids on the Snake River. But beneath—and behind—them was total darkness.

"There you have it, folks," Geezer continued. "You've just experienced the visual equivalent of a sonic boom! Those poor little photons behind us can't keep up. The speed of light is for wimps!"

Zeb awaited Marlie's reaction. She had fixed Geezer in a silent stare. "Looks like our game's been upped, Marles."

Still staring at Geezer, Marlie replied, "Mr. Geezer, I hope that your boundless enthusiasm hasn't made you forget your promise to get us back home. And by 'us,' I'm referring to our flesh-and-blood incarnations."

"I said I'd do my best, and that only after we got to the Recipients."

"We may have a long way to go, so we can hardly afford to drag this out with a lengthy side trip."

"You knew this too was going to happen."

"Well, I hoped. And I figured you'd appreciate this voyage as much as I do."

"Hogwash."

Despite the shock of recent events, Zeb was sufficiently centered to see that his sister was heading further into anti-diplomatic territory that could prove perilous. "Marlie—"

"All he ever wanted was for us to help him get his homemade rocket launched, no expenses, *such as us*, spared."

A cloud of annoyance gathered over Geezer's brow.

"Listen, Punkette—"

"My name is Marlie."

"A little respect, mister," added Zeb with a set chin.

"I'm getting tired of your whining. I had the impression I was recruiting a real astrophysicist for the apprenticeship of the millennium, someone who fancied herself hankering for a run to Jupiter. At least that's the impression I got from Special Agent Nikola. Well, you're an astronaut now, both of you.

We're breaking into territory that's remained hidden from view throughout the known history of intelligent life.

"Yes, I've given some thought to assisting you in your quest to return to your childhood home, but things have changed now, and if that plan becomes obsolete, you should damn well be glad of it. I have enabled you two to achieve liberation from your stunted meat form to one vastly more powerful. *You're virtually invincible!* And if the trip home is no longer on the itinerary, so what?! Now you can remain powerful and free till the day you die! And maybe this way you'll never die—I haven't aged a day in four years!"

Marlie responded, "Gee, Coach—that's swell! I'll make ya proud if ya put me in the lineup, I swear!"

Zeb winced. This was not the tone needed to effect the change in Geezer's mindset she was seeking.

"You're in it, sister," replied the guy who was absolutely not her brother. Zeb was about to take Marlie aside for some strategic brainstorming, when Geezer continued. "More than you realize." Geezer floated in even closer. "Let me clue you in on what I'm pretty sure is going on here.

"Long before this reunion, I suspected that my search for the Recipients was being aided by an unknown physical force. I told you that when I left Neptune on that initial search I could feel the massive signal stream that had been refracted from the planet into deep space, even though, without methane, I couldn't see or hear the imagery it contained. I was riding the groove of a carrier wave that I was sure would lead straight to my destination. And you'll recall that my flight was proceeding a lot faster than I could manage on my own. In fact, it was steadily accelerating. It was inescapable that something was pulling the signal stream with such force that it threatened to exceed the speed of light.

"That whetted my appetite all the more. Once I flashed on the potential synergy of putting an NSAG vessel into that high-powered slipstream, I had to get my hands on this laboratory. And thank God I did, because, as you've seen, we've busted Einstein's speedometer already and there's no stopping us now. We've boarded a non-stop flight to Recipientland!"

Zeb had to stop himself from smiling. A dash of humor helped the Grand Guignol medicine go down, but a glance at his sister brought home the gravity of their plight. He could see that even Marlie felt some excitement about the prospect of solving a great mystery in the very near future, but every second racing in that direction diminished the odds of their ever resuscitating their Earthly lives, and that was disturbing and oppressively sad.

Zeb floated back down to the lab floor, pretending to want a different view of the stars tearing downward into darkness outside the diaphanous tower walls. "Hey, Marlie—check this out," he called. She left Geezer up at the dome, relieved to be away from him, and joined her brother below.

"How're you doing?" he asked.

"Sick to my stomach."

"Specifically because . . . "

"Because I've just recognized the significance of the starscape we saw above us when the tower got on its way, out of Neptune."

"You mean the zodiac?"

"It wasn't just some random part of the zodiac, Zeb. We were headed toward Sagittarius."

"Sagittarius became indiscernible long ago."

"Yeah, because the stars that make up the constellation were relatively close to our solar system, which we've left very far behind. But we haven't changed direction, and there's only one destination I can think of thataway."

"Which is?" Zeb asked.

"Sagittarius A-Star."

"Sounds like a club on the Sunset Strip."

"No, Zeb."

"I didn't really think so," said Zeb. Some glum peeked through his veneer of good cheer.

"The name Sagittarius A-Star was chosen because Sagittarius is the constellation in the direction you'd have to travel from our solar system to get to it. It's the black hole at dead center of the galaxy. The Milky Way's Grand Central Station, with all arrivals and no departures."

Zeb's optimism division shut down. He had nothing to say.

"More than that, what Geezer said makes me think it's a black hole with a special kind of attractor in it."

"Attractor?"

"An attractor exerts a tremendous pull on its surroundings, beyond anything else we know of. One in intergalactic space is called the Laniakea Supercluster, but maybe there's one in the Milky Way that draws in the signal stream that Earth's animal reporters and the solar aurorabirds have been sending out, pulling them in at superluminal speed. Since we're riding the stream's carrier wave, it's pulling us its way too and making us speed past the stars at such an incredible rate. Plus, you see the fuzzy waves in this star stream?"

"I've been noticing them."

"My bet is that, in this high-speed aurorized condition, our vision is picking up on other electromagnetic wavelengths outside our normal visual range, like X-rays and ultraviolet and gamma radiation."

"Trippy." Zeb's comment managed to nudge Marlie's dormant smile muscles, but the effect didn't last long.

"'Trippy' is what the guys in my platoon said about the flares we sent up over the bridges at night in Nam, if they'd gotten into some acid behind my back." The twins looked up at Geezer, who was surveilling them from the mezzanine.

If the twins hadn't already felt off-center, that random remark would have done the trick. For one thing, they could hardly believe the old man had disclosed something about his past besides his astronomical obsessions—that was a first. Worse, he left them feeling uncertain as to whether he'd made his comment in derision, an attempt at humor, a reminder that he was watching them, or expressly to elbow them off balance. On instinct they both chose the same response—none—in favor of maintaining their focus on the crisis at hand.

"I was just trying to look on the bright side," Zeb explained to his sister.

"Trippy, maybe, but scary, definitely. We've got very little time left to come up with a way to avoid being engulfed and no doubt annihilated in a supermassive black hole."

Nonetheless, the crisis they had to focus on was steamrolling them into a state of glumness rather than brainstorming fervor. They looked through the tower walls and stared for a minute at the stars passing by like a waterfall of sparkling hailstones.

Marlie broke the silence. "Whatever we do, we'll have to retain the capacity to achieve superluminal speed. There's a good chance we're already ten thousand light years from the solar system. And that's not all. How is somebody in this shape supposed to survive? What do we eat?"

"Maybe as auroral beings we derive our energy from light. I didn't notice any snack bars on the sun."

"How do we know that our fate isn't to fade away or deflate to tiny nothingness?"

"As Old Geeze pointed out, he hasn't lost a candela in four years. And I doubt that the tower twins will collapse."

"I'd love to get a heaping portion of your cleverness once we find safe harbor. Preferably one on the California coast."

Zeb sighed, acknowledging the gravity of their situation. Then he tilted his head and furrowed his brow in a way Marlie recognized from having observed him many times in the throes of creative inspiration. Then a smile crept slowly over his facial landscape. "Time for an exit strategy, all right," said Zeb in a hushed tone as he put his thousand-foot-long arm on her shoulders, "and I just might have one."

The twins sat together in the dome watching Geezer meander about the mezzanine, apparently—or pretending to be—examining the star flow from different directions. They had the distinct impression he was getting suspicious and trying to overhear them. Zeb started conversing with Marlie about the stellar scenery in low tones, hoping to dissuade Geezer from conflating quiet speech with the murmurings of conspiracy, which was in fact just moments away. They reduced their voices to a level of whisper-plus.

They knew that, in a crisis like this, Marlie's edge in physics and (non-aviation) technology would be matched by Zeb's in creative problem-solving and keeping his cool, a role that included optimizing his sister's state of mind. "Let's work the problem, people."

His subtle reference to Marlie's NASA heroes at the peak of their Apollo 13 crisis had the desired effect on her, shoring up her confidence and determination. She'd need plenty of both to withstand his imminent proposal.

"Hear me out," he began. From his jacket pocket, Zeb plucked the pen and the drawing he'd made of Shangrilarian facing down an enemy fighter pilot. In three minutes, he embellished it with his signature special visual effects that could connote sound and movement with line and shading alone to convey vibrant non-verbal abstractions. The drawing swiftly took on shattering elegance in the creature's dynamic pose, the ear-splitting sound of the aircraft engine going kablooey, and high-powered vibrancy in the expressions of both characters—the pilot's stunned shock and admiration and Shangrilarian's exultation in projecting his martial dance power.

Zeb almost blushed at Marlie's quiet "Whew." He thought she sounded like an aspiring NBA draftee witnessing Michael Jordan on court for the first time around 1984. He hoped that augured well for her being in a receptive mood for his scheme.

"Point number one: Even as a rookie auroraman, I've still got dexterous hands; hold that thought.

"Now if I really want to put Shangrilarian to the test, I could make the pilot and his aircraft into a dynamic duo with their own special powers. In the next panel we could see something like this at the plane's tail." He sketched a quick rendition of the plane ducking away from its tormentor. The pilot had clambered out onto an exhaust plume of vibrating rays of light extending from the tail engine and was turning the plane by pulling on the rays as if they were the reins of a chimerical fighter-jet stallion.

"If the pilot's strong enough, he could exert enough force on those rays to direct his aircraft like a cowboy maneuvering his horse at full gallop." He looked up with a wide-eyed smile at his nonplussed sister, gulping in apprehension. "It can totally work, Marles! This tower is a virtually massless auroral rocket, and I could turn it around with controlled pulls on the tungsten cables beneath it. We can head back to the Orion Arm, which would at least give us a shot at finding our sun. It can't be much harder than some situations I've handled with a sailplane. Did I ever tell you about the time I had to sheer off a landing when a newbie pilot, who was as out of control as a panicked skier, cut me off thirty feet above the landing strip?"

"Yes, dear brother, more than once. And I'd like to be able to hear it many more times over the next eight decades, but I'm quite afraid that this wacky scheme of yours will reduce that opportunity to eight minutes. This isn't a comic book."

"You mean 'graphic novel,' I presume. And I'm well aware that there are risks. But I'm also well aware that we'll have to take some chances if we don't want to find ourselves very far up Shit Creek.

"Now listen: There's a ventilation opening in the basement floor right behind the NSAG, and I can slither through there, climb out on the tungsten cables, and get a good hold of a couple of them in each hand, just enough to put this tower into a turn. You can help navigate to confirm when I've made a one-eighty, and from there it should be a straight shot. Hopefully."

Marlie shook her head in split wonder. Zeb's plan was breathtakingly far-fetched, a surefire bet to break the record for craziest idea-that-just-might-work. Except for one factor.

"Say, brother, that's mighty nifty, but one question lurks: How is your rodeo event going to be affected by Geezer catching you torpedoing the greatest dream of his life?"

"That could prove challenging, but you can put up a screen for me. I've got to steer."

"A screen. Do you remember the term 'SuperGeezer'?"

"Yeah, he's stronger than you, but he's still an old man and you're a twenty-one-year-old gymnast. Outmaneuver him."

"May I remind you that the last time we met up with Geezer he was about as decrepit as Bruce Lee at the height of his powers and, as he has modestly pointed out, he hasn't declined an iota?"

"So, dazzle him. You've got your own Shangrilarian moves. Hit him with an Arabian double half-out."

"Geezer's an auroraman now, Zeb. He can do tricks more dazzling than that, as we saw in his battle with Shang."

"None of that would matter if we can just wrest control of this thing long enough to reverse course. That's got to convince him that we're serious. Now that we've helped him get this rocket off the ground, he shouldn't need us any longer. He'll probably be thrilled to have us out of his hair."

"I have a feeling that your case has a lot of invisible holes in it."

"The only hole you should be thinking about now is the black one straight ahead."

That sank into Marlie's ruminations for a moment, after which she asked, "Well, even if this dicey scheme of yours works to get us back to our solar system, what about the tiny detail of deaurorization?"

"That's got to be faced at some point, so the sooner the better's what I think. Geezer had a theory about how to pull it off back when we were returning from the sun."

"That was with Wardenclyffe 3. Wardenclyffe 2 is a different animal."

"Geezer's the guy to ask about that. He's the expert on all post-Tesla Wardenclyffes. We can work out those details once we're in the right part of the galaxy. Now, the man said he would help us get back, and the time for that has come. At the rate we're going, the danger pile is only getting higher by the minute."

After a pause and a sigh, Marlie muttered, "Ooookay."

"All right, then." Pretending to be enthralled by the starry scenery, Zeb passed by Marlie, muttering, "Cover me as best you can." As he ambled over to the entry to the basement, feigning enchantment, for Geezer's benefit, with the star flow outside, his peripheral vision revealed that the old man was watching him. The tension ratcheted up. *Make your move now or never.*

He dropped into the reactor chamber, and a moment later Geezer shot past Marlie in hot pursuit. After a quick freeze from embarrassment at the fantasy that she could have effectively blocked Geezer—she pictured herself trying to block a star NFL running back—she dove down to the chamber and slipped past Geezer through the vent opening.

Outside on the tendrils stretching many miles beneath the tower, she was caught short again, this time by the sight of the rushing star stream, now more brilliant than ever, unfiltered by the gauzy auroral tower walls. Zeb was already pulling on the tungsten reins, causing the starfield to appear to sweep upward as the tower veered down toward the darkness beneath them.

Marlie crawled across the vibrating tendrils toward Zeb, struck by the weirdness of moving at such astounding speed out in the open without feeling any wind. She heard nothing but a staticky hum of the vibrating wires, topped by the guttural shouts of Geezer, who had anchored himself to the tower's bottom rim above them. "You idiots! Get back in here! This reactor puts out intensifying pulses under pressure! You could lose your grip and never be seen again!"

Realizing she should have anticipated that danger, Marlie hollered to Zeb to abort the mission. He called back, "I'm almost—" but whatever he had intended to say was lost as a jolt of electricity shot through her from her hands and feet right through her torso and head, causing her to lose her grip and her connection to the tower. She rapidly decelerated from superluminal velocity and drifted alone as dark space was repopulated with millions of stars. She frantically called out Zeb's name, but he had vanished, along with the tower, unleashing a chilling tsunami of loss that swept over her. Whether or not death awaited just around the corner was irrelevant, since a life from which Zeb had been permanently excised would be too awful to endure.

19

Marlie's incipient grief began to lift like the fog departing San Francisco Bay on a summer afternoon, for destiny had another trick up its sleeve. As she decelerated from the momentum of the NSAG-powered tower, she beheld something that, for all she knew, had never been seen directly by another living organism. She was nearing an immense nebula of glorious colors, light years across, very like the subject of the revered photograph dubbed *Pillars of Creation*, which was pieced together in the '90s from Hubble photographs aimed at the Eagle Nebula. By comparison, the most stupendous mushroom clouds of hydrogen bomb tests were as impressive as a fluff of dust kicked up by a beetle in her mother's garden back home. Gleaming through the dark and colorful flora of the cloud were infant stars, igniting into life in a stellar nursery. *What a way to go . . .*

Marlie flashed on her brother, perhaps similarly adrift in deep space, and hoped that at least, amidst his own lonely loss, he too could cast his eyes on this magnificent wonder. Zeb's prodigious imagination had produced some amazing treats for the mind's eye, but they can't compare to this feast for real eyes as she entered the nebula.

While the enchanting vista couldn't eliminate the hollow of grief for losing her brother, it did provide a bridge of wondrous distraction that begged further investigation. She flew into the cosmic seedbed arrayed in reds, golds, and purples, where she could see hundreds of stars in various stages of gestation and birth. She continued to slow, looking forward to her first moment of stillness since she had been aurorized. She had almost reached that tempting equipoise when a bright ray of light crossed her path up ahead, a beam that bore an unmistakable resemblance to the one Geezer had introduced her and Zeb to in the upper atmosphere of Neptune. There would be plenty of opportunity for stillness and meditation later on; this pulsing beam demanded examination now.

The closer she got to it, the more enticing it became. If it indeed were a signal stream, perhaps she might yet detect signs of life before she faded out (if that's how aurorized beings give up their ghosts). It was broad in scope, miles in diameter, like the one they'd observed on Neptune. And as she rounded the corner, entering the beam itself and facing it head on, she saw that this one, too, was heaving with a wild flood of images from Earth. In fact, the stream of images depicted home! It was hard to recognize at first her parents' little pocket of Sonoma County, but there it was. In the middle of what should have been yet another silent night, it was crawling with cars and fire engines and satellite trucks and reporters and looky-loos shooting cell phone videos and a helicopter training several thousand watts of searchlight power down on the wreckage of Geezer's cored-out house, with a huge hole in the middle reaching way down into the Earth. Marlie couldn't make out whether or not Relura and her parents were in the crowd, but one thing was clear: the secrecy with which she and her siblings had shrouded the story of their first extraterrestrial extraction could never exist for their second.

By applying her hands to the signal stream as Geezer had on Neptune, Marlie isolated and slowed a small sector of the stream to better absorb its details. A dashboard video from some random car showed their extraction from Geezer's house at the moment Geezer had shaken the tower before enveloping it in its transparent plasma jar and zooming off into interplanetary space. And—*oh, boy*—there at the top in the dome window itself were Zeb and herself looking down at Relura and their parents exiting the car in dismay. Another shot from overhead showed the house's ripped-out core. Geezer had really blown up his secret life now, and perhaps along with it civilization's foundational self-image, for television stations around the world were now broadcasting an abduction of human beings by a strange life form from space.

Other shockers were piling up like a mass collision on an icy freeway. Scenes from Europe, Africa, and Asia, then in daylight, revealed intelligent animals so freaked out that their secrecy protocols were beginning to break down. Amateur and pro news gatherers were broadcasting and live-streaming shots of animal councils in crisis mode, with the likes of bats and snarling canines trying to fend off the photographers. In one, by a savannah riverside, an elephant, a baboon, a gazelle, and a flamingo clustered around a white rhinoceros in heated discussion. Marlie knew that intelligent animals might confer with each other—she'd seen birds do so on the Antarctic iceberg—but a sage rhinoceros elder?! *They had me fooled.* But then she remembered Mock's explanation that high intelligence in animals, while extremely rare, occurred in many different species. Most rhinos were doubtless as dumb as they appeared to be, including the ones hunkered among the scores of nonplussed animals looking on and trying to make sense of the council.

Another scene showed a hawk, a robin, a woodpecker, a sparrow, and a seagull chattering intensely among each other on the Eiffel Tower while dumbfounded tourists stared, agape. In another scene from within the ocean, a sperm whale held court over a motley undersea assemblage including a sea tortoise with a starfish on its back, a steelhead, a surgeonfish, an octopus, and a sea lion, while anxious marine neighbors swam around in ragged circles. On a jungle riverbank, a tarsier with a pen and paper was caught on camera scribbling notes or sketching while a crocodile, a lorikeet, and an elephant gabbled away until the photographer sneezed, causing the animals to scatter. The tarsier first tried to hide the pen and paper under a rock before taking another quick look at the photographer, squeaking, and grabbing his stash and running off.

The timing of this eruption of distress among intelligent animals can't be a coincidence, thought Marlie. Whatever's bugging these creatures has got to have something to do with Mock having witnessed us being been yanked off the planet by an enormous aurorized hand and the gushing viral video streams that followed.

Whatever the cause, the panic was spreading to normal animals too. Bewildered beasts were seeking security and shelter among humans, parking themselves on roads and airport runways and invading indoor spaces like restaurants, hospitals, churches, and private estates. Birds transported small mammals and reptiles over factory gates, seeking comfort in numbers. Their joint cacophony was driving people nuts.

Kicking the pandemonium up several notches, a shaky cell phone video of a talking magpie was going viral. Looking straight at the camera, the bird issued a warning in a hard Australian accent: "The Recipients are coming!" *Unh-hunh!* thought Marlie. Mock had told her and Zeb that intelligent animals believed there had to be some recipients of their worldwide news feed, but the rumors of an imminent advent fueling the present melee must have originated with the late Nikola Bullfrog in the weeks leading up to the extraction.

Now, more and more talking birds—a grey parrot, a starling, and a crow among them—were seen tossing caution overboard and directly addressing humans, squawking about the Recipients. Commentary from newscasters and streamers accompanied the imagery, with certified and self-appointed experts offering up guesses as to what these animals were talking about. Who were 'the Recipients' the birds had mentioned? What had they been receiving? Were they coming? And—in breathy semi-hysterical questions from some—were they coming for us? Maybe it all augurs the Rapture a-comin' in totally unexpected form. Or maybe it's an animal rebellion planned eons ago and now they'll possess us and take control of the machines, their powers of execution no longer constrained by the limits of paws and claws. Or— aliens! Coming at last! Alien monkeys and horses with skinny green bodies and huge eyes and brains. Survivalists are upping their alerts to DEFCON 1, preparing for an onslaught of alien warthogs from outer space, deploying armies of large moths with tiny ultralight but lethal weapons affixed to their bodies.

Marlie welcomed the onrushing deluge from Earth. It tamped down her grief over losing Zeb, an injury on a par with the thought of losing her life. But this—*oh, damn, Zeb, I hope you're seeing this, if it's not too late. This colorful hysteria so suits your style.*

Her bittersweet bemusement didn't last long. A new signal smashed into it with a shot of Relura—*Relura*, trailed by a TV reporter, as their parents, emergency responders, and volunteers combed through the weedy overgrowth on Geezer Island in the dark, hoping in vain to discover the missing twins, perhaps injured from a fall from the tower but at least alive. Wide-eyed, Relura declared, "They can search all they want. I know that my siblings are far away for now but will return as heroes, having solved the great mystery of the Recipients."

More than the unexpected happiness of seeing her family again, more than the reminder that she would probably never see them again in person, Marlie's emotions were overwhelmed by a twinging sense that something was off. A rank odor of *wrong* emanated from that telecast performance and cooked a stomach-churning brew in her innards. Everything about Relura's behavior in that scene—her expressions, her language, her googly-eyed temper—was utterly unlike her. The Relura she'd grown up with was witty reserve personified, an exemplar of cool, calm, and collected demeanor.

Suspicion gripped Marlie by the brain and ordered her to advance deeper into the beam to look for clues that might explain the anomaly.

She flew straight forward, becoming aware that the conical beam was narrowing swiftly, which ill fit the construct that the beam was radiating from a source some light years away. The source could only be close; very close. She lurched forward at top speed till she came across a sight that made her jam on the brakes. The beam came to a point in the clenched hand of another aurorized figure suspended in the nebula. There was someone else in the stellar nursery, and—*thank God!*—it was Zeb! He was calling her name loud enough to reverberate through the nebular methane as he flew toward her with his hand balled in a fist.

"MARLIE!"

They embraced for the second time as aurorized siblings, and it was as reassuring as the hug they had shared when they'd found each other alive on the beach of Puerto Ángel, back when they'd consisted of flesh, blood, and bones. Marlie couldn't speak at first but eventually set her jaw and whispered, "Damn—I was afraid I'd never see you again!"

"I never doubted we'd see each other, especially once I discovered a sure-fire beacon to lure you my way."

"What do you mean?"

"There's good news, Sis, and there's bad news, and they come from the same place. For one thing, Earth isn't slip-sliding to hell—"

"How do you know?"

"—but there's absolutely nothing connecting us to Earth, because none of that news from home was real. We've been played. Bigtime." With that he reached his right hand into his left, allowing just enough space to pick out a thumb-sized translucent plasma jar that was somehow . . . jumping. Marlie's eyes narrowed as she recognized their former travel compartment, the plasma jar Geezer had fashioned to carry them and the core of his old house in their pre-aurorized incarnation. Something was shaking the jar and emitting what sounded like a hacking cough.

"I was agog myself at all the wacked-out news coming through the signal stream till I tracked down its origins to this mini-gnome." Zeb nodded at the animated plasma jar still clutched between his fingers. "I suggest you fish the magnifying glass out of your pocket." Marlie plunged her hand into her pocket to grab the magnifier she'd used on Geezer's NSAG and trained it on the plasma jar.

"Damn it!" she shouted. There, rolling on his back in croaking hysterics, was Nikola. He did his best to make a face at Marlie and turned around to point his froggy butt in her direction. "The little bastard is *mooning* me!" A moment later the signal stream started up again, visible in the methane as a beam of light pointing away from the twins.

"Nik was projecting his own concocted stories all along, the same way he used to project Mock's edited news feeds. I think he made up the whole disaster movie as an ego-bait ploy to get us to rejoin Geezer in Mission Recipients," mused Zeb.

"What a conniving imp! I knew there was something fishy about Relura looking agog bragging on us. There she was, plain as day, but the scene reeked of bullshit."

"I don't know why Nik thought it was necessary to pump up the volume on our motivation to help Geezer, since we'll probably never see him again, but you gotta hand it to him, he doesn't give up easily."

"How did he get here anyway?"

"He must have burrowed his way into my pocket while I was on the cables trying to steer the tower back the way we came. I remember a little tug right when Geezer yelled at us, but I was too preoccupied to pay it any heed. When I entered this wild-looking nebula, out of the corner of my eye I saw something emerge from my pocket."

"How does he manage that? The jar doesn't have wheels."

"He uses his own. He rolls the jar around like a hamster in a hamster ball. When I got here, I wasn't thinking about him or whatever had slipped out of my pocket. I was too absorbed by that phony television broadcast. But once he started in with that ridiculous stuff about Relura, I knew something was fishy and I started following the beam till I tracked him down a couple hundred yards from me in the nebula."

Marlie thought for a moment. "Yeah—Relura gabbling on TV about us solving the great mystery of the Recipients? That was a dead giveaway."

"For all we know, nobody but our family, a few neighbors, and the county volunteer firefighters have any idea that anything at all unusual has happened."

"Or maybe things are actually even worse back there than anything Nik made up."

"Could be."

"Why are you still holding on to the little booger? Let him go so he can make trouble for somebody else."

"You didn't abandon your puppy when it peed on your bed."

"What, you want to keep that little prank perp?"

"Kinda. He's the last vestige of Earth life other than ourselves we may ever see."

The words were barely out of his mouth before a searing bow wave tore through the methane cloud surrounding the twins to unveil the second coming of Geezer Tower, slowing to a pause, now with Geezer himself reaching up to them from the dome window. "Gotcha, kids!" he roared. "Climb back on board!"

20

The twins looked at each other, awash in ambivalence. Their tormentor had found them and was offering them a means of escape from the nebular wilderness. "Zeb, do you really want to sink back into a headlong rush to oblivion?"

"Time's a-wasting, kiddos," Geezer barked. "Our reward awaits us!"

"I know it's the Good Ship Crazy Pop, Marlie," said Zeb, buttoning his pocket over the wriggling plasma jar, "but we've got to take him up on it. At least once we're in the tower we can work on Geezer and maybe get him to turn around. Here, we're stuck for good. Flying home on our own would take thousands of years even if we had a galactic GPS."

Even though Marlie was pretty sure that Geezer had no better idea of what awaited them than she had, she sighed and nodded. Zeb gallantly stepped aside for her to float into the tower.

The twins settled down in the dome while Geezer went below and got the NSAG to lurch the tower back into upward motion with what he called auroral propulsion. Marlie knew that her aviator brother was mighty curious to know how Geezer did it, but now was not the time for NSAG flight instruction. They were still absorbing the first moments of recovery from having been lost in a distant reach of the galaxy. When Geezer rejoined them in the dome, the three of them glanced at each other occasionally while gazing at the ever-thickening flood of stars passing by.

Geezer noticed some agitation in Zeb's jacket pocket. "My man Nikola helped me rescue you two. He doesn't deserve being stuck in the brig."

Zeb unbuttoned his pocket. The frog's plasma jar popped out, rolled along the dome sill, and parked in front of Geezer. Zeb considered using the magnifier to inspect the expression on the frog's face, but it was too soon for that. Probably some combination of triumph and starstruck fealty to his master. But after another minute, Zeb did break his silence.

"So why did you rescue us?"

"You might yet prove useful. Who knows?"

"That's it? After our aborted mutiny?"

Geezer looked at the rushing star stream for a minute, mulling something over. "In Nam I had a troubled grunt in my platoon who threw a grenade that landed so close to me it looked to a few of us like a bungled fragging. I had a lot of options for punishing him, but not many uninjured men left in my squad. On instinct, when things settled down, I gave him a chance to air his grievances, saying nothing about the attempted hit. That night, in another round of firefighting, he took a bullet in the chest. I could have gotten away with leaving him, but I crawled into the kill zone and hauled him back. When he returned from the field hospital ten days later, he was fiercely loyal to me, one of the best fighters I had that whole tour of duty."

Zeb exchanged a look with Marlie. *Oh—now we're redeemed failed assassins?*

"I recognize that you two are agitated adolescents. You're storm-tossed. You love discovery, but you also still love the lives you were leading back at home sweet home, predictable as they were. And you've got your people back there. So, in a moment of weakness, you lost faith that you could serve both loves and made a bad call, but I'm not vengeful. You helped get this mission off the launchpad, after all."

"Under duress," Marlie interjected, against her better judgment. She was in no position to scorn the better instincts of the guy who'd just saved her life.

"Just the same, I still plan to help you get back to your comfy old life—after we get to our destination, of course. Like you said earlier, Zeb-boy, we'll work the problem, people."

Hm, thought Zeb. *So, he did overhear us when we were cooking up our mutiny. Note to self: Never assume that anything can be hushed enough to elude Geezer's hairy auroral ears.*

Marlie turned to Geezer. "So, Mr. G, you never credited any of Nik's phony bulletins from Earth."

"Hell no." Geezer picked up Nik's plasma jar and gave it a good squint. "Mr. Tesla had tipped me off that he was going to tail you and keep you busy while he transmitted your whereabouts."

"Jesus," muttered Marlie. She glowered at the jar, hoping Nik got a good faceful of her.

Nik rolled the plasma jar along Geezer's foot, causing his hero to grant him a grin that carried a trace of respect, perhaps even Geezeresque affection. "Whither I goest, you will go, eh? Just the attitude we like to hear from an enlisted man, Tesla. You've earned yourself a medal for Distinguished Service."

Marlie took the magnifier to get a look at Nik's expression: a visual duet of proud fortitude and restive caution under the looking glass. "Y'know, Nik, with that much imagination and brainpower, you've had the capacity to do something respectable with your life. Why did you turn to the dark side?" The frog broke out one of his signature wide-mouthed smiles. Marlie smiled too, in spite of herself.

Zeb stood up and looked out the dome's apex, entranced by the ever-thickening rush of stars. "I suppose you're navigating by dead reckoning."

"I haven't done a thing to set the course. I was thinking I'd have to align the tower with Nikola's signal stream, but it looks like we're getting a free pull straight to our destination. I lowered the setting on the NSAG already. In fact, I might as well turn it off."

"It does look like we're heading straight for the most star-dense point ahead."

"'Point' doesn't quite describe the black hole, Z. Sagittarius A-Star is tens of millions of miles across."

The thought that he could respond "Tasty infonugget, Sis" flashed through Zeb's mind, but there was little space in her psyche for anything upbeat, or in his own, for that matter. The blues were seeping through him too, or rather a new alloy of the blues, alchemically fusing the anchor weight of doom with breathtaking exhilaration. He sat next to her in silence.

Geezer thought little of the twins' refusal to share in the exaltation the moment called for. He couldn't tolerate it for long. "Look, you dopey-mopes, climb out of your sad cubbies and take advantage of the opportunity at hand. We're on the verge of beholding the greatest secret in the known history of intelligent life forms. I had you figured for a lot more pizzazz and zest for life than this. Yearning for your old California cliques and hangouts is unbecoming."

Coach's final timeout pep talk isn't doing it for Marlie, nor for me. We're down a hundred at the half, dazzling lightshow notwithstanding. Give it a rest.

"Frankly, I don't care for the implication that you're doomed. I told you I was going to help you get home, if at all possible. Summon a little patience! You can't get home without this tower—we're a good twenty thousand light years from your old haunts by now. This tower is headed to the center of galactic action and we're almost there! Seize the minute!"

He's not wrong. I hope he hit home with Marlie. No one who'd had her astronomy jones jacked up the way hers was on the trip to the sun could fail to be at least a little excited about our imminent destiny.

Suddenly a blast of light like a nuclear explosion appeared from somewhere far to the right. It swooshed through the star stream, blurring and stirring it like swirling cream. Before his eyes could adjust and find Marlie, he called out to her, "What's that?!" but her answer, if there was one, was overcome by a second explosion coming from one o'clock that hit them with a powerful wave. For a moment he felt his body stretch in odd contortions and saw flashes of dark smudges the size of baseballs vibrating in intricate arrays flowing past them.

The shock wave subsided long enough to find Marlie and Geezer both plastered against the tower walls before recovering their balance and regarding him and each other in dismay. Zeb's imagination tried to ride to the rescue. He suggested that maybe the Recipients had sentinels on duty to threaten prospective intruders.

Marlie, short of breath, responded, "I don't think so. I'm pretty sure those explosions were supernovae."

"I hear you, missy, but what did you make of those dark patterns?"

The twins were impressed that Wizard Geezer had been obliged to consult a college girl to solve an astrophysical enigma, but Marlie shook her head in puzzlement. "I got nothin'."

Zeb, however, did have something. It was inchoate, stirring about in the well of his memory as he tried to place the patterning he'd observed, when the third blast hit them, this time from straight ahead, punching them with an energy cannonball that momentarily blasted them above the galactic plane in a hyperbolic arc. On the way down, Zeb could see several spiral arms of the galaxy converging on the black hole center of the galaxy and reverberating from the shock wave of the supernova.

While sinking back into the galactic plane, Zeb noticed two plumes of some kind shooting up and down from the black hole. But there was no time for consultation with his fellow voyagers—in another moment they were back in the stream, and in the grip of another strange vision. It was the smudge patterns like those Zeb had seen before, but this time each particle was his size, apparently enlarged by the supernova blast, rotating and gyrating as they flowed past him, heading inward toward the black hole, alongside the tower. Yes, he'd seen patterns like that somewhere in his past. A memory of them was rushing toward his consciousness from an unexpected direction. His eardrums tensed in the tornado-loud deluge of sound, deafening him momentarily and then subsiding just enough for him to hear his sister's voice calling him. She said, "Dark matter, Zeb!"

Between his sister's rhapsodic love of astrophysics and the appeal of that field to his own wide-ranging curiosity, he knew that scientists had long been fascinated by the evidence that much of the Milky Way's mass had earned the moniker "dark matter" for defying measurement and observation by neither absorbing nor emitting light. Marlie's theory only intensified his desire to place the patterning up against some template in his memory that called out to him to dig and dig till he met up with its meaning.

The dark matter rose over his head in a great wave. Still a California surfer boy despite the thousands of light years separating him from his glorious home-state beaches, he couldn't resist placing his hand against the wave as he sped alongside it. Doing so amplified the arrays he touched and brought them closer to his eyes for inspection. Marlie watched him from nearby and saw a joyous smile break out over his face.

"What?!" Marlie called out to him. In the long moment in which she awaited his answer, she noticed a horizontal split in the dense concentration of stars immediately ahead of them, which, it struck her, could be the portal to the black hole of oblivion. "If you know what they are," she shouted through the maelstrom, "speak up! We're about to forever hold our peace!"

The three seconds before they were sucked into the portal were just enough to hear the triumphant result of Zeb's memory search.

"They're nucleotides, Marles—particles of DNA!"

21

*Hell! That jolt hit me like a Mack truck customized for Formula One . . .
but . . . there's no pain. It's like I've been dissociated into randomized component parts of consciousness and body. Bodies, actually. There's my foot, but the
leg is Zeb's. I see him off to the right, but his face has my nose and left eye and—
ack!—Nik's mouth. He's no better off.*

Throughout the dark passage of visual chaos, Marlie moved forward, all
a-jumble, different facets of a crystal in flux, constantly rearranging its parts.
*Oh, God—I've got a genuine hunger for flies. Please don't tell me I'm going to
merge with that smarty-pants slime ball. And what's this, fragments of places
too? There's a floating forest under Geezer's chin, a city of fractalized jewels, bliz-
zards and monks and tropical moths and soccer crowds, all flowing forward
alongside me on a stream of nucleotides enlarged and illuminated by flares of
light. Where's my center?! There's no meditating my way out of this maelstrom.
What if this never ends or gets worse and worse? It wasn't worth it, Geeze. But—
it is insanely fascinating, so whoever I am, I'm lucky too. Thanks, Geezer, but
also, that's enough.*

*Settle down. I've always aspired to be a priestess of rationality, so get a grip.
This mental unmooring can't go on forever (can it?), so an end will come and
then I'll be centered once again, relieved to recollect and reflect.*

But for the time being, Marlie's self-delivered pep talk notwithstanding,
fragments kept a-flying, including especially strange ones in the distance par-
tially hidden by haze: purple mountain kings, their majesties. Lightning
striking mantises, englorying their wingtips with blinding hundred-thousand-
volt arcs. Things that looked human-made and things that looked made, but

not by humans. And landscapes familiar and weird as a tossed salad of canyons and stars.

"Zeb?" She called her brother and was weirded out to hear her voice sounding a little like Zeb's but with Gregorian chant harmonics. *That rumble —don't tell me I've blended Geezer's voice with mine. I'm so confused.* But Zeb answered, from close by, and that helped. *Always I can count on Zeb, thank God for him.* Geezer looked somehow both intense and serene, unconcerned that Nik was maneuvering the little plasma jar onto his shoulder. Aircraft entered seas like submarines and emerged thousands of miles farther on, following direct aerial-marine great circle routes. Antlers of a hundred beasts snarled together in tumultuous rituals. Foolish wars raged between cannon-wielding echinoderms slaughtering but ultimately quelled by intelligent coral. Caterpillarish creatures dancing. Tree-like animals sauntered along a riverside bearing baskets of babies. Fog blobs fell from a speckled mauve sky, enveloping ungulates and plump children skating on a glassy sea . . .

Ah, we're slowing down. I see a dark space up ahead. Marlie guessed that they'd simply been passing through a thin energy field, through which reports from the likes of whales and frogs were tearing at breakneck speed. Whatever it was, the tower emerged from it and came to rest, releasing her from a spell of dizziness and slaking her desperate thirst for stability and the sight of her brother. He was now standing on the tower chamber floor alongside her, reassembled and looking like he must have tumbled through a mental mish-mash like hers. It probably had affected Geezer too, and maybe even Croaky-Face. *Never mind: we've not been annihilated.*

"We're not even scratched," said Zeb, as if in direct response. Had he heard her? Had she spoken? Maybe she wasn't quite back to normal, but with the soothing familiarity of Zeb's voice, a smile gingerly began working its way to her face. "Catch your breath, Sis."

"I'm working on it."

Marlie surveyed their environs from within their enchanted castle spacecraft. They had come to a halt just inside an enormous sphere bounded by starlight, so dense around the middle that individual stars could not be distinguished. *Exhibit A for the thesis that the Milky Way is disk-shaped, with a swollen center nesting a black hole. Score another point for Earth's astrophysicists.*

The sphere's equator was ringed with portals, a kind of zodiac with perhaps twelve million streams showing signs of life on other worlds. Or maybe it was twelve billion—it was impossible to tell with the portals packed together so tightly they looked like flickering points of light. In the nearby ones, which afforded the best view angle, Marlie could see streams of scenes as rapid-fire as the one from which they'd just emerged near Neptune. It was a staggering medley of strange environments and organisms, dozens of reports reaching each portal display every second.

"So much for 'Are we alone?'" said Marlie. "We could save NASA a lot of money on SETI research." She was happy for her brother, whose broad smile reflected some vindication for the output of his vivid imagination. "Now, what was that you were saying before we were so psychedelically interrupted?"

"Oh—nucleotides. Life's raw material, the building blocks of DNA."

"Well, I'd like to know what they have to do with the show we just saw, and who, if anyone, is watching it."

"I've got a feeling we're about to find out, Marles. See the object Geezer's staring at?"

The captain of their vessel was transfixed by a sight opposite from the Portalvision panorama that had preoccupied her. Far in the distance, at what looked like the center of the immense hollow sphere that had been so crudely misnamed a "black hole," a cluster of light sources was engaged in some high-energy activity that demanded further investigation.

Zeb glanced at Marlie out of respect, but he knew she would consent to his next suggestion. He approached Geezer and said, "Let's do it." The old buckaroo was going to do it anyway, of course, but he allowed the twins an approving half-grin. He ducked below deck to the NSAG chamber, where he cranked the tower engine back on. In a moment, the tower slid into flight again for the final leg of their journey from the house by the lake to the center of the Milky Way.

Anticipating an answer to the great question that had consumed Geezer and Nikola for years, the three aurorized humans and Nik arrayed themselves at the dome, facing the hypnotic star-like figure at the center of the black hole, watching tiny, brilliant sparkles erupting from its surface. Geezer radiated a soul-filling satisfaction that justified a lifetime of effort and sacrifice.

Zeb put his arm around Marlie's shoulders for a squeeze in the interest of propping up her morale, but she was fine. Perhaps there could be no greater gift for an aspiring astrophysicist than the revelation unfolding before them.

As the tower approached the object, it became clear that it was not a star but rather a constellation of microstars—a true constellation in that the microstars were actually connected, not merely located near each other in the observer's visual field the way constellations as seen from Earth appear to be connected even though the component stars have no real relationship to each other.

"I wonder if these tiny stars are like body parts of a single conscious organism," said Marlie.

"'Conscious organism' doesn't do this character justice, Marles. This thing is more like a brilliant artist, hard at work." Indeed, even through the gauzy auroral tower walls and dome, the starry artist could be seen operating with hundreds of arms of starlight rays extending from a central point like superfine, incandescent sea anemone tentacles, shaping a dizzying array of organisms and periodically tossing them into vortices suspended above and below its work area.

"You could be right, Z."

"We ought to park and get out for a closer look."

Geezer had come to the same conclusion. He slipped below to the NSAG chamber to bring the tower to a halt at a respectful distance from "the object" (creature? process? colony?) still a few million miles away. Absent any landmarks of known size, the best the twins could come up with for an estimate as they approached was that it must be far larger than the sun but nowhere near as large as the nebula where they'd been marooned with Nikola before Geezer had retrieved them.

The recollection of that episode prompted Zeb to check on Nik. He asked Marlie for the magnifying glass and trained it on Nik's plasma cocoon. The frog was staring at the stellar designer, bug-eyed and agape.

When Geezer returned, he led the way out the dome window, followed by the twins. Nik, whom no one had invited to the outing, nevertheless accompanied them by hopping unobtrusively into Zeb's pocket again.

Absent the gauzy barrier of the aurorized tower walls, the clarity of the scene enlivened their senses like nothing they'd ever experienced before. The sparks emanating from the figure's core were elegant precision instruments engaged in a flurry of high-speed, complex movements, accompanied by a deep, throbbing hum that lit another smile on Zeb's face. *Hunh—the music of the zillion spheres.*

Seconds passed, then minutes. The three observers gazed speechless, beginning to understand more about what the artist was up to. Geezer's eyes glistened as his face became beatific.

Wow, Zeb thought, *I'm not gonna attain Geezer gonzo-gaga nirvana over this scene, but I've got to admit, it is freaking fantastic.* Right in front of them, a creative genius made of mysteriously connected microstars, perhaps a million miles high, was sculpting new life forms at a dizzying pace. This designer-inventor-artist was sweeping up raw matter from its surroundings, dark-matter nucleotides that had remained invisible until the artist went to work on them. As the constant succession of its light-ray arms handled the nucleotides, the artist would glow like phosphorescent phytoplankton, as dark matter did when illuminated by the supernova blasts outside the black hole. Like a jeweler crafting a crown, the artist arranged the nucleotides in long double-helical molecules on its chromosomal construction site, building entire genomes in seconds, employing hundreds of light-ray arms, each with filament-thin protrusions at the ends engaged in finger work so dexterous as to make a virtuoso pianist weep in envy.

The artist—and its four tiny observers from Earth, of which it was apparently unaware—knew exactly how its genetic sculptures would affect the ultimate appearance of the organisms they would give rise to, because, above the workspace in its magnificent Galactic Center Studio, the life forms that would ultimately be created from each genetic design were visualized in real time, in richly colored, sharply defined auroral light.

Zeb was enthralled by the artist's procession of new creatures-to-be: A blobby marine creature with a semicircular array of vision organs and the bulky torso of a sea cow that could write with its fins while waves of color swept along its body from its dodecahedral head to its tail. A butterfly-like creature with two wings was assessed and outfitted with several additional genes that added six more wings spreading from around its trunk. A bird that could build floating nests and was equipped with a single complex eye made of scores of tiny eyes. A humanoid heron . . . feline fish air-swimming in swarms . . . a milk-spouting ginger flower . . . a forest of giant clover . . . an endless succession of strange and wonderful creations.

Zeb sighed in envious admiration. "Genesmithing—man, I could get used to a gig like that."

"You already have one. Or had."

"Not like this, I didn't."

"You don't look the part, but you've got the talent for it."

"Who knows how a Genesmith looks when it first stakes its claim in a young galaxy? On-the-job experience can change anyone. This one must have been at it for a few billion years."

Marlie loved that thought, and not just because witnessing these fine-tuned fireworks of creation brought relief from the doubts and fears that had assailed her ever since their abduction. "At last, a peek behind the curtains. A singular inventor working all by its lonesome." She glanced over at Geezer, but he didn't return her look. He was enraptured by the Genesmith's dazzling genius.

"Must be fun brainstorming," Zeb mused.

"Right—heart above the stomach or below? How fast should the current run from the cerebellum to the fingertips? Double-joint the knee or make it one-way to reinforce stability?"

"Not to mention the creatures it comes up with that have no need of stomach, heart, or knees."

Periodically the Genesmith paused and radial sparks of blue-white light arced between itself and the black hole's equatorial portal displays: the Recipient, checking reports from the field.

When satisfied with the projected denouement of each genetic plan, the artist compressed the prototype and triggered a glowing mitotic reproduction series that produced tens of thousands of copies of its design. These it flung into a shimmering disk-shaped pool in the center of the black hole, which, upon contact, caused jets of gas to be propelled out of its black-hole studio.

Thus, another piece of the three-dimensional puzzle clicked into place: these genome-infused gas ejecta were the plumes the tower astronauts had observed on their way into the black hole. Marlie had heard theories about ejecta emerging like upward and downward geysers from black holes, but none involved a master craftsman's distribution system fertilizing habitable zones throughout the galaxy.

The twins had almost forgotten about Geezer till he departed their company and settled a couple hundred yards away from them, arranging his floating aurorized body in a seated position like a reverent acolyte learning at the feet of his master.

"Finally, an answer to the question of where babies really come from," said Zeb.

"So it appears, indirectly, anyway. Conception on a grand scale."

"Years after he co-discovered the structure of DNA, Francis Crick hypothesized that life on Earth might have been seeded by aliens. Directed panspermia, he called it."

"Sounds like your kind of guy."

"I've got it way easier than Crick. There's no end to the slack people will cut a graphic novelist. It took guts for a Nobel Laureate scientist to come up with life farmers from space."

"'Life farmer' sounds like a dude with overalls, a straw hat, and a corncob pipe—not quite what we're seeing here."

"Either way, someone's spreading around a lot of seeds without knowing exactly which ones will take root."

"But Z—new organisms evolve in stages over many generations through genetic mutations. The Genesmith can't deliver a brand-new giraffe baby where there's no pre-giraffe."

"First off, 'mutation' is a pretty crude term for creations like giraffes, oranges, and us. That aside, the packets the Genesmith sprays around the galaxy may operate as mysteriously as the dark matter they're made of. Maybe they're not macromolecules themselves but, rather, dark matter instruction programs that can penetrate germ cells like cosmic rays, with coding for all the incremental iterations a new organism will require to evolve. It could be programming ten million steps ahead."

"Uh . . . dark matter instruction programs?"

"Darwin knew nothing about DNA. We shouldn't get too arrogant, mouthing supposed laws of nature like your baboon elder pontificating about the speed of a cheetah."

"Yeah, but the Genesmith would face mighty long odds getting a dark matter genetic instruction program into a mammalian germ cell thousands of light years away."

"So? It's got billions of planetary petri dishes to work with and all the time in the universe. If someone with a helicopter dropped ten million redwood seeds over a redwood forest, it wouldn't matter which ones would take root and grow to a height of three hundred feet, as long as some of them do. The Creator probably looks at the big picture."

"'The Creator' now, like God? Mr. Genesmith rules this roost, apparently, but there are a hundred billion other galaxies out there, at least. Maybe this artist is just one member of a *really* big guild." Marlie noticed Zeb nodding. "You think it knows we're watching?"

"If there were a gnat flying around the far end of my house when I was at my desk in creative fire mode, I wouldn't be aware of its existence, much less be concerned with its whereabouts."

That remark gave Marlie the opening she was hoping for. "Well, there are some people back home who are aware of our existence and very concerned with our whereabouts. I trust you don't want to stay here indefinitely."

Zeb hesitated for a second. Marlie was pushing to get down to some tricky business. "Well . . . no."

"Okay. So even if our chances of getting home are just one in a million, you want to give it a go, right?"

"One in a million? You're quite the optimist."

"We can't afford the luxury of lazy pessimism here, Zeb. I shouldn't have to tell you that."

"Yeah, I get it. Sorry. Maybe I was thinking we should prepare for a radical long-term change."

"Who knows what that could mean, Z? We have no idea what staying here or continuing to hang with Geezer would come to, but we do know that this black hole business lacks a lot of treats we've grown accustomed to back home—like family, waterfalls, food, music—"

"Art—"

"Luminous relationships."

"I see you've still got Trey on your mind—but, of course, that too. And we've put twenty-one years into a good run of such treats, which I don't want to give up."

"I'm glad to hear you say that, Zeb. I was beginning to wonder where your head was at, especially when I saw you mesmerized by the ultimate character designer out there." She nodded toward the Genesmith, whose organism-production frenzy continued unabated.

"I was thinking about selling you on touring the galaxy for a century or so. Doesn't that beat a year cooped up on the International Space Station?" Zeb winked at his sister, who sighed, choosing not to dignify his phony proposal with a response. "On the other hand, Alyssa makes some mighty fine French toast, and we are supposed to go backpacking in the Andes next year."

"Good—it's decided. We've got to plan and execute another homecoming. I mean, we got back from the frigging asteroids before!"

"That's like saying we should be able to get home from the bottom of the Indian Ocean because we once got back inside the house from the porch."

Marlie nodded in embarrassment. "Okay, I grasp the scope of the challenge at hand. If you reduced the sun to the size of a coarse grain of sand, Sagittarius A-Star would be more than halfway to the moon."

"Duh. And out by the asteroids we were ten light minutes from Earth and rescued from our kidnapper by an aurorized Good Samaritan neighbor. Now we're twenty-seven thousand light years away and our former rescuer is our kidnapper."

"Come on, Zeb. You're supposed to be a master creative problem-solver. Brainstorm with me."

Twinged by guilt for having dodged a serious question, Zeb looked away from his sister toward the sphere's bejeweled equator. "Okay, Sis—we head back toward the portals, find the signal beam coming from Earth, then crank up the NSAG to propel us upstream along it all the way to our solar system. And we'll have the world's greatest TV show playing all the way."

"You're kidding . . . right?"

"Yeah, yeah, the great attractor effect, stuff goes in but nothing gets out."

Marlie tapped her fingers on her arm, gears whirring, hoping for something a bit more practical in a situation with a dire practicality shortage. She and Zeb observed the Genesmith designing a creature that looked like a cup-shaped brain that rolled on scores of tiny ball-bearing feet. Pleased with its latest design, the Genesmith wrapped it up by compressing the genome, replicating it, and sending it on its way.

Zeb lit up. "Except that's not true! The bit about nothing gets out—the great Genesmith's goodies all make it out of here. We just have to hitch a ride with them on the gas ejecta launchpad! Once the force propelling the ejecta gets us out past the event horizon, with a little luck we can wing it from there all the way home!"

Marlie was relieved to have Zeb in active solution mode, and she desperately wanted her formidable rationality to take a hike for the sake of hope, but no go. "Good swing, Z. If we enter the ejecta at the right angle and with the right speed to optimize our impact without overshooting our mark, we could catapult ourselves bigtime. It would be like constructive wave interference. But, once we're out of here through the top—assuming we survive that—how would we find Earth's signal? There could be billions of signal streams trained on this place. And even if we do find Earth's and make it all the way home, there's still the little detail of our being aurorized."

She had him there, she was sorry to note. While Zeb bit his lip, she allowed her gaze to glide around Sagittarius A-Star's great equatorial belt of signal streams, coming to a stop on Geezer, as rapt as ever in the thrall of the Great Genesmith. "And then there's him. Something tells me Geezer's not going to be too keen to ditch this place for Merlo Lake, or to be deaurorized and reduce his size by a factor of nearly a thousand. It will be hard enough to pull off our deaurorization even without having to reckon with Geezer."

"What's the problem? Geezer's found his Holy Galactic Grail. Now he can deliver on his promise to lend us a hand, with the return and deaurorization both!"

Marlie's doubts were interrupted by the sight of Geezer rising with his arms outstretched, like an ecstatic black Jesus resurrected from the grave en route to the glory. "What's *that* about?" she wondered aloud.

"I guess he's just plain clam-happy, mission accomplished and all. Maybe this is a good time to mosey on down to the NSAG chamber and see about scooting ourselves over to those gas jets."

Before Marlie could respond, Geezer's trance state gave way to his sharp-sheared default demeanor. He sailed over their way, coming to a stop in front of them. "Greetings again, mates!" he offered in a cheerful enough rumble. "Surely you must acknowledge that seeing this virtuoso at work was worth the inconvenience, eh? Who better to appreciate that than a young artist and his inventor sibling, themselves blessed with abundant creative talent!"

Despite her discomfort at their uncertain immediate future, when Geezer nodded at her on the word "inventor," Marlie blushed. She couldn't help taking that as a sign of respect between peers.

But focus: she and Zeb had to improvise a pitch to their potentially recalcitrant rescuer. Zeb stepped up to the plate, prepared to inform Geezer that it was time to go, but before he could open his mouth, Geezer said, "It's been a grand day out, little teddy bears, and it's time to take you home to bed. It's six o'clock somewhere and, after all, I did promise to aid your homecoming upon completion of the mission."

With a quick glance between them, each of the twins knew what the other was thinking. Instead of the complications they'd been expecting in dealing with the old man, he'd shown up as ready for departure as they were, right in the middle of what looked like an ecstatic epiphany.

Geezer put his hands on their shoulders. "I know how eager you are to get moving. A little froggy told me so."

So, Nik had been tattling to Geezer with one of his trademark closed-circuit telecasts, the little scamp. Seeing Geezer's eyes tilt down toward his jacket pocket, Zeb slapped the pocket just a moment too late to trap Nik, who jumped out and rolled over to Geezer, ascending the folds in Geezer's jacket in a jiggle that called to Zeb's mind the Mexican jumping bean Relura had given him when he was six years old. Nik scrambled up to Geezer's shoulder, where he perched, proud and snappy as a pirate's parrot.

"Who cares, Zeb? Nik's gonna do what Nik's gonna do. The point is we're good to go."

"Right on, children. I'll go fire up the NSAG."

Feeling off-balance in several different directions, Zeb defaulted to pilot mode. "No worries, I've got this. You can relax up here. I'll handle the NSAG and throttle it back as we reach the glide path to entry. We wouldn't want to have a nuclear engine cooking at the same time we're subjecting ourselves to a force so strong it can escape a black hole."

"I appreciate the offer, lad, but you can relax up here and leave the driving to me. I built this place, after all. And, forgetting that you entered it at the suggestion of a frog, you are my guests."

Marlie didn't want haste to make waste. "Wait—what about deaurorization, Mr. G? If we make it back to our solar system, it won't do much for our family and friends if we're flying around above the Earth's atmosphere while we're still several times larger than the Empire State Building."

"Fret not, young lady. We'll get to chat about that soon enough." As he jumped down to the chamber floor he added, "Time to hit the road."

A tense look shot between Zeb and Marlie. "That was . . . easy."

"Uneasy's how I feel. Let's get down there and monitor the situation."

Driven by vague anxiety, the twins plunged down to the entrance of the NSAG chamber and squeezed through the trap door. Geezer was manipulating the NSAG's charge level slider and the pulse duration control with the precision of an eye surgeon and the intensity of a fevered cathedral organist manipulating more keys and stops on his instrument than seemed possible with only two hands. The tower was sliding through space, directly toward the energy column leading to the upward funnel for the gas ejection vortex. A succession of the Genesmith's compressed dark matter formulae was entering the column like a steep mountain tributary joining a roiling river, but Geezer wasn't slowing down. A roaring blast like a high-powered wind tunnel issued from the ejection column, becoming deafening as they got closer.

"Hey!" Zeb waved his hand at Geezer to get his attention. "Cool your jets, mister. We've got too much momentum already!"

But Geezer was taking no more notice of the twins than the great Genesmith had. He seemed to be calibrating an arc of alignment that would bring the tower into the ejection column at maximum speed, accelerating and blowing Marlie's alarm-containment system all the way. "Geezer, what are you doing?!"

With a grim smile, the old man slipped the nuclear-powered tower into the column and, at the peak of the gas jet kick, he yanked the engine's power throttle all the way to maximum and looked up as the tower shot upward out of the black hole at stunning speed.

22

An energy whirlwind swirled around them, whipping the surrounding stars into an indistinguishable storm cloud of lights. The twins zoomed out of the NSAG chamber up to the dome for a better view, leaving Geezer alone down below. They'd assumed he would bend the tower's trajectory into an arc over the Milky Way, but instead they were tearing ever higher above the galaxy, high enough to see it spread out beneath them, hundreds of billions of stars, as far as the eye could see.

The twins looked at each other, stilled in the frozen silence that descends upon people who suddenly recognize that they're in very deep trouble. It would have been hard enough to find their way back to the sun's location on the inner edge of the galaxy's Orion spiral arm by tracking the report signals from the solar system. Now, any chance of dead reckoning a path there had just been eliminated by the madman burrowed into the chamber beneath them.

Marlie flashed again on Jim Lovell's voice crossing two hundred thousand miles of space when "a problem" had arisen during Apollo 13. All available thought and action had to be focused on the swift, life-or-death recalibration of the next hour and the rest of their lives, if there was to be any difference between the two. Her eyes stung surveying the tragic gorgeousness of the Milky Way receding beneath them like a pumpkin-sized leaf falling down a well.

For a moment it looked to Marlie like the galaxy was rippling, like a sheet of plankton resting atop a rolling ocean wave. Then she realized that the wave was affecting the tower walls, not what was external to them. She felt a dizzying sense of perturbation course through her auroral body, and it seemed to be affecting Zeb too, and even the entire tower itself. After a minute, their extreme acceleration subsided, and the tower settled into an even, insanely fast cruising speed. Old Geezer's flight engineering had truly advanced from his humble ramjet roots. Synergizing aurorized nuclear-powered thrust with black-hole central gas ejection had shattered their own short-lived spaceflight velocity record. Their speed after breaking the light barrier beyond Neptune, and even their speed as the black-hole attractor drew them into the Genesmith's lair, were leisurely promenades compared to this. This pace made her long-fancied launch from the Florida peninsula on a spacecraft bound for Jupiter look like the trudge of an opium-saturated sloth.

She realized that Geezer must have been well aware of what the impact would be of maximizing the power of his aurorized nuclear-powered engine when they were already in the grip of a gas jet force so strong it could crash through the escape velocities of both a supermassive black hole and the galaxy itself. He *wanted* this to happen.

"But why?" she asked Zeb, there being no need to state what she was referring to.

Zeb nodded up to the top of the dome. "Andromeda's one clue. The helmsman's been busy."

Straight up—i.e., straight ahead—gleamed the fuzzy disk Zeb had seen many times with the naked eye and through binoculars: the Milky Way–class galaxy two million light years from home. "That's M31, all right," said Marlie.

Whatever we call it, it's noticeably larger already, so we must be going hundreds or thousands of times faster than we were before we made it to Sagittarius A-Star. Why has Geezer launched us in that direction?

That question remained unasked as Geezer emerged from the chamber and rose to join them at the mezzanine under the dome. With his instincts for silver-lining detection, proactive problem-solving, and sister protection momentarily stymied, Zeb looked at Geezer, who was standing triumphantly, staring upward, his hands perched on his hips, unconsciously (probably) mirroring the iconic Superman pose.

Geezer's self-absorbed exultation didn't sit well with Marlie under present circumstances. "O, Captain, my Captain," she intoned with audible harmonics of sarcasm, "your Recipient prize is won. You bore witness to the apotheosis of invention. Couldn't you have kept your damned promise to assist our return to Earth before embarking on yet another wacko escapade?"

"The prodigal great-uncle, gone rogue," Zeb added.

"Children, calm down. I said I would aid your return at the completion of our mission, which I shall do. The mission, however, has expanded to incorporate one additional objective. After that it will be your turn."

Marlie was disinclined to put much stock in Geezer's word about helping them get home considering that a hundred percent of his actions had catapulted them ever farther away. With Zeb at her side, she rose to the mezzanine to get in Geezer's face. "Where in blazes have you just flung us?"

Surely she couldn't have thought she could intimidate Geezer. Pausing only to pick Nik's plasma bubble out of his hair, he replied, "If you had the brains of a frog—even this frog—you'd realize that I must have a powerful reward in store for you despite your predictable tantrum." *This guy's got a lot of nerve, comparing my brain to an obnoxious toad's.* "With a little luck, I should soon be able to present you two the chance of a lifetime. If you still want to go back where you came from, I'll say bye-bye, birdies, you're free to return to Mother Earth's nest, but at least you'll know that my having drafted you into this expeditionary force came with an offer of a grand prize."

"So you say. Your word doesn't count much, Geezer."

Zeb had to admit to himself that this new development in their adventure excited him at some level. Marlie, too, had to be deriving some kind of charge from being one of the first three human beings to travel abroad extragalactically. *(Do we still count as human beings?)* But he knew she was wounded by Geezer's betrayal and he was pissed that the old troublemaker had forced him to wrest her back from anguish. "We had a deal!" he exclaimed. "We help you; you help us."

"Your lack of respect notwithstanding—you are troubled youth, after all—I am still prepared to support your dream of returning home, but, sticking with me, you might find yourselves no more interested in returning to your old lives than a reincarnated tiger would fancy repeating his past life as a banana slug."

Zeb muttered, "Here we go again with Geezer's 'great prize behind door number three' trick." But he was finding it difficult to focus on Geezer amidst a growing fear that they might lose track of the Milky Way. Their galactic home was diminishing every second in the rear-view mirror, while dozens of other galaxies belonging to the so-called Local Group were becoming visible in a "night sky" devoid of individual stars. Marlie noticed Zeb's puzzled expression as he observed several soft, tiny clusters of light appear in the general vicinity of the Milky Way. "Satellite galaxies. Major galaxies often have a brood of them under their gravitational influence."

Under normal circumstances, Zeb liked chewing on Marlie's astronomical tidbits, but at the moment he was preoccupied. He turned back to Geezer and remarked, "Whether hanging with you or living on Earth is more banana sluggish is a matter of opinion."

Looking Marlie in the eye (and ignoring Zeb), Geezer remarked, "I've been impressed with your potential, lassie. When I got my start in engineering, young ladies like you were few and far between. High intelligence and moxie can be a potent combo in applied science."

The twins had little appetite for compliments. Seeing two great flocks of stars in opposite directions was a visual treat, but it didn't much compensate for the stress of being in the grip of a mad skipper sailing nowhere—or somewhere worse than nowhere. For someone who prized his navigational skills as much as Zeb, getting lost was unacceptable. To prevent that from occurring, he'd long known that, in trailblazing, it can be unwise to entrust every visual landmark to memory. Employing a safety measure he'd not been taught in flight school, Zeb retrieved his Shangrilarian drawing and his pencil from his jacket pocket and sketched into the background sky an image of the galaxies he could see from their current vantage point, attending to their arrangement and approximate sizes and magnitudes.

The task was burdened by growing hopelessness, however. If they went much farther, his document wouldn't be much help. A sketch of their car's position at a trailhead isn't much help to hikers who have wandered five hundred miles off course, but Zeb was never one to denigrate backup planning.

Geezer looked over Zeb's shoulder as he built up his map alongside his Shangrilarian drawing. "As for you, laddie, I see your sister's not the only creative one in the family. Handsome supercreature you've got here. I remember that clever note you made for me way back when, with the seeker poking his head through the sky. Your talent ought to be transferable to other environments."

"Zeb is a creative genius, Geezer," said Marlie, ignoring for the moment the cryptic reference to "other environments." "His imagination leaves mine, and I daresay yours, in the dust, and he's got the chops to share it with others, given some paper, ink, and pixels."

"Thanks, Marles," said Zeb. He valued her opinion, especially now that there might not be any others in a position to share it in the future.

Geezer nodded, respecting their sibling bond. He made a move toward the dome, but a second thought brought his attention back to Shangrilarian. "Quite the humdinger, that creature is. I believe I was a witness to his conception—in good old Sol's asteroid belt. Who could have guessed that a tiny protozoan's aurorized emergence from a Wardenclyffed splash in the surf augured great things for all of our futures?" He patted Zeb on the back. "I'm proud of you, son. Never let a good inspiration go to waste."

Zeb was too grateful for the praise to give Geezer a hard time, but also too wrought up about his and Marlie's possible intergalactic doom to respond with more than a two-percent smile. Apparently, Geezer didn't expect any more. With a captain's look at M31, he slipped away to re-enter the NSAG chamber, leaving his companions to wonder what was next.

By now the Milky Way and M31 seemed to be of similar dimensions in the young astronauts' field of view. Each was noticeably larger than the apparent size of the Andromeda Galaxy as seen from Earth. Since the two gigantic galaxies are not very different in size, Marlie realized that the travelers had already traversed about half the distance from the one to the other, about one million light years.

Then a new puzzle appeared atop the existing one. Geezer, who had gone below and not yet returned, must have set about pulling on his tungsten cables to effect a slight turn in the tower's flight path. They were now close enough to M31 so that it appeared to be about twice the size of the full moon as seen from Earth, but they were no longer aligned with it, and no alternate destination was visible other than, possibly, one of the several dozen much smaller satellite galaxies hanging just outside the hinterlands of M31.

"What's up with the change in heading?" asked Zeb.

"And the deceleration? Geezer's turned off the NSAG."

"He's homing in on his next destination."

"Next? Or final?"

"Good question. We can't just stand around passively while Geezer hurls another high-speed knuckleball at us."

"Hold on." Marlie pointed at the thumbnail-sized plasma jar that Geezer had set down on the mezzanine bench. She'd noticed it inching closer to them out of the corner of her eye. "That little punk's spying on us again."

"Scram, Nik." The frog was smart enough to know that defying Zeb wouldn't end well. He rolled his plasmic hamster ball over to the steps and bounced his way down to the tower floor. Zeb's sharp vision could have tracked him there without the binoculars, but he didn't care as long as Nik was out of hearing range.

"Removing the NSAG thrust from the equation isn't going to bring this spacecraft to a halt in the vacuum of space," Marlie pointed out. "There's no friction out here."

"Newton's First, at your disservice."

"Right. But he's cooking up something, so we've got precious little time to strategize a way out of this trap—though I have a sinking feeling Geezer will know in advance whatever we come up with."

"Why? We just booted his little croak-and-dagger buddy out of our huddle. You think Geezer's got telepathic powers now?"

"It's not telepathy that lets a grandmaster know your chess strategy ten moves in advance."

"So be it. We need a plan to take control here; probably a radical one."

"That won't be easy," Zeb replied. "Geezer's not about to cave after crossing intergalactic space. And our last effort to depose the crazy king didn't go very well."

"That's because we weren't prepared for jumping jolts in those tungsten cables. This time we can wrap them around our bodies just long enough to throw this truck into reverse. I can distract him while you handle the steering, but it'll all be for naught unless you're willing to reach out with your foot and kick him off."

"You're suggesting we throw him overboard into interstellar space? That's a little harsh, doncha think?"

"'Golly, gee, Gretl, it would be awful mean to put the witch in the oven.' We're kidnap victims, Zeb, headed for a fate worse than an oven!"

"The witch wanted to eat those siblings, Marlie. Geezer genuinely believes he's offering us a beautiful gift."

"Oh, yeah?"

"And don't forget, he saved me on the iceberg when it meant possibly bollixing his great eclipse play. If it weren't for Geezer, I might have come back from Antarctica as a paraplegic or a corpse."

"A, we repaid that debt when we pulled him out of Shang's sea; B, that was a long time before the monster intergalactic travel bee got into his bonnet buzzing him cuckoo; and C, it's not like we'd be killing him. Geezer's a big boy. He'll find a way to amuse himself. This place is his ultimate dream come true. We'd be bestowing upon him fabulous opportunities to frolic around as a satellite galaxy tourist. He'll be happy as a pig in slop."

"I can't see him getting very far without his pride-and-joy NSAG spacecraft. But if we stick together, maybe he'll see how serious we are and agree to take a run at Earth first. After we disembark, he can carry on with his galactic grand tour to his heart's content."

"Ultra-chancy, Zeb. Sure, it would be groovy if Geezer agreed to take us back home first, but he's made it clear that that's not high on his agenda, if it's there at all. If we threaten him, he'll never let his guard down. From his point of view, he's in the penultimate moment of his lifelong quest. From mine, he could be stumbling into an act of involuntary manslaughter and unwitting suicide—with reverberations of agony for Relura and the parents as they keep waiting, day after day, decade after decade, for another phone call from Mexico that will never come."

"So, you think it would be smart to dump the dude without finding out what he's got up his sleeve to help us out? Maybe finding out whatever help he's got in mind could prove crucial. We're raw rookies here. Unless he comes up with something that's a direct threat to our lives, we're better off avoiding a fight and working as a team."

"What could Geezer do that we couldn't do for ourselves? Increase our odds of success from one in a million to two in a million? And think: if we let him in on the plan, he might put a humongous kibosh on it. We shouldn't play into Geezer's hands any more than we have already. He keeps moving the goal posts back, thousands of light years at a time. We've arrived at the last resort!"

A little taken aback, Zeb avoided his sister's look. He was torn between the equally troubling alternatives for dealing with Geezer: Marlie's realpolitik abandonment scheme versus some potentially risky outcomes from negotiating, or tangling, with the old man. And if it came down to severing their ties, he didn't think much of the aggressive bouncer approach Marlie was pushing. He thought it would be wiser to tell Geezer that they felt it would be unfair to pressure him to leave the high altar of invention after his long search, that they'd be happy to bid him Godspeed and be on their way, that they could take it from here after he cleared out.

Amidst these ruminations, the Team Twins huddle was suddenly busted up by the rolling vocal thunder of a Geezer warning from below, slicing through their hushed chatter. "Stand back against the walls, you two!" The twins knew their erratic companion well enough to act fast. They barely had time to squeeze up against the tower walls before an NSAG charge from the chamber below blasted to the top of the dome. Within moments, the tower slowed appreciably as Geezer guided it into position over the center of one of M31's young satellite galaxies, a move that prompted Zeb to say, "I think we'd better get down there and get into it with Geeze before he sucks us into another black hole."

As soon as Geezer terminated the charge, the twins descended to the NSAG chamber, where they found Geezer studying the starscape below. This new galaxy was a lot smaller than M31, much younger and less developed, but it did show spiral arm development and the beginning of a gas ejection stream pouring up from the center. Geezer stared at the ejecta and mused to himself, "I wonder what life forms might be aborning in that plume."

Marlie interrupted his train of thought. "Mr. G, I strongly suggest that you not attempt to dunk us into another black hole. If this place is on your bucket list, you can check it out after you deliver on your promise to help us get back to Earth." In the pause that followed, it occurred to her that she could counter his power trip by threatening trouble, but before she opened her mouth again, Geezer began moving the tower away. "What now?" she demanded.

Geezer fired the NSAG back up to a higher velocity and navigated a course farther to the side of M31. Zeb looked back for the Milky Way before their view of it became blocked. It was more difficult to locate it now because, at their distance, M31's dozens of satellite galaxies, though much smaller, were also much closer.

"Stand back," Geezer barked again, before shooting another braking blast from the chamber up to the dome. He angled the tower toward another, smaller satellite galaxy on the back side of M31, affording them in the process another visual thrill never before seen by human eyes: a head-on view straight down into the center of an embryonic galaxy. They marveled at the view of a rhapsody of primordial celestial beauty swirling in slow motion, with new stars collapsing into each other in beds of dust and gas. Judging from the stillness of Nik's plasma jar, which was poised on Geezer's left shoulder, even the frog must have been dumbstruck.

The new galaxy appeared to possess a black hole, though of much smaller proportions than Sagittarius A-Star. It emitted a nubbin of a gas stream from its center that bore little resemblance to the geyser pumped out by Sagittarius A-Star, and it reminded Zeb of the time he'd flown his sailplane four miles above the peak of Mount Shasta, looking straight down at the snow-capped volcano that dominated the landscape over a swath of Northern California more than five hundred miles in diameter. Even though this was a black hole, the diminutive size of the galaxy and its distance beneath them allowed the astronauts to remain beyond the grip of any attractor force it was exerting upon stellar material nearby.

But there were limits to how long the twins were prepared to sit around and admire this new splendor, because they were now farther from home than ever. As the thought passed through Zeb's mind that they might never see their home galaxy again—let alone their *home*—he became increasingly perturbed by Geezer's continuing disregard for their desire to get homeward bound. "Look, old buddy, the time has come for you to make good on your promises or reckon with the possibility of some real interference with whatever future you're scheming for."

"All right, children, it's time for school. Since your longing for Earth is killing any appetite you might have had for the astronomical feast I'm offering you, I'm prepared—despite your unpleasantness—to share some words of wisdom in the interest of getting you back where you came from."

The twins' attention was riveted on Geezer, for deep down they knew they were unprepared to climb the mountain of uncertainties looming above them on their own. This journey would require intricate teamwork; a detailed briefing from the ship's captain was critical to survival.

"Your first priority is power. We got here by synergizing the maximum power of the NSAG with the force of the black hole ejection geyser. Skip either component and you're stuck.

"Your problem here is fuel. Even an essentially massless spacecraft operating in frictionless space needs some oomph to cover the distance back to the Milky Way, and my uranium oxide supply is getting low." Marlie rolled her eyes. *It's just one thing after another with this guy.* "But I've got a workaround for that.

"Uranium isn't the only metal suitable for the ceramic fuel matrix needed to power this reactor. Tungsten should work fine, and there's plenty of it in the cables dangling beneath the tower—all the raw ore anyone needs to whip up a batch of nuclear fuel to power the NSAG. Once this fine spacecraft has launched, you just chop some samples off a few of those cables and mix them with ceramic material lying about in the lab—the sink, cookware, anything ceramic down to the teapot. Then you cook the ingredients in the reactor oven and, presto-bango, you've got a homemade breeder reactor capable of churning out enough juice to get this baby back to its crib. Once we guide the tower low enough to reach the ejecta geyser, it'll be time to pull the trigger."

Marlie allocated a moment to share a glance with her brother. Getting home was going to take a lot more than clicking their heels three times. Zeb's nod was a sign that read, "We can do this—(*gulp*)—right?"

Recognizing a couple of cases of dry mouth in front of him, Geezer added, "Granted, this is a bit of a long shot, but you've proven yourselves pretty ballsy. Even competent! Between the two of you, you ought to be able to manage."

The same unsettling question popped into both twins' heads. "Hold on, Mr. G," said Zeb. "What do you mean 'between the two of you'? You're the one who invented this contraption—how about your operating it?"

"Because, lady and gentleman, this is my stop. I've got an opportunity to get in on the ground floor of something big here, and I'm gonna seize it."

"What?!"

"Ah, where's your old self-confidence, kids?" He gently patted Nik's plasma bubble with a fingertip. "With a little luck, you and Mr. Tesla could be lazing about in your backyard in no time."

Zeb joined his sister in raising his voice in protest, only barely conscious of Nik leaping his plasma bubble off of Geezer's shoulder. "So, your grand help scheme is to desert us?! You're going to sacrifice our futures for the sake of some loony *carpe diem* caper?!"

Geezer ambled over to the portal at the bottom of the NSAG chamber. "No whining, Pilot Man. You need to be in crisis management mode. Look up there at the rim of the dome. There are some latches you'll need if you decide to blow the hatch."

The tower lurched. Everyone's attention turned to the NSAG's power switch, where they discovered Nik jumping up and down on it. The switch was fifty times the size of his plasma jar, but Nik outweighed the aurorized switch a hundred-thousandfold, and with one more jump the engine started up, causing the NSAG to emit a charge blast straight at the dome, lifting the tower up and away from Geezer's destiny.

"Whoops—gotta go, friends! Our froggy friend has forced the hand of fate." Geezer poked his head down into the net of cables, positioning himself for a dive, scarcely noticing Nik thrusting himself right into the thick of the blast. Its supercharged cool fire stretched from the wire lacing in the dome down to Nik's bubble, filling it with phosphorescent silver light. Nik's frog-gish outline glowed and expanded second by second until it cast off its bubble shell and finally emerged as AuroraNikola, now the height of a strapping eucalyptus tree.

Geezer grinned at his most (and only) devoted fan. "Well, look at that: Froggy plucked his magic twanger!"

The twins neither understood nor cared what that meant. Their attention was on Nik. No one needed a magnifying glass to see his smiling mouth stretched wider than ever, a seeming impossibility rendered possible by an all-time record for amphibian pride. Nik performed a triumphant quick-hopping strut, concluding with a leap onto Geezer's shoulder. Geezer didn't welcome the presence of a frog nearly the size of his head right next to it and batted him away. Not to be deterred, Nik bounded onto Geezer's back and clutched his jacket. Geezer eyed his new self-appointed pet over his shoulder and murmured, "Hmmm."

Turning back to the twins, he added, "We mustn't waste your precious fuel. It's time for me to move on up in the world; the apotheosis of invention ain't observing somebody else inventing. I do thank you young folks for helping me get this far. Au revoir, friends!"

Geezer dove down through the NSAG portal and flew toward the center of the satellite galaxy, with Nik riding him like an ecstatic jockey of Pegasus. Marlie shouted at the top of her lungs, "Geezer! How are we supposed to deaurorize ourselves?!" but the roar of the charge stream still blasting through the tower rendered his reply almost inaudible, except for the phrase *"Wardenclyffe 3!"* And then he was gone forever from their sight, falling into a virginal black hole.

23

Zeb and Marlie stared at each other, utterly speechless. They were in their neighbor's house, very far from their own house, with barely a germ of an idea as to how to find their home galaxy, and now they were rising into deep space at an accelerating pace.

Zeb cleared his throat. "All right, the atomic clock is ticking, Marles. If we don't want our odds of survival to slip from slim to none, we've got to get on it. Let's get tungsten-cooking."

"Not till we set our course. Right now, we can't even see the Milky Way."

"I'm ready to take the reins if you want to navigate."

"It's a little hard to navigate since Geezer's stuck us behind a view-blocker that's hundreds of light years across. You'll have to steer us to the starboard side till we can get a clear sight line."

Zeb lit out for the cables streaming beneath the NSAG and pulled on several starboard cables. Just as he was easing the tower away from its position centered over Geezer's galaxy, he heard Marlie shout, "Zeb—that methane cloud to the left—get over there!" That meant going a bit off course if the aim was to get out from behind the satellite galaxy, but Zeb knew she wouldn't have issued that command without good reason. Seeing her face lit up with a most unexpected smile hastened his maneuver. As he approached the cloud, he throttled back the engine, bringing the tower to a near halt as he beheld a vision he would never forget.

A signal beam emanating straight from the satellite galaxy revealed a burgeoning Genesmith designer operating in the great star-lined cavern of a black hole. "I think Nik is back in the transmission business, Z!" said Marlie.

Though the black hole was smaller than Sagittarius A-Star, it was unmistakably the workplace of a being very like the one they'd visited before at the heart of the Milky Way. The new constellar designer was evolving before their eyes, made of stars conforming to the appearance of Geezer himself, handily wielding a dozen light-ray arms as he crafted a new life form from a surrounding sea of dark-matter nucleotides. His motions were so fleet as to obscure his handicraft in a blur, but after another minute he pulled back his light-ray hands and permitted the projection of his newborn design to shine in all its glory: it was *Shangrilarian*, a dazzling ninja Baryshnikov protozoanto-be, a cosmic homage to the creative talent of Zeb Morell. The twins watched Nik's projection as Genesmith Geezer compressed the design and whisked it into a geyser of ejected gas that the twins could see both in Nik's projected signal beam and in reality, shooting up from the center of Geezer's own satellite galaxy and out to who knew how many young worlds hungry for living things.

"Damn!" exclaimed Zeb, his spirit tickled and his eyes gleaming. "Glad to be of service, Geeze!"

"You've been published bigtime, Z!" Marlie high-fived him.

"Can't deny it: I'm touched." Zeb took care to modulate his voice to a timbre he imagined might issue from the mouth of Captain Woodrow Call on his cattle drive hundreds of miles north of Lonesome Dove, but the sight of his artistic baby en route to real life made his heart sing. His fantastical masterpiece would soon inhabit a real world of unknown dimensions. "How provincial it was for me to think of Shangrilarian protecting truth, justice, and the Milky Way."

"Eyes on the prize, my brother."

"Shangrilarian alive is a great prize."

"I'm hoping you'll be able to relish that joy while continuing to create new tales about him from home, but to do that we'd better get on with finding it ASAP."

"Here we go, then. We should be past the Geezer Galaxy in a minute."

As the tower emerged from behind the baby galaxy, they beheld M31 looming overhead. Taking guidance from Marlie, Zeb switched the direction of the NSAG charge beam, steering the vessel toward the side of the galactic parent.

Slipping through the tower's bottom portal, Zeb wrapped his legs around some of the central tungsten tendrils and gripped several of those to his right and left. Piloting a vehicle as wildly designed as any he'd ever come up with for his own stories, he felt a kinship with the Apollo 8 astronauts beginning the first voyage to Earth from beyond the moon. *Those guys had it a lot easier, though. They could see the Earth and they had helpers down there.*

After skirting the outside of M31, they could see several dozen fuzzballs of light hanging in the blackness of space at varying distances from the mothership galaxy. As Zeb had noted shortly before Geezer's departure, some of M31's satellites were easy to confuse with the far more distant Milky Way. He pulled his hastily sketched Local Galaxy Group map from his pocket and tried to make sense of it. "Any help?" asked Marlie.

"Hard to say. When I drew this, we were at a different angle." He would have said more on the subject but he was distracted by the uneven cadence of an engine running low on fuel—an observation that's disconcerting for a pilot two miles from a landing strip, let alone two million light years.

"Well, figure it out," Marlie prodded. "I've got an answer to our fuel problem, but it won't be any use if we can't set our course."

Zeb returned his attention to the map and brought it to Marlie. By turning it seventy degrees, the drawn layout bore some resemblance to the array of distant galaxies spread out before them. He pointed to a spot on the map and compared it to a small star cloud they could see beneath them and to the right. "That one that's a little more oblate—I think that's how the Milky Way looked when Geezer launched us out of it."

"Go for it." She followed Zeb back to the tower's tendrils, talking along the way. "Here's the thing. Relying on Geezer's fuel-breeding scheme alone would be way too dodgy. Before that we should call the play the Soviets came up with on one of their first space missions: the gravitational assist."

"That's the deal where a spacecraft uses a planet as a slingshot by tearing by it at top speed?"

"Right. NASA's used it countless times. You hit a planet's gravitational field with enough velocity to get sped up and slung around without being captured into orbit."

"I'm not seeing any planets around here."

"I'm talking about using the entire Andromeda Galaxy as our slingshot."

Zeb considered his sister's outlandish proposal, initially at first to inspect it for holes and then to behold its elegant audacity. "Marles, that rocks! You just might score us a free ride all the way back home. Plus, you can put it on your resume when you apply to the astronaut corps."

"You'll deserve at least half the credit, Z. As the only pilot on board, you're going to have to direct this spacecraft near M31 without getting us sucked into it with a near-empty fuel gauge."

Zeb cleared his mind to focus on priming his instincts for the challenge ahead. The most important flight maneuver of his life filled him with excitement. Being the first pilot in the known universe to execute a galaxy-scale gravitational assist would be a sublime coup, plus this one came with a view to end all views.

Zeb's instincts at balancing forces, well-honed by flying sailplanes for five years, stood him in great stead. He got the tower to sweep around the Andromeda Galaxy at superluminal speed, taking in the view that would momentarily paralyze any lover of gorgeous skies. *As Marilyn Monroe's lovers would have undoubtedly agreed, an eyeful of the real thing beats the pants off fantasizing about it.* There were a couple of gravitational wobbles along the way, but Zeb corrected for them on the fly with subtle panache, his peak flight skills kicking in when needed most. They careened around M31 with the fluid grace of an Olympic figure skater, drinking in the sight of billions of stars never before seen by Earthlings. When Zeb kicked the NSAG energy blast to a still higher level, he steered Wardenclyffe 2 onto a path exiting the galaxy sphere of influence and reached a superluminal speed matching that of Geezer's escape from the Milky Way. They had left port on a voyage across the Intergalactic Sea.

The next order of business was whipping up a batch of NSAG fuel. Zeb went around the lab with a hammer and chisel scrounging ceramic material wherever he could find it, a few pots and the sink proving the most fruitful as ingredients for Geezer's tungsten recipe. Meanwhile, Marlie found some carbide-edged cutters in Geezer's tool cabinet and used them on a few selected tendrils suspended from the NSAG chamber.

Once Marlie fed the ceramic matrix into the NSAG "breeder chamber," the twins settled into a rare moment of tranquility. The scenic spectacle of M31 had receded into the distance and now held forth over only about a sixth of the "sky" behind them. They ascended to the mezzanine and let their minds wander while they looked out the dome.

At first, Marlie's train of thought veered toward the abyss of life-threatening what-ifs. *I'd better find a happy place, quick,* she told herself. Determined to visualize success, she imagined the joyous reunion that would unfold upon their return home. *Mom will embrace us as joyfully as Aunt Polly hugged Tom Sawyer on his return from the imaginary dead, minus the ear boxing. Dad'll try to not show how badly he's been thrown for a loop; for a short while, he'll be speechless. Sean has surely driven back up from the city to support Relura. Maybe Alyssa will be there too, and Zeb's sailplane buds, and the cousins, and maybe even my aurora-inducer crew, including Trey. Quite the wild setting that would be to get asked on a first date.*

She noticed Zeb giving her an inquisitive look. "I was just imagining the boisterous party scene back home when we show up." She appreciated Zeb's letting "when" slide without wedging in the correction *if and when*, but to establish her reality-grounded bona fides, she added, "I realize it could be a real mess."

"*Could* be?! Absolutely *will* be! That scene will turn prickly quickly, girl! Everyone will want answers to some whopping-big questions. There'll be TV news satellite trucks and maybe the sheriff and the DA on hand and a county fire department squad with a boat and divers and detectives looking for explosives, helicopters nosing around for shots of the cored-out hole in Geezer's house, and legions of *ooo-wooooo*ing ArtBellites descending on us."

"All right, I get it—Nik's phony nightmares coming true after all." Though she felt it incumbent upon her to acknowledge the iffiness of her assumption that they would make it back in one piece, another thought shoved that one out of the way. *What if we make it back in a great many pieces, whether in California or the bottom of a Mexican cliff or the Southern Ocean? Or maybe we get prematurely deaurorized back to our flesh-and-blood selves without the protection of a handy-dandy plasma jar to keep us from being freeze-dried at minus two hundred seventy degrees kelvin, vulnerable to a meteoroid smacking us to smithereens? Maybe the poets were blinded by binarism and failed to imagine that the world could end with both a whimper and a bang, by both fire and ice.*

Nothing against life after death, but if our passing thus comes to pass, I hope we'll be spared Mock's reports on the scene back home. Relura crumpled flat, if not by a botched landing of our freshly deaurorized tower then by grief unfairly laced with guilt over having enabled our Geezer chase four years ago. No thank you. And by the way, how long is it before missing people are declared deceased? Just how many hours or decades will Relura keep praying she'll receive another phone call from us that can never be placed because we're drifting in a remote part of the galaxy, helplessly ignorant of where home is, much less able to get there? Oh, Lura, your dilemma—torn between telling the authorities what you know (on the one in a thousand chance they'd believe you and the one in infinity chance they could help) and keeping quiet to protect your reputation and the family from those same authorities (and cable TV vultures).

Whoops. I think I've slipped out of my happy place.

Zeb patted her on the foot. "Come on, Marles. Defunk your mindset." *Was it that obvious?* "If anybody can dig their way out of this kind of trouble, it's us. Besides,"—*uh-oh, there's that impish grin; brace yourself*—"think on the bright side. Maybe we'll make it back home still in all our auroral glory, visible at night from fifty miles away. Showing up like that at a meeting with your venture capitalists would have to convince them you're the next big thing."

"You mean if the meeting's in Stanford Stadium, which might have room for my nose?"

"Well, think this through. If we manage to get deaurorized just from the neck down, you could sit on the fifty-yard line and they'd get a really impressive view of your two-hundred-story-high head."

"Couldn't go clubbin' no more."

"No, but a nighttime campfire party at the beach would be cool."

"Yeah, you could join us after appearing at Comic-Con. You wouldn't be able to sign autographs with a pen that's a hundredth the size of your fingertips, but you could thrill your fans by giving them plasma jar rides up the outside of the auroral author skyscraper—Hey!"

Marlie had been so caught up in chatty musing, she hadn't noticed that they were getting mighty close to the Milky Way. It was filling a good eighth of the visual field already. She knew that the rate of change in the proportion of the field taken up by a destination on approach follows a hyperbolic curve and they were hitting that upward swing. "We'd better snap to, Zeb."

Looking around at the change in scenery accomplished that. "You know which spiral is the Orion Arm?"

"Best guess is that wispy feather at about eleven o'clock, dangling off the second spiral. I suggest you get down below and steer us in that direction. I'll stay up here since the view out the dome is clearer."

"Roger."

One of Zeb's favorite moments in flying was the descending glide from clear skies above into fluffs and wisps of clouds. For that fraction of a minute, the brilliant white figures stood around him like hills, trees, or even living sentries watching his descent. But the fond memories of those moments could hold no candle to the stunning bliss of settling his surreal spacecraft into the ocean of stars comprising a universe-class galaxy. No such transitional view had been possible when Geezer had blasted them out of the galactic center in ejected gas at an insane speed. Though no words passed between Zeb and his sister, he knew she was as breathless as he in the thrall of such unsurpassable natural beauty. *Get a good grip on this image; I'm certain that the memory of it will come in handy some day, if we get the chance to remember things.*

He focused on strategizing how to find their home sun and its planet family amongst the millions of stars in the Orion Arm. He came up with a methodical search strategy and was about to pitch it when Marlie beat him to the punch. "Z—we can narrow this search way down by applying some clear-cut filters to the glut of candidates.

"From our current position, our skyscape consists of about seventy degrees of azimuth and fifty of right ascension, so that's about thirty-five hundred square degrees. If we figure Sol's distance from the galactic center at about a third of the way to its edge, with the sun being probably in the middle of the disk's thickness, that fine-tunes the target zone way down to maybe a dozen square degrees right up ahead of us.

"Once we eliminate all the blue, orange, green, and red stars, and any double star systems, I think we'll have cut the number of candidates down to the low three figures. So, between the two of us, we can pick out the best ones and cruise by those in maybe as little as an hour, checking for the number of planets in each one and their brightness and distances from each other and the home star. I'll bet few will match the Sol family pattern. When we come across a hot prospect, we can go in for a close-up look at the third planet from the star and hope for the best."

"You'll make a good navigator when NASA goes interstellar, Sis."

Marlie knew Zeb was fully aware that by the time humans engineer spaceflights beyond the solar system, NASA and America might no longer exist and so-called manned spaceflight will be in a form they wouldn't recognize. She accepted the compliment as presented. "Thanks, Bro. You'd be a top gun pilot on that mission, for sure."

When Zeb brought the tower down close enough to see a star's whole system for the first time, Marlie's face lit up in delight. Of the twenty or so planets in the system, almost half of them, and even a few of their moons, had polar auroras of varying colors.

"Celestial crowns of electromagnetic jewels, babe. A sign of your glowing future!"

"More to the point, they could determine our immediate future. Auroral pattern recognition can help us speed up our solar system IDs. Picking out Sol from all these stars is as hard as sexing Mom's chickens."

As their grand tour of the Orion Arm continued, the twins got into a groove enabling them to determine if a yellow-white star might be Sol with a swift fly-by at a distance of about a billion miles above the orbital plane. Some had only gas giant planets, a few had none. Most had a mix, with colors and arrangements that didn't square with the observations humans had made of Sol's planets over centuries, and at no time did a single familiar constellation come into view. The twins knew that even if many familiar stars were nearby, the formations Earth's stargazers were used to wouldn't appear unless one was fairly near Sol.

Along the way, Zeb became skilled at finessing gravitational assists to power each step of the voyage while preserving their fuel, a necessity since the NSAG engine had to be kept alive for navigational fine tuning and deaurorization. But after checking out more than a hundred solar systems in less than an hour, Zeb noticed that the original fuel supply in the NSAG was getting low. He told Marlie, "If we don't make it home soon, we may have to put Geezer's wacky NSAG fuel recipe to the test."

"Let's not panic about crossing a bridge we might not get to."

"Not panicking—just sayin'."

"If we're going to worry about something, it should be what we're going to tell the hordes when we get back home. Questions will be coming at us with tsunami force. We've done zero planning for that little possibility." She paused as they passed by a series of green, blue, and orange stars. "And I'm beginning to think it might be a very little possibility."

Gotta keep Marlie's mind from getting sucked into search-failure worries. Better go for a tried-and-true thought-deflection strategy. "I say we tell all, Marlie. Let it all hang out. Give people some credit. They might take it in stride."

"In stride?! Wittydumdum, you're nuts!" Zeb's satisfied smile failed to cool her fervor. "This story will make the Mississippi fishermen alien abduction story sound about as wild as a Geyserville Women's Club ice cream social. We'll be hounded by freaks and geeks for the rest of our lives!"

"Okay, so we won't bring it up. We've managed with one outer space secret for the last four years."

"There's no comparison, Zeb! The iceberg was a thousand miles from Antarctica and there was no damage. This time people saw us lifted into the night sky above a standing house that had just had its insides ripped out!" Zeb let her rattle on, content that at least he'd gotten her mind off the dearth of Sol candidates. "*They're* going to bring it up. The point is we've got to find a way to keep our traps shut, regardless. The more we tell them, the worse it will get—the wackos, the cultists, the paparazzi—our lives will become primo tabloid fodder."

"Fine—we'll stonewall the media. But the people we care about—"

"We can't tell them either. Except Relura, maybe. Others would blab, in time."

"I agree with you there. Alyssa accuses me of thinking all ears are parts of public address systems."

"*You* should think that way, *lovers included.*"

"Of course, we *could*—"

"Hold on, there's a yellow-white one up ahead." Marlie's voice had instantly remodulated from worry to excitement. "Let's check that out!"

Zeb brought the tower over the top of the new solar system, but the view revealed no brood of planets. Instead, its entire field was littered with thousands of asteroids strung out in concentric circles, sparkling in the star's light like a nighttime view of a city designed by circle-obsessed planners. "Nice view, you've gotta admit," said Zeb.

"Quite a beauty," Marlie replied, with more disappointment than pleasure. You were saying?"

"I was going to suggest that we tell people that the incident was an experiment with proprietary technology in development by a colleague of yours and that you're not at liberty to discuss it publicly. The homeowner is aware of the damage to his house and it will be handled at no cost to the taxpayers. You could sell that—you're a physicist!"

"Your naïveté is almost as staggering as the truth, and the truth would set the world free to go crazy."

"Fine, mum's the word—except for Relura and the parents." At the mention of their parents, Marlie's face contorted in dread. "We have to tell them, Marlie, if Relura hasn't already. They *saw* us." Marlie sighed and let her gaze fall to her shoes, thus missing an intriguing sight Zeb spotted some ten light years ahead. "Marlie—check that constellation out. It looks a lot like Scorpio! We're in the zone, baby!"

"There's a yellow-white one, at eighty degrees. Hit it!" Zeb turned the tower toward Marlie's find.

In another minute Marlie exclaimed, "Oh my God! It's the sun! There's Saturn! We're nearly home!"

The twins enjoyed all of two seconds' jubilation before their party was interrupted by a disturbing sputtering lurch. Zeb frowned. "Uh-oh—we're running on fumes."

"Hell, I'm not giving up on a two-million-light-year journey with a stinky nine hundred million miles to go!"

"Well, get on with refueling, Sis. You and Geezey must have some kind of mind meld for inventions like this, right? Besides, even if we can manage to reach Earth's orbit by balancing braking with the tower's inertial velocity, we're going to need the NSAG power if we're to have a prayer at deaurorization."

"I'm on it, Zeb. Keep your eyes open for a friendly blue planet, and I'll figure out how to refuel Geezer's reactor with our tungsten blend." Marlie combed over the surface of the NSAG to suss out how the NSAG fueling mechanism worked. "And start decelerating!" she added.

"You don't have to tell me, Marlie. If we deaurorize after waiting too long to hit the brakes, our landing would make the Tunguska meteor crash look like a butterfly alighting on a lily."

"There's a fix for that. We can aim the NSAG blast against the dome in the direction opposite to our main propulsion."

"Ah—you mean use the dome like a sail?"

"Right. That was a key concept for an interstellar nuclear spacecraft engineering fantasy from decades ago, called *medusa*."

"Because a sail like this is shaped like a jellyfish?"

"Exactly," said Marlie as she continued perusing the control panels on the NSAG. "Okay—I think I see how this contraption works."

"Be prepared, they told us in Scouts. Always have an applied physics major on board when traveling in outer space."

"Got it! The tungsten matrix is flowing right into the fuel chamber!"

"I knew you could do it. Hey—off to the left—Io and Jupiter!"

"I feel like blowing them a kiss."

"Do it fast, because we've got to figure out a deaurorizing plan. It won't help to land on Earth in a form that would be invisible to people in daylight and shock them to death at night."

"Wait—a quarter of the way around the sun—is that Earth?!"

"Mars, Marles. Even I can see that. It's red."

"Yes, obviously." Her overeager astrophysicist's embarrassment vibe was palpable.

"Keep your cool. Deaurorization."

"Righto. Well, all we've got to go on is what Geezer told us four years ago, before he went after Shang, about how we might deaurorize him later using Wardenclyffe 3."

"You don't think that was a load of b.s. to get us to aurorize him?"

"Even if he were bullshitting, that doesn't mean it's wrong. Besides, it's the only theory on the table and it does kinda make sense. He thought that we could get the strong intra-atomic forces in his auroral self to take hold if we set up a spark gap with him in the middle between the sun and the Wardenclyffe blasting with reversed polarity."

"Well, duh!"

"Okay, maybe it's nutso, but—Hey!" Her throat caught. "Earth, for sure!"

It was unmistakable. The gleaming blue spot beyond Mars could be nothing else. "Thank God!" As she caught her breath, they felt another lurch.

"I think we just crossed the light barrier going the other way," said Zeb.

"If we're still just barely slower than the speed of light, we've got a helluva lot of braking to do before we reach Earth." Marlie continued her examination of the NSAG. "Plus, at the rate this thing is devouring our tungsten home brew, we don't have much fuel left. And as for your smarty-pants 'Duh!,' unless you want to engage in deaurorization R&D till we run out of fuel entirely, Geezer's method is all we've got."

"Fine, but hold on to your rear because the tricky landing factors are really piling up. We're going to have to align the whole tower with a direct path from the sun to Earth, and if we want to survive, it's got to be over water near a shoreline." With Earth already looking larger than the full moon, he added, "And at the moment we pull that trigger, we'll have to have halted forward movement completely."

Landforms began to be discernible surrounding an ocean. "That's West Africa, Z. Move us north and west to our own West Coast."

"That could be a problem too, if it's nighttime there. Millions of people would witness our arrival. Success or a disaster, we don't want that."

"Check it out. Worst case, we can aim for a sparsely populated island in the Caribbean."

As he steered the tower westward, Zeb's voice got more clipped. "As for Geezer's theory, we've got a lot more to deaurorize now than just one old kook. Plus, Wardenclyffe 2 is a whole lot more powerful than its miniature version was. If deaurorizing works on us, it's likely to take the whole tower with us, which could lead to a very iffy landing. This thing isn't exactly built like a sailplane. The moment it becomes normal matter, it'll sink like a thirty-thousand-pound stone. We're going to have a tricky balancing act on our hands, angling the tower to face the sun, lowering it so that we're at a dive-able distance from the water so we can eject and survive, and deaurorizing ourselves *while* slowing to a stop, all at the same time."

By now they'd crossed the Americas. The night-shadow terminator lay just off the West Coast. "Look—it's sunrise in Northern California. That should work out great."

"Think quick, Marles."

"First thing is to head out over the Pacific and then turn a one-eighty so that we can fly toward the coast, eventually turning the tower horizontal so the basement is facing the sun, all the while slowing down."

"Aaaand . . . slowing it down how, exactly?"

Zeb left it to Marlie to solve their simultaneous four-part equation while he concentrated on operating his bizarre spacecraft. Her eyes, having narrowed for a moment, suddenly opened extra-wide. She snapped her fingers. "We should try to get the auroral propulsion split both fore and aft, balancing a medusa sail technique—basically hitting the dome with some of the charge beam while the rest is exiting the back. We should be able to guide our velocity downward with complete control!"

"Which has the advantage of having the beam already aimed at the dome when we're ready to deaurorize."

"Exactly."

Zeb considered her brainstorm, nodding his head with increasing vigor. "Nice economy of motion, girl!" Marlie's vibrating relief at her brilliant solution didn't last long before being checked by Zeb. "But it's still no cakewalk, Marles. If we don't titrate the descent with the deaurorization perfectly, we could end up as regular human drowning victims or as half flesh-and-blood/half aurorized drowning victims, which would be grotesque, or maybe anoxic aircraft ejectors falling from outer space to our deaths. Or we get deaurorized too soon in the upper atmosphere without a handy plasma jar to protect us from suffocating and freezing. Or maybe the tower gets deaurorized before we do and we end up floating around as auroral monsters with the only remaining Wardenclyffe in the world weighing fifteen tons and sunk at the bottom of the ocean."

"That's your final time-out pep talk, Coach? Sometimes I'd rather you kept your imagination penned up."

"Touché. I'll apply it instead to aviation's cardinal rule: No matter how rough the circumstances, visualize a successful landing."

"Okay. I'll visualize a cylindrical sailtower that's as flightworthy as a sailplane."

"No complaints, Can-Do Woman. We need you to get that blast up to the dome, strong enough to slow us down, and be ready to hit the polarity switch when the time comes for deaurorization. Our D-Day landing is just a few minutes away."

Zeb was more intensely focused than Marlie had ever seen him. She felt fortunate indeed to have him as their pilot. She felt less confident about her own role, since she would soon be responsible for an unprecedented life-or-death technological transformation that she couldn't exactly study up on with YouTube tutorials.

As soon as Zeb had made the turn over Hawaii's million lights glittering in its night, Marlie directed the NSAG charge at the dome. Seeing the glowing jellyfish canal pattern in the dome's tungsten veins, she breathed a sigh of relief.

Their declines in speed and altitude intensified immediately. Having studied countless pictures from the International Space Station and scored a session in a spaceflight simulator during a field trip to the Johnson Space Center when she was nineteen, Marlie felt confident in assessing their altitude at about two hundred miles and dropping fast. The West Coast was rolling into view over the curve of the Earth.

Zeb began tilting the tower from its vertical orientation toward the horizonal. He pointed out San Francisco Bay, ahead and down on the right. "We're probably three hundred miles north of the bay, but we'd better head straight for the nearest shore."

"Hell yes, that'll still be a lot closer to home than I thought we'd get. Keep it simple."

"Can't get much simpler than landing a house-core spacecraft with no wings or wheels in the ocean. But if we're lucky enough to find ourselves back in human form dropping into the ocean, what happens then? No dinghy, inner tube, or life jackets on board. Have you thought about that?"

"As a matter of fact, I have, flight commander. The dome can serve as our life raft. Geezer has it latched into place. We'll unhook the latches when we're close to the water, jump out, and retrieve the dome once we're in the water." Marlie noted with pleasure that Zeb was nodding in approval of her scheme. "Now make a good visual note of everything around you before we enter the atmosphere—"

"—which will be in less than a minute—"

"—because we're about to enter sunlit air, where it will be nearly impossible to see anything that's aurorized—

"—including ourselves, unless the Great Deaurorization works. Till then, we'll be part of an invisible, inhabited nine-mile-long ghost ship." Marlie didn't respond. She was staring back up at the night sky. "What's up?"

"Tell you later." They entered the hazy top of the atmosphere, illuminated by blue skylight for the first time since they'd traveled to their parents' house to meet Relura. Overhead it was indigo but brightening by the second, in synchrony with their diminishing visibility. "Our altitude must be less than twenty miles. I can barely see you, but I hear you fine. When do you think we should begin deaurorization?"

"If it's going to be any use, it's got to reach completion when we're close enough to survive a dive but high enough to allow us a little leeway for an imprecise—"

"Unprecedented—"

"Okay, a never-before-imagined landing. We should aim for completing the process when we're between forty and eighty feet above the sea. Keep your hands on your throttle system and try to modulate it accordingly. We've got nothing to go on but intuition, and mine says start cranking it at eighteen thousand and pray."

"And you'll tell me when that is."

Zeb could barely see his sister. She was a faint glow in the now-clear blue sky. "I will . . . and that would be *now! Hit it!*"

After years of managing aircraft descents, Zeb smoothly guided the huge auroral vehicle toward the coast and braced for a charge that would bring his sister and him normal physical life or auroral death. Though he could no longer see Marlie, nor even the NSAG and the tungsten cables he was using to control the flight, he knew she had reversed the polarity and intensified the charge beam because he could feel its zinging build-up throughout his body. He remembered to call out "I love you, Marles!" in case it should be his last opportunity, and he was pretty sure he heard her reply in kind, but it was hard to tell because of a roaring static in his ears.

At ten thousand feet, he heard Marlie's voice calling to him through the static. "Not to worry, Z—our aurorization followed a hyperbolic curve, and this may as well. Expect big changes in the last few seconds!"

Marlie heard Zeb call out, "Thirty-five hundred . . . three thousand," and then she lost his voice altogether in the noise. Suddenly the charge intensified so brutally she feared she'd pass out. She could feel tremendous tingling compression taking place throughout her body from head to toe. As she noticed a small boat about a thousand yards offshore and half a dozen people on shore entering the water with surfboards, the tower and her body and Zeb's took on a thickening spectral glow. She and Zeb were now only a hundred feet tall and the tower had diminished to the size of a tall office building, descending on its side with tungsten tendrils hanging from the back like the tail of a giant horse. Along with the tower, they kept shrinking by the second and began to solidify and become visible enough that she could see Zeb leaping toward her. He grabbed her hand and scrambled toward the dome.

At some eighty feet above the water, deaurorization jacked into its climax in one sudden heave and then, at last, returned them to the fully normal flesh-and-blood form they'd lived with from birth until their hopefully-not-final night. Zeb yanked on the dome latches. When he released the last one, the dome dropped off the tower and drifted down to the waves in the lazy pattern of a falling maple leaf. Zeb gave Marlie a look that meant business as he shouted, "Jump!" He pulled her with him into the air for a forty-foot drop into the cold Pacific. When she came up and swept the water out of her eyes, the first thing she saw was Geezer's bottom-heavy tower sinking, almost upright, below the waves.

When she felt Zeb's hand on her shoulder, she turned to see his grinning mop-haired face and wrapped her arms around him in sheer joy. They still had a long, cold swim ahead of them, but they'd kept their wits about them and held on to their lives, thanks in part to Geezer's spectacular contraption, which was at that very moment finding its final resting place beneath a pod of startled gray whales making their way north.

Zeb pointed to the tower dome, which floated upside down some seventy-five yards away. They pulled off their water-soaked jackets and began swimming toward it, avoiding the soaked papers, books, tools, and other detritus of Geezer's lab. They welcomed the flood of neuromuscular signals and stress required to interface their trillions of living cells with four-foot swells, not minding a bit when the rising sun lit up the water around their eyes, momentarily blinding them.

When they reached the dome and began to reckon with the challenge of overturning a huge polycarbonate dish, a rumbling sound overtook them from behind. They turned around to see the fisherman making his way toward them in his motorboat loaded with fishing gear and an excited black Lab. "Don't you worry!" he called out. "I gotcha." His next words were unintelligible, directed into his cell phone, but when he came within five yards of them, he cut his engine and shouted, "What in the blazing hell was that fuselage thing you fell out of?! The damn thing was hovering there like a long, wiry kestrel!"

Marlie swam a few strokes to the side of the boat, where the fisherman reached out to give her a lift. Her attempt to join the fisherman in assisting Zeb was obstructed by the furious sniffing of the curious dog.

"Many thanks, mister. The water's cold."

"Name's Wyatt Krebs," said the fisherman. "My assistant there is Sparky. I was just heading in anyway." Squinting at them he added in a squeak, "Are you kids *okay*?" The twins assured him they were fine and gratefully accepted the blanket he offered, which they wrapped around their shoulders.

"Damnation!" he cried. "Does this have something to do with that weird house explosion down in Sonoma County that's been on the radio and the TV?!"

The moment of truth or truth avoidance had come, and yet, despite their preparations, neither Zeb nor Marlie could come up with an answer. Besides, they were distracted by the shouts of the surfers, who were paddling their way, emitting hoarse calls of "Crazy!" and "Friggin' insane, dudes!" and "What happened?!"

The twins waved to the surfers and thanked the fisherman again as he headed toward shore, skirting around the surfers. Zeb asked to borrow his phone.

"Sure enough," he responded, reaching into his poncho pocket. "Now what the hell was that thing you just jumped out of?"

Zeb shrugged, "Hard to say, Mr. Krebs. It was like a dream."

As Zeb began punching in Relura's number, Marlie looked up to the northwestern sky, where she'd been staring when they entered the Earth's atmosphere. While waiting for Relura's phone to ring, Zeb asked her, "What's out there, Sis?"

She glanced back at him, smiling. "Andromeda." She lifted a finger and pointed at a spot of clear blue sky about thirty-five degrees above the horizon. "He's right . . . *there.*"

Zeb saluted in that direction. "You think Geezer and our local Genesmith might ever share news?"

Marlie arched an eyebrow in caution. "Who knows, Z? Who will ever know?"

A brown pelican that had been wheeling overhead flew down just above the water, eyeing her and Zeb as the chorus of panting dog, lapping waves, puttering motor, and approaching surfers was joined by a couple of sirens and the *thwop-thwop-thwop* of a helicopter appearing over the tree line on shore.

Staring back at the pelican, Zeb replied, "Maybe Mock can clue us in." He smiled at Marlie, who reached over Sparky for a discrete low five.

Acknowledgments

I am deeply grateful to Patricia Dedrick, Kathryn Dulin, Craig Lambert, John Newmeyer, Gurney Norman, Mark Terry, and Jennifer Scott Teton for their comments on the material; to copy editor Lisa K. Marietta and book designer Dickie Magidoff for their assistance in preparing the text for printing; to Michael Ray Allison for contributing generously to the design of this book's cover; and to Justin Mikkelsen, Aidan Terry, and Melanie Gendron for their help with it. I am lucky to have *The Book of Geezer* make its way to the world supported by the wisdom, dedication, and keen instincts of Scarlet Tanager Books publisher Lucille Lang Day. Most of all, I appreciate my good fortune in being immersed in the wonderful waves of love and wit from my late parents, Shirley and Joseph Teton; from my children, Sage, Ben, and Zoe; and especially from my boundlessly gifted wife, Jennifer.

About the Author

John Teton was born in Chicago and earned degrees from Harvard and the San Francisco Art Institute. He has directed the international film festival award-winning short films *Thunder Head Clearing* and *B'raesheet* and produced the cosmology film program *Visions at T Minus Zero*. In addition to *The Book of Geezer*, his fiction includes *Appearing Live at The Final Test*, *Upsurge*, and *ELEVATION: The Cave Logs of New Hale, Tibet.* He is the founding director of the International Food Security Treaty Association, which arose from notes for *Upsurge.* On behalf of the IFST, he has made many public appearances at universities and U.S. congressional briefings, and he was featured as a non-government presenter in conjunction with the annual plenary session of the United Nations Committee on World Food Security in Rome. He has written numerous articles, including "On the Origin of a Hunger-Free Species," published in the *Harvard International Review*, and "The Armless Hand," in the *Yale Journal of International Affairs*. He and his wife, Jennifer, are the parents of three and live in Oregon.

Praise for

ELEVATION: The Cave Logs of New Hale, Tibet

"Virginia Woolf said that it is a rare gift in our days for a storyteller to be able to make us want to learn the end of the story. John Teton has that gift; as I read *ELEVATION*, I very much wanted to know how the story would end, and turned each page quickly and eagerly so as to be able to find out."

Lawrence Rosenwald, Anne Pierce Rogers Professor of English,
Wellesley College

"John Teton's novel *ELEVATION* is an adventure story and a love story, but above all it is the story of a spiritual quest. Terma Den Sherab and Cali Zigana Moss journey deep into the human psyche to discover and combat the source of evil. Like Teton's previous novels, this is socially conscious fiction at its best, addressing humanity's most significant problems, and suggesting that, through radically new ways of thinking, these problems might be solved."

Lucille Lang Day, author of *Married at Fourteen* and
The Curvature of Blue

"Read John Teton's literary-quality work of speculative fiction, *ELEVATION*. Travel on a search for heritage and 'soulspace' to Tibet and beyond, and meet characters who take us on a journey to a higher plane, a place where our imagination creates an exciting new realm of what is humanly possible."

David Rottman, past president of C. G. Jung Foundation of New York

Praise for

Upsurge

"An artful blend of well-crafted science fiction, revealing social criticism, and an engaging love story, John Teton's *Upsurge* will strike an immediate chord with anyone who has experienced outrage at the persistence of hunger in the midst of potential abundance. At once a sci-fi fantasy and a thoroughly engrossing love story of family relationships, this book . . . raises fundamental questions about the fate of humanity and entertains at the same time. Bravo!"

Janet Poppendieck, Professor of Sociology, Hunter College,
City University of New York; author of *Sweet Charity?*
Emergency Food and the End of Entitlement

"*Upsurge* is a great, evocative, thought-provoking book . . . an engaging and personal drama that takes us on a voyage of inner discovery of moral and scientific transformation."

Tyler Volk, Associate Professor of Biology, New York University;
author of *Gaia's Body: Toward a Physiology of Earth* and *Metapatterns*

"*Upsurge*, like its predecessor, *Appearing Live at The Final Test*, proves again that literary realism can hold its own when interwoven with fantasy elements, even those as wild and original as those in these books. Teton's characters and their emotional complexities are so firmly established early on that by the time readers are transported to his dizzying alternate realities, we're hooked for the duration."

Debo Kotun, Producer, Pacifica Radio Network; author of *Abiku*

"*Upsurge* brings real family dynamics and real politics together in great science fiction."

Eric R. A. N. Smith, Professor of Political Science and
Environmental Studies, University of California, Santa Barbara;
author of *Energy, the Environment, and Public Opinion*

Praise for

Appearing Live at The Final Test

"Fantastic . . . defies typecasting . . . a grounding in everyday human fears and troubles, along with mind-blowing scenes which venture into questions about creation and the role of human beings in it."

Santa Barbara News-Press

"Appearing Live at The Final Test is a genre-breaking story unlike any other. Its scenes range from a scarily realistic depiction of an urban nuclear event to mind-stretching intergalactic travel—all related in the author's savvy, wise-cracking, original, and sometimes hilariously hyperbolic voice."

Craig A. Lambert, Deputy Editor, *Harvard Magazine*

"Appearing Live at The Final Test is an extremely well-written novel—a pleasure to read, a wild ride of depression at some points, exhilaration at others. John Teton has raised some serious concerns regarding the fate of civilizations, and our consciousness is raised with this thought-provoking work."

Eric Chaisson, Professor of Astronomy and Physics, Tufts University; Director, Wright Center for Science Education; author of *Cosmic Evolution*

Scarlet Tanager Books

Bone Strings by Anne Coray
poetry, 80 pages, $15.00

Fire and Rain: Ecopoetry of California
edited by Lucille Lang Day and Ruth Nolan, poetry, 462 pages, $25.00

The Rainbow Zoo by Lucille Lang Day
illustrated by Gina Aoay Orosco, children's book, 26 pages, $18.00

Wild One by Lucille Lang Day
poetry, 100 pages, $12.95

The "Fallen Western Star" Wars: A Debate About Literary California
edited by Jack Foley, essays, 88 pages, $14.00

Catching the Bullet & Other Stories by Daniel Hawkes
fiction, 64 pages, $12.95

Luck by Marc Elihu Hofstadter, poetry, 104 pages, $16.00

Visions: Paintings Seen Through the Optic of Poetry by Marc Elihu Hofstadter
poetry, 72 pages, $16.00

Embrace by Risa Kaparo, poetry, 70 pages, $14.00

Catch and Other Poems by Richard Michael Levine
poetry, 82 pages, $18.00

crimes of the dreamer by Naomi Ruth Lowinsky
poetry, 82 pages, $16.00

red clay is talking by Naomi Ruth Lowinsky
poetry, 142 pages, $14.95

The Number Before Infinity by Zack Rogow
poetry, 72 pages, $16.00

Red Indian Road West: Native American Poetry from California
edited by Kurt Schweigman and Lucille Lang Day, poetry, 110 pages, $18.00

Call Home by Judy Wells, poetry, 92 pages, $15.00

Everything Irish by Judy Wells, poetry, 112 pages, $12.95

Turning a Train of Thought Upside Down: An Anthology of Women's Poetry
edited by Andrena Zawinksi, poetry, 100 pages, $18.00